"Ah know what happened! She had a baby! She disgraced me! She disgraced this family! She had that baby in the school's toilet. ... Do yuh believe that? There ain't no forgiving that."

"Disgraced you! John, she's yuh daughter. She's a child. How can yuh judge her without speakin' with her?" Loretha was stunned. "No! No!" She held up both her hands with her palms facing John and shook her head to emphasize her words. "Let me rephrase my statement. We need tuh know how this happened."

"Ah don't care how this happened. It happened, and that's all that matters!" He scowled back at her. His ugliness grew, cloaking his face and filtering into the rigidity of his body language.

REHOBOTH ROAD

ANITA BALLARD-JONES

Genesis Press, Inc.

Black Coral

An imprint of Genesis Press, Inc.
Publishing Company

Genesis Press, Inc.
P.O. Box 101
Columbus, MS 39703

ISBN: 978-0-7394-7098-5
Manufactured in the United States of America

DEDICATION

To my mother Alice Idell Parker
In memory of my father, Robert Parker Sr.
and my brother
William Neil Parker

ACKNOWLEDGMENTS

First and above all I need to thank my Lord and Savior for the inspiration and creativity to write this book. Thanks to my loving husband Joseph Jones who has to be the most supportive, understanding and encouraging husband in the world. I love him so much. Thank you to my loving children and grand children for their belief in me and excitement over my endeavor, Thomasina Hurtt, Carmena Murphy, Michael Jones, Melanie Hurtt, James T. Hurtt, Britney Ballard, Kai E. Lewis and Malik Jones.

Thanks to my only sister and best friend, Anna F Jackson. Without her I would be a very lonely person. Thanks to my favorite uncle and aunt, Mr. & Mrs. Leroy and Shula Davis—two people other than my parents who made the most difference in my life. Thanks to my two brothers, Rober L. Parker Jr. and Leon H. Parker, who have made my life interesting. Thanks for the encouragement I received from my cousin Gwen Starr, my neice Adele Philips and her daughters Shardel Collins and Bedelia Hall.

Thanks to my special friends, Kristi Williams, Annette Jamison, Joann Smith, Elsa Espanosa, and my dearest friend Sharon Elizabeth Gambrell, author of *Caroline*.

CHAPTER 1

In Georgia, the promise of spring is a promise that's always kept. The evening dew cleanses the air and lies on the new leaves in tiny beads, waiting to quench the thirst and nourish the trees that hibernate during the mild winter months. The aroma of the wild honeysuckles, jasmine and Cherokee rose mixes with the array of other wild flowers to sweeten the air and hold the dew until the sun's rays store the moisture until the next evening's dew.

In 1950, Rehoboth was a small community about twenty miles south of Macon, Georgia. A nine-mile stretch of dirt and gravel laid road that the blacks called Rehoboth Road and the whites called Rural Route 822. The community not only spanned the length of Rehoboth Road, but also branched off onto a maze of back dirt roads; usually divided and bearing the name according to family ownership, such as Lansing Road, meaning the road would lead to the Lansing's property. Now on the way down Lansing Road, there were other roads, such as Bains Road off to the right and Wren Road off to the left. The one thing they all had in common is they were all called "Roads."

As with most Southern communities, the Church was the center. The Concord Baptist Church was the spiritual foundation for Rehoboth. An invitation to the Lord's house traveled from the opened window and floated on the ribbon of song, prayer and ministering, touching every ear, with or without an invitation to do so. The white wood frame church was visible just as you reached the bend in Rehoboth Road where the old magnolia tree stood strong, deeply rooted in the Georgia soil. The same ribbon of spirituality was equally captivating if approaching from the opposite direction, from where the ancestors rested eternally in the church's cemetery.

Reverend Turner held his handkerchief in one hand while he gripped the podium with the other. Reverend Oliver, his young and charming assisting pastor, sat in the pulpit to his right. Reverend Turner stomped his right foot and threw his head back. "Listen, Church!" he screamed out. He jumped back from the podium and threw both hands in the air, and then out to his side. The sleeves of his maroon robe draped about him like wings readying to lift him into flight. "Yes, Church!" he shouted, holding his arms forward and fanning them wide again. "We have a friend in Jesus!" He used his handkerchief to wipe the pearls of perspiration from his face. "Where can we find a friend so faithful, who will all our sorrows share?" He nodded toward Thea Oliver, and an upbeat arrangement of "What a Friend We Have In Jesus" rang out from the piano and filled the church. Reverend Turner sang and strutted across the pulpit. His arrangement allowed him to be repetitive and place emphasizes on certain verses. He clapped his hands, jumped, and the congregation roared.

While they worshipped and shouted in the spirit evoked by Reverend Turner, Reverend Oliver caused fifteen-year-old Elizabeth Turner to sit bashfully pinned to the pew with his penetrating eyes while he visually assaulted her in plain view. Eyes barely blinking, his lips slightly separated as he stared, Elizabeth's appearance resembled signs of intimidation, enough to pull her head down until her chin met with her chest. Innocence, inexperience and shyness left her ill-prepared to deal with his forward behavior.

Reverend Turner moved between Reverend Oliver and Elizabeth and sang out at the top of his voice, "Precious Savior, still our refuge— Take it to the Lord in Prayer."

Loretha cried out, "Yes, Lord. Thank you, Jesus," Reverend Turner continued to preach. With Loretha standing and Reverend Turner at that side of the pulpit, Elizabeth was completely shielded from Reverend Oliver's visual assault.

"Yes, Lord. Yes. Yes. Yes, Lord. Folks—Precious Savior, still our Refuge. Take it to the Lord in Prayer," Reverend Turner sang.

Most of the congregation was standing and Loretha, Reverend Turner's wife, held her hanky between her fingers and clapped her gloved hands as the spirit filled her. She used her hanky to capture tears generated by his inspirational message. She was a slender woman with a honey-brown complexion, free of facial makeup and the glitz of jewelry, the lack of which added to her natural beauty in a homespun, Godly manner. She wore her hair neatly pulled into a bun on the back of her head, and always presented herself with perfect etiquette.

Twelve-year-old Sarah stood with her mother and enjoyed the preaching and singing of her father. She used a funeral parlor fan to cool herself and occasionally turned the fan on her mother to add to her comfort. Loretha gave her a warm smile and returned her attention back to her husband. Sarah had her mother's complexion, and was a shy and timid child. She was beautiful in her own special way, sharing both parents' attractive features. She considered Elizabeth her father's favorite, and longed for the day when she would hold that place. Reverend Turner loved both girls equally.

Reverend Turner preached, sang and danced to the other side of the pulpit. Reverend Oliver was acting as if he were in the spirit, and his eyes were no longer pinning Elizabeth to her seat, but she didn't know that. She was afraid to raise her head.

An arm touched her on the shoulder. "It's okay, honey. He ain't got a fix on yuh now," Mrs. Collins whispered in Elizabeth's ear, and then sat back on her pew.

Elizabeth turned to Mrs. Collins and mouthed, "Thank you." It was a relief knowing someone else saw him.

Elizabeth thought of how hard it was for Mrs. Collins to be at church in spite of her weeks of ailing. She was in her early seventies, and Elizabeth was concerned about her recent illness. It was impolite for her to question what malady had stricken her, but she seemed so sad, Elizabeth believed her illness was loneliness. Mrs. Collins seemed to struggle just to get through her day, but she was always ready on Sunday morning for church when Reverend Turner arrived in her driveway.

Loretha leaned forward until she got Elizabeth's attention. "Are yuh all right?"

"Yes, ma'am," Elizabeth whispered. Reverend Oliver was now standing alongside Reverend Turner while the deacons stood on the floor below the pulpit, during altar call.

"Are yuh all right, Mrs. Collins?" Loretha asked.

"Yes darlin'," Mrs. Collins said before she locked eyes with Elizabeth.

As soon as the service was over, Sarah and Elizabeth offered to assist Mrs. Collins to their father's car.

"Thank yuh, young ladies, but dis be da only time Ah have tuh do a little fellowshippin'. Y'all can go on now. Ah'll be waitin' fer yuh right here on dis back pew."

"Yes, ma'am," Elizabeth said. She was a beautiful, slender, honey-brown skinned young lady, with dark brown hair that reached about five inches below her shoulders. She had just celebrated her fifteenth birthday on April 10, 1950. She possessed youth and innocence, and for her parents' sake, she presented herself with poise and dignity.

Before the girls left the church, many of Mrs. Collins' friends came to greet her, and some made empty promises to visit her at her home. Elizabeth smiled as she passed through the open church doors.

Mrs. Collins moved down the left aisle of the church, holding to the back of each pew for support as she greeted her longtime friends. "Lawd have mercy. It's so good tuh see y'all tuhday," or "Ah been waitin' fer that visit yuh promised." Or she might say, "I missed yuh last Sunday. Ah been prayin' y'all be well?" She'd smile, shake a hand, give a hug, or even accept a kiss to her cheek. By the time she reached the last pew in the church, she'd ease herself down to rest. She sat quietly and observed Reverend and Mrs. Turner and Reverend and Mrs. Oliver exchanging words in the area below the pulpit. They had just returned to the sanctuary after personally greeting the congregation as they left for the day. The dynamics of the two couples captured the interest of Mrs. Collins as she watched the way Loretha and Reverend Turner related to the tall and handsome Reverend Owen Oliver.

A 24-year-old young man with the tan skin and keen features, Reverend Oliver was the new assistant minister, just out of seminary school, as well as an elementary school teacher. Thea, his young and stunningly beautiful wife, was the pianist and organist and led the choir in their inspirational music. Married a little more than a year, she had not yet developed the homespun appearance of a minister's wife. Thea was also tall. Her caramel colored skin was highlighted by the radiance of her second month of pregnancy.

Mrs. Collins sat quietly and continued to observe the dynamics of the relationship among the ministers and their wives. It was obvious how pleased the Turners were to have such a young minister practicing in their church. Reverend Turner believed Reverend Oliver's youth was an inspiration to the young people in the congregation and community, but it bothered Mrs. Collins. She knew it would be difficult to convince Reverend Turner that Reverend Oliver was staring at Elizabeth improperly. She decided to watch him and gather more evidence before she spoke up.

The Turner family and the Oliver family lived on Rehoboth Road, three miles from each other. The Olivers lived two and a half miles west of Cornerstone, and the Turners lived a half mile east of the church.

The Turner family enjoyed the comfort of their two-story home with a large country-style front porch. There were four spacious bedrooms and a bathroom located on the second floor. The first floor was laid out with a center hall, a large living room on one side and the dining room on the other. A spacious den and kitchen were located at the rear of the house.

The Oliver home was equally as comfortable. Their white shingled ranch-style home was set back a hundred feet from the road and was surrounded by a variety of tall trees, the most impressive being the large weeping willow that canopied their driveway.

It was the evening of that second Sunday in May, May 14, 1950, when Elizabeth's life changed forever. Reverend Turner called for the girls to take Mrs. Collins her daily meals. Elizabeth was in the den listening to the radio while her parents where entertaining the Olivers on the front porch. They had just enough time to deliver the food and return home before dark. Loretha had been preparing meals for Mrs. Collins for weeks and would continue to do so until she had completely regained her strength. Elizabeth and Sarah made frequent trips to her home to help her with her chores and keep her company. Mrs. Collins had always been in their lives, and spending time with her was as natural as spending time with each other.

"It's okay, Daddy. Ah'll take it. Sarah is playin' with her friends," Elizabeth said.

"All right, but hurry. Ah don't want yuh tuh be out alone after dark."

Elizabeth knew darkness would fall in a little over an hour, and figured if she took the short cut through the woods she could deliver the food and return home before night fell. A warm breeze whispered through the trees, and the evening dew had begun to fall. The path through the woods was narrow, familiar, and solely used by the Turners.

It was only half a mile to Mrs. Collins' home. The walk down Rehoboth Road was one and a half miles, and the turn onto Collins Road to her house was half a mile.

As Elizabeth left the house, she turned around and saw her father and Reverend and Mrs. Oliver sitting and talking on the front porch. She waved at them and began pacing herself at a moderate stride, hurrying on her way. When she reached the edge of the woods near Mrs. Collins' home, she slowed her pace to catch her breath and used her hanky to wipe the perspiration from her forehead.

Mrs. Collins' house was a small wood frame, three-bedroom ranch with two small bedrooms approximately 15 x 10 feet each, separated by a 15 x 20 foot living room. There was an opening on the right side of the living room that led into the kitchen, which was the same size as the two front bedrooms. The back door opened into the kitchen. Across from the kitchen was a small sitting area and a door that led to the 15 x 20 master bedroom. An old well remained in the backyard, ten feet from the kitchen window, and the outhouse toilet was still standing behind the shed that housed a dusty black car that once belonged to Mr. Collins. Back in 1947, Mr. Collins had modern plumbing added to the house as an anniversary present to his wife. A standard size bathroom was built off the side of the kitchen near the middle of the house. It stuck out like an awkward appendage, so Mr. Collins extended the front porch to wrap around to the side of the house.

Elizabeth tapped on the back door and then entered Mrs. Collins' home. She knew she was welcome, and never felt the need to wait to be invited in. Mrs. Collins was sitting in her favorite lounge chair in her sitting area reading her Bible when Elizabeth kissed her gently on her cheek. She knew it was Elizabeth, but believed the verses she was reading were too sacred to allow any interruption. Elizabeth stood patiently and waited for her to put her Bible aside and look up at her.

Mrs. Collins was always very happy to see Elizabeth, though today she seemed tired; it appeared attending service earlier had been very draining. She was a wise, delightful and responsive senior. The fullness of her five feet, two inch tall frame left no evidence of the signs of her years, from her ageless face to her smooth soft hands, to the defined curves of her body. Her long, silver-white hair, worn neatly corn-braided around her full, dark brown face, removed years from her appearance.

"Ah'll fix yuh dinner and put the rest away for yuh." Elizabeth walked across the hall into the kitchen and reached in the cupboard for two plates. She removed the cover from the waxed paper lined lunch pail and removed each portion of the meal. There was enough for Mrs. Collins' dinner and for lunch the next day. Each item of food was separately wrapped, because Loretha knew the girls would be shaking the pail in their haste to make the delivery.

Loretha had prepared fried chicken, potato salad, string beans, sweet rolls, and sweet potato pie. Elizabeth placed a leg and thigh on one plate with half the side dishes, and the breast and wing on the second plate with the remainder of the food. She covered the second plate with wax paper, set it on the shelf in the refrigerator, and removed the pitcher of lemonade. There was a lightweight end table near Mrs. Collins' chair. Elizabeth placed her food, drink, and utensil on it.

"Oh, thank yuh, chile. And thank yuh mama fer me."

"Yes, ma'am. Ah can't stay long. It's gittin' dark. Ah'll come back after school tomorrow and we can talk a while."

"Oh, Liz'beth, hurry home. Did yuh come through dem woods?"

"Yes, ma'am. If Ah hurry, Ah'll be home before dark."

"Ah got a bad feelin' 'bout dem woods. Ah don't think y'all should be walkin' through 'em. Y'all is young, the walk down Rehoboth Road will do yuh good."

"Yes, ma'am, Ah'll be just fine. It's still light. Ah'll run and be home before dark."

Elizabeth kissed Mrs. Collins again and hurried out the door. She ran along the path until she was tired. Slowing her pace, she continued to hurry along, taking notice of the rustling sounds echoing through the trees. Thinking it only a scurrying squirrel, she continued on her way, but Mrs. Collins' warning echoed in her head. She hurried at a fast pace, trying to move as far away as she could from the crumpling, rustling sounds. As she approached the middle of the woods, the sounds were louder. She stopped, stood still, quiet, and tried to reassure herself that the noises were those of small animals. She allowed herself to believe a small deer might be lingering nearby. The sounds were louder, startling, and before she knew it, a hand was covering her mouth. She felt a tightness surround her body.

"Don't scream, and Ah won't hurt yuh!"

It was Reverend Oliver. She stood still and nodded her head in the tiniest of motions. She was concerned, remembering how he gaped at her during church. She didn't like the way he was holding her, but in her innocence, she believed she was overreacting and would be safe. "Reverend Oliver?" she whispered as though she was committing herself to keeping a secret.

"Yes, Elizabeth." His voice was soft and non-threatening. "Don't be afraid. Ah'm not gonna hurt yuh."

She inhaled a swoop of air as her body relaxed. "Why are yuh here? Why'd yuh grab me?" Then her thoughts took over before he responded. *This ain't right. Ah need tuh be afraid. His eyes are crazy. He's not playin' with me. He said he won't hurt me, but why did he say that? Please God, let this be a game.*

"Elizabeth. Ah can't help it. Ah've been watchin' yuh for a long time. Yuh so beautiful. Ah need yuh."

Fear rose in her throat. She looked at his familiar face and reassured herself that he was a minister. *He wouldn't hurt me, but what does he mean, "Ah need yuh?"*

Reverend Oliver cut off her thoughts, putting his finger to her mouth and whispering, "Shush, shush," before she asked the question. He began to massage her back and shoulders, and then rubbed her behind and legs.

Speechless, Elizabeth pulled away and tried to scream, but before her cries could pass from her lips and echo off the trees, he covered her mouth, muffling her sounds.

"Don't scream," he demanded. "Ah'm gonna love yuh. Ah need tuh have yuh!"

Again, she felt his hand on her legs, and then under her dress, tugging at her underwear. His other hand slipped away from her mouth, down her blouse, and gently caressed her left breast.

She pulled back, trying to escape his touch, and felt his manhood against her backside.

"Please stop! Stop!" she cried softly. She crossed her legs, twisted and pulled away from him, only to be pulled back and held tighter.

"Elizabeth. Please." He covered her mouth again and forced her to the ground. Her body was stiff and rigid, her eyes wide and searching. She was in a state of shock, not believing, or not allowing herself to believe, this was happening to her. The things he said, the way he said them, confused and frightened her.

"Elizabeth, Ah need tuh show yuh how much Ah love yuh. Ah know yuh don't want this tuh happen like this, but Ah can't help it. Ah want tuh make love tuh yuh. Ah want tuh make yuh feel good and forget yuh fear. Ah won't hurt yuh."

Elizabeth was terrified as his unbridled desire seemed to remove any rational thoughts or judgment. He touched her with one hand. When she resisted, he pinned her to the forest floor with his other hand. He spoke softly, lovingly, then powerfully and demanding. She wanted to scream, but was more frightened that any rescuer would find her in a compromising position, believing the shame of that would be greater than the impending rape. He continued to remind her he would have his way and soon she would not want to struggle. He touched the sensitive areas of her body with his hands, tongue and lips. She twisted in the struggle to be released. He continued his touching until he lifted her inner pleasures against her will. Her twisting was of passion—a surprised passion. She submitted to her innocent lust. Her body was ready to receive him. He stole her innocence and blossomed her desire.

When Reverend Oliver finished, he rolled over and laid beside her, holding her hand. He told her he loved her more than he could ever express. He told her he only wanted her to want him and love him the way he loved her, if just for a moment.

Elizabeth slid her hand from his grasp. His touch repulsed her. She knew his continued hold was to remind her that he was still in control. She used both hands to pull down her skirt, while she sobbed quietly. Fear had left. He took, he raped, and he made her forget she was being raped. She felt violated and angry. The only fear she felt was the fear of her mounting hatred for him. She tried to deny the pleasure she experienced, but only succeeded in accepting the blame for her own violation.

"My father will be missin' me," she cried.

"No, he won't. Yuh mama and daddy went tuh the church. Ah have tuh meet them there soon." He stared at her with questions in his eyes, and seemed to be unrealistically surprised that she would pull her hand from his with such a force.

"But what about yuh wife? She's gonna have yuh baby."

Reverend Oliver turned away. She knew he loved his wife. He looked into Elizabeth's eyes and saw hatred flow from the inner depths of her soul. His body quivered with fear, and he held his head low.

"Ah'm so sorry. Please forgive me. Ah don't know what came over me. Please forgive me. Ah've loved yuh from the first time Ah saw yuh. Ah didn't mean for it tuh be like this. Ah allowed my passion tuh rob my judgment. Please don't think of me as a bad person. Ah wanted yuh for so long. Ah took yuh because … Ah love yuh. There's no other way for me tuh have yuh. Ah'm sorry, please forgive me."

"Ah wanna go home! Please let me go home!" Elizabeth whined. "Ah won't tell anyone … please let me go home!"

"Ah'm not worried about yuh tellin' anyone!"

In the pulse of a moment, Elizabeth saw his emotions switch. The tone of his voice deepened. His jaws clinched. He scowled. "No one will believe yuh," he growled. "Do yuh think yuh daddy will believe Ah raped yuh? Believe me, he won't." His words were cold and brash.

Elizabeth's posture was jerked back to rigidity, and Reverend Oliver was successful in reinforcing his control. He seemed to be admonishing himself for his last remarks, while his eyes continued to tell her how sorry he was and how much he loved her. Tears were running down his face. He adjusted his clothing, stood and ran from the woods.

Elizabeth watched him run. He didn't look back. She wanted him to, so he could see the reality of what he had done. She gathered her things and slowly staggered on the moonlit path toward her home.

Sarah was in her bedroom. Elizabeth tipped into her bedroom, removed her soiled clothing, rolled them into a ball and hid them between her bedsprings and mattress. She grabbed her bathrobe and slipped into the bathroom. Sarah came out of her room when she heard the water running in the bathtub.

"'Lizabeth, is that you?"

Elizabeth didn't respond. Sarah pounded on the bathroom door. "'Lizabeth! 'Lizabeth!"

Elizabeth knew she had to answer. She yelled out, "Yes, it's me. Ah'm takin' a bath."

"Where yuh been? Why'd it take yuh so long tuh get back from Mrs. Collins?" Sarah was annoyed with Elizabeth for making her worry.

"Oh, Sarah, yuh know how Mrs. Collins is. We got tuh talkin' and time just slipped away."

"Okay, Ah'm goin' tuh bed. Daddy and Mama went tuh the church."

"See yuh in the mornin'." Elizabeth tried to sound like her normal cheerful self. It was important to her that no one know what happened until she had time to sort things out. She slid her body into the warm water and cried. The sounds of her sobs were hidden behind the sounds of the water still trickling from the tub's faucet. *The man Ah respected took me, and Ah liked some of it. Ah don't have no business likin' none of it. Ah shoulda fought more. Ah shoulda screamed loudah. Ah coulda gotten away from him, but Ah didn't try hard enough. Ah musta wanted it to happen. How can Ah face my father? Ah've sinned, and God won't forgive me.*

Her mind ran wild, reflecting on the terrible events of that evening. When she reached her bed, it was difficult to quiet her thoughts.

CHAPTER 2

The days led into weeks, and Elizabeth's ordeal continued to trouble her. No one knew of her pain, mental anguish, anger and guilt. Before this incident, she had no reason to hate. She had felt the realm of human emotions, including what she thought was hate, but until that evening, she never knew what the real experience was like. Believing no one was to blame but herself; maybe she looked at him the wrong way or said something she shouldn't have. She smiled when he stared at her in church. Maybe she led him on. She thought he was handsome and charming. He lifted her spirits, and she enjoyed being in his company.

Being raped was more emotionally painful than the act itself. The physical pain subsided within hours, but emotionally, the crisis seemed to grow with each passing moment. She was confused and angry. Still numb and traumatized, facing Reverend Oliver wasn't difficult. She could feel his eyes on her, but he was transparent to her, and she never allowed her eyes to meet his. She believed this caused him to hate himself and fear her. The solid, soul-worthy substance of this man she once admired was suddenly only recognized by the shadow of his being. Somehow, she assured herself that what he had done was festering at who he believed himself to be; festering at his goodness, morality, and virtue. That was all she had to feed the anger she was allowed to feel. There was no one to talk to. If she allowed her anger to seek revenge, she believed she would have the punishment turned on her. She was confused over the whole ordeal, and only prayed it would go away. Reverend Owen Oliver had raped and threatened her, and she knew her silence was the only way to survive. He was a man of the cloth. She thought no one would believe he would do such a thing, and it would all come crashing down on her. The passing of time, prayer, and meditation allowed her to understand that her teenage bashful smile did not deserve the theft of her innocence.

Weeks passed, and Elizabeth had not told her father. She knew Reverend Oliver was right. Her father would blame her, and she understood that rationalization because she also blamed herself. It was best to just let it pass with time, but time wouldn't let it pass. Although she was innocent, she knew that sexual intercourse could lead to pregnancy, but she didn't think it could happen the first time. The facts of life were something her mother had no intention of explaining to her until she was ready for marriage.

"'Lizabeth!" Loretha said, "Sarah has her 'time.' What about you?"

"Yes, Mama, Ah got mine tuhday." Elizabeth bit down on the inside of her mouth as soon as the lie passed her lips. She thought for a brief moment and couldn't remember having a recent period. Loretha always asked the girls if they had their periods. Describing it as "time" made a biological function, which Loretha considered a necessary nasty, seem acceptable. The church revival took up so much of her time the month before, she hadn't asked about their periods. For some unexplained reason, both girls always had their periods during the same time of the month.

For the first time, Elizabeth thought she might be pregnant, and the frightening thought weakened her knees. She took a sanitary napkin from the box in the bathroom, walked back into the den and spoke briefly with her mother. It was just small talk, just to get her mother's attention. Her main objective was to hold the sanitary napkin openly so her mother could see it. She had felt the tenderness in her breasts and experienced morning sickness, but she figured she was coming down with something.

"Chile, hide that thing," Loretha scolded. "Young ladies don't walk around holdin' them things for anybody tuh see."

Elizabeth tucked the napkin in her dress pocket and excused herself before going to her room. She threw herself to the floor and cried, trembling in fear. *My God! … My God! … Ah've been good. Why is this happenin' tuh me? Ah know yuh love me, Lord. Yuh my protector. Be with me now. Ah need yuh now more than ever.* When she finally stood up, she went over to the full-length mirror, removed her dress and examined her front and side profiles while standing in her undergarments. Her stomach was flat. It had been nine weeks since the rape, and there was no sign of a bulging belly. *Maybe God ain't forgot me. Maybe Ah missed my "time" 'cause Ah was taken. It musta been the shock tuh my body that made it stop comin'. It'll come.*

For the next couple of months, Elizabeth's belief in God sheltered her from her dilemma, and from the messages her body was sending. She went on, day after day, week after week, pretending all was right. She was a child of the Lord, and He would never forsake her.

"Chile, yuh sure is shapely. Ah guess my little girl is growin' up," Loretha said.

Elizabeth's hips and breasts had added womanly curves to her body. She had a small potbelly, but it wasn't noticeable under her full skirts. Her mother's statement was meant as a compliment, and that was how she took it. It was time for her to develop from that slender child into a woman.

A few weeks later, Elizabeth was startled by a tender punch to her stomach. It was during dinner. She glimpsed over at her parents to see if they noticed her reaction. She slid her hand over her small bulging belly and waited. Relieved there were no more tender punches, she dismissed the incident as a gas pocket. Later, during the still of the night, she lay awake, and the tender punches came again. The fluttering taps continued even after she rolled from her bed to the floor.

"Oh my Lord! Yuh have forsaken me. Ah believed Yuh'd never leave me alone. Why'd Yuh let this happen tuh me? Why don't Yuh love me the way Ah love You?" she prayed.

Elizabeth cried and prayed until she couldn't cry any more. She asked Him to come back to her—to make the changes in her life that only He had the power to do. But the more she prayed, the more she was convinced her God had forsaken her, and that was shattering to her existence. She chose to announce to herself that her Lord didn't exist, but she allowed a tiny bit of faith to remain with her.

It was late October, and as the leaves dried up and fell away from the trees, Elizabeth's faith had completely fallen away from her, and she lived in fear of what was to come. One evening only Elizabeth and Sarah were home. Sarah was downstairs in the den listening to her favorite radio program with the volume turned up louder than necessary, while Elizabeth was in the privacy of her bedroom.

Suddenly, a feeling of irrepressible anger came over her, and she refused to call on her Lord to hold it at bay. "See what yuh did tuh me," she whisper-screamed at the wall near the door. The veins in her neck became pronounced at the same time her eyes widened in a glaring stare. "Yuh stole my life. Ah didn't do anything wrong! It was yuh evilness! Yuh took me! Only bad things gonna come tuh yuh!" Her body was rigid; her arms stretched down at her side with her hands balled into a fist. She reached for the empty pottery flower vase and hurled it at the wall where she believed she saw a glaring apparition of Reverend Oliver. It shattered, and shards of thin baked clay sprayed across the wooden floor, along with a picture of a white Jesus Christ in a glass frame and a wooden cross.

Elizabeth knelt down on the circular braided area rug near her bed and banged her fists against her legs. Tears ran down her face, and she felt them tickle as they dripped from her chin. She wiped them away with the back of her hands. "Ah didn't do anything wrong," she repeated in a softer whisper. She cried and hugged herself, rocking herself to calmness. "Ah didn't do anything wrong, but Ah'm gonna wear all the blame." She rested her head on her bed and pulled her quilted bed cover around her tight enough to give her a sense of security.

An hour passed, and Elizabeth was still on the floor wrapped tightly in her quilt when she heard Sarah's footsteps coming up the stairs.

"Good night, 'Lizabeth,"

"Night, Sarah," Elizabeth called out. She stood behind her door, holding the doorknob tightly and propping her foot against the bottom, just in case Sarah tried to come into her room. She was calmer now, and when she looked around her room, it was startling to see its condition: the Jesus picture laid in its frame with a shattered glass cover, the cross on the floor midway of the room, her favorite vase shattered, and her bed covers pulled to the floor. She felt her face, and it seemed swollen, and her hair appeared to be wild and loose about her head. She didn't want to look at herself in the mirror. As soon as she was sure Sarah was in her own room, she combed her hair, made her bed, and hurried downstairs for the broom to sweep up the broken glass. She hung the cross and the Jesus picture, without the glass covering, back on the wall. She was in her bed before her parents returned home, but sleep didn't come easily.

Elizabeth's parents were so involved in the church they didn't notice her saddened spirit. She was very skilled in hiding the physical changes in her body, but the happy, outgoing child was no more. Each day there was a special preparation to select the clothing and undergarments to hide her changing figure. She was fortunate her body had filled out and continued to hide what was growing inside of her. It was easy getting her mother to purchase the girdles and bras she needed. Loretha was always lecturing that it wasn't proper for young ladies to have their behinds quivering and bouncing when they walked. One full line bra-girdle and one size small panty girdle were all she needed to hide the shame she believed to be hers alone.

Elizabeth would have taken her life rather than face her inevitable shame, but the reason for her shame was the very reason that saved her from doing the unforgivable, believing her child's life was not hers to take. It wasn't about God. She didn't know what she believed anymore. It was about the innocence of her unborn child, and as long as it existed inside her, it should have the right to live outside of her.

The days of November were rapidly passing, and Elizabeth's secret was soon to be revealed. She had to talk to someone who would believe her and understand: someone who could give her direction and offer a shoulder for her to cry on, someone who would keep her secret. That person was Mrs. Collins. Elizabeth wasn't sure if she would keep her secret, but she decided to visit her anyway.

Elizabeth reminded her mother that Sarah had band practice and asked permission to have the school bus drop her off at Collins Road after school. Loretha agreed, and volunteered to pick her up when she called.

Elizabeth thought about calling her mother, about the openness of the telephone, about the successions of three rings that let her and her family know the call was for their household and not for any of the other three or four families sharing the telephone line, about the "party line." Anyone could pick up the telephone at their home and listen to another family's conversation. The secrets of personal information and the loss of privacy often turned to gossip were a side effect of the party line.

Elizabeth spent her time at school thinking about her upcoming visit with Mrs. Collins. Her mind was busy forecasting what her life would be like before that year's winter season ended. Most of the day she appeared to be in a daze. Her thoughts were confusing, and that frightened her, but it frightened her more when she realized she wasn't able to sort and order her thoughts. It made her feel better knowing she could go to Mrs. Collins, but it troubled her not knowing if Mrs. Collins would keep her secret. She knew adults supported each other. Asking her to keep her secret was the same as asking her to employ the silence of a lie, and she wondered if it was fair to place that burden on Mrs. Collins. She also wondered what she would do if Mrs. Collins refused, telling her that informing her parents would be in her best interest. She wondered if it really mattered; her secret was about to become undone by the courses of nature.

Ah ain't got nowhere else tuh turn. When the baby's time comes … Daddy's gonna throw me outta the house. He ain't gonna believe Ah was taken. Reverend Oliver knows my father. My shame is gonna grab Daddy and hold him tight. He's bound tuh think Ah was like them bad girls … doin' nasty things and havin' babies. Ah shoulda gone on tuh the church that night … and … in front of my daddy and the deacons, and everybody … Ah shoulda told Daddy what Reverend Oliver did tuh me. Oh! … Ah shoulda did that. But Ah was tuh scared. Ah was too shame-faced. Ah was so shame-faced, Ah didn't scream for help or nothin'. So now Ah been thinkin' maybe 'Ah shoulda shamed Reverend Oliver at the church; humph … what a silly thought. If Ah knew then, what Ah know now … silly thought or not … Ah woulda went tuh the church instead of home. Ah reckon Daddy still wouldn't have believed me … but … Ah coulda shamed that man the way he shamed me. Ah coulda shamed him in front of everyone and later when Ah come up with a baby, they'd believe me then. Ooooh … what am Ah gonna do?

At the end of the day, Elizabeth sat behind the bus driver and asked him to let her off further down on Rehoboth Road at Collins' Road. She was quiet and ignored the loud noises and laughter of the other kids. When the bus arrived at Collins Road, Elizabeth thanked him and waved the bus on. Clutching her books close to her chest, she began to walk the long dirt road to Mrs. Collins' house. Her scrambled, rambling thoughts spoke to her from within the bouncing rhythm of her footsteps. When her fingers touched Mrs. Collins' front door, she had a limited memory of the half-mile walk.

"Hello! Mrs. Collins! It's me, 'Lizabeth!" She poked her head inside the front door, then waited for a response before walking in the house.

"Yes, chile. C'mon back here. Yuh know where Ah lak to be."

"Yes, ma'am." She walked from the front door through the living room to Mrs. Collins' sitting area.

"Ah's so happy yuh came tuh sit wit' me."

Elizabeth had held her misery for so long her defenses began to fall apart the moment she entered Mrs. Collins' sitting room. At first, tears gently streamed down her cheeks, then she burst into open sobs just as she approached Mrs. Collins' chair.

Mrs. Collins sat up in her chair as if something startled her. "Whut be botherin' yuh lak that, chile? Whut's the mattah wit yuh?"

Elizabeth was hurting so much her body vibrated with fear. "Ah need ..." Elizabeth began but suddenly her lips were stilled by fear. When she noticed the concern in Mrs. Collins' face, she summoned the courage to continue speaking. "Ah need tuh ... talk tuh yuh. It's ... it's real bad," Elizabeth stuttered, "but ... but ... Ah been hoping yuh can help me, and yuh won't tell anyone."

"Ah cain't tell nobody? Not even yuh folks? Whut if'n whut yuh be tellin' me goes 'gainst yuh folk's teachin'? Honey, Ah cain't tell yuh nothin' fer sho' 'til Ah know whut yuh be talkin' 'bout. C'mon down here where Ah kin reach yuh so Ah kin hol' yuh. Honey-chile, yuh sho' need some holdin'."

Slowly, Elizabeth bent down to her knees. She needed to be held, but that wasn't what was important to her, but because Mrs. Collins told her to come and get some holding, that was what she had to do. She gently laid her head on the softness of Mrs. Collins' full bosom. Her tears were absorbed by Mrs. Collins' house-dress, and she sniffed back the mucus sliding down her nasal cavities. It was comforting to feel Mrs. Collins arms wrap around her, rocking and soothing her body to stillness. She was at peace with herself for a short while, but just as she wiped away her tears, reality returned.

"Mrs. Collins, Ah don't want tuh ask yuh tuh do somethin' that's bad. Ah just need yuh tuh keep my secret. Ah ain't got nobody tuh talk tuh, and Ah'm hurtin' real bad. Please! Please! Gimme yuh word. My secret won't be a secret for long, anyway. Please promise me!"

'But, 'Liz'beth, honey, Ah cain't be makin' nary a promise til Ah know whut 'tis."

Elizabeth's streaming tears turned to sobs again. "Can Ah just sit with yuh for a while? Mama said she'll come and pick me up when Ah call her. Ah don't wanna go home yet."

"Yes, chile. Yuh company is always welcome. Would yuh lak somethin' tuh eat or drink? Yuh must be hongry."

"No, ma'am, Ah'll be all right. Ah just wanna sit here for awhile."

Elizabeth dried her tears and made attempts to compose herself. "Ah'm sorry for comin' here and upsettin' yuh like Ah did."

Mrs. Collins nodded her head. "Ah'm here, chile." Then she was quiet and only patted the back of Elizabeth's hand, calming her and giving her the time she needed. She was a wise old lady. Elizabeth knew Mrs. Collins understood she was deeply troubled. Elizabeth could see she was worrying her because of the expression on her face, but she was still too emotional to speak. She took deep breaths, waited and continued to accept the comfort of Mrs. Collins' touch. She was beginning to think a little clearer and knew her secret would be out eventually, so it really didn't matter if Mrs. Collins kept it or not.

Wanting to speak and holding it back was another struggle she fought within herself. All she could do in those moments was allow her eyes to follow the paisley pattern of Mrs. Collins' favorite chair. She thought of how comfortable that chair must be, and she believed it held Mrs. Collins as tender as Mrs. Collins had held her. Then, within a heartbeat, her thoughts flashed back to the reason she was there, and she heard herself speaking. "Ma'am. Do yuh remember tellin' me not tuh go through them woods last spring?"

"Yes. Ah 'member."

"Ah shoulda listened tuh yuh."

Mrs. Collins sat up in her chair, and her eyes fell on Elizabeth as if she knew what she was going to say. "Whut happen', chile?"

"That night, when Ah was goin' home, Ah went through the woods, and Reverend Oliver was waitin' there for me." Elizabeth's swollen eyes released another stream of warm tears, and her voice trembled as she spoke. "He took me!"

"C'mere, chile," Mrs. Collins beckoned. "Mah God! Lawd have mercy!"

As Elizabeth moved closer to receive more comfort, her crying broke into emotional sobs again. "Ah shoulda listened tuh yuh and took Rehoboth Road, but Ah think he woulda got me anyway. It's still a long walk down yuh road, and it was gittin' dark."

"Are yuh tellin' me Reverend Oliver took yuh, chile? Am Ah hearin' yuh right?"

"Yes, ma'am. He took my body, and now Ah don't know what tuh do."

"Did yuh tell yuh daddy?"

"No, ma'am! Ah know my daddy. Reverend Oliver said my daddy wouldn't believe me. Ah thought Ah'd feel better and the memories would go away … but …"

Before Elizabeth could go on, Mrs. Collins whispered softly, "Now yuh gone have his baby."

Elizabeth let out another sob. "Yes, ma'am! And Ah don't know what tuh do!"

"Oh, chile, yuh shouldn't be carryin' this burden by yuhself." She closed her eyes, and her lips were moving while she counted back the months. "Lemme see now, that wuz … five … no, six months ago. Oh baby, yuh been holdin' all that misery in fer six months? Yuh ain't tol' no one?"

"No, ma'am. Ah was afraid they wouldn't believe me. Now Ah don't know what tuh do when the baby comes."

"Do yuh want me tuh talk tuh yuh folks? I shoulda spoke tuh them dat day he was staring at you in church."

"That was the same day it happened," Elizabeth cried. "Please don't tell 'em now. Ah'll find a way. Please don't even tell 'em Ah told yuh." Elizabeth cried and cried as she pleaded. "Yuh the only one that knows. Ah had tuh talk tuh someone that would believe me. Ah didn't do anything wrong, but Ah know this is gonna disgrace my family."

"Chile, yuh daddy loves yuh, and he'll be there fer yuh."

"No, he won't ... and Mama ... Ah don't know 'bout Mama."

"Why didn't yuh come back tuh mah house? Ah woulda called yuh daddy. He woulda believed me." Then Mrs. Collins caught herself. "Oh baby ... Ah'm so sorry. It be too late tuh be speakin' 'bout whut yuh shoulda done. We need tuh be thinkin' 'bout whut we gone do now." She rested her head on the back of her chair, and her eyes moved up and set upon the rows of grooved wood in her sitting room ceiling. It seemed like she was counting each board. "Lemme see now ... yuh is 'bout five months 'long. No, Ah believe yuh is in yuh sixth month." Seemingly satisfied with her calculations, she turned back to Elizabeth in a quick, smooth move. "Chile! How yuh hidin' this baby?"

"Ah wear two girdles and always a full skirt. If Ah wear pants, Ah always wear a big shirt."

" 'Liz'beth! Chile! Yuh could be hurtin' the baby lak dat."

"Ah have tuh do it this way. Ah don't know what else tuh do."

"Ah'm here fer yuh. Ah'll keep yuh secret. Ah gotta give this mattah some mo' thought. Yuh sho' gone be in mah prayers tuhnight."

"Mrs. Collins, please don't be praying for me. There ain't no God for me. If He loved me the way Ah loved Him, He wouldn't let this happen tuh me. There ain't no such thing as a God." Elizabeth spoke with some conviction. She was angry with Reverend Oliver, but her hurt and disappointment seemed to be more with God.

"Oh baby! Yuh mus'n speak out lak dat 'gainst the Lawd. Oh, chile! Oh, chile, the Lawd, he got a plan. He got a mighty big plan fer yuh. He ain't gone leave yuh 'lone. He ain't fergotten yuh. Now, He be walkin' beside yuh. Keep the Lawd in yuh life. Honey, He got plans fer yuh baby too. He didn't do dis tuh yuh. The devil did it, but the Lawd gone make it right."

Elizabeth let Mrs. Collins preach to her out of respect, but she continued to believe there was no longer a Lord to protect her. For the next few weeks, she spent a great deal of time with Mrs. Collins. It was only when she was with her that she had moments of peace. Mrs. Collins pleaded with her to tell her parents. Preparations had to be made, but the conversation always ended the same, with Elizabeth saying, "Ah'll tell them next week."

"Ah'll stand wit' yuh; Ah'll have 'em tuh come tuh mah house. Ah'll tell 'em fer yuh. Ah know dey is gone be mad wit' me, but dat ain't important now. Ah'll be wit' yuh, chile."

"No, Ah'll tell them. Ah don't want them tuh know that yuh know. Yuh helped me to be strong, and Ah can't ask yuh tuh do no more. Believe me, yuh'll know when Ah tell 'em. Yuh'll probably hear them screamin' through them woods."

"Ah s'pose so, chile. Ah s'pose so," Mrs. Collins mumbled.

CHAPTER 3

Spending time with Mrs. Collins gave Elizabeth the strength she needed to speak to her parents. For the past four weeks, she visited her during the evenings and helped her with her chores on Saturdays. Loretha and Reverend Turner thought it was very nice that she shared her time with a well respected Christian woman instead of hanging out with the local teenagers. Elizabeth and Mrs. Collins rarely spoke about the rape or the baby. Elizabeth had promised Mrs. Collins she was just waiting for the right time to tell her parents. They were friends, so they talked about the things friends talked about. Whenever Elizabeth wasn't with Mrs. Collins, fear and anxiety plagued her; at times she was frozen in a whirlwind of thoughts and worry.

It was a Tuesday morning, December 12th, 1950, and Elizabeth went through her normal early morning routine preparing for school. When the school bus honked, she and Sarah left the house. Elizabeth took her regular seat behind the driver, and Sarah hurried to the middle of the bus where her friends were waiting.

The old, hand-me-down bus from the white kids' school pulled away, rattling and bumping down the road. When the white school received new buses, their old buses were passed down to the Negro school. The brakes on the bus made a grinding sound whenever it was pulled to a stop. All the kids bounced in their seats when the bus was in motion, and the gears clanked into place as it lurched forward. There was no attempt to add a fresh coat of yellow paint to the rusty-old-rickety vehicles, but they did manage to paint over the lettering to let the community know the buses were now transporting the colored children. There was no doubt about it, passing down the old buses as well as any other equipment made a statement. It yelled loud and clear, "We are above you, better than you, superior to you." That had a definite effect on the young people, but the elders said, "Never mind, we got schools and we got buses."

The elders could remember when they walked miles to the dirt floor, one room building with the pot belly stoves where they sat on wooden benches and used slate to copy their letters, where a whole family shared textbooks that they had to work so hard to earn the money to buy even though they were worn, tattered and passed down from the white schools.

Elizabeth endured the bouncing and shaking every day and never gave the condition of her transportation a second thought. It wasn't important. She sat quietly and hugged her books. She watched the road, but not at anything in particular, while her mind was involved in noisy and busy thoughts. Just then, she felt a pain that grew stronger as it traveled from the lower pit of her back, around and across her stomach, squeezing her. She held her breath and was jerked into reality. *Oh my God! What is this?*

She bent forward and clutched her books even tighter. She bit down tightly on the corner of her notebook to hide the pain. Within the minute, what she thought was a stomach cramp had passed. Elizabeth hoped she didn't have to experience that kind of cramp again. She was first off the bus. Still clutching her books, she moved aside to allow the other kids to pass. Feeling better, she pushed the cramp incident to a corner of her mind and walked slowly and alone toward the high school building.

The Booker T. Washington Campus educated all the black children in Bibb County. The all brick elementary school building was the newest building on campus and was located to the right of the main driveway and extended behind the bus parking lot. It was the largest building, "L" shaped, with the auditorium and cafeteria sharing the same space. Classes for the sixth, seventh and eighth grades were held in three separate wood frame buildings that once served as the elementary and intermediate school. Wood burning stoves heated each classroom. On those cool mornings, the janitor would have all the classrooms warm for the start of the school day.

The high school was a single story building that was about a hundred and fifty feet long. It had a center corridor and a girls and boys bathroom at each end near the exit doors. The nurse's station and the campus' general office were located in the center of the building. The agricultural building and gymnasium were located in a large cinderblock building with a tin roof behind the high school building.

The first period of the day was Physical Education, and Elizabeth had been fortunate in hiding her figure under the large bloomer-type gym suit and oversize high school sweatshirt. She went through a moderate version of the activities without another cramp. Relieved, she felt confident she would be okay, and she made it through the second period. But midway into the third period, intense low back pain tightened like a band around her stomach. The pain was more severe, but, like before, left within the minute only to return, again and again, at regular intervals. Each time lasting for longer periods. She had to appear composed and hide her fear more than her pain from her teacher and the other kids in her class.

Elizabeth raised her hand to get the teacher's attention. "Mrs. Colsen, may Ah leave the room?"

Reaching for the hall pass, Mrs. Colsen gestured her approval while continuing to lecture about the mathematical equation that was written across the blackboard.

Elizabeth stepped into the empty corridor. Its overwhelming depth appeared before her. The girl's bathroom, which was only two doors away, now seemed to be located out of her walking reach. Her heart pounded, and pain grabbed her so tight she could barely breathe, much less walk. She wanted to get down on her hands and knees and crawl, but she remained erect and struggled along on her feet, allowing herself to be supported by the wall. Just as she reached the door, her pain released her.

As soon as she entered the toilet stall, a gush of fluid soaked through her undergarments. She fought desperately to remove her outer clothing so she could remove the girdles. Another cramp grabbed her while she stood naked, holding her blouse and skirt. Her full slip, long line bra-girdle and panty girdle lay in a soggy clump on the floor. She knew she was going to have the baby. She wanted to cry, but crying would only cloud her mind with useless self-pity. Struggling with the pain and the determination to dress was all her young mind had time for.

When the pain subsided, she managed to replace her blouse and fasten her skirt before the contractions came again. The next contraction was so severe it caused her to sit on the toilet, and compelled her to push. She could feel the baby coming. Petrified with fear and overcome with pain, she lost consciousness and fell from the toilet to the floor. It was near the end of the third period, Elizabeth was alone, unconscious, giving birth, and bleeding severely.

—∿—

Within the moments that followed, the school bell rang, signaling the changing of classes. Three girls entered the bathroom. "Look! That's Elizabeth Turner. Go get the nurse," one of the girls yelled.

Stunned! None of the girls moved. Although Elizabeth was unconscious, the birth of her baby was continuing. "Oh mah God! She's havin' a baby. Quick! Pull hur out of the stall. The nurse is gonna need tuh get tuh hur," another girl demanded.

"No! We shouldn't move hur," said the more timid girl.

"We have tuh move hur so the nurse can help hur. Move … Ah'll pull hur out into the open! Yuh go get the nurse!" The more dominant girl took charge. The tone of her voice demanded compliance. "Yuh go block the door so no one else can come in! She doesn't need a bunch of people gawkin' at hur." She grabbed Elizabeth by both arms and pulled her out and away from the toilet stall. Then she noticed the baby had been born, but he wasn't breathing or moving and was covered in vaginal fluids and blood. He was lying between Elizabeth's legs on the bottom section of her wet skirt.

The girl didn't want to touch the baby, but she knew if she didn't, he would die. She took the front section of Elizabeth's skirt and pulled it down to cover him. Using it as a barrier between her and the baby, she picked him up and placed him belly-down on Elizabeth's stomach. Holding him in place, she gave him a whack on his bottom. He coughed and let out a wailing cry. His purplish-pale skin pinked up to the color of a walnut, and the girl knew she had done the right thing.

The nurse arrived and noticed the wailing and trembling baby. "Lawd have mercy! Oh mah God! Did y'all deliver that baby?"

"No, ma'am. When Ah pulled hur from the toilet stall, the baby was already there. Ah just put 'em on hur stomach and smacked 'em on the bottom. Ah don't think he was breathin' too good."

"Yuh did good. Yuh may have just saved that baby's life. Now, Ah need yuh tuh go tuh my office and bring as many towels and blankets as yuh can carry. The ambulance is on the way," the nurse said.

The umbilical cord was still intact, so the nurse removed her shoelace and tied it tight near the baby. She placed him on Elizabeth's stomach and pulled the corners of her skirt over him to help keep him warm. Elizabeth was unconscious and had lost a great deal of blood. She pulled Elizabeth by both legs back into the stall and elevated her feet on the toilet bowl. The baby was still wailing, giving out good, healthy sounds. The nurse knew he was in no immediate danger. Her main concern was with Elizabeth's color and the large amount of blood that stood in a pool and had begun spreading out, traveling along the grouted tracks of the tile floor. She knew it was conceivable that Elizabeth could die if help didn't arrive soon. It was no secret that the one ambulance emergency system would give preference to a white person in need before coming to the aid of a Negro. She closed her eyes and prayed to God. She prayed that there were no other emergencies.

The girl returned with her arms filled with towels and blankets. She helped the nurse cover Elizabeth and the baby. Two paramedics barged in with a gurney and a large box containing medical supplies. The nurse raised her head toward the ceiling and mouthed, "Thank yuh, Jesus." She believed that immediately thanking the Lord for granting a prayer request cleared the way for the next prayer. Then she stood back and gave them room to work.

A paramedic separated the umbilical cord and clamped it off before wrapping the baby in a towel and handing him to the nurse along with her shoelace. Elizabeth was placed on the gurney. As one paramedic was covering her with warm blankets, the other was setting up the bottle of intravenous fluids.

Outside the girls' bathroom door, teachers were ordering students to their classrooms. The three girls who found Elizabeth were allowed to remain, and they continued to block the door.

Elizabeth and the baby were ready to be transported to the hospital. Elizabeth was covered with blankets, and an oxygen mask covered her face. In spite of the teacher's orders, the students continued lagging in the halls.

"What happened?" a student asked.

"Somebody had a baby in the bathroom," someone else answered.

"Who is she?" another questioned.

"Go tuh class!" a teacher yelled out, directing her orders to all of the students. "Go now or Ah'll see tuh it that yuh'll be disciplined."

The students began walking away. Some of them walked backward to satisfy their curiosity.

"Move it! Move it now!" another teacher yelled out.

The paramedics raced down the corridor, pushing and guiding the gurney. The nurse was right behind them, carrying the baby bundled in towels. She turned to the three girls and spoke softly, "Thank yuh for yuh help. Now if one of yuh would ask the janitor to lock this bathroom until he can clean it. Another one of yuh go tuh the office and have the secretary call Elizabeth's parents. Tell 'em tuh meet us at Macon General Hospital. As soon as the bathroom door is locked, Ah want yuh tuh call yuh parents and have 'em pick yuh up early if they can. Don't talk tuh any of the other children, and stay in the office 'til yuh parents come."

Reverend Oliver watched Mr. Lacy, the campus principal, walk toward the elementary school building with a hurried, stressed pace. Mr. Lacy was a slightly built, fidgety little man with an ashy mushroom complexion and feminine mannerisms. He switched and twittered as he took his tiny little steps and mouthed, "Lawd have mercy!" He spoke to himself at the audibility of a whisper. The expressions of his words were etched all over his face and into the wrinkles of his brow.

"What's wrong with these young gals? Can't they keep their panties up and their legs crossed? A man can't help being a man, but a woman can resist. Their mamas need tuh teach 'em tuh save themselves. Elizabeth Turner. Ah thought she wuz different. Well … that's whut's tuh be said of a quiet chile, a minister's daughter … Yuh never know whut's going on in their heads. Now Ah have tuh tell hur daddy whut happened. Dammit! Dammit! Dammit! The superintendent is gone have my head. A pregnant gal in school contaminating other girls. Hur teachers sure bettah be ready tuh answer tuh me. How could they let a pregnant gal in school?" He hurried along, allowing the rhythm of his rude words to quicken his pace even more.

Reverend Oliver approached Mr. Lacy just as he entered the elementary school building and stood in his path. "What's goin' on over there?"

"Elizabeth Turner. Mah God! Of all girls! Man … that gal had a baby in the girl's room. Do yuh believe that? Reverend Turner's gal." He started to say more, but seemed to remember he was speaking to Reverend Oliver and quieted down.

The shocking news of Elizabeth's dilemma caused Reverend Oliver to require the assistance of the wall to maintain his balance. Mr. Lacy was so deeply cloaked in the events of the past thirty minutes, he didn't notice Reverend Oliver's blood-drained complexion. After stopping for only a few moments to give the initial information, he walked away, never looking back, and he never stopped talking. "Right now, Ah'm going tuh get hur sistah. Ah believe it'll be best for hur if Ah take hur along wit' me tuh the hospital tuh wait for hur parents. Ah'm only goin' tuh tell hur hur sistah was sick, and she'll be okay. Let hur parents tell hur about the baby."

Loretha answered the call from Mr. Lacy. The urgency in his voice caused Reverend and Mrs. Turner to fear the worst. When they entered the colored emergency waiting room, they noticed Sarah sitting in one of the three wooden chairs, being consoled by the nurse. Mr. Lacy was still twitching, pacing, fidgeting, and practicing the words he should use when he spoke with Reverend Turner.

"What happened, Sarah?" Loretha asked.

"Oh, Mama," Sarah cried out in loud sobs.

"Sarah, everything will be all right. Let me talk tuh yuh parents. Ah'll explain everythin' tuh them," Mr. Lacy said. He beckoned them to the side of the room and began to whisper as though something that was out in the open could suddenly be hidden again. "Ah spoke with the doctors, and Elizabeth will be all right." His mannerism allowed the Turners to feel at ease, but they still needed to know what happened. It was very difficult for Mr. Lacy to tell them. He began to twitch, and fidget with his hands, scratching his head and the corners of his nose repetitiously. He didn't know where to begin or how to break the news gently.

At first, he stumbled over his carefully selected and rehearsed words, which made him sound like he was babbling. On his second try, he was blunt, to the point, and crystal clear. He closed his eyes and the words, "Elizabeth had a baby," rolled off his lips.

"Had a baby! Yuh must be mistaken. 'Lizabeth wasn't pregnant. How dare yuh say such a thing about my daughter," Reverend Turner said.

Mr. Lacy opened his eyes and looked at Reverend Turner while he spoke, but when he needed to respond, he closed his eyes again. He always closed his eyes when talking about a sensitive situation. "Please,

Reverend Turner. This is very difficult for me. Yuh daughter delivered a baby boy in the girls' room at school. What else can Ah tell yuh?" By the time Mr. Lacy opened his eyes again, the nervous fluttering stopped.

"Ah resent yuh tone of voice, Reverend Turner. Ah'm here because it's my job tuh be here. Ah didn't cause this problem. Ah'm only trying to help." Now he was angry. He looked at Reverend Turner, and this time his eyes didn't flutter. He glared directly in Reverend Turner's eyes. "Maybe yuh didn't know she was pregnant, but the fact is, she had a baby while at school."

Loretha was weak with disbelief. She leaned back and propped herself against the wall in the tiny room.

Mr. Lacy watched Reverend Turner, whose threatening demeanor appeared to cause him to swell in stature. He towered with anger over the frail Mr. Lacy, and he snarled down at him. "Ah don't believe yuh." He turned abruptly and walked over to the nurses' station and demanded to speak with one of the doctors and to see his daughter. Mr. Lacy exhaled the air from his lungs and his body slumped into a chair.

"Ah'm sorry, Elizabeth Turner is in surgery, yuh can't see her now," the nurse replied.

"Did my daughter have a baby?"

"Yes, sir. She had a healthy baby boy, but there were some complications from the birth, and she had tuh be taken in for emergency surgery. The doctor will come and speak with yuh as soon as possible." She turned away and continued with her duties.

Loretha hurried to the nurses' station. She bent down so her eyes could meet with the nurse's. "Is my daughter goin' tuh die?" She stared into the nurse's eyes to judge the truthfulness of her reply.

"Ah don't know that answer, ma'am."

Knowing the nurse gave her an honest, but empty, answer Loretha thanked her anyway. A cold, numbing sensation gripped her, and she held tightly to the corner of the desk. By the time her balance returned, she remembered the school nurse. It came to her that she didn't know her name. She needed to question her.

"Mrs. Turner," the school nurse began, "Elizabeth was unconscious when she was found in the girls' room, but her breathin' was very good. Ah believe she'll be okay. The baby was a little small, but he had a strong healthy cry. Try not tuh worry. There were only about ten minutes between the time she left the classroom, tuh the time the girls found her." She didn't tell her how pale she was, how much blood she had lost, or how she was afraid Elizabeth would die before she arrived at the hospital. "Please don't worry, Mrs. Turner. Ah know she'll be all right." She silently prayed that what she was telling her would be so.

Loretha apologized and asked the nurse her name. After learning it was Mrs. Mitchell, she thanked her for the information and for being there for Elizabeth. Then she thanked her for giving her hope.

Reverend Turner took a few steps in the small room, and he was back in Mr. Lacy's space. He seemed to be in a hurry, and was gruff in his expression. "Thank yuh for all yuh help. Ah know yuh have other things yuh need tuh do. We're here now. Yuh can leave us." He was rude, hurt, and painfully embarrassed. He just wanted them to leave. "Ah'll call yuh tomorrow and tell yuh how she's doin'."

Mrs. Mitchell kissed Sarah on the forehead, and winked and nodded at Loretha. She stood and walked closer to Mr. Lacy while he shook Reverend Turner's hand. Reverend Turner began to escort Mrs. Mitchell and Mr. Lacy to the emergency room door as though he were escorting them to the door of his home. He walked close behind them, and that seemed to suggest that they should not turn around. He watched them walk toward Mr. Lacy's car.

―∿―

As soon as Mr. Lacy and Mrs. Mitchell drove away, Reverend Turner went over to Sarah.

"Who's the father?"

"Ah don't know nothin', Daddy! Ah didn't know she was goin' tuh have a baby."

"What do yuh mean, yuh didn't know? She's yuh sister. How could yuh not know?" Then he heard himself, and reality flashed across his mind; it came to him that he was expecting Sarah to know something he should have known. He wanted to be still, to be quiet, to stop the rage growing inside of him, but he was unrestrained and loose. There was no one, or nothing, to hold him back; he needed someone to strike out at, and Sarah was the chosen candidate.

"Daddy, Ah didn't know. She didn't tell me anything."

"Don't lie tuh me! Sisters talk tuh each other! Ah know yuh know, and yuh gonna tell me!"

"Please, Daddy. Ah don't know anything. She didn't tell me anything."

Sarah had only been humble, and showed no sign of disrespect, but that didn't stop Reverend Turner. He stood over her and raised his hand to levy the blow he intended for Elizabeth.

"Stop, John! The chile said she didn't know anything! Please! Leave her alone!" Loretha pulled Sarah close to her.

It was very clear to Reverend Turner that Loretha wouldn't allow him to hurt Sarah, physically or emotionally. He recognized her defiance and lowered his hand. He was stunned and thankful she stopped him from doing something he would regret as soon as the act was committed, but defiance from Loretha was something he had never experienced. He had no defense against her. Her defiance embarrassed him in front of Sarah; it pushed him back to a strange and unfriendly place, but he was thankful to be there. He stood before both of them with a confused, torn, and twisted expression, then stormed out the room.

Loretha and Sarah remained, waiting for news of Elizabeth's condition. They were emotionally tired. More than an hour passed. Loretha sat with her eyes closed. When she opened them, she glanced at the clock, then at the nurse's station. Sarah, who sat with her head on her mother's shoulder, straightened up when Loretha decided to walk over to speak with the nurse again.

"Yuh told my husband my daughter had a baby. May we see the baby while we wait for news?"

"Sure. The baby is in the isolation nursery on the third floor. He's on the maternity ward. When yuh daughter returns from surgery, she'll be placed in the ward on that floor. Ah'll give yuh a pass and have the doctor meet with yuh upstairs."

"Oh, thank yuh. We'd like tuh see the baby."

When Sarah and Loretha arrived on the maternity wing, Loretha asked the nurse if she could see the Turner baby. She was directed to go down the hall to the isolation nursery.

"Ah'll call down and tell 'em tuh move the baby tuh the window," the nurse replied.

The incubator with the small baby was waiting at the window of the nursery when they arrived.

"Oh. Mama, he's so tiny!" Sarah whined.

"Yes, and he seems to be healthy. They call him, 'Baby Boy Turner.' The card says he weighs four pounds and two ounces," Loretha said.

Sarah stared at the tiny baby and began to cry again. "Mama, Ah didn't know 'Lizabeth was gonna have a baby. Why'd Daddy blame me?"

"Honey, he's just hurtin'. He didn't mean tuh take it out on you. We'll all be blamed for this. But, we'll get over this, too." Loretha told Sarah what she needed to know to keep her from worrying. She wished there was someone to comfort her. There had never been a serious dilemma in her family. For as long as she had been married to John, they had never had their foundation shaken.

"Mama, the baby looks like Daddy."

"Like Daddy and 'Lizabeth," Loretha responded. She wiped the tears from the corners of her eyes.

"Mama, he's all wrinkled, but Ah think he's beautiful."

"Sarah, does 'Lizabeth have a boyfriend?"

"Ah don't think so. She always stays tuh hurself. Mama, she didn't even spend time with the girls at school. All she did was study and read. Ah never, ever, saw hur talkin' tuh a boy."

Loretha stood quietly, staring at the baby and keeping her thoughts to herself. *How did this happen? What will John do? Oh Lord, help my family get through this. Lord, we need yuh now.*

The commotion at the far end of the corridor caused them to turn in that direction. The large double doors swung open, and a gurney was guided into the maternity wing.

"Mama, it's 'Lizabeth," Sarah said. She rushed toward Elizabeth, turned back and beckoned her mother to hurry.

Loretha wasn't far behind. "Is she going tuh be all right?" she asked the aide.

"The doctor will be in tuh talk tuh yuh," was all the aide could answer.

Looking down at the still and sleeping Elizabeth, Loretha thanked the aide. She kissed Elizabeth gently on the forehead, then stood back and allowed the aide to take her to the bed assigned to her. She wanted to cry when she saw her child unconscious, wearing a frightening pale-ashy complexion and connected to bottles and tubes. It was clear one of the bottles was half filled with blood. For Sarah's sake, Loretha remained composed.

"Mrs. Turner, y'all can go tuh the waiting area down the hall, next tuh the elevator. Ah'll let yuh know when yuh can come tuh hur bedside," the aide said.

Loretha thanked the aide and began to walk toward the waiting area, directing Sarah through the swinging doors.

"Mama, 'Lizabeth is so pale. Is she gonna be all right?"

"Yes, honey, she's been through a lot. She'll be fine." Loretha prayed that was what the doctor would tell her.

While they sat in the waiting area, they entertained themselves, watching the elevator doors open and close. Loretha took notice of the happy faces of the families visiting the maternity wing. *Birth is supposed to be a happy occasion,* she thought. *Life is happiness. Ah'm goin' tuh love this baby like Ah love my own, no matter what.*

The elevator door slid open and a tall, white man stepped off. He approached the waiting area, "Mrs. Turner?"

Loretha stood up. "Yes, Ah'm Mrs. Turner."

"I'm Doctor Pernell. Let me tell you where we stand. Your daughter delivered a baby boy at seven months gestation. I mean, seven months along. The baby is healthy and strong, except for a low birth weight. Elizabeth will be fine, but she experienced some serious complications. She lost a lot of blood, and we had to transfuse her twice. We almost lost her. It was as though she didn't want to live. She wouldn't fight with us, but we won. She's out of the woods for now. I'm afraid she may never have another child." He spoke quickly, trying to give all the details before any interruptions.

"Did she have tuh have a hysterectomy?"

"No, no, but her chances of having another baby are very slim. But with faith, anything is possible. She may be in the hospital for a couple of weeks, but you can take the baby home in a few days."

"Thank yuh. Will yuh be around if Ah have more questions? This was such a shock. Ah'm havin' trouble sortin' things out," Loretha said.

"Yes. I understand. My name is Doctor Raymond Pernell. Just ask the nurse to give you my card. I have regular office hours, and you should feel free to call me with any questions. I want to see Elizabeth at the clinic for follow-up after she's released from the hospital. I'll be her physician while she's here."

"Thank yuh, so much."

"I'll be talking with you." Doctor Pernell excused himself with a gentle bow.

Immediately, Loretha summarized that Doctor Pernell was not from Georgia. His speech was proper, or so she thought. He sounded like a Northerner, and he was nonjudgmental. It seemed to Loretha that Doctor Pernell believed Elizabeth wasn't just another colored girl bringing another colored bastard into the world. He didn't seem to care how she became his patient. He treated Elizabeth like she was a person, and sympathized with her mother.

Loretha and Sarah picked up the doctor's card and returned to the waiting area. They were tired. Sarah snuggled up close to her mother and closed her eyes. It was early evening. Sarah had not eaten since breakfast, and she was hungry. Loretha was too tired and drained to even think about food, not even for Sarah. It wasn't long before the nurse came over to inform them that they could go to Elizabeth's bed, but she warned them that she was still asleep, and she didn't think she would wake up before morning.

"Thank yuh. C'mon, Sarah. Ah want tuh sit with 'Lizabeth for a while, then Ah'll find a way tuh take yuh home, but Ah have tuh come right back. Ah don't want hur tuh wake up and be alone."

"Mama, Ah want tuh stay with yuh. Ah don't want tuh go home and be alone with Daddy. Can Ah stay with you and 'Lizabeth tonight?" Sarah pleaded.

"Ah know the nurses will let me stay, but Ah don't know if they'll let you. Ah'll ask them. If they say yuh can't, then we'll think of something else tuh do," Loretha whispered.

Sarah watched with pleading eyes while her mother called to the nurse who was leading them into the large room.

"Would it be okay if my daughter stayed with me in the hospital tonight? Ah don't have anyone tuh leave her with, and Ah don't want Elizabeth tuh wake up and be alone."

"Well, it's against hospital policy tuh have visitors on the ward after eight o'clock. Parents and husbands are allowed, but … let me talk with the charge nurse. Ah'll get back tuh yuh."

Loretha knew this place well. Sarah and Elizabeth were born in this hospital. She remembered it as being a place of happiness. But Sarah had never seen a hospital ward before. She was immersed with the many beds lined neatly in a row on both sides of the room. This was the colored maternity wing. She could feel the eyes of the other new mothers following them as they made their way to Elizabeth's bed. She nodded at each one as she walked passed. Each bed had curtains hanging from tracks attached to the ceiling. The drawn curtains provided privacy, but the sounds of the ward filtered through.

Sarah was frightened by Elizabeth's condition, and she clung tightly to her mother's arm. Loretha led her to the chair next to the window, and then pulled the other chair close to Elizabeth's bedside. After spending a few minutes with Elizabeth, the two left for the small restaurant across the street from the hospital. They ordered chicken sandwiches and ice tea, and ate quickly at a small table in the greasy back room kitchen area, then hurried back to Elizabeth's bedside before the announcement that visiting hours were over. The nurse forgot them or pretended to forget, but Loretha pulled the curtains tight and didn't question for fear she would tell her Sarah had to leave.

Loretha, tired and weary, laid her head on the corner of the bed. Sarah sat curled up in the chair and soon fell asleep. Filled with emotions and afraid of John, Loretha tried to sort things out. *How did Ah fail my daughter? Why didn't she come tuh me? What am Ah goin' tuh do about John? He's goin' tuh be so unreasonable. If Ah knew she was pregnant, Ah could've sent her tuh live with my sister in Virginia. She could've come back home and no one would've known. Ah don't know what we would've done with the baby … but that doesn't matter now. Now … Ah must try tuh figure a way tuh bring John around. Oh Lord, please keep us near yuh!*

Loretha didn't know when the thoughts ended and the dreaming began. Before she knew it, daylight peeked through the slits of the closed draperies. The nurse entered between the privacy curtains and began changing the bottles and making notes on Elizabeth's chart. Sarah began to rouse, but Elizabeth remained asleep.

"Good morning," Loretha said, looking up at the nurse. "When do yuh think she'll wake up?"

"Its hard tuh tell. She's been though a great deal, but she's doing just fine. Ah've been checking on hur throughout the night. The doctor will be in tuh see hur soon. We'd like tuh freshen hur up and change hur bed. Yuh could wait in the waiting room, and we'll call yuh when we're through. When we change hur, she may wake up. Ah'll tell hur yuh here and that yuh been with hur all night," the nurse said.

"Thank yuh very much. Come, Sarah."

The agony of this experience was evident in their posture and their facial expressions. Loretha was confident Elizabeth would be all right, but she was troubled over John's attitude. They had spent the night with Elizabeth and he hadn't called or revisited the hospital to inquire about his daughter's condition.

"As soon as 'Lizabeth wakes up and sees that we're here, Ah'll take yuh home."

"Mama … please … Ah don't want tuh go home. Ah don't want tuh be alone with Daddy."

"Honey, yuh don't have tuh be afraid of yuh father."

"Yes Ah do, Mama. Yuh saw how he was yesterday. He'll still be mad at me. Can yuh just take me tuh Mrs. Collins' house? Ah'll be ready tuh come home when yuh come back for me. Pleaseee … Mama … Pleaseee?"

Sarah's pleading was etched with fear. Loretha knew she was right. John might continue to go after her. She found it very hard to admit to Sarah that she agreed with her, but John's behavior was unpredictable.

"Okay, honey. If yuh feel so strongly about this, Ah'll take yuh tuh Mrs. Collins."

"Okay, Mama."

It was time to go back to Elizabeth's bedside. When they passed the nursery, they stood for a while and took a long quiet look at the baby. "He's so beautiful and innocent," Loretha whispered. "What kind of life will he have without a father?

"Come, Sarah, we need to get back tuh the ward." She turned from the window and Sarah just as tears began to form in her eyes. As they approached Elizabeth, they noticed she was still in a twilight sleep. Not knowing if she could hear her or understand, Loretha leaned over and kissed her on the forehead.

"Are yuh awake, honey? Can yuh hear me?"

Elizabeth opened her eyes briefly, and then closed them. This little gesture was enough for Loretha to realize that Elizabeth knew she was there. She was awake and coherent, but found it difficult to face her mother. She wanted to tell her what happened, but didn't have the strength to explain.

"Listen, honey. Ah want tuh take Sarah home. Then Ah'll be back tuh stay with yuh."

Elizabeth briefly opened and closed her eyes again.

"Ah'll be back soon, Okay?"

This time, Elizabeth just pretended to be asleep. This wasn't difficult, because before they could leave her bedside, the lingering effects of the anesthesia pulled her back into unconsciousness.

Just as Loretha and Sarah reached the end of the corridor, Loretha remembered John had taken the car.

"Sarah, we don't have any way tuh get home. Ah don't want tuh call yuh father."

"Mama, maybe Reverend Oliver will pick us up?"

"Oh … he's probably working, but Ah'll call his house anyway," Loretha said.

CHAPTER 4

The telephone rang. Reverend Oliver hurried to answer it before Thea. He had a two-ring signal. He wasn't sure what news he would hear, and he was afraid, believing Elizabeth would eventually tell her parents. When he heard Loretha's calm and tired voice, he felt relieved; if she knew anything, he didn't believe she would have been so relaxed.

"Yes, Ah'll be happy tuh pick yuh up. How's Elizabeth?"

"She's still asleep. She opened her eyes for a moment, but she's still under the effects of the anesthesia. Ah'm surprised tuh catch yuh home."

"Ah took a few days off tuh be with Thea. Her time is near, yuh-know. Ah'll be there in twenty minutes. Wait at the main entrance. Okay? Bye." He fell back in the chair, holding his head in his hands. A few moments passed before his panic subsided.

"Thea," he called out. "Ah'm going tuh the hospital tuh pick up Loretha and Sarah."

"Okay," Thea said. "Owen, why isn't John pickin' them up?"

"Ah don't know, honey. That was Loretha on the phone. She just said they needed a ride home."

Just as Reverend Oliver pulled up to the hospital's main entrance, his fears worsened. He had to be careful about what he said, and decided to let Loretha and Sarah do all the talking, but they were weary and quiet. Reverend Oliver drove, and they all took advantage of the mental space they seemed to need. He drove slow, savoring each moment of peace before the truth came out.

"Reverend Oliver, would yuh take us tuh Mrs. Collins' house first?
"Sure."

———ɯ———

Reverend Oliver waited in the car while Loretha and Sarah entered Mrs. Collins' house, watching as they walked from the circular, reddish clay-dirt driveway, along the overgrown stone path. His fear took him on a mental tour while he searched for patterns in the stone walk. Patterns meant order. He needed the return of order to provide relief from suffering the punishment of fear and confusion. The guilt of his thievery remained with him, beating him and attacking his conscience with a vengeance. His guilt had mellowed somewhat over the months, and the stabbing pains had dulled, especially when he began to believe he would never have to experience the social consequences of his action.

He continued to search for the patterns in Mrs. Collins' walkway, allowing his eyes to trace each stone and separate them from the weeds and blades of grass that found life and managed to survive from beneath the edges and cracks of the uneven masonry. The word "Life" slipped through his lips. *It was time for this child tuh be born. Lord, it was yuh purpose that this child should live. But, why me, Lord?* Then he scolded himself for insinuating the Lord had anything to do with his behavior. *It was the devil's work. Oh Lord, please don't let this child be of the devil's making, but of yuh turnin' around the devil's work and creatin' the grandeur of this life. Oh Lord! Please Lord! Will there be no end tuh my sufferin'? Oh Lord.*

Mrs. Collins stood in her opened door. "What y'all doin' here so early?" she asked.

"Ah should've called yuh," Loretha said, "but yuh know 'bout that party-line." When Loretha explained about Elizabeth, John and Sarah, and why Reverend Oliver drove her to her house so early in the morning, Mrs. Collins remained straight-faced. She turned toward

Reverend Oliver and gave him a wave of her hand, because it was the neighborly thing to do.

Reverend Oliver waved back, knowing waving wasn't the correct behavior for a minister. He should have walked with Loretha and Sarah to Mrs. Collins' door. He should have greeted her with a handshake or a cheek-to-cheek hug. He should have asked her how she was doing, or if there was anything he could do for her. He should have greeted her in a proper manner that the privilege of her age demanded, but he didn't. He couldn't.

Loretha and Sarah sat on the swing on Mrs. Collins' front porch. Mrs. Collins reached inside for her heavy knit sweater and joined them on the porch. She pulled her sweater tight around her and sat in the wicker chair.

"Ah don't understand John. Ah know this was a shock tuh him, but it's a shock tuh me, too," Loretha said.

Mrs. Collins nodded her head and reached for and patted Sarah's hand. "Go on inside, baby."

Mrs. Collins sat next to Loretha and listened while Loretha rambled on out of weariness. Reverend Oliver remained in his car and strained to hear their conversation. Mrs. Collins didn't speak a word. She didn't pretend; she didn't ask why or how or who did this to Elizabeth.

Reverend Oliver wished the ride to Loretha's home was longer. When he saw John sitting on the front porch without a sweater or coat to hold back the cold morning air, his heart pounded with the kind of rhythm the body used to put all of its systems on protective alert. He took a few cleansing breaths and reminded himself that it wasn't time, and he didn't need the defensive posture he had involuntarily prepared for.

"Thank yuh, Owen." Loretha whispered as she turned toward him.

"Just call me if yuh need me for anything." He put the car in gear, backed out onto Rehoboth Road, and waved at Reverend Turner as he drove away.

Loretha walked toward John, not knowing what to expect, but she was ready. Her weariness had moved aside to make room for "mother-love." Mother-love was more powerful than Daddy's denial, shame, hurt, pain, disbelief, confusion, and any emotion he might allow to rise within him to further injure her wounded child. They had never known each other this way. They were new to each other, a kind of newness that put them on alert to stand and defend their positions.

Loretha was angry: he should have remained at the hospital, he didn't call to find out if his daughter was all right, and he didn't seem to care how she and Sarah would get home. She wanted to take a warm bath and go back to the hospital, but she had hoped John would go back with her. She wanted to ask him to drive her back, but was afraid to say anything that might cause an argument. She didn't have time for an argument. She was in a hurry, and didn't want Elizabeth to be alone when she was fully awake. She walked past John and into the house, but mother-love turned her around and directed her back to the porch. Mother-love asked him to come back to the hospital and spend some time with his daughter. Mother-love wasn't going to argue. Mother-love would just ask him.

"Ah only have one daughter now!" John's words were harsh and heavy. This beautiful man had transformed into something ugly and difficult for Loretha to look at.

"John! Yuh don't know what yuh sayin'. We don't know what happened. She's our daughter, and we need tuh be with her."

"Ah know what happened! She had a baby! She disgraced me! She disgraced this family! She had that baby in the school's toilet. … Do yuh believe that? There ain't no forgiving that."

"Disgraced you! John, she's yuh daughter. She's a child. How can yuh judge her without speakin' with her?" Loretha was stunned. "No! No!" She held up both her hands with her palms facing John and shook her head to emphasize her words. "Let me rephrase my statement. We need tuh know *how* this happened."

"Ah don't care how this happened. It happened, and that's all that matters!" He scowled back at her. His ugliness grew, cloaking his face and filtering into the rigidity of his body language.

"Yuh-know John … Ah don't want yuh tuh come back tuh the hospital. 'Lizabeth don't need yuh upsetting her. Ah'll drive myself back."

"No, yuh won't! Yuh can go, but yuh won't take the car!"

Loretha just stared at him. He was a stranger. A mean, twisted-faced, red-eyed stranger, who looked up at her from the porch swing. Loretha pulled at the screen door with an unexpected force, crashing it against the side of the house. She pushed the front door open and slammed it before the screen door clapped back to its closed position. The angry doors made John flinch, but he didn't remove himself from the swing.

Loretha hurried to the bedrooms and selected personal items and a complete change of clothing for herself and Sarah. She put on her hat and coat, picked up her pocketbook and the two small bags, and walked out the door. She was angry, and had never defied John before. She walked past him toward the road and toward the car. Without warning, she climbed into the car, tossed her suitcase on the passenger seat, positioned the keys she held in her hand, keyed the ignition, pressured the clutch, shifted the gears, backed out of the driveway, and drove off.

Her movements weren't erratic, but slow, steady, smooth, and syncopated, leaving no room for fumbling or mistakes. John watched her for a few moments until it registered what she was doing. He jumped to his feet and yelled out her name, but there was no way he could stop her. Mother-love had taken over. Mother-love said to hell with John, she had to get back to the hospital. Mother-love took the car.

Loretha drove up Rehoboth Road in the opposite direction of Mrs. Collins' house. She didn't want John to know where she was going, but she had to get Sarah's clothing to her without his knowledge. It was a five-mile drive, traveling in the opposite direction around the back roads to Mrs. Collins' house.

It bothered Loretha that John never asked about Sarah, but that was just another discovery of whom he had become. Mother-love told her he would have to find another way to get around. A little voice—the voice of reason—reminded Loretha that John would find a way to come after her, but, in that moment, Mother-love refused to allow her to think rationally as long as her objective was met.

—◆—

Sarah had not expected to return to the hospital, and was surprised when her mother told her to get in the car. "Sarah, yuh have tuh go back with me. Yuh father wouldn't drive me back, so Ah took the car. He might come here tuh get yuh. Thank yuh, Mrs. Collins. Ah'm sorry Ah've involved yuh. Ah'm not afraid of John, but in this last day, Ah've seen a side of him that Ah didn't know he had. He needs time tuh come tuh his senses, and Ah have tuh get back tuh 'Lizabeth!"

"Y'all is mah only family. As long as the good Lawd leaves mah soul on his good earth, Ah'll be here fer yuh," Mrs. Collins said.

Loretha kissed Mrs. Collins on the cheek and hurried Sarah out the door. Soon they were raising the dust on Collins' Road.

Mrs. Collins remembered Elizabeth telling her how she would be able to hear her parents' screams. "Yuh was sho' right, chile," she whispered.

"Mama, Ah've changed my mind. Ah don't want tuh go back tuh the hospital. Ah'd rather go home. Ah'm not afraid of Daddy anymore. Please stop the car and let me go home. Ah can walk home from here."

Loretha was taken back by Sarah's change of heart, but figured it probably had something to do with spending more time at the hospital. "If yuh want tuh go home, then Ah'll drive yuh and let yuh out at the end of the driveway. Call the hospital and ask for the Colored Maternity Ward if yuh need me," Loretha instructed. "Ah don't believe yuh daddy has the energy tuh mess with you and me too, but if he gives yuh a hard time, try tuh get back tuh Mrs. Collins' and call me."

"Okay, Mama. Bye now. Don't worry, Ah'll be okay," Sarah spoke softly, trying to calm her mother and reassure her that she would be okay.

Loretha waited at the end of the driveway and watched Sarah approach her father, who never stopped swinging. He looked up at Loretha, and then at Sarah. Loretha was prepared to go after her if he gave her cause. Sarah was a wounded child also, and Loretha was ready to risk her getaway if he gave her cause. But John just sat on the swing, allowing the wind and cold to punish him.

Sarah approached the house cautiously, then she ran to him, wrapping her arms around his neck. "Daddy, please don't cry. Ah'm here."

John held her and continued to weep. "Yuh my only lil' girl now. Ah'm so sorry Ah hurt yuh."

"It's okay, Daddy. Mama will be home as soon as 'Lizabeth is all right."

"Ah know, Sarah."

Loretha watched Sarah position herself on the swing next to her father. She cuddled up close and rested her head on his chest. The rocking motion of the swing seemed to be soothing to both of them, but the cool weather soon drove Sarah inside.

Loretha drove away.

Loretha tried not to break the speed limit, but she was already late. *'Lizabeth will be thinking Ah'm angry if Ah don't get back soon. She needs me now more than ever. John made it clear he didn't want anything tuh do with her.* Loretha prayed for God to protect her family, and wondered how long it would take before John found a way to come after her. She just prayed he didn't come to Elizabeth's ward and upset her. He had his keys, and she prayed he would just take the car and leave.

When Loretha reached the maternity ward, the mattress was turned back on Elizabeth's bed. Startled, she rushed to the nurses' station.

"My daughter, Elizabeth Turner, she's not in her bed. Where is she? Is she all right?" She was shaken, weak with fear and had to hold tight to the ridge of the desk, her legs were buckling beneath her.

"Oh yes, Mrs. Turner, she's okay. She was running a fever, so we had tuh move hur tuh a private isolation room. She probably has an infection, and we don't want hur around the other mothers, especially when we bring the babies on the ward. It's just a precaution. The doctor placed her on antibiotics," the nurse replied. "She's down the hall in room 307."

Loretha thanked the Lord before she thanked the nurse, then she went back to talking with the Lord as she walked briskly to Elizabeth's new room. *Yuh knew 'Lizabeth needed her privacy. Gettin' her in her own room was a good thing. Ah know yuh goin' tuh take care of that fever and infection, too. Thank yuh, Lord.*

Elizabeth was still asleep when her mother entered the room. Loretha backed out and walked toward the nursery. *There's my new grandson.* The blue card at the head of the incubator read, "John Robert Turner." Loretha put her hand to her mouth. *'Lizabeth must be awake. She named the baby … and she named him after her father.*

She hurried back to Elizabeth's room. "'Lizabeth, honey, are yuh awake? 'Lizabeth? 'Lizabeth?" she whispered softly and gently rubbed and patted her hands.

Elizabeth turned and looked at her mother. Staring at her with teary eyes, she didn't know what to say.

Loretha, being a sensitive, forgiving person, rubbed her hands. "Honey, everything will be all right. Don't worry, we'll talk about it another time. Please, just get better."

"Mama … is Daddy here?" Elizabeth's voice was so weak, and she whined when she spoke.

"No, honey, but we'll talk about it later." Loretha tried to change the subject. "Have yuh seen yuh new son? He's so beautiful. Ah see he's got you and yuh father's features."

Elizabeth began to cry. Loretha knew she would talk to her when she felt stronger, but she needed to do something.

"'Lizabeth, do yuh think it would be all right if Ah ask the nurse tuh bring the baby tuh us? Ah would like tuh feed and hold him. Oh, honey, don't cry. Everything will be all right."

"No, it won't. If everything will be all right, Daddy would be here with yuh, Mama. If everything was all right, Ah wouldn't be here. Mama, Ah want my life back. Ah didn't ask for a baby. Ah didn't do anything wrong."

Loretha had a problem understanding how Elizabeth believed she didn't do anything wrong, but she knew the time wasn't right to get into that kind of discussion. She tried to ignore her comment. "But yuh named him, Lizabeth."

"Mama, Ah didn't name him. Ah was thinking about Daddy. Ah was thinking he would never hug me again, he would never kiss me or hold me again. Then the nurse insisted Ah name the baby, and 'John Robert Turner' just came out. Ah just want tuh see my daddy."

"He'll come, honey," Loretha said, but she secretly prayed he wouldn't.

Elizabeth's eyes shifted from her mother to her father as he walked through the door and closed it behind him. Her tear-filled eyes stretched wide open, and her body shrunk with rigidity.

"How could yuh do this tuh me? Ah gave yuh everything!" Reverend Turner angrily whispered. He was seething. His facial expressions and rigid body movements caused Loretha to move closer to Elizabeth.

"John, stop! She's tuh weak for this. We can talk about this when she's stronger," Loretha pleaded.

"No! We'll talk about it now!" His words were slow, deliberate and threatening. "Who's the boy?"

"John!" Loretha pleaded.

The volume of Reverend Turner's voice steadily increased. "Shut up, Loretha, let the girl talk! She disgraced this family. Don't yuh realize she had that baby in school? The whole town is talking 'bout us." He turned and gave Loretha a gaze that she immediately interpreted as a plea for her to understand and see things his way.

"John! Please! The nurses will come in."

Reverend Turner held back his rage and made an attempt to calm down.

Love, shame, fear, and disappointment pushed tears to Elizabeth's eyes. She wasn't emotionally or physically ready to go through this, but her father's will was stronger than her own.

Loretha pleaded with Elizabeth to talk to her father and tell him what he wanted to know.

"How did this happen, 'Lizabeth?" he asked in a calmer voice.

Elizabeth knew he wouldn't leave her alone until he had some answers. She knew he wouldn't believe her and, at that point, since the situation had peaked, she believed she had nothing else to lose, so she used what little energy she had to tell him what had plagued her for so long. "Daddy, Ah was raped! It was Reverend Oliver! He's the baby's father!"

"Reverend Oliver!" Reverend Turner yelled. "Yuh expect me tuh believe Reverend Oliver did this tuh yuh! What do yuh think Ah am? He's a fine young man, a fine young man. He wouldn't do this. He has a beautiful wife, and they're going tuh have a child. Yuh ruined yuh life, and now yuh want tuh ruin his family?"

"John, yuh daughter is a fine young lady. Yuh goin' tuh put him before her?" Loretha had to hold on to the headboard after hearing what Elizabeth said, but she still had enough strength to question John.

"Shut up, Loretha! Just shut up!" Reverend Turner yelled loud enough for his voice to escape through the closed door.

"Daddy! He said yuh'd never believe me. He was right. Why don't yuh just ask him? He'll probably lie, but ask him anyway. Look in his eyes when yuh ask him," Elizabeth pleaded and cried.

Reverend Turner spoke a little quieter after realizing he had been yelling. "Don't yuh tell me what tuh do! Ah'm not goin' tuh ask him anything. Yuh planned this well. Yuh think everything will be all right if Ah believe Reverend Oliver raped yuh. Ah'm not going tuh ruin his family the way you've ruined mine."

"John, why don't yuh just ask him? This is yuh daughter! She's a good girl. Why would she lie?" Loretha begged.

"If he raped yuh … why didn't yuh say something then?"

"He said yuh wouldn't believe me. Ah was afraid, so Ah believed him. Ah just wanted it tuh go away. Ah didn't know Ah'd be pregnant." Elizabeth began to sob. "If Ah didn't get pregnant, yuh woulda never known … because … because he was right. See, Daddy, yuh don't believe me."

"Well, yuh right … Ah don't believe yuh. Yuh no longer welcome in my house … Loretha, if yuh want tuh side with her … yuh can stay here and never bother coming home again."

"John … she's our daughter! How can yuh be so cruel? Yuh a minister. Why is it so hard tuh believe her? Yuh know her, why can't yuh listen tuh yuh own daughter? Why can't yuh forgive her? If she's lying, she could have said some other person did this, or she could have said she didn't know who did it …"

"Cruel?" Reverend Turner said, cutting her off. "Elizabeth's been cruel tuh us. She's disgraced us, and now yuh call me cruel. It's cruel for her tuh blame this on Reverend Oliver. Why would Reverend Oliver rape her? She's lying tuh cover up her sin, and now … now, she wants tuh bring down a fine young man like Reverend Oliver. Yuh either come with me now, Loretha, or never come home again. Ah don't ever want tuh see 'Lizabeth again or her bastard child. She got herself intuh this, so she'll have tuh get herself out."

"Please stop," Elizabeth cried. She'd never spoken against her father, but through her physical weakness, somehow she found the courage. "Mama, Ah don't need tuh be forgiven. Ah didn't do anything wrong. If Ah wasn't so afraid of Daddy, Ah would've told yuh. Ah went through this alone, so if yuh want tuh disown me because yuh feel Ah've shamed yuh ... then ... yuh never really loved me anyway."

Reverend Turner stormed out of the room.

Loretha hugged and kissed Elizabeth. "Ah love you, baby." She kissed her again. "Oh God, help my baby. Please Lord, shelter her from any more pain," Loretha prayed. "I believe yuh, 'Lizabeth. Ah'll come back, honey. Ah have tuh go with him now, but Ah will be back. Just let me talk tuh him," Loretha said as she rubbed Elizabeth's hand.

"Ah know, Mama. Ah know yuh love me. Please go." Elizabeth continued to cry.

Elizabeth was blinded by her emotions as she watched her mother run from the room. She had been through a long and difficult time. Now the misery of this day would be added to the time already served. It seemed like a million things were running through her mind, confusing her. The weight of hopelessness was crushing her. She knew her mother loved her. Witnessing the effects of the stress her mother was feeling added to her emotional pain. Misery shrouded her. She loved her father too much to hate him; when she should have been angry, disappointment almost suffocated her, capturing air in her lungs and holding it until it was dead air and no longer able to feed her body, then exploding outward with a flood of tears and unbearable heart pain.

She couldn't disguise it as anger, because anger spewed outward and required energy and a target, and she had neither. Her father was a proud man, but she never realized how weak he was. All that had happened was more than he could bear, so he took out his anger on her.

Carefully, she disconnected the intravenous tubes, rolled over, and lowered herself from the bed. The floor and the walls felt like they were moving, like they were rubbery and springy like a soft cloud, like she was in a large air bubble. She pulled herself up on the foot wide windowsill. The air was sweeter than the stale hospital air, and she took in deep breaths. Her arms felt heavy, like they were weighted down, but she managed to push the window open wider, and the sweet air bathed her face. She was weak, and could feel herself losing her fight to remain conscious. When she looked down the three stories, the ground appeared to be spinning, with patches of black streaks passing before her vision. She turned up to face the gray-blue sky and tried to blink away the blackness, but the streak passed before her vision with a greater frequency until there was more black than natural view.

A nurse, who was walking past her room, noticed Elizabeth sitting on the windowsill. First, she wondered what she was doing there. Within her next heartbeat, she realized Elizabeth was trying to get out of the window. "Miss Turner! Whut yuh doin' up there?"

Elizabeth was straddling the window ledge, one leg in, and the other out. The blackness was increasing, and the sweet air was beckoning her to fly on the cool, clear breeze and free herself of the troubles that plagued her. Sounds and voices seemed far away, hollow and echoing. She had enough strength to hold up her right hand to gesture the nurse to stop, to stay back. She fought against the black streaks that were overtaking her consciousness. Suddenly, her body went limp. Her head was still inside the window, braced against the window frame and preventing her from tumbling to the grassy surface below.

The nurse ran to her, screaming as loud as she could for help. She grabbed Elizabeth and pulled her back through the window. Overpowered by her weight, she slid to the floor, dragging Elizabeth down with her.

Another nurse ran to the room and helped to get Elizabeth back to her bed. "She was trying tuh jump out the window. Call her doctor," the first nurse ordered.

"What happened?" the other nurse asked.

"She's fifteen, unwed, and had a baby! That's whut happened! Ah don't know whut hur daddy said tuh hur, but hur parents just left here." It was evident she was more annoyed with Elizabeth's parents than with her.

CHAPTER 5

During the drive home, Loretha had very little to say to Reverend Turner. All she could think about was Elizabeth. Mother-love compelled her to help her daughter, but she didn't know how. She had never had any real uncontrolled crisis in her life before. Mother-love told her to act, but not to think. Taking the car had only made things worse. There were other ways to get back to the hospital. She had friends who would have helped her. She could have even asked Reverend Oliver to take her back, but when she considered what she had recently learned, she believed that wouldn't have been a good idea. Taking the car, even though she believed she had just as much right to use it as John, was definitely a bad idea.

She knew John would come to the hospital to get it, and that was all the excuse he needed to come to Elizabeth's room and attack her. She had to be careful and calculating. She couldn't afford to make any more mistakes that could hurt Elizabeth. It served no purpose to continue to anger John. She had nothing of her own except a little "mad money" she'd been saving that John didn't know about. She knew that wouldn't go very far if she had to find someplace to live. She prayed Elizabeth would understand why she had to leave with John, and know that she would return as soon as she could.

It was a long drive. Loretha was weary and so was Reverend Turner. She felt no pity for him, only a sense of loss. For that moment, his depraved attitude stripped her of all the love and respect she had for him. She couldn't distinguish her anger from hate, but she knew she would never love him the way she had, ever again.

—⚭—

Not long after Reverend Turner and Loretha arrived home, Dr. Pernell called from the hospital. Sarah answered the telephone. "Yes, my daddy is here."

"Daddy, it's 'Lizabeth's doctor. He wants tuh talk tuh yuh."

Dr. Pernell had asked to speak with Elizabeth's parents, not specifically Reverend Turner, but Sarah made the decision as to whom he should speak to. Loretha rushed to the telephone, but Sarah passed her mother and handed the phone to her father. Loretha's eyes dictated to Sarah her disappointment in her decision. Sarah's eyes spoke for her, too, and she moved closer to her father. Loretha understood what she was saying, but she only moved closer and put her arm around her in a way she hoped would express that she understood her suffering, too. Then she listened with concern to Reverend Turner's responses to Dr. Pernell.

"She did what?"

"What, John? What happened tuh 'Lizabeth?" Loretha said, a frightening concern flavoring her voice.

Reverend Turner waved his hand at Loretha to quiet her without telling her what the doctor was saying. She was angry and frightened, so she rushed to the telephone in the kitchen. She listened with quiet intensity as the doctor questioned what may have led to Elizabeth's suicide attempt. Her heartbeat throbbed all over her body, and the air she breathed seemed thinner.

"Yes, Ah was angry with her. She disgraced this family. She's played a lot of games and believe me, this was just another one of them," John spoke abruptly.

The doctor was angrier than Reverend Turner. "You listen to me, Reverend Turner, this was not a game. I almost lost her in the operating room. She had lost her will to live. Speaking with you, I understand why. You call yourself a man of the cloth? If all ministers were like you, I would never step foot in a church again. I don't want to talk with you any longer. I spoke with your wife at the hospital, may I speak with her now?"

"No! My wife has nothing tuh say."

"Yes Ah do," Loretha said. She knew John would be furious for going against him, but she was not going to let her daughter die. "Is 'Lizabeth all right?"

"Get off the phone, Loretha!"

"Yes, I have an aide staying with her," Dr. Pernell said over Reverend Turner's voice. He heard John, but it was easy to dismiss him.

"Get off the phone, Loretha!"

Loretha spoke over Reverend Turner's voice, "Dr. Pernell! Please tell 'Lizabeth Ah love her, and Ah'll get there tomorrow. Ah'll call yuh. Ah have yuh card. Bye." She hung up the phone, hoping John realized he couldn't stop her. She had said what she needed to say.

Reverend Turner hung up the phone and rushed toward the kitchen. "Don't yuh ever go against me!"

Loretha was startled and backed away from his rush toward her. Sarah began to cry and ran between them. John was crazy with anger, and had that same crazy appearance he had when he threatened to hit Sarah.

"Daddy! Please! Please stop!" Sarah put her arms around his waist and held him. "Ah love yuh. Ah love yuh, Daddy!" She kept repeating herself. Every time he tried to look around her at Loretha, she swung her body, hoping to get his attention. She continued repeating her love for him. Soon Reverend Turner was forced to attend to Sarah. It bothered him to see the terror in her face.

Sarah only wanted to stop the madness, but Loretha took her action as siding with her father. Sarah had taken sides, but this time she was afraid for her mother, it had nothing to do with siding. Loretha believed she was Elizabeth's only hope. She went to Elizabeth's room to get away from John and Sarah. She believed John was crazy enough to strike her. This was the first of the many nights she would spend in Elizabeth's room.

Early the next morning, the chilly air bit at Loretha's face and legs while she walked to Mrs. Collins' house. It was just before daybreak, about six o'clock, too dark for her to take the short cut through the woods. She knew Mrs. Collins would be up, and it was too early to call the hospital or Dr. Pernell. She just didn't want to see her husband or Sarah. She wanted them to miss her. Mrs. Collins always offered a warm inviting smile and a greeting that made her feel there was no problem so terrible it didn't already have a solution. All Loretha had to do was slow down and give her troubles some thought. Of course, telling Mrs. Collins didn't hurt either.

"Oh, chile, yuh don't hav'tuh worry. 'Liz'beth kin come stay wit' me," Mrs. Collins' offered.

"Thank yuh so much, but Ah can't worry yuh with our troubles … and if John finds out …"

"Whut if Reverend Turner finds out? So whut if he finds out! Dis here mah house!"

"But, Mrs. Collins, John's her father. He could have the State of Georgia take her away from me."

"Where dere be a will, dere be a way. When yuh talk tuh dem folks over at dat hospital, ask 'em tuh help yuh protect 'Liz'beth from hur daddy."

Mrs. Collins wanted to keep Elizabeth's confidence, but there was a time for everything, and she realized this was the right time to tell Loretha what she knew.

"Loretha, Ah need tuh tell yuh somethin'." When Mrs. Collins knew she had her full attention, she began. "Ah know who the baby daddy be. Yeah, Ah know and Ah shoulda tol' yuh. It be Reverend Owen Oliver … dat buzzard. Dat conniving buzzard stol' dat chile's innocence. Didn't 'Liz'beth tell y'all?"

Loretha was startled. Reverend Turner didn't want this to get around. If Mrs. Collins knew, John would think she told her. "How'd yuh know that?"

"Oh, yuh did know. She tol' yuh. Well Ah'm glad she did."

Mrs. Collins walked over to her kitchen table and eased herself into her woven straw-bottom chair. Loretha followed her, almost on her heels, and positioned herself behind a matching chair on the other side of the table. With the wave of her hand, the lowering of her eyes, the nodding of her head, and her soft crackling voice, Mrs. Collins told her to sit down. It wasn't that Mrs. Collins thought Loretha needed to be sitting when she told her what she knew, she was tired of standing in her living room and wanted to take a seat in her kitchen.

"Listen, honey, Ah kin tell 'Liz'beth tol' yuh somethin'. Ah don't know how much she tol' yuh, but lemme tell yuh whut Ah know. It be weeks ago, 'Liz'beth come tuh me. She was heavy wit' troubles. Looked lak hur soul was turned inside out. She tol' me 'bout bein' raped by Reverend Oliver, and she bein' pregnant. She was scared and didn't know whut tuh do. Ah talked hur intuh tellin' y'all. She said she was scared of hur daddy, and she said he wouldn't believe hur. But she still promised she would tell yuh, but the baby come tuh soon."

"Why didn't yuh tell me?"

"Ah know, Ah shoulda come tuh yuh, but Ah was scared, too. It's hard tuh bring bad news tuh a-body. Ah gotta say, Ah be happy when she begged me not tuh tell. She promised tuh tell yuh. Ah believed hur, and Ah still believe hur. She jest didn't git the chance."

Loretha asked, "How'd yuh know she was telling yuh the truth?"

"Oh chile ... Ah be seein' the way he be lookin' at hur in church. Dat night it happen', Ah warned hur 'bout walkin' through dem woods alone and dat same day at church, Ah saw him gawkin' at 'Liz'beth. Yuh know, the way a man can undress a woman wit' his eyes. Ah wuz gone tell yuh 'bout dat, too, but Ah wuz sacred. Ah sat in the back of dat church and saw how y'all took tuh Rev and Mrs. Oliver, and Ah wuz scared tuh speak 'gainst them. Tell yuh the truth, Ah ain't think he'd do nothin' but look at her, so I ain't say nothin'. Dat was back when Ah was sick, 'bout mid-May, but Ah 'member tellin' 'Liz'beth 'bout dem woods. But, yuh-know, when Ah think 'bout it, it didn't mattah 'bout dem woods out back, 'cause he wanted hur, and he coulda got hur in dem woods jest off the road. He had a mind-set to git dat chile, and he did jest dat. Honey, hear me when Ah speak … yuh chile … she don't know no other man."

Loretha felt enlightened. She loved her child, but John was trying to convince her this was Elizabeth's way of shifting the blame. She really didn't care how Elizabeth became pregnant, she knew she would stand by her, whatever the reason. She believed Elizabeth would have told them about being raped as soon as it happened if anyone other than Reverend Oliver was involved. And she knew her father wouldn't believe Reverend Oliver would do such a thing, but he would have believed her if it was someone else or even if she said she didn't know who the person was.

"Well … John didn't believe her," Loretha responded

"'Liz'beth said he wouldn't. Ah knew he wouldn't, too."

"John refuses tuh ask Owen about it."

"Ah figured dat much. Dey be makin' dey own peace wit' God one day. We cain't change 'em. If yuh speak tuh Reverend Oliver, John gone disown yuh, too. Believe me, one day, dey time gone come. Tuhday we need tuh be spendin' our time makin' plans for 'Liz'beth and dat baby."

Mrs. Collins stood up slowly then walked over to her black, wood-burning kitchen stove to put more wood on the hot embers. "Lemme fix yuh some coffee. Yuh seem tuh be mighty low. We'll be thinkin' clearer after some coffee."

"No, Mrs. Collins. Let me fix the coffee."

"Ah ain't hep'less, and dis here mah house. Didn't Ah tell yuh dat befo'? When Ah come tuh yuh house, den yuh fix the coffee. If yuh weren't here, Ah be fixin' it, so lemme be. Yuh jest sit there and be still. Ah'm gone fix the coffee." She was firm and feisty, because she was loving and gentle, and that was the way she was.

Reverend Turner came into the dining room expecting to see Loretha. It was Thursday morning, he had his ministry duties to attend to, and Sarah had not been to school since Tuesday. The table had not been set and breakfast had not been prepared.

"Yuh mother must've walked over tuh Mrs. Collins. She was upset, but she'll get over it. Do yuh want tuh go tuh school?" John said, acting as though nothing had happened. That was his way of handling his problems, denial. Except for the sporadic flashes of the daughter he loved so much, he couldn't deny her, so he slammed her memory away like slamming the door on an unwelcome stranger. It was unbelievable that he even suggested Loretha would get over Elizabeth, that she should just forget her. He really believed he could control her mind, body, and soul, but he didn't understand the power of mother-love.

"Ah guess so. Ah have tuh go back sometime," Sarah replied.

"Yuh know … whenever yuh go back, the other kids will question yuh, but the sooner yuh go the better."

"Ah know yuh right, Daddy. Ah guess tuhday is as good as any other day. Ah'm scared, but Ah'll be okay. The sooner Ah get this over with, the better. Ah'll just tell them what they already know and keep my head up," Sarah said. "Don't worry, everything will be all right, Daddy."

Reverend Turner snapped out of his deep thoughts and responded, "Oh, Ah'm all right." He slammed Elizabeth out of his thoughts again, then he stood up and announced. "Let's fix something tuh eat. Yuh don't want tuh miss yuh bus, and Ah have a few things tuh do." He paused for a moment then added, "Would yuh like me tuh drive yuh tuh school?"

"No, Daddy, Ah can take the bus."

Reverend Turner was happy to hear this, knowing Sarah was brave enough to do something he wasn't able to do. He didn't insist. He was relieved he didn't have to face the students, teachers, and school officials. He had not called Mr. Lacy to let him know Elizabeth and the baby were going to be all right. He was too embarrassed, and didn't know how to apologize and thank him for helping Elizabeth.

Loretha spent most of the morning with Mrs. Collins, and had planned to return home when she was sure John was gone. She had friends and would ask one of them to drive her to the hospital, but she knew she would have to return before John was due back home. Before she left for home, she called Dr. Pernell and explained what happened between John and Elizabeth. Dr. Pernell made arrangements with the hospital social worker to meet her in Elizabeth's room at eleven-thirty that morning. He explained that an aide had been assigned to stay close to Elizabeth around the clock, and the psychiatrist had a scheduled visit with her for later that afternoon. Loretha thanked him for his help and prepared to go home so she could find a way to get to the hospital.

"Yuh lissen here, Loretha … yuh go on fer now, but don't fergit Ah'll always be here fer yuh and 'Liz'beth," said Mrs. Collins.

"Ah don't know how tuh express how thankful we are tuh have yuh," Loretha said, kissing her on the cheek. "Ah'll give yuh a call this evening and tell yuh what happened."

As Loretha walked home, she thought of her friend Janet McCray, who had two cars. Her son bought a car, but then lost his driver's license, and Janet took the keys. Driving without a license was treated like a capital offense for a colored boy. It was just a piece of a car when he bought it, but her boy knew how to fix it up, and it ran like a charm. She hoped Janet would allow her to use it to get to the hospital. As soon as she arrived home, she called Janet.

Janet had heard about Elizabeth and was more than willing to help Loretha, agreeing to pick her up to get the car. On the way back to Janet's house, Loretha explained everything to her. That is, everything but who the baby's father was. She just told her Elizabeth was too weak for her to question her. Janet, being the mother of teenagers, was very understanding, and reminded Loretha she could borrow the car for as long as she needed it.

———⟋⟍⟋———

Loretha arrived at the hospital just in time to meet Miss Davies, the social worker. Elizabeth was surprised, and very happy, to see her mother. Loretha removed her scarf and gloves, placed them in her coat pocket and folded her coat over the back of the chair.

Miss Davies told Elizabeth that Dr. Pernell had explained her case, and she was there to help. "Ah have tuh ask yuh a few questions. Please don't get upset. Ah'm here tuh help yuh and protect yuh wishes," Miss Davies explained. "The first thing Ah need tuh know is, do yuh want tuh keep yuh baby?"

"Yes ma'am," Elizabeth responded.

"Then yuh can keep yuh baby. Yuh goin' tuh need some help, and we're here tuh help yuh," Miss Davies continued.

"'Lizabeth, honey, Ah'm happy yuh want tuh keep him. If yuh'd decided not tuh, Ah would've found a way tuh keep him myself. He's family, and he belongs tuh his family, but Ah want yuh tuh know, Ah got nowhere with yuh father. So, we'll have tuh make plans without him. Yuh can keep yuh baby, and Mrs. Collins wants yuh tuh come and live with her," Loretha added, then she turned to Miss Davies for consultation. "If my husband has anything tuh do with it, he might force 'Lizabeth tuh put the baby up for adoption. Can yuh help hur?"

"Mrs. Turner, the law is clear regarding minors, but yuh daughter can file for an emancipation. If yuh husband objects, the state will provide a lawyer tuh represent hur, and the matter will have tuh be settled in the court. Sometimes, things don't always go the way we plan for colored girls. Ah have tuh be honest with yuh, but Ah really like yuh, and the judge is a personal friend of mine. If she wins, yuh husband will have tuh support Elizabeth until she's eighteen. If he agrees not tuh fight, she can obtain the status of an 'Emancipated

Minor' without the court's involvement, but if she files for public assistance, the court will force yuh husband tuh provide for hur care. The baby will be eligible for Public Assistance Program."

"But … what if Ah lose?" Elizabeth questioned.

"If yuh daddy wins, he can either take yuh home, or request the court tuh send yuh tuh a shelter, or have yuh placed in foster care. Either way, the court will still require him tuh pay for yuh support, which will be based on the family's income. Believe me, it would be cheaper for him tuh agree tuh the emancipation without allowing this matter tuh go tuh the court."

Loretha listened to what Miss Davies was saying, and couldn't believe a white woman would go so far to help a colored girl and her baby. She didn't have to tell her about the emancipation. She could have just pulled Elizabeth and the baby away from her family, placed them in separate foster homes and to hell with them; what did it matter to her? Elizabeth was just another colored unwed mother who brought another bastard into this world. Why was this white woman helping and doing for them what they had always done for white families? Maybe she was a truly good person, or maybe she wanted to pull down a popular, uppity colored preacher.

What Loretha didn't know was Dr. Pernell asked Miss Davies to treat this family special. He was tired of the self-righteous fathers hurting their injured daughters. Making sure Elizabeth got the best of her father gave Dr. Pernell the satisfaction akin to beating the living hell out of the good Reverend John Turner. It also helped that Miss Davies was in awe of Dr. Pernell. Every time she mentioned his name, her facial expression brightened up. She was too eager to please him. Loretha didn't know what the reason was, she just thanked God for Miss Davies.

"Honey, Mrs. Collins wants you and the baby tuh come and live with her," Loretha interrupted. She didn't think Elizabeth heard her when she mentioned it earlier.

"Mrs. Collins wants us? Mama, that's great. Ah want the emancipation." Elizabeth was beginning to feel better. Dr. Pernell had ordered the nurse to take her to the nursery window, and hoped that would give her more of a reason to live.

"Could yuh help us do this? Ah can't let my husband know Ah had anything tuh do with this, but Ah want yuh tuh know Ah'm going tuh be there for her," Loretha pleaded.

"Oh yes, that's why Ah'm here. Ah'll drive out and discuss all the details with yuh husband. Ah'll bring a lawyer friend with me and all the forms. If he signs them, we can take it from there. With all that's happened tuh this child, Ah'm sure the court will grant the emancipation. Maybe it won't get that far. Ah've handled cases like this before, and most of the time the parents sign. Georgia is a poor state. The courts try tuh handle issues like this with respect tuh the best interest of the child and what's the most cost effective. Elizabeth, yuh very fortunate, many young girls don't have as much goin' for them as yuh have. If yuh daddy continues tuh insist that yuh can't go home, the lawyer will present yuh case and make him feel it's in his best interest tuh sign the papers. After that, we'll set yuh up with Mrs. Collins and make sure yuh have what yuh need tuh take care of yuh baby. Of course, we'll need tuh speak with Mrs. Collins tuh confirm her offer. Ah'll need her address, and if she has a telephone, Ah'll need the number."

Loretha wasted little time jotting down the necessary information and handing it to Miss Davies. "Ah don't want my husband tuh know she'll be livin' with Mrs. Collins until everything is settled. If he knows, he won't sign the paper."

"We are not obligated tuh tell him what hur living arrangement will be, but we must tell him we'll find hur a place tuh live. Elizabeth … is this what yuh want? If it is, I'll begin the process."

"Ah want the emancipation," Elizabeth answered. She turned to her mother for confirmation that she was making the correct decision. Loretha nodded.

"All right then. Ah'll be on my way. Don't worry, Ah'll keep yuh informed. Ah'll be talkin' with yuh more." Miss Davies stood up and prepared to leave the room. Handing Elizabeth her card, she added, "Call me if yuh need tuh."

"Thank yuh," Elizabeth said. She smiled and reached down for her mother's hand.

Loretha stood and patted Elizabeth's hand, then turned to Miss Davies. "Yes, thank yuh so very much," she added, now using both of her hands to shake Miss Davies' hand. "Oh, Miss Davies." Loretha's eyes widened, and she held tighter to her hand. "Oh, Ah'm sorry." She turned Miss Davies' hand loose and clasped her own hands in front of her. "We have a party line telephone, and being that my husband is the minister for our community, Ah'm sure all ears are listenin' for our ring. Ah don't mean tuh be takin' up yuh time, but ..."

"Ah know what yuh tryin' tuh say," Miss Davies said, cutting her off. She smiled and nodded at Loretha and Elizabeth. "Let me make a few telephone calls, and yuh go on with yuh visit with yuh daughter. Ah'll try tuh work out a plan. Call me from the nurses' station when yuh ready tuh leave, and Ah'll meet yuh in the visitor's lounge."

"Thank yuh so much." Loretha wanted to extend her hand and shake Miss Davies' hand again, but she had over stepped her boundaries once, and believed it was improper to be too familiar with a white person, so she gave her a broad smile and a modest bow. She never expected Miss Davies to invite her to her 'White only' office.

Elizabeth's eyes shifted between Miss Davies and her mother. A timid smile slightly curved her lips, but the way she was twisting the bed sheets gave an indication of the concern she was feeling.

"Don't worry, Elizabeth. Yuh mama and Ah will work everything out. It's gonna be all right." Miss Davies placed her hand over Elizabeth's hand to comfort her.

Miss Davies left the room. Loretha turned to Elizabeth and kissed her on the forehead before sitting back down in the chair. "Honey, the doctor called the house and told us what happened. Yuh won't try that again, will yuh? Never feel that all the doors are closed. When the Lord closes one door, he always opens another. See ... the Lord sent Miss Davies."

"Mama, please. Don't feel Ah'm disrespectful, but the Lord has forsaken me. Ah don't pray anymore. If the Lord loved me, He wouldn't have let this happen tuh me."

"Honey, He hasn't forsaken yuh. The Lord has a grand plan for y'all. Yuh gonna be proud of Johnny one day. Honey, let go and let God. Okay?"

"Mama, yuh called him 'Johnny.' That's the first time yuh said his name."

Loretha and Elizabeth smiled at each other and were silent for a moment. The strain on both of them was apparent, but neither spoke of Reverend Turner or Reverend Oliver. There would be time enough for that.

Elizabeth's nurse entered the room. "Yuh lab test came back and yuh infection is not contagious, but the doctor wants yuh tuh stay in this room 'til yuh discharged. Would yuh like us tuh bring yuh baby tuh yuh? The doctor just removed him from the incubator. He's a strong, healthy baby, and is having no trouble breathin' on his own."

Loretha sprang to life. She would be able to hold her grandson for the first time. This would be the first time Elizabeth held her baby, and she knew every moment Elizabeth spent with him would take her further away from her suicidal thoughts.

The nurse entered the room and placed Johnny in Elizabeth's arms. He smelled so sweet, the way babies are supposed to smell. He was very light skinned, but the color of his ears and fingertips indicated that his true complexion probably would be a little darker, closer to her father's color.

"Oh 'Lizabeth, he is so beautiful," Loretha said. "We don't have any baby things. Ah did pack away the crib. Ah guess, Ah thought, Ah would have another baby. It's in the attic, but Ah gave away all the blankets and baby clothes. Yuh'll need blankets, diapers, bottles and a sterilizer for his formula … and he's a new baby, so he'll need new clothing tuh wear home from the hospital. Ah'll start gathering the things yuh'll need."

"Mama, how yuh gonna get all that stuff? Daddy won't let yuh buy it."

"My mother always told me to save a few dollars every month for myself. For years, Ah been putting a little money away for a rainy day. It's not that much, but there's still goin' tuh be some left over after Ah get the things yuh need."

Loretha reached over and kissed Elizabeth and the baby. "Ah have tuh go now. Ah won't see yuh tomorrow, but Ah'll call yuh if Ah can. Now yuh enjoy yuh baby and take time tuh get tuh know him." She put on her coat and picked up her pocketbook.

"Okay, Mama. Mama, Ah love yuh … and Mama, Ah still love Daddy."

Loretha smiled, turned and walked to the door, "'Lizabeth, if you need the nurse tuh come for the baby, just use yuh buzzer. Ah love yuh, 'Lizabeth."

"Thanks, Mama, the aide will come back when yuh leave."

———ᵐ———

Loretha walked from Elizabeth's room to the nurses' station and asked to use the telephone to call Miss Davies. She held the card in her hand and stared at it as she spoke.

"May Ah place the call for yuh, Mrs. Turner?" The nurse held out her hand for the card and smiled.

Loretha turned, looked up at the nurse and handed her the card. She watched in silence and smiled, thanking the nurse when she handed her the telephone.

"Thank yuh Miss Davies. Ah'll be waitin' for yuh in ten minutes." Loretha held the phone to her ear until she heard the call disconnect, then she pulled the handset away and stared at it.

"Mrs. Turner? Are yuh all right?" the nurse said. She placed her hand on Loretha's shoulder.

"Oh yes. Ah just have so much on my mind. Thank yuh for placing the call for me." She smiled, nodded, hugged her pocketbook, and walked toward the waiting area.

"Yuh welcome," the nurse said. She placed the handset on the cradle and watched her walk down the corridor.

Miss Davies arrived at the waiting area in less than ten minutes, or so it seemed to Loretha, who had her back to the door and was looking out the window. She was still hugging her pocketbook.

The colored waiting room was small, about the size of a standard bathroom, with six chairs, two on each side of the walls, except the wall near the door. The window was located at one end, and the door to the room at the other. Miss Davies sat on one chair, and Loretha sat in a chair facing her. She rested her pocketbook on her lap, but stress lines creased her forehead. She prayed what Miss Davies would tell her would be helpful.

"Mrs. Turner, Ah spoke with Stan Bruen. He's the lawyer friend Ah was talkin' about. He said he's available anytime tomorrow. Do yuh know what yuh husband's schedule is for tuhmorrow?" Miss Davies sat with her legs crossed. She held a clipboard that supported a yellow legal pad, and tapped her pen against it while she waited for Loretha's response.

"Well Reverend Turner usually doesn't leave the house until after nine in the mornin'. Sometimes later, but Ah really don't know his schedule. Ah believe the best time tuh catch him home would be in the mornin'. Would that be tuh early for y'all?" Loretha sat forward with her hands clasped on top of her pocketbook.

"Would eight o'clock be tuh early for yuh? Mr. Bruen suggested we drive tuh yuh home at eight. We both live out yuh way, and we could come tuh yuh house before we come intuh Macon. How would that be?" Now Miss Davies was leaning closer to Loretha's space.

"Ah believe that's a good time tuh catch Reverend Turner." Loretha knew Miss Davies was wondering why she continued to refer to her husband so formally. Every time she said his name, Miss Davies gave a clinched lip and distasteful blink.

"Okay, Mrs. Turner, we'll be there by eight. Are yuh sure that's not too early?"

"No. That's the best time. It won't matter when yuh come, John won't be happy tuh talk tuh yuh."

"Don't worry. We have a great deal of experience in this area. Believe me, maybe he won't want tuh meet with us, but he won't have much of a choice. It's simple, meet with us tomorrow morning, or meet us in court. Ah already have the paperwork in the process for a subpoena. All Ah have tuh do is have the judge sign it," Miss Davies explained with confidence.

"All right then, Ah'll see yuh in the morning. Please, don't let John know Ah met with yuh or had anything tuh do with this," Loretha reminded her again.

"Ah'm gonna give yuh my home number. Will yuh call me if yuh husband isn't available tuhmorrow mornin'?" Miss Davies wrote the number on the bottom half of the yellow pad, tore it off, and handed it to Loretha.

"Ah sure will, and yuh can call Mrs. Collins at the number Ah gave yuh earlier if yuh need to reach me if yuh plans change. Ah'll tell her yuh may call. Just tell her that yuh can't keep our appointment. The noisy-bodies won't know what yuh talkin' 'bout."

"That's great. Ah have her number. Now don't worry. Ah'm an expert at being discreet. So long, now."

Miss Davies reached to shake Loretha's hand. Loretha switched her pocketbook to her left hand and shook Miss Davies hand with her right. "Thank yuh," she called out as Miss Davies stepped onto the elevator.

CHAPTER 6

Loretha arrived home around four o'clock. Reverend Turner was still out. Sarah was home, and noticed her mother getting out of Mrs. McCray's car. She ran to the bedroom and threw herself on her bed, hoping to avoid a confrontation with her because of her behavior. The little scene the night before was to protect her mother from her father the only way she knew how, but the arrogant way she handed the telephone to her father, even though her mother was closer to her, was what gave her cause to be concerned.

She had chosen whom to side with for her own gain, allowing her gaze at her mother to communicate this. She couldn't describe it, but her heart kept reminding her that she was betraying her sister. Had she stood by her mother, maybe her father would have softened his attitude. Now it was difficult for her to face her mother only because she feared having to explain her behavior.

Loretha called out for Sarah several times when she entered the house. When she didn't answer, she went to her bedroom and lightly tapped on her door. When she opened the door and found Sarah asleep on her bed, she pulled the door closed to a crack and went back down stairs to start dinner.

Sarah was pretending to be asleep. She had successfully deceived her mother, and laid in bed thinking about her terrible day at school. She knew it would be difficult until the excitement over Elizabeth's ordeal no longer held any interest for the other kids. She questioned the actions of some of the teachers, her friends, and those kids who were not close to her, the curiosity seekers. Her youth and immaturity added to her difficulty distinguishing between cynical curiosity and genuine concern. Sarah was angry, confused, and suffering the punishment of her sister's dilemma, her mother's discontent, her father's sulkiness, and her own selfish motives. Tears came to her eyes, and soon she was sobbing.

Loretha had just walked upstairs to change her clothing when she heard the whimpers coming from Sarah's room. Quietly, she tipped closer to her door and listened intensely. Moved by the sobbing, she entered the room without knocking.

"Sarah, yuh crying."

Loretha sat on the side of her bed and opened her arms to hold her just as Sarah moved to be comforted.

"Mama, Ah'm sorry." She had to say something; she couldn't say, "Mama, Ah'm guilty," or, "Mama, Ah'm ashamed of myself." Saying she was sorry was what she knew would lay softly on her mother's ears and get her a little sympathy.

"Honey, why are yuh sorry? Yuh didn't do anything wrong."

"Yes Ah did, Mama. First, Ah was scared for 'Lizabeth, but then Ah felt glad. Ah wanted tuh have Daddy all tuh myself. 'Lizabeth has you, but Daddy was all alone. Ah know what he's doing is wrong, but Ah can't help it."

"But that's normal. Ah know how everything must've embarrassed yuh. Ah can't imagine how yuh managed tuh go tuh school tuhday. That took a lot of guts. What yuh felt … and, what yuh did … well honey, that was a normal first reaction. Yuh weren't happy about what happened tuh 'Lizabeth, yuh were just happy it wasn't you. And yuh shouldn't feel yuh daddy loved her more than you, or that her misfortune put yuh first in his eyes. There is no first or second, he loves yuh both the same, that's why he's hurting so much."

"But, Mama, Ah turned against yuh and sided wit' Daddy."

"No yuh didn't. Yuh just found yuhself caught in the middle. Yuh know Ah love yuh, and no matter what, Ah'll be there for yuh. Yuh father still loves 'Lizabeth very much. He's still in shock, and Ah know he believes the shame is more than he can bear. He says he doesn't want tuh see her again because he's hurting so much. No matter how he acts from now on, remember that his pain goes so deep, he may never recover. He has tuh find his own peace, and wants his pain tuh go away.

Remember, yuh not giving him fuel to act that way, he has enough of his own."

Sarah held her mother tight, her sobbing decreased to quiet weeping. "Did yuh see 'Lizabeth today?"

"Yes, honey, she's all right, and she's going tuh keep the baby."

"Daddy won't let hur come home. What's she gonna do?"

"We have tuh work out the details. But don't yuh worry. Everything will be all right … and Ah know yuh thinking about her trying tuh kill herself, she's all right with that, too," Loretha said. Then she pulled back to look into Sarah's eyes. "Believe me, "Lizabeth will be all right, and so will the baby. Now get up and come down stairs and be with me while Ah fix dinner. Okay?"

"Okay, Mama."

Loretha had put on a great show for Sarah. During the past few days, she had paid her little or no attention. Now, she realized that she was suffering, too. She wanted to give her all the details of the plans so she wouldn't worry, but she knew she would tell her father. After all that had happened, poor Sarah was left to face the questions alone.

"Mama, can Ah help yuh with anything?" Sarah asked.

"Yes, come over here and help me peel these potatoes, and we can talk. It's a good idea that yuh went back tuh school as soon as yuh could." Loretha spread out a few sheets of old newspaper, then put a few potatoes in one of the two bowls and set two knives nearby. They sat at the kitchen table and peeled potatoes while they talked.

"Yeah, but it was hard. Ah think the worst is over. A lot of kids really like 'Lizabeth. They wanted tuh know if there was anything they could do tuh help. Even the teachers said tuh ask yuh if there was something they could do."

"Did anyone say anything bad that hurt yuh feelings?"

"A few kids were troublesome, but most of the day Ah had a lot of friends with me. They stood up for me and 'Lizabeth." Sarah finished peeling a potato and placed it in the bowl, then reached for another. She began to remove the skin and was quiet for a moment before asking if Elizabeth would return to school when she was better.

"Oh, Ah haven't thought that far ahead. Ah know she won't be allowed tuh go tuh her same school. If a girl has a baby, she's not allowed tuh go tuh public school. But there are other types of schools. Lord knows, she's gone need her education, but we must take first things first. Ah'm so happy yuh day wasn't tuh difficult. Yuh-know, it really makes me angry, the boys never get put out of school if they become fathers. Nothing happens tuh them, even if they don't marry the girl. But the girl has tuh do all the sufferin'. That makes me so mad," Loretha said.

"Mama, did 'Lizabeth tell yuh who the baby's father was?"

Loretha held her head down and paused. "No, honey, she will tell me when the time is right. She did tell me she was raped."

"Raped? Mama! Ah don't know what that means. Ah mean … Ah know it's something bad a man does tuh a woman. Ah know it has something tuh do wit' yuh private parts, but Ah don't really know what the man does."

"Honey, what yuh know is enough." Loretha held a knife in her right hand, a half-peeled potato in her left and smiled at Sarah as she continued peeling.

Sarah thought for a moment, shrugged her shoulders. "Mama … when was 'Lizabeth raped?"

Loretha stopped peeling the potatoes and gave Sarah her attention. "It was last spring. She was ashamed and didn't want tuh tell us because she was afraid. She has suffered so much …" Loretha was beginning to get a little teary. She had to take a few deep breaths and push her emotions back to a quiet place before she could say anything else. "Honey, she suffered through the rape, the pregnancy and the birth alone. We must be there for her now."

Sarah could see how much her mother was hurting, but that didn't stop her from asking her how she knew Elizabeth was telling her the truth.

Loretha closed her eyes for a brief moment and opened them slowly. "Sarah, why would she lie? At this point, with all her troubles, she had no reason tuh lie, besides, Mrs. Collins knew, and she told me what happened. Well, 'Lizabeth told her a few weeks ago, but Mrs. Collins remembered telling her not tuh go through the woods alone. It happened the same day she warned her. So remember, never go through the woods by yuhself."

"Mama, 'Lizabeth was raped in them woods out back? Why did she tell Mrs. Collins, and not Daddy or you?"

"Yes, honey, in them woods. She didn't tell anyone because she was so mixed up and afraid. We aren't the most open parents a chile could have. She was just afraid. We'll never understand what she went through, so all we can do now is be there for her."

"Daddy said she can't come home. Does he know she was raped?"

"Yes," Loretha said with a sigh. "But he doesn't believe her. He thinks she was just a bad girl. That's why she tried tuh commit suicide, and why Ah was so upset last night." Weary in her mood and movements, Loretha picked up the bowl of peeled potatoes and walked toward the kitchen sink.

"Mama, what's 'Lizabeth gonna do?"

"Well … she'll be in the hospital for a while, so Ah have time tuh work things out. Yuh've worried enough. Don't worry. Everything will work out."

Loretha and Sarah stopped talking when they heard John's car pull into the driveway. Before Loretha could say another word Sarah was already out the door, ready to give him a big hug. Loretha continued to prepare dinner.

"Hello, John," she spoke with a cold tone. Without turning to look at him, she worked harder. The bowls and utensils were no longer being handled gently, but slammed and banged, demonstrating her anger. She wondered why he bothered stopping by the kitchen, and turned to face him.

"Hello." John had no more words for her than she had for him, but her pleas for Elizabeth were etched all over her face. He stood in the kitchen and allowed his eyes to meet with hers. His eyes spoke, but only told her he had something to say. It was something important, something he had given a great deal of thought, then his eyes said never mind. Important or not, it would never be said, only he would ever know what it was. He blinked a flutter of blinks that separated his visual tie from Loretha, turned and walked from the room. Loretha knew what he had to say was something she would not be receptive to. He was so emotionally drained, he didn't have the strength to argue his point, or hear what Loretha had to say.

When dinner was ready, Loretha called to John and Sarah, and they all sat at their places at the table. Other than the traditional blessing, there was little, if any, conversation. All that could be heard was the clanging of the flatware against the dinner plates. Their thoughts were heavy with conversation, enough conversation to create a low pressure that kept their heads bowed and their eyes shifting away from each other. After dinner, Sarah cleared the table and cleaned the kitchen. Loretha and John retreated to the den.

"Did yuh speak with Owen tuhday?" Loretha spoke out, breaking her silence.

"No, and Ah don't intend tuh," John responded adamantly.

"Are yuh going tuh let 'Lizabeth come home with the baby?"

"No! … She can't ever come tuh this house again, with or without the baby."

Loretha stared at John with compressed lips and clenched teeth. Stress wrinkles appeared between her eyebrows. She shook her hand rapidly, trying to shake off her anger as she got up and walked to the kitchen. She had to remind herself it was John who angered her, and made a special effort to be civil toward Sarah when she kissed her on her forehead. Again, she retreated to Elizabeth's bedroom for the second night. She spent most of the remainder of the evening reading her Bible and on her knees, praying to God to help her daughter.

Loretha was up at her usual time on Friday morning. She was anxious, but successful at hiding her feelings from John. Using her compounded energy, she bathed and dressed before coming downstairs to prepare breakfast. John sat at the table reading his Bible. Loretha glanced at him in periodic bursts, but didn't say anything. Sarah's bus would arrive around 7:30 A.M., and she wanted to send her off after having a positive morning.

"Sarah, this is the last day of the week, and Ah'm sure it will be better than yesterday. Remember, no matter how tough it might get, just stay with it. Each day will be better," Loretha said.

"Ah'll be okay, Mama."

The school bus honked, and Sarah grabbed her belongings, kissed both parents, and hurried from the house. Loretha cleaned the kitchen and went about straightening up the living room and den. Next, she went upstairs to work in the bedrooms. She didn't want to be in the same room with John, and wanted the house to be neat when Miss Davies and Mr. Bruen arrived. All was in her favor. John was still sitting at the kitchen table, reading the Bible as though he didn't have anything on his schedule for the day.

Loretha watched the clock and made several trips to the bedroom window that gave the clearest view of Rehoboth Road in both directions. It was about ten minutes after eight when a black car pulled in the driveway behind John's car. She ran down the stairs and stopped at the third step from the bottom. John was standing at the door, watching the two white strangers approach the front porch. They were both carrying briefcases, and appeared very professional.

"Reverend Turner?" Miss Davies said.

John nodded his head and seemed puzzled. He wondered who they were, and why these two white people were standing at his door so early in the morning.

"My name is Lillian Davies, and this is Stan Bruen. Ah'm the social worker at the hospital, and Mr. Bruen is a legal aid attorney assigned tuh work with yuh daughter Elizabeth. May we come in? We have some very important issues tuh discuss with yuh and yuh wife. Is yuh wife home?"

Still puzzled, John stood back, nodded, and gestured for them to enter his home. He didn't appear to be the master of all that surrounded him. The very sight of white people coming to his door at eight in the morning transformed his demeanor to just another Negro who was uneasy in the presence of white people, even in his own home.

"We're sorry tuh call on yuh so early, but we called several times yesterday and weren't able tuh reach yuh. We just took a chance coming out early, hoping tuh catch yuh before yuh left for work," Mr. Bruen said.

"Come in … come in," John said, even though they were already standing in the foyer of his home. Loretha walked down the remaining steps and went over to greet them. She acted as though she had never met Miss Davies, wiping her hands on her apron before shaking their hands.

"Would you like to come into the den?" Loretha offered. Before they could respond, she was leading them into the room and fluffing the pillows on the sofa, indicating that was where she intended they sit. John followed them and sat in his lounge chair.

"May Ah take yuh coats?" Loretha asked, holding out her arm as though it were a rack. She returned to the room carrying a chair from the kitchen and placed it close to John, pretending to offer him support and keeping her demeanor as close to his as possible.

"How can we help yuh?" John asked.

"We need tuh speak with yuh about yuh daughter Elizabeth and the baby. We want yuh tuh know Elizabeth wants tuh keep her baby. She's told us yuh're not willing tuh allow her tuh return home. Is that the case?" Mr. Bruen said in a matter of fact tone. He was a handsome man, close to John's age, and pleasant to look at. He had a strong build, mixed gray-black hair and a black mustache. His quiet demeanor could have put John at ease if he were a black man, but he was white, and all white men made John stand on guard.

John was sharp with his answer, not softening even though Mr. Bruen made the hairs on the back of his neck stand erect. "Yes, Ah can't allow her tuh come back. She's brought shame on this family."

"Reverend Turner, Elizabeth told us she was raped. Rape is a serious crime in this state. She refuses tuh tell us who the rapist is, but we'll find out. It will be easy tuh prove in court, because we have the baby's blood type. Even if she changes her mind, she's a minor, and the man who raped her is subject to criminal prosecution, whether she wishes tuh press charges or not. This is a rape case, and at the least, a case of statutory rape," Mr. Bruen explained.

"But," Reverend Turner blurted out, before being sharply cut off by Mr. Bruen.

"No. Hear us out. We are not connected tuh the District Attorney's office. We're here tuh represent Elizabeth's wishes," Mr. Bruen continued.

John was weak with anger. He had just been cut off by a white man in his own home. Loretha sat closer to him, and was steaming with her own reason for her anger. She knew John didn't want Reverend Oliver to face criminal prosecution, but it was okay that his daughter had been violated and her life changed forever. Loretha knew John wanted to blot all that had happened from existence, but now it was slapping him in his face. Loretha wished she could slap him, but the satisfaction she was receiving from this meeting was revenge enough.

"We don't know what's happening. Please continue," Loretha said. John was too anxious over the possible outcome, and found it difficult to respond.

"Elizabeth said yuh don't want her tuh come home, and yuh just confirmed that. Elizabeth would like tuh come home, but she knows that wouldn't be a good idea. She's tried tuh commit suicide, and is currently under the care of a psychiatrist. Because of her medical status, she will be in the hospital at least another week. If she can't come home, it's the responsibility of the Social Service Department tuh find a foster home for her and the baby," Mr. Bruen continued.

John and Loretha continued to listen intently, but John wasn't willing to offer his home back to Elizabeth. Loretha knew he wouldn't bend, just as she knew what the two were leading up to.

Now the small, shapely, not very attractive white lady that had the serious crush on the prosperous Dr. Pernell spoke up. "We're not in the business of keeping families apart. Time is all yuh have tuh heal yuh wounds. But for now, we want tuh offer a solution that may be comfortable for all involved. We have explained the options tuh Elizabeth. Now we are here tuh explain them tuh yuh. Yuh must know that when we find out who the father of the baby is, we are obligated tuh notify the District Attorney's office for criminal action."

"What solutions are yuh offering? 'Lizabeth has gone against the preaching of the church and shamed herself and this family. She must pay the consequences," John answered in a quiet but definite tone.

"As we said. We represent Elizabeth. We've explained tuh hur the 'Emancipated Minor Law.' This law supports the responsible child that has irreconcilable differences with their parents. Yuh can grant Elizabeth an emancipation from yuh care, but yuh must continue tuh support her until she is eighteen years old. Yuh have the option of doing this with Elizabeth's counselor, or yuh'll receive a subpoena tuh appear in court. The family court judge will decide the case. Yuh contribution tuh her care will depend on yuh financial status. The Public Assistance Program will provide support for the child," Mr. Bruen explained.

"Where will she live?" Loretha asked.

"We'll find suitable housing for her, but as an emancipated minor, she will not be required tuh enter the foster care system. She will become the head of her own household. This is possible because of the infant. We don't want tuh pressure yuh, but we would like tuh have as much time as possible tuh find her a home before she's discharged from the hospital. We brought all the necessary papers with us, and yuh can call us with yuh decision when yuh ready. If we don't hear from yuh in three business days, we must file a petition with the court on her behalf," Mr. Bruen continued.

John sat quietly for a while. He pinched his fingers over his eyes and appeared to pretend he was someplace else. Miss Davies and Mr.

Bruen stood, suggesting they were ready to leave. Loretha leaned closer to John, pretending to give him her support.

"What are we goin' tuh do, John?"

"Ah don't know. Ah suppose we should let her have the emancipation."

Loretha wondered if John was giving Elizabeth her way to ensure she would be taken care of, or was he more concerned with giving in to remove her from any legal action that might implicate Reverend Oliver? He was truly shaken. Loretha made positive eye contact with Miss Davies and Mr. Bruen. She knew John wouldn't let them leave without signing the papers.

"Thank yuh for coming way out here. Ah'm sure yuh'll hear from my husband in a few days," Loretha said, winking her right eye. "Ah'll see yuh tuh the door."

"We'll be waiting tuh hear from yuh, Reverend Turner. Thank yuh for giving us yuh time," Mr. Bruen said, extending his hand for the traditional handshake.

John stood, shook their hands, then sat back down. Loretha walked them from the den to the small closet in the hall near the front door.

"Mr. Bruen, Miss Davies, yuh said yuh have the papers. Ah would like tuh take a few moments tuh read them."

"All right. We'll wait. If yuh have any questions, we'll try tuh answer them," Miss Davies said.

"Let's go tuh the dining room and sit around the table," John suggested.

Loretha led the way to the dining room. John took his time reading each word. The papers were very clear. The only question he had was the issue of financial support.

"If yuh can find yuh income tax papers from last year and yuh current essential expenditures, that'll be yuh mortgage or rent, yuh electricity and gas, what yuh spend for heat and food, yuh-know … what yuh need tuh live on, but not the luxury things like yuh car or telephone. We can give yuh an estimate of what the support charges will be," Mr. Bruen stated.

"Mr. Bruen, Ah'm exempt from paying taxes because my whole income is from the church, and havin' a car and a telephone is essential for my work, it's not a luxury," John said.

Loretha knew John felt it was degrading having to explain to this white man his personal and private business. She also knew he had internalized his anger to appear submissive, but he blamed Elizabeth for the invasion into his personal life and making him feel like he was begging the state for something.

"Yes, Ah understand, but Ah have tuh go by what the law allows. Now if yuh exempt, each year yuh file for that exemption, Ah have tuh see what yuh filed and yuh monthly bills."

"John, do yuh want me tuh get the papers?" Loretha offered.

"Yes, please do," John said. He turned and directed his next question at Miss Davies. "Where will 'Lizabeth and the baby live?"

"We don't have a residence for her yet, but we do have some options tuh follow-up on. We will have a place for her before she's released from the hospital."

Loretha returned to the dining room carrying a small briefcase with the necessary information. The lawyer reviewed the annual earnings from the tax forms, mortgage, utility bills, medical and insurance expenses and made tabulating notes on his yellow pad. He removed a formulary sheet from his briefcase and continued to tabulate the figures. John attended to Mr. Bruen's equations intensely, hoping the support cost wouldn't be more than he could manage.

"Support cost will be in the ball park of … approximately, $58.00," Mr. Bruen said.

"We can't afford that kind of money each week," John responded.

"No! A month … until her 18th birthday."

John appeared relieved. "That's $17.00 a week."

"Do yuh want tuh pay more? Yuh can give as much as yuh want, but this is the minimum the court will set based on yuh income. A judge could set it higher after the county's accountant reviews yuh financial status and submits a report. We can prevent that if this matter doesn't go tuh court," Mr. Bruen added.

Loretha was amazed how they handled John. This proud pillar of the community was reduced to the lowest level of meekness. He was ready to sign the papers.

"Yuh need tuh know if you and yuh daughter come tuh terms, the conditions of this settlement can be reversed. Ah hope everything works out for all of yuh," Miss Davies added.

John had nothing else to say. He thanked them only because it was the correct thing to do, but his indignation laid just a layer below his politeness. He wasn't happy. For the first time in his life, as a family man, he had lost the ability to maintain control. While Loretha escorted them to the door, John retreated to the den and sunk into his lounge chair.

When Loretha, Mr. Bruen and Miss Davies approached the door, they secretly smiled at each other. Loretha whispered that she would be in touch with them as soon as she could. She asked them to tell Elizabeth that she would call the hospital later that day. "Ah just want y'all to know that Ah'm truly thankful for yuh help," a jubilant Loretha whispered.

CHAPTER 7

John felt an emptiness about him while he tried to relax in the den. His head rested on the back of his chair, his feet were propped up on the footrest, he was still, trying to concentrate and centralize all of his energy on his prayer. He asked God to show him the way, to give him a sign.

Loretha was busy moving around the house. She refused to be a part of John's self-imposed anguish or share in his reasoning and misery. She was hurting, too, but hurting from worry, in spite of the recent victory. Elizabeth had endured seven months of mental agony alone. Reverend Turner's pain was his fear of disgrace. He thought he would be better off distancing himself from the source of the problem. Loretha felt sorry for him. Not the kind of sorry that came with pity, but sorrow because he was unable to see clearly and heal himself. She looked in on him each time she passed the den.

Although she hated what he was doing, she still recognized that his pain was real. Her anger had subsided, but she still bore the weight of his attempts to alienate the family from Elizabeth. She wanted to visit Elizabeth and tell her the news. Seeing Elizabeth and the baby would lift the heaviness she was feeling and allow her spirit to breathe.

It was after eleven o'clock, and Reverend Turner seemed to have no duties on his agenda for the day. His depression overwhelmed him and pinned him to the lounge chair. Revenge had saddened Loretha. It was the good in her that made her feel for him. She entered the den, pulled the small foot hassock close to him and sat on it. Intentional or not, her seating position was perfect. It allowed him to feel in charge. She was presenting herself in an humble, non-threatening manner.

"John. There's no need for yuh tuh suffer like this. Yuh acting like yuh daughter suddenly died."

"She did."

"No! She has not died! Yuh know the last thing she said tuh me yesterday? She said, Mama, Ah love Daddy."

"It won't work, Loretha."

"Please, listen tuh me. Yuh a man of the cloth. Only God can take a life. Elizabeth is an innocent chile who has suffered a terrible ordeal. And she went through all that because she didn't want tuh hurt yuh. She was raped! My God … John … she was raped. Yuh could never know how she must have felt … and … yuh would've never known if she didn't have a baby. That's because she loves yuh and didn't want tuh hurt yuh. Yes … now she has a baby. He's a new life, a gift from God. This child will be something wonderful with or without yuh love and acceptance. That's because Elizabeth is something wonderful."

Reverend Turner didn't say a word. He had already been whipped that day and was still recuperating. It was clear he heard her, but her words passed through him like the breeze blowing through the window curtains.

She sat there for a short while just looking at him. Then she removed both his hands from the sides of his chair and cupped them in her hands. When their eyes met, he read her pleas and turned away. He didn't pull his hands back to the arms of the chair, because he enjoyed the comfort of her touch. Loretha held on for a while longer before slowly removing herself from the hassock. She stood over him, placed her hands on his shoulders and whispered softly, "Ah'll pray for yuh, John." She turned and walked from the room.

Loretha was heavy with burdens. For the few moments that she sat with John, she realized how much she loved him, but she loved the blood of her blood more. She would pray for him. If it was in the Lord's great plan, he would come around. If he never did, she knew Elizabeth and the baby would be cared for. Having her most monumental accomplishment for the day completed, there were still a few other tasks on her agenda. She had to contact Elizabeth, visit Mrs. Collins, and go shopping for groceries and the things Elizabeth would need for the baby. She returned to the den and asked her husband if she could use the car to go food shopping. She knew if he refused, she would use Janet's son's car that was still parked in her driveway. Reverend Turner agreed, but only if she promised to return before three o'clock.

Reverend Turner continued to sit and stare off into the distant corner of the room. He thought about Miss Davies and Mr. Bruen. Like Loretha, he wondered why white people cared what happened to a colored family. Why were they going out of their way to help Elizabeth? They never cared before. He knew. He had helped other colored families through the church because there was nowhere else to turn. The white officials didn't care if a colored girl and her baby lived or died. He believed it was because they wanted to find the colored man who raped Elizabeth, but it really had nothing to do with Elizabeth, it was a way to get at a colored man, to prosecute and jail him so there would be one less colored man in Bibb County. He believed they wanted to get this man because he made another colored baby.

Reverend Turner allowed his mind to wander into confusion, before he began to talk with God. He asked why this terrible burden was placed on him and his family. He pleaded to be freed of this sickening feeling. He doubted he would be able to meet with the deacons later that evening. He also doubted that Reverend Oliver was responsible. But he did wonder why he hadn't heard from him. He refused to allow Reverend Oliver's golden boy image to be tarnished on the well-thought out plans of his teenage daughter.

Lord, help me through this. Help me see the way. Ah've been faithful tuh yuh and tuh my duties in the church. Ah've been a good husband and father. Why this? Help me, Lord. Please help me.

He cried as he prayed. He was thankful Loretha left the house. He wanted and needed to be alone. There were no plans for three o'clock that afternoon, but he knew if he gave Loretha a deadline she would not have time to go to the hospital. Never realizing selfish thoughts would remove bits and pieces of him from God's grace.

It was as though Reverend Turner and Reverend Oliver were on the same plane. They were suffering their own separate miseries over the same dilemma, and both lacked the compassion and morals to do the right thing. They prayed, but received no revelations. It was likely God had turned his back on them. He was testing them, and they failed. Nowhere in their prayers were there any pleas for God to help Elizabeth.

Reverend Oliver had not seen or called Reverend Turner all week, and he continued to have mounting anxieties. He was sure Reverend Turner and Loretha knew he was the father, but he hadn't heard anything from them. He and Reverend Turner usually spoke daily about their personal lives and church matters. He was sick with fear, and tried to believe since Reverend Turner had not contacted him, maybe Elizabeth didn't tell him what happened.

Thea noticed a change in Reverend Oliver. His leave from school allowed him to be home. He sat in their living room in a stupor and only responded to her when she moved close to him. When she questioned what was bothering him, he told her he was afraid she would be alone when their baby was born. Thea was comforting, and assured him she would be fine.

"Do yuh think yuh mother can stay with yuh when Ah have tuh go out?" Owen asked. "Yuh due date is in two days."

"Don't worry, Owen. Ah think yuh worrying yuhself sick for nothing, but if it'll make yuh feel better, Ah'll call my mother."

Reverend Oliver's main concern was not for Thea. He had to find a way to rid himself of his overwhelming fears and anxieties. He was at the breaking point, and was faced with losing his wife, job, church, and the respect of the community, not to mention the possibility of criminal actions. In a moment of weakness, he had committed a criminal act and a transgression against Elizabeth and the church. He knew, if not today, there would come the day when he would pay dearly for his actions. It was tearing him apart.

Ah should call John. If Ah don't call, and Elizabeth told him what happened, it'll give him reason tuh believe her. One way or another, Ah have tuh get this over. Ah can't go on like this any longer. It was about twelve thirty in the afternoon.

"Hello," John said.

"Hello John, it's Owen. Ah've been trying tuh reach yuh for two days," Owen explained as the lie rolled off his tongue. "How are Elizabeth and the baby?"

Immediately, the things Elizabeth told her father about Reverend Oliver raced through Reverend Turner's head. He took a few deep breaths before he responded. If he could have seen Reverend Oliver at that moment, he would've known Elizabeth was telling the truth, but Reverend Oliver was composed in his conversation.

"Ah was out during the day, but Ah've been home every evening. You could've called me later in the evening," Reverend Turner said.

"Ah've been praying for yuh family. Is Elizabeth all right?" Owen asked about Elizabeth again, evading John's question just as John had evaded his.

"Yes, she's fine, and the baby is fine, too," John answered in a quiet distant manner.

Reverend Oliver felt a sigh of relief. "Ah've been so worried about Elizabeth … and all of y'all. Yuh-know, Ah picked up Sarah and Loretha at the hospital and brought them home. Ah would've come in, but Thea was home alone, and Ah'd been away from her tuh long. It's just a matter of time before she delivers, and she's been having false labor. Didn't Loretha tell yuh?" Reverend Oliver bit his lip and waited for John's reply.

"Ah wondered why yuh didn't come in, but Ah understand. Ah wasn't much for company anyway. We have a meeting with the deacons tonight at eight o'clock. Could yuh meet me at the church at seven?

Ah'd like yuh tuh pray with me before we start. It's goin' tuh be very hard facin' the deacons after all that's happened."

"Of course. Thea's mother will be with her. Ah'll see you at seven."

"Thanks, Owen, Ah'll see yuh then."

Reverend Oliver felt better. He was convinced Reverend Turner didn't know anything. He wondered why Elizabeth didn't tell him. Even if he didn't believe her, if she told him anything, Reverend Oliver believed Reverend Turner would have questioned him. He believed he was safe for the time being, but knew it would be difficult facing John. He didn't know how he would do it, fearing his guilt would slither through any attempts he made to appear his usual self. He hadn't prayed for God to forgive him since the weeks after the act, when nothing happened, he believed he had been forgiven and thanked God for his mercy. Now he was a witness to the mysterious ways in which the Lord worked his wonders. His agony was compounded by overwhelming fear. While he sat trying to gather his emotions, Thea entered the room. He looked at her round pouch belly and up at her beautiful face.

"How do yuh feel?"

"Ah'm all right," Thea said. "How do you feel? Yuh look terrible. What's been wrong with yuh these past few days?"

"Oh, it's Elizabeth and the Turner family. They've been through so much. Ah'm worried about them. Ah just spoke with Reverend Turner, and he's taking it so hard. Ah feel so bad. Ah'm supposed tuh be a minister, and Ah don't know how tuh comfort him. He wants me tuh pray with him tonight before the deacon's meeting. Ah don't know what tuh say."

"It would mean a lot if yuh prayed with him. He's not handling this tuh well. Ah've heard … he's not letting Elizabeth and the baby come home. Ah called yesterday tuh speak with Loretha and Sarah told me she wasn't there. She wasn't sure where she was, but she told me John was very upset about this whole thing. She was upset because he wasn't goin' tuh let Elizabeth and the baby come home."

This was the first Reverend Oliver heard about Elizabeth and the baby not coming home. It made him feel even worse. He had to hide his emotions from Thea, but his posture sank down and inward.

"How could John be so hard on her? Everyone makes mistakes, yuh just don't throw yuh children away!" Thea rationalized.

"Ah don't know, honey. Ah just don't know. Maybe he'll have a change of heart. Would yuh please excuse me. All this is more than Ah can bear. Here we are, all excited about bringing a new life intuh the world, and Reverend Turner is throwing his child away." Reverend Oliver acted as though he was being stifled by the stale house air. He removed himself from Thea's presence, quickening his pace toward the door. "Ah need tuh get some air."

It was a brisk, cold day, but Reverend Oliver didn't bother getting a coat or even a sweater. He went outside and sat on the bench located at the far end of his backyard. Tears streamed down his face. He was responsible, but he wasn't man enough to go to Reverend Turner. He prayed for forgiveness, but the only way he could rid himself from the pain would be to tell Reverend Turner and hope for the best. He decided against that option and rationalized that he deserved to suffer because he was the cause of Elizabeth's suffering.

Thea grabbed her coat and Reverend Oliver's jacket and headed out of the back door. He didn't want her to come out. He wiped away his tears.

Thea yelled from the back porch, "Owen ... why are yuh taking this so hard?"

"That family is like my family. It hurts so much tuh know they're suffering. Ah don't understand John's behavior. She's his daughter, his blood. Maybe Ah can talk some sense intuh him."

"Yuh can pray with him, but he has tuh find his own way. Time will heal his wounds. Now come back inside. It's cold out here."

"Ah'll be in shortly."

"Well, put yuh jacket on." She wrapped the jacket around his shoulders. She walked slowly toward the house, turning, facing him and wanting to return to his side.

Reverend Oliver wanted to remain outside. It was easier. The cold numbed his fear. He had enough wits about himself to realize he couldn't return to the house knowing Thea would continue to question him. His eyes scanned the yard for some way to relieve his tension. He knew he needed a clear head before he met with John. *The wood pile. Ah'll cut wood.* The rack on the back porch was filled with split logs, but he always seemed more relaxed after chopping wood.

It puzzled Thea to watch Reverend Oliver from her kitchen window as he chopped large sections of wood. Most of the time, she had to remind him that the wood pile was low. She returned to the backyard.

"Owen! What is wrong with you?" she yelled in a concerned tone.

"Ah'm okay. Ah'm okay," he said, trying to convince her his actions were fulfilling his need to be busy and, at the same time, convincing himself of his need to release tension.

"Why yuh choppin' all that wood?" Thea said. She turned and waved her hand at the pile of wood neatly stacked near the back porch. "There's no place tuh put it."

"Then it'll stay out here 'til we need it!" Reverend Oliver yelled out coldly. "Ah'm sorry, honey. Ah'm so worried about yuh."

"There's nothing tuh worry about. The doctor said the baby is healthy and Ah feel fine. Ah'm just tired of being pregnant and disappointed from false labor." Hoping to relieve some of his anxieties, she chuckled lightly and rubbed her belly. "Come inside. That's enough for today."

"Yuh right. Ah'm acting foolish. After Elizabeth had her baby alone, Ah keep worrying that it could happen tuh yuh." His eyelids quivered, and he turned away as he lied.

"Yuh should've gone back tuh work. Ah don't need yuh hangin' 'round worryin' 'bout me. Besides, yuh-know Mama will be comin' tuh stay with me when yuh not here."

"Well, my leave has already been approved, so Ah guess yuh stuck with me." He put his arm around her shoulder, and they walked back into the house.

CHAPTER 8

Loretha's first stop was at Mrs. Collins' house, but, just as before, she traveled the back roads so John wouldn't know where she was going. She knew she didn't have much time. She had to get to Mrs. Collins so she could tell her John signed the papers, and then she would get in touch with Elizabeth.

Mrs. Collins saw the puff of dirt trailing Loretha's car. She was waiting at the front door.

"How's mah girl?'

"She's doing fine, but the good news is, John signed the papers."

"Ah know."

"Yuh know?"

"Oh yeah," Mrs. Collins said with a grand smile. "Dem folks came here when dey left yuh house. Ah signed dem papers so 'Liz'beth and the baby can live wit' me."

"Yuh did?" Loretha said while she followed Mrs. Collins through her living room, into her kitchen.

Mrs. Collins eased into her kitchen chair and nodded for Loretha to take a seat. "Yeah, so it's settled. Be happy chile. Ah jest wanna he'p 'Liz'beth, but Ah don't wanna hurt yuh. Ah know yuh want yuh chillen home. The lady said she can go home anytime she wants, that's if the good Reb wants her and the baby ... Ah know she be goin' home. Ah jest want yuh tuh know, Ah's here fer yuh and yuh family as long as yuh be needin' me."

"Ah love yuh," Loretha said.

"Well ... Ah love yuh, too. And don't worry 'bout talkin' tuh 'Liz'beth. Dem folks said dey is gone see hur as soon as dey get back tuh the hospital."

"That's good. It would be so hard not knowin' if she got my message. Well … when Ah leave here, Ah'm goin' food shopping, and Ah want tuh buy things for the baby. Ah think Ah'll buy 'Lizabeth a new night gown, robe and slippers. Would yuh like tuh go?"

"Sho' would. Will it be all right? Ah mean, can yuh wait? Ah gotta change."

"Yuh go ahead. May Ah call the hospital and try to get a message to 'Lizabeth? Ah'll pay yuh for the call," Loretha spoke louder to catch Mrs. Collins' ear as she walked around the table toward her bedroom.

Mrs. Collins stepped from her bedroom and into her sitting area. She didn't want to yell out when she answered Loretha. "Yuh don't need tuh be payin' me for no phone, and do yuh want yuh business out? Yuh know 'bout dem party lines."

"Yuh're right? Ah'm sure Miss Davies told her what happened, and Ah'll see her tomorrow."

———𝔪———

Mrs. Collins didn't get out of the house much. Loretha walked with her out the back door, and they walked around the house to Loretha's car. Mrs. Collins looked back at her husband's car parked in the shed, covered in three years of dust. The 1943 sedan used to be a beautiful black shining automobile. It was in excellent condition when Mr. Collins died. As Loretha turned around in Mrs. Collins' circular driveway, Mrs. Collins could still see the side of the car.

"Ah don't even 'member whut kinda car dat be. It jest got me where Ah wanted tuh go. Dem white folks, dey jest stared at us when we go by. Ah guess colored folks wasn't s'pose tuh have no car lak dat. It was kinda scary, so Mr. Collins … he didn't drive it much. Didn't wanna be showin' off none. Wasn't too healthy fer a colored man tuh be showin' off. Kept dat car in the colored section, wipe it down and polished it most ever' day. Take the hay wagon tuh town when he had tuh go. He treated it like it was his baby. Ah'm gone have the mechanic come git dat car."

"Ma'am?" Loretha responded. Her mind was somewhere else, but she responded out of respect.

"Fred's car. Ah'm gonna have it fixed up. Yuh can use it when yuh want tuh, and maybe yuh can teach 'Liz'beth tuh drive. It's shameful. Fred's love dying out in dat old shed," Mrs. Collins said in a low voice.

"Yuh want tuh put Mr. Collins' car back on the road?" Loretha said.

"Well, chile! We's sure gone need a car."

"Yuh right about that, but let me pay for the repairs. Ah don't want tuh burden yuh with an added expense."

"Whut makes yuh think Ah'm a po' ol' lady? Ah'm an ol' lady … and Ah ain't rich … but Ah ain't po' either. Fred left me a few dollars. Ah think dat man saved ever' penny he made. He never put a penny in a bank, but Ah did when he died. His pension ain't much, but the money Ah stashed in the bank jest keeps a growin' and a growin'. Ah don't bother it. Ah don't need much. The house and land is free and clear. Ah jest make a wit'drawal each year tuh pay the taxes. Then, Ah jest kinda forget 'bout it."

"Ah don't know how Ah'm gonna thank yuh," Loretha said.

"Yuh already done thanked me. Ah'm gone be a mama 'gain before Ah die. Last year when Ah wuz ailin', Ah think it wuz jest loneliness. Ah was preparin' tuh die. There be nothin' fer me on dis earth; 'cept fer y'all, Ah ain't have nothin'. Ah'd go tuh church to ask the Lawd to make a place fer me. Now, Lawd done give me a purpose. Yuh-know … mah baby girl died when she was jest ten years ol'. Dat be over forty years ago. She had dat leukemia. The Lord ain't give me no mo' chillen. He knowed best, 'cause Ah had too much pain tuh give good lovin' tuh another chile." Mrs. Collins was opening up some of the private parts of her life. She had no way of making Loretha understand how grateful she was for allowing her to be a significant part of her family.

"Ah'll see her 'gain when it be mah time … but now … Ah'm gonna have yuh girl and yuh gran' baby 'round the house, and Ah'm gonna die a happy ol' lady, so yuh don't have tuh thank me fer allowing me tuh share yuh chillen lak dey mah own. It's me ... Ah be needin' tuh thank you. Ah use tuh wonder why God was keepin' me 'round so long ... and all alone."

All that Mrs. Collins expressed swelled Loretha's emotions. She wouldn't say thank you this time, but she was grateful, she knew the words would slip out from time to time. This time she would rub Mrs. Collins' hand. Between her tingling bits of sorrow, she managed to say, "Ah didn't know yuh had a little girl."

"Yeah, Ah sho' did. But enough 'bout dat now." Mrs. Collins grew quiet. It was still too painful to speak of memories so close to her heart.

"Mrs. Collins, do yuh have paper and a pen? We have tuh make a list of all the things we need for the baby." Loretha was trying to change the subject.

"Lemme search in mah pocketbook ... Ah think ... Ah believe ... Ah kin find a piece of paper, but Ah ain't sure if Ah got a pencil."

"In my pocketbook, Ah think Ah have a pen or pencil."

"No. No. Ah found somethin'. Ah jest hope yuh can read mah writin'," Mrs. Collins said.

"If Ah can't, yuh can read it."

"What if Ah cain't read it either?"

"Oh, come on now," Loretha said, and both ladies laughed.

The baby's list was made. Loretha had pushed the family's troubles deep inside. She was lifted by the many blessings she had received that day. Proud to be a grandmother, she was not willing to allow the damaging tones of anyone to bring her down. This attitude was conveyed everywhere she went, and her highly lifted spirit was worn like a banner, a message to everyone she met. She was not ashamed of her daughter. Her carefree spirit shadowed her, and she was appalled by the comment of a church member she met on the street.

"Ah'm so sorry tuh hear 'bout yuh misfortune," the lady said.

Loretha's eyes widened and her head tilted slightly to the side. "What misfortune? We have a beautiful grandson. Yuh-know, the good Lord works his wonders in many ways. We must always accept his gifts and never question the mode of delivery."

"Yuh so right, Sister Turner," the lady said, tempering her tone of voice and attitude.

Mrs. Collins and Loretha nodded their heads in a gesture of farewell before moving on.

"Oh, Ah lak dat. Ah couldn't a done better mahself. Yuh all right, chile … Mrs. Loretha Turner. Yes darlin' … yuh all right."

They smiled at each other and went about their duties. Saturday was the shopping day for Loretha's family, but because she was so excited about buying baby things, she couldn't wait for Saturday. She had planned to spend Saturday at the hospital. She knew as soon as she began selecting baby clothes time would slip away, so she decided to shop for food first. After putting the food in the trunk of the car, she and Mrs. Collins walked to a small department store. She bought Elizabeth two nightgowns, a bathrobe, and a pair of slippers. They didn't have time to get the baby's things, so they decided to make a special trip at another time.

Loretha dropped Mrs. Collins off at her home, then she hurried home, knowing John would be watching the time.

Reverend Turner checked at his watch when Loretha entered the house. He was right where she'd left him. She walked back to the den and remarked in a subtle, sarcastic tone, "Would yuh help me get the groceries in the house?"

Reluctantly, Reverend Turner removed himself from his chair and walked directly to the car without speaking to her. Loretha broke the silence.

"John, do yuh have tuh leave right away?"

"No. My plans have changed. Ah have tuh meet Reverend Oliver at the church at seven."

"Are yuh goin' tuh speak tuh him about 'Lizabeth?"

"No! Ah told yuh Ah'm not goin' tuh drag him intuh our problem!"

"Okay! Okay! Yuh do what yuh have tuh do, and Ah'll do what Ah have tuh do!"

"Loretha, Ah forbid yuh from talking tuh anyone about this."

"John, Ah'm not goin' tuh say anythin' tuh Reverend Oliver. Ah don't have tuh. Ah'm sure he's in his own private hell, and for now … that's where he belongs. Ah want some time with you and Sarah. Ah want us tuh pray together. Will yuh pray with me?"

"Yes, Loretha, Ah'll pray with yuh, and Ah'll pray for 'Lizabeth and the baby, but Ah won't change my mind," John said.

"Very well, John, we'll sit together before dinner. Ah'm not goin' tuh try tuh get yuh tuh change yuh mind. That's somethin' yuh'll have tuh live with. Yuh could accept 'Lizabeth and the baby without speaking tuh Reverend Oliver, but that's yuh decision. She loves yuh, but she doesn't want tuh come home. Yes, now it would be so simple for yuh tuh have her home, but Ah don't want her here tuh be tormented. What yuh did this morning was the right thing tuh do under the circumstances. Ah'll stay with yuh, even though yuh asking me tuh choose between you and 'Lizabeth. Ah'm here with yuh and Ah'll stay with yuh, but if yuh ever try tuh forbid me from seeing 'Lizabeth or our grandson, Ah'll leave yuh tuh wallow in yuh misery alone."

"Loretha! Ah forbid yuh tuh speak tuh me in that tone."

"Ah'm yuh wife, yuh best friend, the mother of yuh children. Ah've honored, respected and obeyed yuh. Up 'til now, Ah believed in yuh, but Ah don't have tuh agree with yuh. Respect is always best received when it's also given. We've had our differences … and in the past … Ah've always let yuh have yuh way. Ah have a right tuh speak for the sake of the chile Ah carried and brought intuh this world. Ah know the only reason yuh wanted the car back by three o'clock was because yuh knew Ah couldn't get tuh the hospital, do the shopping, and be back in that short time. If Ah had planned tuh go tuh the hospital, Ah would've used Janet's car. Ah just wanted tuh see what yuh were gonna do tuhday. When Ah need the car tuh visit 'Lizabeth, Ah will tell yuh and Ah expect tuh get it." Loretha's body language accentuated every word she spoke. For the first time, for as long as she could remember, she felt good, strong, and in control of her world.

John was seeing a new Loretha. He wasn't quite sure how to respond to her. He felt threatened, and didn't want to lose her or her love. She never challenged him before, and she made it quite clear she'd accepted the fact that Elizabeth was not coming home. Their eyes locked; Loretha's attitude was clear. She knew the battle was over, and she had won.

"Ah understand how yuh feel. Ah'll respect yuh wishes, and Ah'll never try tuh stop yuh from visiting her. Ah'm sorry Ah was trying tuh keep yuh from her. Ah won't do that again," John apologized.

"Thank yuh, John. Ah appreciate yuh understanding. Ah'll be visitin' 'Lizabeth tomorrow, and Ah'll need tuh use the car ... now, if yuh have some church duties, Ah'll use Janet McCray's son's car." Loretha was angry, determined, and she wasn't finished. "Now there's one more thing before Sarah comes in. Ah think yuh should let her decide if she wants tuh visit 'Lizabeth. Even if yuh think she shouldn't, yuh shouldn't try tuh influence her decision."

"Sarah is only thirteen years old. Ah still have a say in what she does. 'Lizabeth may be a bad influence on her ..."

"Oh, come on, John!" Loretha said, cutting him off. "If that was the case, Sarah would have known 'Lizabeth was pregnant. If yuh don't allow hur tuh decide on what she thinks is right or wrong, yuh may lose her, too. She may want tuh visit 'Lizabeth, but she won't if she thinks yuh'll be mad at her. Ah'm just asking yuh tuh respect her wishes, too."

"All right, Loretha! Al l l l l right!" He appeared tired and defeated. He had been studying the situation so intensely. "We'll sit together and talk about 'Lizabeth and the baby. Ah'll tell Sarah it's all right if she wants tuh visit her."

"Ah'm home," Sarah announced as she entered through the front door.

"How was school tuhday?" John asked.

Loretha was in the kitchen preparing dinner. She walked into the dining room and sat at the table to hear about Sarah's day.

Sarah sat at her place at the table. "It was better than yesterday. Yuh're right, Daddy. Ah guess it will get better and better."

"That's very good, Sarah. It will get better. Yuh'll tell us if yuh having a problem, won't yuh?"

"Yes, Mama."

"John, this is as good a time as ever tuh speak with Sarah."

Sarah seemed puzzled and unsettled. "What's the matter? Is 'Lizabeth okay?"

"Yes, honey, she's fine." Loretha winked and nodded for John to start.

"'Lizabeth won't be living with us when she gets out of the hospital."

"Ah know, Daddy, but why?"

"Yuh know why." John didn't want Sarah to question him, but he wanted to be gentle with her. "Tuhday, Ah signed papers declaring her an adult. She can live wherever she wants."

"But where will she live? How will she take care of herself and the baby? Don't yuh love her anymore?"

John evaded her question. "Listen, she can't come home. The social worker at the hospital will find a place for her tuh live."

"John!" Loretha interrupted abruptly. "Sarah ... honey, yuh father is still having trouble accepting all of this. He doesn't want 'Lizabeth tuh come home, but he won't stop us if we want tuh visit her. Ah will visit her as often as Ah can. We've decided it's yuh decision if yuh want tuh visit her."

"Mama, Ah'll visit her, but Ah'm not sure when. Ah'm not ready yet."

"That's fine, honey. Just tell me when yuh are," Loretha reassured her.

A small smile appeared on Reverend Turner's face, as though he'd won. Loretha returned with a pleasant smile, knowing it wasn't about victories. If it were, she would have been gloating.

Without saying another word, Loretha removed herself from the table and returned to her kitchen duties. Just as Sarah was about to leave the dining room, she called to her, "Could yuh help me for a few minutes? Ah want tuh get yuh old crib from the attic after dinner. We need tuh bring it down tuh the garage so Ah can wash it down and get it ready for 'Lizabeth."

"Mama, where are they gonna live?"

"Ah don't know, but the social worker will find her a nice place, somewhere near by," Loretha said, knowing Sarah would find out the truth soon enough. Then, she remembered Mrs. Collins would be going to the hospital with her. If Sarah went along, she would find out Elizabeth would be living with Mrs. Collins. *Ah won't do anything tuh encourage her tuh visit 'Lizabeth tomorrow. If she says she wants tuh go, Ah'll think of something tuh change her mind.*

"Okay, Mama, Ah think Ah can get the crib by myself."

"No, Sarah, we'll do it together. Ah don't want yuh tuh fall. Yuh go on … we'll do it after dinner."

Sarah nodded and left the room.

Reverend Turner was very quiet during dinner. He was worried about meeting the deacons, but most of all, his meeting with Reverend Oliver. Reverend Turner knew all he had to do was confront Reverend Oliver, but he didn't want to know the truth.

"Loretha, Ah'm going tuh the church, Ah have a meeting with the deacons. Ah'll see yuh when Ah return."

"See yuh later." She didn't say good luck or that she hoped everything would go all right. She knew John knew what he needed to do.

Reverend Turner arrived at the church and noticed Reverend Oliver's car parked in its usual place. The lights in the church were already on. Reverend Turner took his time getting out of the car. Just as he closed the car door, he saw Reverend Oliver standing at the top of the steps. The lights illuminating from the door of the church gave Reverend Oliver the appearance of a black shadow. He knew it was Reverend Oliver, but his appearance in silhouette gave him an uneasy feeling. He stood for a few moments longer and stared at his black, sordid image. *Maybe this is the sign from God.*

Shaking his head in disbelief mixed with not wanting to believe, he allowed his mind to accept a rational, self-serving conclusion. *No, it's not clear enough.* Slowly, he walked toward the church steps. He kept his head low, his eyes toward the ground, afraid to look up at Reverend Oliver again.

Reverend Turner's demeanor increased Reverend Oliver's apprehension. Reverend Oliver needed to see his eyes to reassure himself that he was safe. He reached inside the doorway and turned on the outer lights.

When Reverend Turner looked up again, he saw Reverend Oliver in the luminous radiance of the bright lights. Confused, he stopped again and stared at Reverend Oliver. He was just given two signs, and he selected the brighter one, which lifted the burden of his confusion.

"John? Is that you?" Reverend Oliver yelled.

"Yeah Owen. It's me ... yuh early."

"Yuh said seven o'clock. Well ... it's ten after seven. Ah decided tuh open the church while Ah waited."

"Is it that late? Ah guess time just slipped away." Reverend Turner hurried up the steps, and the two men entered the sanctuary together. They walked to the front pew, sat, and clasped their hands in their laps. At first, it seemed that each was waiting for the other to speak.

"Reverend Oliver, Ah need yuh help. You know the circumstances about 'Lizabeth. Well, Ah'm not handling it very well. Ah have tuh meet the trustees and deacons tonight, and Ah don't know how tuh face them. Ah don't know what tuh say. Ah feel so ashamed."

Dreading being with Reverend Turner, Reverend Oliver had to say something. "John, it really troubles me tuh see yuh so torn. Don't worry about the deacons. Face them. Start out by being open. Ask them tuh pray for you and yuh family."

"They may not want me tuh pastor the church any longer."

"John, they are men with skeletons in their closets, too. They know life. Yuh've been the pastor of this church for fifteen years. They know that most of the congregation will follow you if yuh were tuh leave. But, be unassuming and let them believe it's their decision tuh keep yuh on. Yuh know yuh have my support, and yuh also have the support of the majority of the deacons and trustees."

"Ah hope so."

"Come on. Let's pray. We don't have much time. They'll be coming soon," Reverend Oliver said.

As Reverend Turner prayed for the deacons to be understanding and the Lord to give him guidance, Reverend Oliver prayed silently that Reverend Turner would never know he was responsible.

Reverend Turner and Reverend Oliver heard the church door open. Deacon Harris, and Deacon Tutley entered. John felt weak, and leaned on Reverend Oliver's shoulder for support. Reverend Oliver's posture dipped slightly from his weight. He needed all of his strength to hold himself up.

"Good evening, brothers," Reverend Turner said.

"Good evening," both men responded simultaneously.

"Reverend Turner, we've been hearin' a lot of things about Elizabeth, troublin' things. Do yuh want tuh talk about it?" Deacon Tutley questioned.

"Ah would like tuh talk about it … and Ah need tuh talk about it, but it's very painful. Ah prefer tuh wait until everyone arrives. Ah don't think Ah have the strength tuh go over it more than once." John held his head low and tears filled the corner of his eyes.

"It's all right, Rev," Deacon Tutley murmured.

Deacon Harris put his hand on Reverend Turner's shoulder, signaling his confirmation of Deacon Tutley's statement. That helped

Reverend Turner to know he had their support, but he wasn't so sure about the support of the other deacons. He excused himself from the room, leaving Reverend Oliver standing with them. He went into the pastor's study and just sat quietly. After seeing Reverend Oliver, he was convinced he had nothing to do with Elizabeth's accusation. And just having the support of two deacons relaxed him with the belief that he would have all of their support. Now his biggest concern was facing the congregation on Sunday.

It wasn't long before Reverend Oliver was calling Reverend Turner to start the meeting. At most meetings, there was always someone unable to attend, but for the obvious reasons, everyone was present on this night. Reverend Turner stood from his chair and took a deep breath. He was prepared to step down if asked, but he prayed that wouldn't happen.

"Good evening, brothers," he began. "Brother Dotson, would yuh lead the opening prayer?" The men stood and bowed their heads.

"Let us pray."

"Dearest Lord, thank yuh for the opportunity tuh meet in yuh place once again. We come before yuh as humble men, asking for yuh guidance and direction. He'p us tuh follow yuh teachin', and keep us on the path of righteousness. We ask these and all other blessin' in Jesus' name. Amen."

"Amen," the other men sang out.

Reverend Turner thanked Brother Dotson before addressing the men. "Ah know yuh all want tuh hear what's happening in my family. Ah think we should put this issue at the top of our agenda. Before yuh begin with yuh questions, Ah'd like the opportunity tuh give yuh information first hand and tuh the best of my knowledge. When Ah finish, if yuh want me tuh step down as yuh pastor … Ah will."

Reverend Turner turned from the men and walked to the opposite side of the church. It was as though he needed more time to think about what he would say, but that was not the case. He needed more time to compose himself. He felt he had lost a daughter, was losing his wife, and now, may lose his church. But he believed if this was God's will, then His will must be done. With this, he felt a surge of inner strength.

"Gentlemen, as yuh know my daughter had a baby. And yes … she delivered this baby in school. No one knew she was pregnant … and we don't know who the father is." John had said it all in three sentences. "Somehow, Ah … Ah must have failed. Ah'll understand if yuh all want me tuh step down. If Ah can't instill the 'Word' in my family, yuh must be wondering how can Ah lead my congregation."

"Reverend Turner," Deacon Tutley said, "we all is got our crosses tuh bear, and each and every one of us is livin' in a glass house. We is all human, and our wives and chillen is human, too. Ah think we need tuh clear up yuh most important question. Everyone here done heard whut happened. Ah know it be a heavy burden, but it happened, and that gotta be God's will. Ah would lak tuh open the floor fer discussion if yuh be thinkin' this needs tuh be done." He turned to the other deacons and trustees and held open the palms of his hands toward them, gesturing for their opinion.

"Ah don't think there be any need fer discussion. Ah would like tuh make a motion that Reverend Turner remain as our pastor," Deacon Johnson added.

"Ah second it," Deacon Wren shouted. The other men harmonized, "Amen."

"Those opposed?" Deacon Tutley said. No one opposed, the motion passed.

"John," Deacon Bains said. He called him John instead of the more formal "Reverend Turner" because they had been life-long friends. "Yuh christened mah granddaughter. Mah daughter wasn't married. It was hard fer me tuh take, but Ah survived. Now that lil' girl is the light of mah life. My Theresa tol' me that Sarah said yuh won't let 'Lizbeth and the baby come home. Yuh're a man, a husband, and a father. If this is true, I don't understand yuh decision. It really worries me."

"Yes, Reverend Turner, Ah heard the same. Whut's happenin' here?" Deacon Dotson posed the question that was on everyone's mind.

"Ah'm praying. Ah'm asking God tuh help me through this. Yuh're right, Ah'm just a man," Reverend Turner said.

"No. Yuh not just a man. Yuh our spiritual leader," Deacon Harris said. "Times is hard for a colored person. How's a chile with a chile s'pose tuh survive?"

"Okay, let's lighten up. Each man handles his private affairs in his own way. We're only men, and don't have the right tuh judge anyone," Deacon Tutley interrupted.

"Rev's gotta find his own way. We'll keep him in our prayers. Now Ah make a motion that we move on tuh church business," Deacon Carrington said.

"Ah second," Reverend Oliver said.

"Second motion or not, that's still worrisome tuh me, but Ah'm gonna let it go fer now," Deacon Bains added.

Reverend Turner pretended to be thankful for the men's understanding, but he recognized the discontent expressed by Deacons Bains, Harris, and Dotson. He began to entertain allowing Elizabeth and the baby to return home.

"Okay. Now that the motion has been seconded, let's move on. We can always bring a motion tuh open the subject if we need tuh," Reverend Oliver said. "Now this is December, and the children are working on their Christmas pageant. Mrs. Oliver has been working with Mrs. Jenkins because our baby is due on the 20th …"

The deacons continued with the church meeting, but John's mind continued to wander off. He considered Reverend Oliver, but questions remained in his mind. *Who else could it be? She never lied tuh me before. Ah can't go tuh Owen unless Ah'm sure. The Lord will give me a sign. How can Ah get 'Lizabeth tuh come home now that Ah've signed the papers? How can Ah look at 'Lizabeth and that baby and not show contempt for the disgrace she's caused? Ah'll leave the matter alone and see what happens. Ah need tuh see what the congregation is gonna say.*

CHAPTER 9

Mid-morning had crept up on Loretha, but John was still sleeping. Loretha and Sarah worked briskly to complete their chores before going to the hospital. Loretha asked Sarah if she wanted to visit Elizabeth? At first Sarah was speechless, but then she simply explained she was tired and wanted to catch up on her napping that afternoon. Loretha was disappointed and happy at the same time. When Elizabeth asked for Sarah, Loretha would remind her that it was best for Sarah to stay away from the hospital because she didn't want her to discover their plans. She knew Elizabeth would understand. The phone rang, and Loretha hurried to answer it.

"Hello." Loretha sat on the telephone bench in the hall. She crossed her legs at her ankles and pulled the hairpin from her hair, allowing her bun to unravel and fall to her shoulders.

"Hello, Loretha, it's me … Mrs. Collins. Ah called the mechanic yesta'day, and he come and got the car this mornin'. He's gone call me 'bout noon and tell me how much it cost tuh fix it. Let's jest pray he can get it runnin' again."

"Did he try tuh start it?" Loretha ran her fingers through her hair and massaged her scalp. Then, she placed the phone in her other hand and began to massage the other side of her scalp.

"Yeah, but he got nothin'," Mrs. Collins said.

"Well, we'll just pray he can get it started."

"What time yuh wanna go tuh the hospital?"

"About noon," Loretha answered. "Ah don't want tuh have tuh hurry back, so Ah'll use Janet's car today. Ah'll come and pick yuh up. Let's not talk too much on the phone. Yuh know how this party line is. We can talk when Ah pick yuh up. Is noon okay for yuh?"

"That'll be good. Maybe Ah'll be hearin' from the mechanic by then."

"Well, we'll just wait for his call. If he doesn't call, we'll call him before we leave. Ah'll see yuh at noon."

"Okay, baby. See yuh in two hours."

Loretha hung up the phone and walked upstairs to the master bedroom. Her hair rested about her shoulders, and she liked what she saw when she looked in the mirror, but she had work to do. She parted her hair down the middle and braided each side before wrapping her head in a head rag. She put on an old work dress and heavy sweater before going back downstairs to prepare the bucket of soapy bleach laced water and carried it to the shed where she scrubbed each section of the crib until it sparkled like new. She could see Reverend Turner watching her from the bedroom window, and it made her feel good to know he didn't dare try to stop her. As soon as she finished, she hurried back to the house to change her clothes.

"John, Ah know yuh have some things tuh do tuhday. Ah've decided tuh use Janet's car."

It wasn't long before Loretha picked up Mrs. Collins, and they were on their way to the hospital.

"Ah told John Ah would be visiting 'Lizabeth today. Ah got the crib cleaned up this morning, and now Ah need tuh pick up a new mattress after we leave the hospital."

"Mah, mah. What's goin' on wit' the Reb? Why he help'n' now?"

"Well he ain't exactly helping, but Ah had a little talk with him last night, and Ah put my foot down. Ah told him he could do what he wanted tuh do, but he wasn't comin' between me and mine. Ah told him Ah'd leave him if he tried. He understood … yuh-know whut Ah mean?" Loretha was proud of herself, and it felt good telling Mrs. Collins of her accomplishment.

"Good fer yuh, chile." Mrs. Collins had no more to say on that subject. She was too wise to say anything about a husband and wife's business. "Now why don't yuh bring the crib over here? We could set it up in the bedroom."

"That's not a good idea. Ah don't want John tuh know where Ah'm taking it. Ah have this feeling he's watching my every move. Ah'll bring it over when the time is right."

When they got off the elevator, Loretha took Mrs. Collins directly to the nursery.

"Oh! There's little Johnny." Loretha pointed her finger in his direction and smiled.

Mrs. Colins squinted, tracing the path of Loretha's fingers. "Ah can jest barely see him. Dese ol' eyes ain't what dey use tuh be." She shifted her head and squinted again.

Loretha tapped on the glass to get the nurse's attention, then she beckoned her to bring Johnny's crib closer to the window.

"Oh, he's precious. Ah cain't wait tuh get mah hands on him." Mrs. Collins seemed as excited as a new mother with new responsibilities.

"Yeah, Ah feel that way, too."

They both smiled and admired Johnny through the window. They squeezed each other's hands thoughtfully. Loretha was first to pull her thoughts away, and led Mrs. Collins toward Elizabeth's room.

Loretha and Mrs. Collins stood in the door and watched Elizabeth, who was busy talking with the nurse's aide. The quiet, tense, introspective person that Loretha had come to know over the past several months was gone, and the old Elizabeth had returned; her old Elizabeth with her bubbly, quiet, peaceful personality was back. It was only at that moment when Loretha realized there had been a noticeable change in her daughter. She thought of the heaviness that surrounded

Elizabeth like an invisible cloud. A cloud so thick it levied a low pressure on her and her surroundings.

Loretha remembered times when she was affected by Elizabeth's cloud. The low pressure made her feel heavy and saddened her own spirit. Watching Elizabeth with her aide, Loretha realized her daughter had suffered enormous emotional pressures. Then she heard the harmony of Elizabeth's voice.

"Mama! Mrs. Collins! We didn't know yuh were standing there. This is Adele Jones, my nurse's aide. We were just talking about my school. Adele graduated from there two years ago."

"Is that so? Well it's very nice tuh meet yuh," Loretha said. Mrs. Collins acknowledged her with a smile and a nod of her head.

Adele stood when they entered the room and smiled. "It's nice tuh meet yuh, too. Ah'll be at the nurse's station if yuh need me."

"Thank yuh." Loretha wanted to say more. She wanted to tell Adele how grateful she was for her helping lift her daughter's spirits.

Loretha gave Elizabeth a kiss on the cheek, and Mrs. Collins gently squeezed her hands. Loretha handed her the present and stood close, waiting to see her face when she opened it.

"Oh, Mama, they're so pretty. Ah'll put one on now. Ah'm so tired of these old hospital gowns. Why don't you and Mrs. Collins go out in the hall, and Ah'll call yuh when Ah'm ready. Ah want tuh get pretty for yuh."

"Oh, Ah almost forgot, Ah brought yuh a small suitcase with some things yuh'll probably need."

"Thanks, Mama." Elizabeth rummaged through the suitcase. "You're right, Ah need all these things."

Loretha knew Elizabeth would never change in front of them. She had taught her to be private with her body. It didn't matter that they were all women, or that she was her mother.

Mrs. Collins and Loretha were standing in the hall when they noticed Thea being rolled in on a stretcher. She appeared to be still under the effects of the anesthesia when the aides pushed her past them. Loretha didn't see Reverend Oliver. She heard Elizabeth call for them.

When they entered the room, they couldn't help making over Elizabeth's appearance. Whether it was the new gown or the way her life was coming back together, it didn't matter. It made her sparkle. Loretha stood a few feet from the bed, and tears collected in the corner of her eyes. *My God, yuh certainly work yuh wonders in mysterious ways.*

"There's another surprise," Mrs. Collins announced. "Ah got Mr. Collins' car fixed. When yuh well, yuh mama will teach yuh tuh drive, and the car will b'long tuh yuh."

"Mine? … Yuh givin' me yuh car? Yuh been so good tuh me … yuh don't have tuh give me yuh car."

"Ah know Ah don't, but Ah wanna … and besides, yuh can drive me 'round. Ah'll never learn tuh drive at mah age."

Loretha faced Elizabeth and smiled. "She's just too good tuh be true." Then, giving her attention to Mrs. Collins, she said, "Ah forgot all about the mechanic. Did he call yuh?"

"Yes, and Ah figured Ah'd tell yuh both the good news when we is all tuhgether. All it needed was a lil' engin' work, a new battery and new tires. Now, all Ah got tuh do is git it insured and git the tags, and we be on our way."

"Mrs. Collins," Elizabeth said, "may Ah call yuh MaDear? Yuh're real family now, and that's what Ah called my favorite grandma. Ah really loved her, but she died. Would yuh be my new MaDear?"

"Loretha, do yuh hear this chile?" Mrs. Collins said. "Yes 'Liz'beth, yuh may call me MaDear. Ah love it, and Ah love yuh chile."

Elizabeth was thrilled. "It seems like the wrinkles in my life are smoothing out. Ah have little Johnny, MaDear, my mother and sister, a place to live, and now a car."

"'Lizabeth, when we were in the hall, we saw Thea. She musta had her baby. Ah didn't see Reverend Oliver. Ah have tuh find out if she had a girl or boy."

"Mama, Ah hope she had a healthy baby." Elizabeth's voice was warm when she spoke of Thea. "Ah hope Reverend Oliver realizes he has two babies in the nursery at the same time." A touch of sarcasm was added when she spoke of Reverend Oliver.

"Ah know how yuh feel. Ah was thinkin' the same thing," Mrs. Collins said.

"Let's not talk about Reverend Oliver," Loretha said. "So ... when are they gonna let yuh out of here? What did the doctor say?"

"Ah don't know. He didn't say, but the psychiatrist is still coming tuh see me. Ah still have an aide sitting with me all the time. Ah think they don't trust me. They think Ah'll still try tuh hurt myself. Ah still feel bad, but now Ah have something tuh live for, and Ah wouldn't do anything tuh hurt yuh. Yuh-know, Mama ... yuh use tuh tell me, 'it was always darkest before dawn.' Ah really didn't understand what yuh meant, until now, and Ah wanna tell yuh that Ah just went through the longest, darkest night before Ah came tuh my dawn. It would be nice if Ah could make the psychiatrist understand that Ah'm okay now."

"Jest keep dat positive attitude and dat doctor will see yuh is okay," Mrs. Collins added.

"Listen, honey, there are two things that are not within our power tuh resolve. Reverend Oliver will probably come tuh the hospital tuh be with Thea. Yuh shouldn't let anything steal yuh good mood. Yuh sure tuh see him. Then there's yuh father, yuh must realize he may or may not come around. Ah just don't know. Ah've never seen him act this way, so Ah don't know what tuh tell yuh."

"Mama, Ah'm not worried about Reverend Oliver. Ah've had tuh face him all of these months. He's invisible tuh me. But, Ah love Daddy so much, it hurts. Ah'll never stop loving him. Ah know, no matter how he acts, he really loves me, even if he never speaks tuh me again. He loved me too much before this happened. Daddy hurt me more than Reverend Oliver, but Ah can't let him hurt me any more. Right now Ah don't have time tuh hurt, Ah have tuh think and plan. Ah've been hurting too long."

Loretha reached over and gave Elizabeth a warm hug. "Yuh have a very good attitude."

"Mama, my only regret is that Ah thought God didn't love me anymore. Ah was ready tuh give up. But God was carrying me when Ah thought Ah couldn't go on, and Ah didn't know it. Ah'm so sorry. Ah just didn't know any better. Ah couldn't think straight. But Ah'll never understand. Why me? Why did God let this happen tuh me?"

"Honey, don't blame God. Yuh-know … when he created us, he gave us something wonderful … he gave us 'free will.' All of God's creatures are free tuh live and make choices. What Reverend Oliver did tuh yuh, he did of his own will, his 'free will.' And, honey … because of yuh fear and innocence, yuh used yuh own 'free will' tuh hide yuh pregnancy. But God was always there next tuh yuh, and when yuh were falling, he was picking yuh up. Be happy, honey … God has a grand plan for you and yuh baby. Yuh been through so much. When yuh thought yuh were all alone, He was there with yuh. Ah know He understands how yuh were feeling and has forgiven yuh without yuh asking."

Loretha and Mrs. Collins were preparing to leave the hospital. As they walked toward the door, they saw Reverend Oliver standing at the nursery.

"'Lizabeth, Reverend Oliver is here,' Loretha said. "He's at the nursery window. Ah guess he's staring at his children. Ah'm sure he's scared tuh death, so let's go shake his nerves a little more. We'll pretend we don't know anything, and we'll have the satisfaction of knowin' what he did. That must be eatin' him alive."

"See you later, Mama. See you later, MaDear." Elizabeth smiled at Mrs. Collins and repeated her new name again. "See yuh later, MaDear, my MaDear."

Mrs. Collins gave Elizabeth a smile and whispered, "Ah love yuh."

"C'mon, MaDear," Loretha said, a smile gracing her face. "Lets go stand next tuh him and show him Johnny. Ah wanna show him how proud Ah am of my new grandson." Loretha blew Elizabeth a kiss. She felt a little guilty over her plan to taunt Owen, but she couldn't let an opportunity like this one pass.

"Ah think both of us can make him squirm. See yuh later. This is gone tuh be fun," Mrs. Collins added.

Loretha and Mrs. Collins walked up to Reverend Oliver without him hearing their approach. They stood quietly on each side of him for some time. Loretha could see he was so deep in the moment he didn't realize they were standing there. When Loretha and Mrs. Collins looked into the nursery window, they saw little Johnny and his new baby brother pulled close together. It was impossible for Reverend Oliver to enjoy the moment of seeing his son by Thea without seeing his blessing from Elizabeth.

"Hello, Reverend Oliver. What yuh doing here?" Loretha asked as if she didn't know.

Startled, Reverend Oliver turned and looked at both women. "Ah … Ah … Ah was admiring the babies."

"Yuh came tuh visit 'Lizabeth and see her baby?" Loretha gave him a coy smile. She was sharp, and had picked up his comment that he was admiring the "babies."

"No, but Ah will visit Elizabeth while Ah'm here. Thea had the baby. It's a boy. Ah was wondering if this was Elizabeth's baby?"

"Oh Yes! Isn't that wonderful? 'Lizabeth's baby and yuh new baby are in cribs side by side. It's wonderful. Yuh get tuh see both babies at the same time. They're both beautiful. What name will yuh give yuh son?" Loretha taunted with pleasure.

Reverend Oliver was wearing his badge of guilt. "We … we … we were … we were thinking of Mal … of Malcolm," he stammered.

"Malcolm? Oh, that's a lovely name. How is Thea?"

"She's do … doing just fine. Ah … Ah'm on mah … mah … my way tuh her room now. Ah'll visit Elizabeth after Ah … Ah … Ah see Thea."

Reverend Oliver gave clear signals about the effects the women were having on him. Loretha only promised she wouldn't say anything to him about the rape, she never promised not to be neighborly. "Yuh-know, Ah think the boys show some favoritism, don't yuh think? See their little noses and the way they turn their little heads tuh the side. Don't yuh think so, Mrs. Collins?"

"Ah sure do, chile. Dey is sho' some favoritism dere." Mrs. Collins bent forward slightly and smiled at Loretha.

Reverend Oliver was speechless. He began to shift his weight, rocking from side to side. He loosened his tie and opened the top button of his shirt to allow a cool whiff of air to bathe his neck and face. Loretha knew he wanted her to leave, and he knew if her torment didn't end soon, he would be forced to excuse himself from the gathering at the nursery.

"Oh! Reverend Oliver … Mrs. Collins … Oh! They're smillin', don't yuh see some resemblance?" Loretha smiled and tapped several times on the nursery window as if she were trying to get the babies' attention, but she was drawing Reverend Oliver's attention, and watching his reaction to her taunting through their reflection in the window.

Mrs. Collins allowed her eyes to shift between Reverend Oliver and Loretha. She smiled and admired Loretha's talent at being tactfully cunning and the subtle way she pinched Reverend Oliver's conscience.

"Yuh-know, Reverend Oliver, yuh closeness with John seemed tuh have rubbed off on the babies. Isn't that something?" Loretha added before she smiled at her accomplishment.

"Yes, ma … ma'am," Reverend Oliver continued to stammer, unbuttoning the next button on his shirt.

"Oh, well. Ah think its time for us tuh leave. Don't yuh think so, Mrs. Collins?"

Mrs. Collins took a moment to pull her attention from Reverend Oliver's reflection and respond to Loretha. Her smile of admiration for Loretha shifted toward cynical when she smiled up at Reverend Oliver.

"Ah'll visit Thea when Ah come tuh see 'Lizabeth again," Loretha added. "She's probably too weak tuh see us now. Will yuh tell her that Ah'll pray for you and yuh new family tuh be healthy and live in the ways of our Lord?"

Mrs. Collins gave Reverend Oliver her congratulations. The women walked down the long corridor and didn't look back.

Reverend Oliver could feel the perspiration seeping through his pores. A flash of heat had swelled inside of him, and his shirt felt like it was sticking to his skin. "They know. Ah know they know," he whispered. He felt weak and frightened. His heart was pounding. He couldn't go to Thea until he was composed. He backed up and positioned himself against the adjacent wall and prayed no one noticed his discomfort.

Noticeably shaken, and almost in tears, he finally decided to go to the men's room. He wasn't sure if the ladies were out of the building, so he found his way to the end of the corridor and peeked through the crack of the swinging doors. After seeing the elevator doors close, he ran to the men's room. Bursting through the door, he ran to one of the toilet stalls, making it just before spilling the contents of his stomach. Beaded with perspiration and weak from vomiting, he sat on the toilet and cried.

Loretha and Mrs. Collins walked briskly from the hospital. Loretha thought about their treatment of Reverend Oliver and smiled. Both ladies clutched their coat collars against the cold wind and walked toward the car. Loretha believed it would have bought pleasure to their souls if they knew the actual impact they had on Reverend Oliver. She glanced over at Mrs. Collins, who had a gentle smile on her face, too.

It was mid-afternoon when the ladies finally left the hospital. Time had slipped away. They had to hurry if they were going to accomplish all the things they had planned to do.

"Oh, MaDear." Loretha liked calling Mrs. Collins MaDear, and Mrs. Collins enjoyed hearing it. "Ah have tuh buy the crib mattress and the rest of the baby's things, then figure a way to get the crib tuh yuh house, and Christmas is in less than two weeks," Loretha rambled on.

"Honey. Please stop worryin'. All we gotta do is git the car on the road. So much done happen', and yuh been movin' tuh fast. Now, yuh jest gotta slow down 'fore yuh make yuhself sick."

Loretha smiled with the little nod of her head that expressed, "Yuh're so right, what would Ah do without yuh." She drove and listened to Mrs. Collins' plans, giving her own mind a rest. When they reached their little town, Loretha followed Mrs. Collins to her insurance broker, then to the garage, where she asked the mechanic to get the license plates and deliver the car to her house on Monday.

"Okay, baby, yuh can take over now. Ah did what Ah had tuh do. Now yuh can git yuh baby's things," Mrs. Collins said.

It was still early when they arrived at Mrs. Collins' house, and everything, including the mattress, was placed in the front bedroom. Loretha sat with Mrs. Collins for a while.

Later in the evening, Reverend Oliver visited Thea's bedside. She was awake, but resting with her eyes closed. He sat close to her bed and held her hand. She opened her eyes and smiled at him. He continued to hold her hand, thanking her for their beautiful son and kissing her on her forehead. Their eyes locked, and they smiled at each other for a moment. Reverend Oliver whispered sweet and funny things that made her smile, then laugh. Thea begged him to stop, telling him it hurt when she laughed, then she laughed some more. When they finally stopped laughing, Reverend Oliver sat back in the chair.

Within the span of two heartbeats, a serious expression shrouded his face, and Thea had been thrust from his mind and replaced by Elizabeth. Thea's eyes were set to the ceiling and resting from her exhausting and painful laughter. It wasn't a long rest, only the time it took for her to take several deep breaths, but time enough for Reverend Oliver to undergo another panic attack, but less severe than the one he suffered after meeting Loretha and Mrs. Collins at the nursery window. Trying to hide his discomfort from Thea, he excused himself, telling her he had to go to the men's room.

Reverend Oliver hurried from behind the privacy of the drawn curtains and rushed from the ward. He passed the nursery, then Elizabeth's room. Perspiration popped out across his forehead like tiny pearls. He believed air was being sucked out of his surrounding space. Sweat soaked his shirt collar. He loosened his tie, unbuttoned his collar again, took panting breaths, and continued to move toward the double doors. He pushed the doors with such a force they slammed open and smacked into the back wall, making a terrible bang. Suddenly, there was crisp, cool air. He could breathe again. He was startled by his panting and the hot air as it passed through his nostrils and over his upper lip. His journey to the men's room was over.

He turned on the faucet, captured ounces of water in the cups of his hands and splashed it on his face, continuing until his rapid breathing returned to normal. He walked to the same stall he used earlier, plopped himself down on the toilet, and latched the door. He had to think, he needed to think.

He knew he couldn't continue to be at the mercy of the sudden panic attacks. He realized his greatest fear was his lack of control over future events, and that was the cause of his anxiety attacks. Only God could change the future, but he had some control.

What is it that Ah need tuh do? It doesn't have tuh be much. Just change one simple thing. What am Ah doing tuh draw suspicion? Having these panic attacks ... yeah ... that's a sure giveaway. But Ah can't stop it

… they just come on me. But earlier it didn't just come on me. Ah let Loretha, and Mrs. Collins scare me almost tuh my death. Ah been doin' stupid things, like not stoppin' tuh speak tuh John when Ah dropped Loretha off. Now that was stupid. Then waitin' so long tuh call him, not givin' Mrs. Collins a proper greetin', and now not visitin' Elizabeth even though Ah'm only a few feet away.

Ah have tuh stop actin' like Ah'm guilty. Ah have tuh make myself believe their troubles are not my fault. Ah have tuh act normal. If Ah wasn't guilty, Ah would be right by John's side, Ah would've been his rock. So, don't be stupid: be the rock, be with John, speak without fear tuh Loretha and go visit Elizabeth. If Ah were innocent, Ah would've visited her by now. Now the first thing Ah have tuh do is go visit Elizabeth. Ah know Elizabeth has a lady sittin' with her all the time. Ah don't think she'll say anything out of the way. It doesn't matter, Ah have tuh go.

Reverend Oliver was sure his next move would take him to Elizabeth's room, but first he had to tidy himself. He removed himself from the toilet stall and walked back to the sink. The mirror over the sink was scarred and cloudy. He couldn't see if his eyes were red and swollen, or if his hair was neat. He ran his hands over his hair, smoothing and patting it into place. He buttoned his collar, straightened and tightened his tie, then wet his handkerchief and wiped his face. Wetting his handkerchief again, he squeezed out the excess water and folded it into a small square that could be partially concealed in his hand and used to cool himself if needed. He stood at the door, taking a few deep breaths, then left the men's room.

Just as he reached the open door to Elizabeth's room, Reverend Oliver slowed his steps and took another deep breath. He quietly strolled into her room like he belonged there, and was standing at the foot of her bed before he noticed she was sound asleep.

The aide stood at attention when she saw him. As soon as he was still, she whispered, "Miss Turner is sleep. Would yuh like me tuh wake her?"

"Oh … no … please don't. Just tell her Reverend Oliver came tuh visit," he whispered.

"Yes, sir, Ah sho' will."

"Please don't forget. My name is Reverend Oliver. Ah'm the assistant minister at her father's church." He had to be clear about whom he was, just in case the aide forgot his name.

"Yes, sir, Reverend Oliver."

Reverend Oliver took a few steps backward, nodded his head while he thanked the aide, then turned and slowly walked from the room. As soon as he cleared the door, he took his wet handkerchief, wiped his face, and walked back toward the ward. He didn't know if it was luck or the will of God. He leaned toward the latter, because he believed he should always place his luck in the Lord.

Yes, don't act like a guilty man, he reminded himself. *Ah hope the aide doesn't forget tuh tell Elizabeth Ah visited her. Ah did good. A guilty man would never visit her. Now Elizabeth will tell her mother and her mother will tell her father. Maybe Ah'll try tuh visit her again. This time with Thea; maybe tomorrow afternoon. Thank yuh Lord.*

John was sitting at his desk, completing the finishing touches on his sermon, when Loretha entered the den. He knew he had to acknowledge the events of the past few days and ask the congregation to pray for him and his family. He would leave it at that.

Sarah was in the kitchen and had started dinner. She had helped with the cooking many times, but never planned and prepared a whole meal. Her cooking added a homely aroma to the house. Loretha went to the kitchen and complimented her by blowing her a kiss before returning to the den.

Loretha peeked in and casually greeted John. "Oh, by the way, Ah saw Owen at the hospital. Thea had a baby boy," she announced in a matter of fact way, then turned and headed back to the kitchen. John just nodded as she left the room.

"Hi, Mama." Sarah smiled with pride over her prepared meal. "How is 'Lizabeth and the baby?"

"Oh they're comin' along nicely. But look at you. Yuh so smart. Yuh've just about finished dinner. Oh, guess what?" Without waiting for a response, she announced that Reverend Oliver and his wife had a new baby boy.

"Oh, Mama, that's so nice. Ah guess he was really happy."

"Ah didn't get tuh see Thea, but Reverend Oliver was as happy as the good Lord wanted him tuh be."

"Well, Ah kinda felt bad because Ah didn't visit 'Lizabeth. Ah wanna go with yuh the next time. Then, Ah can see Mrs. Thea and Reverend Oliver's baby."

"Don't yuh want tuh see 'Lizabeth and her baby?"

"Mama, yuh know Ah want tuh see them. Ah just meant Ah could see them all."

"Yes, honey, Ah'm sorry. Ah'm just tired. Ah know what yuh meant."

"Mama, Ah knew yuh'd be tired. So, Ah thought Ah could at least be helpful and try tuh fix dinner."

Loretha stroked Sarah's hair, thanking her again. "Ah'm gonna change my clothes, and Ah'll be back tuh help yuh."

"That's okay, Mama, Ah want tuh do this myself. Yuh seem tired. Ah'll call you and Daddy when dinner is ready."

———⌇———

Loretha was quiet during dinner. She couldn't hold a conversation and indulge in her private thoughts at the same time, and there was so much to think about.

Ah have tuh find something tuh wear tuh church. This is gonna to be a special Sunday. Ah wonder how the congregation is gonna react tuh us? … Ah don't care how they act. Ah wonder how John's deacon meeting went? Well … Ah don't care about that either. Tomorrow Ah'm gonna tell

'Lizabeth what we did tuh Reverend Oliver ... no ... revenge isn't healthy ... but it sure will feel good. Mrs. Collins is my blessing and my rock. God, what would Ah have done without her. Thank yuh, Lord. Thank yuh for loving us so much.

"Mama ... Mama!" Sarah called.

Loretha blinked and swung forward, looking at Sarah.

"Yuh were really thinking hard. Didn't yuh hear me calling?"

"No, honey. My mind was somewhere else."

John and Sarah glanced at each other and back at Loretha. The remainder of the dining time was sprinkled with bits of unrelated chitchat.

———✷———

The daylight rolled into Elizabeth's room and roused Loretha, leaving her feeling rested without the heaviness that came with worry or stress. Instantly her thoughts settled on Elizabeth. Did she have a good night's sleep? Had her burdens been lifted? Did she feel as bright and eager to get on with her life as Loretha wanted her to feel?

Loretha planned to go to the hospital that afternoon. She knew she would have to tell Sarah she couldn't go. Elizabeth needed people around her who would be excited about the baby and her new life. Sarah didn't know the plan and couldn't know. Loretha envisioned Sarah and Elizabeth just sitting in the room and speaking only sporadically for the sake of politeness, and then Sarah leaving and spending more time on the ward with Thea. Loretha had made up her mind, she couldn't find any positive reason for Sarah to visit. She would tell her where she was going, and if Sarah wanted to go, she was prepared to discourage or even forbid her visit.

Loretha planned to invite Mrs. Collins again, begging her if she had to. Mrs. Collins was good for Elizabeth. She was the grandmother her girls missed so much. John's parents lived in Savannah, and they only saw them once, or sometimes twice, a year. When they visited their grandparents' home, they were treated like special company. That was nice, but grandchildren are not supposed to be treated like special guests, they are supposed to feel like they are at home—a home away from home.

When Loretha's mother died six years earlier, the girls lost the person they called "MaDear." Actually, they only called her "MaDear" for a very short time, because it was easier for them to simply call her "Dear." Dear lived in Macon with Papa, Loretha's father. The family visited each other often, but when Dear died after a short illness, Papa went to live with her sister in Virginia. Now Elizabeth had named Mrs. Collins MaDear. It was a wondrous compliment. Elizabeth and Sarah loved Dear and it was difficult for them to adjust after her death. When Elizabeth named Mrs. Collins, MaDear, she was saying, God gave Dear back to her, and she would love her forever.

Mrs. Collins wanted to make the trip, but it was Sunday, and she wanted to go to church. Her body told her she needed to rest. This disappointed Loretha too, but she understood what being tired meant to an inactive woman in her seventies.

Sarah decided against going to the hospital.

CHAPTER 10

John, Loretha, and Sarah picked up Mrs. Collins and arrived at church a half an hour before service was to begin. Usually, they arrived in time for Sunday school, but this Sunday John made the decision not to attend, for obvious reasons. Deacon Bains had been sitting in his car waiting for John for some time.

"Good morning ladies." Deacon Bains tipped his hat.

Mrs. Collins, Loretha, and Sarah nodded, greeting him.

"Good morning, Reverend. Ah wonder if Ah could have a few words wit' yuh befor' the service begins?"

"Yes ... sure, Deacon Bains. ... Come, let's go tuh the study ... Uh ... Loretha! Ah'll be in my study if yuh need me."

The men walked through the sanctuary and down to the study on the lower level. Deacon Bains didn't say a word until the study door was closed, and that caused John to feel apprehensive.

"Yuh-know, Rev," Deacon Bains began, "after the meetin' the other night ... some of the deacons met again at mah house. Ah ... Ah ... just want yuh tuh know that most of us is uncomfortable wit' yuh fer not lettin' 'Lizabeth and the baby come home. We don't want tuh be tellin' yuh what tuh do, but Ah think it's gone cause yuh some problems ... wit' ... wit' bein' the pastor of dis here church ... and all that. Yuh-know what Ah mean? But yuh got time. Yuh got tuh think 'bout yuh decision," Deacon Bains adamantly stated.

Reverend Turner looked startled. He stood up and walked to the window. Deacon Bains knew he had upset him. He waited for Reverend Turner to respond, and he was prepared to stand against him if his response was contrary to his position.

"Yuh-know, Deacon Bains, Ah been hurt really bad. My family has been hurt real bad. 'Lizabeth told me she'd been raped, but Ah found it hard tuh believe."

"Hard tuh believe? Rev! How could yuh? She's yuh 'Lizabeth ... a fine young lady. Who raped hur? Did yuh call the po'lice?" Deacon Bains was angered more than ever by his remarks.

"'Lizabeth doesn't know who did it. It happened some time ago, and there's no use telling the police now. Besides, the hospital reported it as a rape. Ah don't know why Ah didn't believe her. Ah guess, maybe, that's why she didn't tell me when it happened. She told me she didn't think Ah'd believe her. God's been helping me, and Ah've been given that decision a lot of thought. When a person hurts, they say a lot of things they really don't mean. Ah'm the pastor, and Ah should've known better, but, Ah'm still a man."

"So yuh changed yuh mind?"

"Ah'm asking God tuh help me. Ah'm thankful for this discussion, it's also helping me. Ah was planning tuh go tuh the hospital after the service and apologize tuh 'Lizabeth and ask her tuh come home. Ah wanna thank yuh again. Loretha wants her home. Ah haven't seen the baby, and Ah said some terrible things. Ah'd like tuh have them home ... but 'Lizabeth may not want tuh come home after the way Ah've acted."

"Yuh-know, people are not questionin' 'Lizabeth. They is questionin' you! Wit' all respect ... Ah think ... it be in everyone's best interest ... if yuh ... uh ... if yuh worked it out." Deacon Bains didn't say anything else. He turned and left the study.

Reverend Turner placed his hand over his face and slouched down in his chair. His ministry had just been threatened. He knew Deacon Bains was angry, and if he had anything to do with it, he could get the others to turn against him.

"How could they meet behind my back?" he spoke aloud. *Ah have no power over 'Lizabeth anymore. There must be a way tuh get her and the baby tuh come home, but Ah won't beg, not even tuh keep my church.*

Entangled in a web of emotions, Reverend Turner feared losing his position in the church. It crossed his mind to place the blame on Reverend Oliver only to protect himself, but he couldn't visualize the outcome. It frightened him that he could think of such a drastic act without considering Reverend Oliver's guilt. But it wasn't about his guilt, it was about protecting himself. The church loved Reverend and Mrs. Oliver. If he wasn't careful, Owen could win his seat as pastor. He held back the tears only because he didn't want the congregation to see him with reddened eyes. He wanted to be comforted, but there was no one, not even Loretha.

Deacon Bains called Reverend Turner to let him know the service would begin in five minutes. Reverend Turner thanked him, removed his suit jacket, put on his robe, and walked toward the sanctuary entrance. Just as he reached the door, his heart skipped a beat, and then took triple beats to get back in rhythm. Weakness pinned him to the wall, and a cold sweat dampened his undergarments. Only perseverance gave him the strength to take a deep breath, push his fear aside, and compose himself.

He straightened his slouched posture, and that added inches to his height. He still felt small and vulnerable when he opened the door, clutched his Bible close to his chest, and approached the pulpit. Reverend Oliver was sitting to his right. Loretha and Sarah were sitting in the front pew, and Mrs. Collins sat behind Sarah. The sanctuary was filled to capacity. Reverend Turner nodded, signaling the senior choir to begin their march. The congregation stood as the choir began to sing to the words of "We're Marching to Zion," and the church came alive with music.

It seemed that with each step of the choir's march, Reverend Turner's spirit calmed, relaxation took over, and he was a little stronger, but his fear of uncertainty remained. *They're all waiting tuh hear what Ah have tuh say. And Lord, Ah ask yuh tuh forgive me for the false words Ah may use. Ah need time tuh find the truth, but the congregation wants answers now. Ah don't mean tuh be deceiving, but confusion still plagues me. Please forgive me, Lord, don't let them take the church from me. Ah've*

always been yuh faithful servant. Ah don't know what tuh say. Allow me,
and forgive me for using the words that they will believe or need tuh hear.
Lord, please forgive me. He closed his eyes and silently prayed for God's
help while he rocked his head to the melody. When the music stopped,
he opened his eyes and stood quietly at the podium for a few moments.

"Before we begin our service, Ah'd like tuh speak tuh the church.
Ah'm sure yuh all heard about 'Lizabeth. If there are any of yuh who
haven't … well … my oldest daughter … 'Lizabeth … had a baby last
Tuesday. And yes, tuh all of our misfortune, the baby was born in the
girl's bathroom at the high school."

The congregation let out a moan followed by subtle chatter, but
there was no one in the congregation who had not heard. He believed
everyone that knew him or his family had heard the news. Loretha and
Sarah sat with their eyes fixed on Reverend Turner and gave no
acknowledgment to the sounds behind them.

"Yuh all know my 'Lizabeth. She's a good girl. Ah don't believe she
ever had a boyfriend. Those of yuh who know her would agree with
me. My poor 'Lizabeth was the victim of one of the most vicious
assaults a man could do tuh a woman. She told me and my wife that
she was raped."

The congregation sang out for the injustice. Reverend Oliver
turned gray, as if all the blood left his face. Loretha glared at him, their
eyes met, and he turned away. John never turned in his direction, but
Reverend Oliver appeared to be ready to run from the church for fear
of what he would say next. He held tight to the arms of his chair and
seemed to hang onto John's every word.

"Okay … okay … let's quiet down," Reverend Turner said,
gesturing with his hands toward the congregation to compose themselves.

"Who did that tuh Elizabeth?" someone yelled out.

"Tell us, Rev. Tell us," another person called out

"Okay! C'mon church … settle down. Settle down," Reverend
Turner continued. "Listen! People … please listen!" The congregation

was almost out of control. He continued waving his hands and shouting, trying to quiet the church.

Reverend Oliver continued to hold tight to the arms of his chair. His feet were planted firmly on the floor. He appeared frightened and ready to flee from the pulpit and church if he had to.

Reverend Oliver studied Loretha closely. She allowed her eyes to scan the congregation, then turned to face him. He clearly understood what her eyes were saying, and he sank inward in despair. Loretha stood and slowly turned away from Reverend Oliver, but she kept her eyes on him until the rest of her body was half way facing the congregation. Reverend Oliver stood from his chair and waited with apprehension at what she was going to say. Tiny, unnoticeable beads of perspiration made his clothing feel clammy. He looked toward the door at the back of the pulpit, then turned back and concentrated on Loretha.

"We don't know!" Loretha yelled out, taking control.

At that moment, Reverend Oliver felt weak all over. He plopped back in his chair. His heart was pounding against his chest wall in a wild frenzy, and the air he held in his lungs was allowed to leave his body in tiny bursts. He held tightly to the chair and prayed his discomfort wasn't noticeable to the congregation.

"We don't know who the man is!" Loretha yelled again. The noisy congregation quieted, and she was able to continue in a quieter tone. "'Lizabeth doesn't know who he was. Now, please ... let Reverend Turner finish." Loretha nodded and gave a "thank you smile" to the congregation, then she turned back and gave Reverend Oliver a glaring, tormenting, "Ah got yuh," smile.

Reverend Oliver continued to hold tightly to the arms of the chair. He glanced at Mrs. Collins and was startled by her "knowing eyes." He placed his eyes on Reverend Turner's back and would not allow himself to make eye contact with Loretha or Mrs. Collins again.

Gradually the congregation began to quiet down. Loretha returned to her seat. Reverend Turner smiled at her with the same type of love and admiration he had before this ordeal began.

"Listen, people. 'Lizabeth told me she was raped as soon as she was well enough to talk, but Ah committed an even greater sin. Ah didn't believe her. Ah told her she couldn't come home or bring her son home. Because … because … Ah was so ashamed. Instead of loving and comforting her, Ah was ashamed."

"No, Reb," said a woman who stood waving her hand.

"Yuh didn't mean dat, Reb," a lady wearing a wide black hat called out and was heard over the loud rumbling of the congregation.

"People! Please!" Reverend Turner waved his hand trying to calm them down again. Loretha didn't attempt to help him this time. "Please folks, hear me out," he shouted over the roar of the congregation.

Deacon Bains stood and walked to the place just below the pulpit. He held up his hands and yelled out to the congregation. "Can we quiet down here? Ah think Reverend Turner has more tuh say! Don't yuh think we should hear 'im out?"

The rumbling of the congregation gradually quieted. Reverend Turner thanked Deacon Bains, then held up both hands to the congregation. "Thank yuh for allowing me tuh finish. As Ah was saying, Ah was ashamed. Ah was in shock. Ah didn't believe her. Ah thought if a woman was raped, they would report it immediately, but, Ah was wrong. My 'Lizabeth …" he held his head down, shaking it and squeezed the edges of the podium so tight the veins of his hands popped out. His theatrical display of false emotions was convincing as he held back his words, appearing to be on the verge of sobbing, then suddenly returning to a state of composure.

"My 'Lizabeth thought she had done something wrong, and she didn't tell anyone. Now … Ah'm ashamed of my behavior. My 'Lizabeth suffered alone. She carried her baby without anyone knowing, and even gave birth alone. And then … Ah didn't believe her."

The congregation whispered with each other, moaned and fidgeted in their seats, but as Reverend Turner continued to speak, they seemed to make a combined effort to control themselves.

"But, our Lord, my wife, and the deacons have helped me. Ah only pray 'Lizabeth will forgive me … and Ah ask yuh all tuh forgive me. And people … be there for yuh children. Don't do what Ah did. Don't make them afraid tuh come tuh yuh when they're troubled. Don't judge them. Just be there for them. As soon as service is over today, Ah'll go tuh 'Lizabeth and ask her tuh forgive me. Ah want her tuh come home, but Ah've been so ugly, Ah can only pray she will."

Deacon Bains stood again. "People, let's bow our heads for a special prayer for this family."

"Amen! Amen!" filtered through the low murmuring of the congregation. Then a hush preceded Deacon Bains as he led them in prayer.

―⁂―

Reverend Turner addressed the congregation again, "Ah would like tuh thank yuh for yuh love and understanding. My new grandson's name is John. Now, if yuh were not aware, there was another baby born this week. Reverend and Mrs. Oliver had a baby boy just this past Friday. Ah believe his name is Malcolm."

Reverend Turner led a prayer for the Olivers. For their health and God's blessings, and without further interruption, the Sunday morning services officially began.

―⁂―

After the service, Reverend Turner told Loretha and Sarah he wanted to go to the hospital. A smile grew on Loretha's face, probably at the same time one was forming in her heart. She believed Reverend Turner had found his way, and knew she owed this to Deacon Bains. It didn't matter what he said, or how he said it, he had gotten through to him. Now, maybe her family could be together again and celebrate Christmas with their new addition.

Sarah, on the other hand, wasn't as excited as Loretha. She enjoyed the increased attention from her father. "Mama, can Ah stay home? Ah just got my 'time,' and Ah have some cramps."

"Will yuh be all right?"

Sarah nodded, and Loretha asked John to take her home. They dropped her off in the driveway and waited until she was in the house, then drove Mrs. Collins home.

Loretha was feeling better than she had all week. She knew Elizabeth wanted to be home with the baby and her family. Reverend Turner seemed so sincere, and in time, everything would be all right. Just as they turned onto the main road, Loretha asked Reverend Turner what Deacon Bains said to him. She wasn't trying to pry. She was just feeling so good she wanted to know everything.

"He said the church was not passing judgment on 'Lizabeth, they would be judging me for not accepting my grandson or letting 'Lizabeth come home."

"Are yuh going tuh the hospital tuh tell 'Lizabeth yuh love her and how much yuh want her tuh come home, or did yuh just say those things tuh satisfy the deacons and the congregation? Don't yuh believe Owen raped her?"

"Loretha, please, Ah've been through so much today. Ah don't need yuh pressuring me, too."

"John! If yuh didn't mean what yuh said, then yuh only want 'Lizabeth tuh come home so it will be easier for yuh at church. Ah won't let yuh put her through that. Yuh just want tuh spare yuhself from the hell yuh created. How could yuh do this tuh her? You're a liar and a hypocrite. Yuh even fooled me. Believe me, you'll pay dearly for your dishonesty."

"Yuh want her home, don't yuh? Well … Ah'm gonna let her come home. What else do yuh want from me? She can come home, but don't think everything will be the same."

"Then Ah don't want her home."

"My Lord! Loretha! What do yuh want?" Reverend Turner questioned as if he didn't have a clue that what he was doing was wrong.

"Ah want 'Lizabeth and the baby home. Ah want tuh be with them. Ah want yuh tuh love them. They're family. Ah don't want them tuh come home so yuh can continue tuh practice yuh hypocrisy. How can yuh call yuhself a man of the cloth? Yuh don't care about people, not even yuh family. Yuh only care about yuhself. Yuh can say what yuh want tuh 'Lizabeth, but when yuh finish, Ah'll give her the other side of the story and let her make the decision. Don't forget, she's an emancipated minor."

"She's my daughter, too. Ah'm sorry, but Ah'm still not convinced she was raped by Owen. But, Ah do want her home. In time, Ah know Ah'll get tuh love her baby. Ah just need time."

"Then ask her tuh come home when yuh believe her and yuh love her baby. Because Ah don't believe yuh. You've lied so much, Ah'm beginning tuh find it hard tuh believe anything yuh say."

"Loretha, yuh stood by me at church. Why can't yuh stand by me now?"

"John … John," Loretha said calmly. She was genuinely saddened and disappointed. "Ah believed yuh then, so If yuh don't know why … then Ah have nothing else tuh say."

Loretha remained silent for the remainder of the drive. Periodically, Reverend Turner would glance toward her, hoping for a change in her demeanor, but she continued to maintain a constant stare on the road ahead. She couldn't understand how he could be so deceptive with the church's congregation and so honest with her. He simply had to say the words she wanted to hear, and she would have believed he was speaking from his heart.

Now, Loretha understood that John had an image to uphold. It wasn't about Elizabeth or the baby. It was all about John. It wasn't the shame he believed she brought to the family. The shame was gone; the church erased the shame. John was still protecting Reverend Oliver. Elizabeth and the baby would be a constant reminder of what she said

Reverend Oliver had done to her and, somewhere in John's consciousness, he believed her. She was sure of it.

Elizabeth was standing at the nursery window when she noticed her parents entering the maternity wing. She was filled with mixed emotion at the sight of her father. As he came closer, the rigidity of his posture caused her to feel uncomfortable. Loretha, on the other hand, always greeted her with a smile. A calming smile that let her know she would always be loved and protected.

"Hi, Mama." Elizabeth gave her mother a big hug and exchanged a coy smile with her father. While in her mother's embrace, she had a closer view of her father and wondered what he wanted. He was there, but he didn't have an apologetic demeanor, nor did he seem overjoyed to see her. She gave him a contemptuous glare before pulling her attention away from him and changing the subject to being overjoyed and surprised to see her mother. *Daddy seems to be softening. Ah bet they gave him a hard time at church. Why else would he come tuh the hospital? He said he never wanted tuh see me again. Ah wish Ah could ask Mama what happened, but he'd hear and probably get mad. Maybe he came tuh see Mrs. Thea or Reverend Oliver's other son.*

"Mama, Ah didn't expect tuh see yuh here today, but Ah have good news," Elizabeth announced just before being caught up in her father's gaze again. "Daddy, it's nice tuh see yuh," she said in a warm, but distant and guarded, tone.

"It's nice tuh see yuh too, 'Lizabeth. Can we go tuh yuh room? Ah have tuh ask yuh something."

Elizabeth sensed he really didn't want to be there, and she was confused about his motives. She held her mother's hand while he followed her to her room.

"Mama, is something wrong?" she whispered.

"No, honey. Yuh father just wants tuh talk tuh yuh."

Reverend Turner had paced himself and remained some ten feet behind the whispering women. By the time he reached the room, Elizabeth was sitting on her bed, and Loretha was sitting in the chair facing her.

Reverend Turner walked to the foot of the bed and stood quietly for a moment. Elizabeth was quiet and wondered why her father, a man of many words, was having trouble speaking. She also noticed his attitude had changed from mild mannered to arrogant, but her newly-granted emancipation made her an even match for him. She waited to hear what he had to say.

"Elizabeth … Ah … Ah want you and the baby tuh come home. We can work out our differences. It's important for me, if yuh would consider comin' home." Reverend Turner's request was simple, but he appeared cold and robotic. His voice lacked the warmth and sincerity Elizabeth had become accustomed to. He didn't even smile.

"Why, all of a sudden, do yuh want us tuh come home? Yuh made it clear yuh didn't want me anymore. When yuh passed the nursery, yuh didn't even go see yuh grandson."

John flinched at the word grandson. Elizabeth's keen sensitivity absorbed and translated his actions. For the first time in her life, she recognized her father had a shallow, self-centered personality.

"Daddy, have yuh spoken tuh Reverend Oliver?" She tilted her head and her eyes glazed over as she reached for her mother's hand for support. She knew the answer before she asked the question.

"No, honey. A man has tuh be sure when confronting a man on a sensitive subject like this."

"Oh … Ah see. Yuh don't have tuh be sure, and it's not a sensitive subject when yuh hurt me, when yuh call me a liar, or when yuh tell me yuh ashamed of me. Yuh didn't have tuh be sure, and it's not a sensitive subject when yuh tell me that me and the baby could never come home." She pulled her hand from her mother's and lifted the bed sheet to blot her tears. "Daddy, do yuh find pleasure in hurtin' me? Am Ah not impor-tant enough tuh be considered a sensitive subject? Now yuh here asking me tuh come home."

"'Lizabeth, Ah don't know what's gotten intuh yuh. Yuh lost all respect and decency ..."

"No, Daddy, yuh put a man yuh only known for a few months over me, and yuh don't think all the horrible things yuh said tuh me weren't painful and sensitive? Ah love yuh with all my heart, and Ah don't mean tuh be disrespectful, but Ah know yuh're not sincere." She blotted the remaining tears and lowered the sheet, smoothing it out while she continued to speak. "Something must have happened at church. The congregation probably questioned yuh and gave yuh a hard time," Elizabeth turned her attention back to her father, "so tuh look good for them, yuh want me home. Daddy ... when you meet with Reverend Oliver ... and yuh talk tuh him man-tuh-man ... no mattah the outcome, Ah'll come home. But right now, Ah really believe yuh still think Ah willingly gave myself tuh some boy." Elizabeth had all she could do to hold back her anger.

"Honey, Ah was upset. Yuh know how people will talk. Ah said and did things Ah shouldn't have. Will yuh forgive me?" He bent his back slightly and used both hands to support himself on the bottom frame of the bed as he turned his face up at her.

"No, Daddy! Not until yuh meet with Reverend Oliver. Ah love yuh and Ah always will. Ah know yuh still don't believe Reverend Oliver raped me. It hurts me just knowing he was right."

"Honey, will you and the baby come home?" John's words were warmer, but his expression continued to be aloof. He stood up and pushed his hands deep into his coat pockets.

"Daddy ... it's not about Reverend Oliver, is it?" She kept her eyes on him while she slid herself from the bed and slipped her feet into her slippers. "It's the church. What did the church say, Daddy? Are yuh here because of the church?" Elizabeth looked at her mother, knowing she wanted her home more than ever, but Loretha didn't have that supportive, pleading appearance. Her face was bland, expressionless, and she knew something was wrong.

Reverend Turner took a deep breath, his eyes shifted and his lips closed tight, forming a frown, giving his motive away. "'Lizabeth … Ah … Ah …" He was speechless. He held his hands out before him.

"Daddy, Ah shoulda known it was something else. Now it's all about you. How could yuh trade me tuh save yuhself? No, Daddy. Yuh hurt me, and Ah know if Ah came home, yuh'll keep hurtin' me and the baby. Ah wish Ah could turn my back on you that easy. Ah love yuh so much, even though yuh not the person Ah thought yuh were." She used the heels of her hands to wipe the new tears from her eyes. When the tears continued to flow, the sleeve of her robe was an excellent substitute.

Loretha was sitting with her back to Reverend Turner. She knew John couldn't see her face, so she gave Elizabeth a prim smile and winked her eye. Elizabeth glanced at her, in an instant, she had read her expressions and her assumptions were confirmed.

"Daddy, we need to build our relationship again. Mrs. Davies, yuh-know, the social worker, well she explained that yuh signed the papers givin' me the right tuh decide what Ah think is best for me and my baby. Ah think it's best if we don't come home when we get out of here."

"Where will yuh go? How will yuh live? Yuh just a chile."

Elizabeth was puzzled. *Now he's worried about us? Where was this concern last week … when Ah needed it?*

Loretha gave her a nod, confirming it was okay to speak freely.

Loretha decided to speak up, "John …"

"Loretha! Please," he scolded, cutting her off. "Let me do this. If yuh don't have anything tuh say tuh help me, then don't say anything."

Elizabeth looked up at the ceiling, gritted her teeth, and slammed her arms on the bed. *Damn him*, she thought. *If Ah didn't love him so much, Ah could hate him with so much fury Ah could curse him.*

"John! Yuh have tuh listen tuh me," Loretha interrupted again. "Mrs. Davies made arrangements for 'Lizabeth and the baby tuh live with Mrs. Collins."

"Mrs. Collins? Loretha, did yuh have something tuh do with this?"

"No, Daddy, Ah had something tuh do with it. Mama knew, because Mrs. Davies and Mrs. Collins told her. What did you think, Daddy? Did yuh think the state would put me in a home and take my baby away from me? Did you think that would be enough punishment for me, while your precious Reverend Oliver and his family have a normal wonderful life, because speaking tuh him would create a sensitive situation?" It made Elizabeth feel good to tell her father how she felt. Any other time she would have been beat down for speaking to him like that, but now she was emancipated, and it was illegal for him to strike her. They both knew that, but the way she spoke to him was like slapping his face.

"Elizabeth, Ah forbid you from speaking tuh me like that."

"Ah understand how you feel, Daddy, but you have to understand that Ah have feelings, too."

"Loretha!" Reverend Turner called out.

"Listen, John, yuh can't keep hurtin' people and not expect them to speak up. Ah understand how 'Lizabeth feels, and she's right. You need to do the right thing. Peace will never come tuh yuh until yuh do. Ah think yuh know that. And yes, Ah was told about 'Lizabeth movin' in with Mrs. Collins, and Ah supported the idea. When yuh said she couldn't come home, Ah wasn't gonna let them live in some dingy shack down in 'the bottoms,' in the hell pit of town. Mrs. Collins volunteered, Ah didn't ask her. It's a good arrangement, and my chile will be safe and close tuh home."

"How could yuh?" John said with disappointment. "Why didn't yuh tell me?"

"Don't ask me how Ah could! She's my daughter, that's how Ah could! We'll talk about the 'why' later," Loretha said in a calm, firm, and defiant tone.

"All right, but why Mrs. Collins?" John surrendered.

"Because she spoke with 'Lizabeth, and 'Lizabeth told her yuh wouldn't let her and the baby come home. So Mrs. Collins asked her tuh come and live with her. John … It was real easy. It was an ideal arrangement. Yuh didn't want her home, now the final decision is up tuh 'Lizabeth. Ah didn't betray yuh, Ah was protecting my chile. Ah told yuh Ah wouldn't let anyone hurt my chile. Ah still mean it," Loretha stated clearly.

"Daddy, Ah'm gonna go tuh Ms. Collins. If yuh love me, we can work it out. Maybe Ah'll come home someday, but Ah really don't think yuh want me, and Ah know yuh don't want my baby. If it was just me, Ah probably would come home, but now Ah have tuh think about Johnny, and what's best for him. Maybe, when yuh speak tuh Reverend Oliver, Ah'll know yuh ready tuh accept us."

Elizabeth could see her father was upset. He'd lost, and legally there was nothing he could do. In her next breath she had turned away from him. Loretha glanced in his direction, and Elizabeth turned back and saw him with his eyes fixed up toward the ceiling. His lips were clenched tight, and his jawbones were twitching. His hand gripped the edge of the footboard so tight, Elizabeth thought he was going to snap it in two. She repositioned herself and absorbed the pleasure that accompanied revenge and smiled. She didn't want to lose the moment, but neither could she afford the luxury of preserving it, so she moved on.

"Mama, Dr. Pernell said Ah could probably leave the hospital by next Tuesday or Wednesday."

"That's wonderful, honey."

Trying to change the subject, Loretha asked Elizabeth if she had seen Thea and her baby.

"Yes, Mama. The aide told me Reverend Oliver came tuh visit me, but Ah was asleep, and he didn't want her tuh wake me."

"How convenient," Loretha said.

"Ah walked down tuh the ward tuh visit Miss Thea," Elizabeth continued. "Ah think she'll be going home Monday. Ah also saw Reverend Oliver. He was real quiet when he saw me. Ah guess he thought Ah was gonna tell Miss Thea. He's the one suffering now."

"Did yuh say anything tuh him?" John asked, blinking his eyes rapidly. It was a subtle gesture he did when he was annoyed and had no other release.

"No, Daddy!" Elizabeth's response was sharp. "Ah don't have tuh say anything. Yuh-know, maybe yuh shouldn't say anything tuh him. He's so haggard and frightened. Ah guess he's wondering when the truth will come out. Maybe it's best tuh let him continue tuh suffer. When Ah glare at him, straight in the eyes, he seems tuh shrink with fear. It felt good. Ah remember when Ah couldn't, or wouldn't, look at him."

When Elizabeth spoke of Reverend Oliver in that tone of voice, her father turned away. A few more sprinkles of salt in his wound would make her day.

"Daddy, would yuh like tuh see Reverend Oliver's son?"

"Ya-ya-yes, 'Lizabeth, Ah would." Defeated, he removed his handkerchief from the inside breast pocket of his suit and swiped it over his upper lip. He walked from the room with Loretha and Elizabeth following him. When he reached the corridor, he stopped. Loretha stood by his side and gave Elizabeth another confirming smile.

"We could stop by the nursery before we get to the ward." Elizabeth walked between her parents as they walked down the hall, and she gently squeezed her mother's hand. She stopped when see reached the nursery.

"See, Daddy, there's Johnny. He's yuh grandson," Elizabeth said. Instantly, she knew he didn't want to be there. "Okay, Daddy … come over here. There is Reverend Oliver's other son."

In a swift move, Reverend Turner bent his elbow and positioned his hand to lay the back of it across Elizabeth's face.

"John!" Loretha screamed out and grabbed Reverend Turner's arm.

Elizabeth stood firm, her eyes watching her father's movements. She never flinched.

"Okay, Mama. Ah'm going back tuh my room." She gave her mother a gentle kiss on her cheek. Elizabeth wondered if there would ever come a time when her father would believe, love and accept her and her son, but at that moment, she was as angry with her father as she was with Reverend Oliver.

Reverend Turner and Loretha spent a brief time with Thea and Reverend Oliver. Having them visiting in the same area placed a thickness in the air.

"Elizabeth visited me today. We walked tuh the nursery together. She seems tuh be handling her situation very well, but yuh both seem very stressed. Are yuh okay?" Thea asked.

"Sure, Thea," Reverend Turner said. "It's been trying, but the Lord is with us."

"Reverend Turner, Owen told me Elizabeth and the baby weren't coming home. Is that true?"

"Yes, Ah'm afraid so. Ah said some harsh words tuh her when this happened. Things Ah wish Ah could take back. So ... she has made arrangements tuh live with Mrs. Collins. Ah'm gonna do my best tuh convince her tuh come home."

"Thea, yuh and Reverend Oliver have a beautiful baby," Loretha said. "'Lizabeth's son is beautiful, too. Thank God he's healthy. She'll only be a short distance from us, so we'll see her and the baby often. Ah really believe everything will be all right. Yuh-know ... my grandson and yuh son will go tuh school together. Who knows, they may even be in the same class, maybe best friends." Loretha broke out with a silly chuckle. "Ah'm really thinking ahead, but Ah hope they'll be close ... yuh-know ... like brothers." She gave a sly, intentional glance in Reverend Oliver's direction. Her smile was so grand, her beautiful front teeth twinkled.

Loretha knew Reverend Turner recognized the implication of what she had said, and she watched to see if he noticed Reverend Oliver's nervous twitch.

Thea gave a sincere smile, "That will really be nice."

Reverend Turner's eyes met with Loretha's and conveyed he was ready to leave before she threw any more subtle digs at Reverend Oliver. Then he turned to Thea, the quickness of his moves allowed him to avoid any signs of guilt he might have received from Reverend Oliver. "It's getting late, and we really have tuh leave because Sarah is home alone."

Loretha continued to watch Reverend Oliver. He was quiet during the entire visit, and appeared to welcome Reverend Turner's announcement. He stood slowly, and Loretha recognized he was careful not to express any ardent signs of relief as he walked them to the entrance of the ward.

Loretha wasn't happy being confined in a car with Reverend Turner, and it wasn't long before he began to question her.

"Why didn't yuh help me out? Yuh knew Elizabeth would've come home if yuh asked her." John held the steering wheel with both hands and shifted his eyes between the road and Loretha. "Yuh didn't support me!" His eyes glared with anger. "What's happening tuh this marriage and this family?"

Loretha sat hugging her pocketbook. She never bothered to look at John, and didn't finch from his jerky movements and voice inflections. She wanted him to hear her and be clear about what she was saying, so she spoke in a calm clear voice. Her tone was deeper than usual and each word was spoken slowly and demanded his attention. "Ah told yuh once, and Ah'll tell yuh one last time. Never try tuh come between me and my children."

She continued to look at the road and hug her pocketbook. She was angry, and spoke through her clenched teeth, never turning to look at John. "When 'Lizabeth needed yuh, yuh weren't there. Mrs. Collins was. Ah knew, but yuh weren't ready tuh help her. Yuh said she was dead. Remember! So if she was dead, why should Ah try tuh tell yuh what was happening?"

Loretha couldn't hold her eyes on the road any longer. She snapped around to face John and unclenched her teeth, speaking firmly, but wanting to yell at him. She sat straight and audaciously pulled her head back. "All yuh wanted tuh do was hurt her. It only began tuh matter when the church questioned yuh. Ah know Deacon Bains posed some serious questions tuh yuh this mornin', and yuh probably lied tuh get him out of yuh office. John, these last few days have caused yuh tuh tell lies or act out lies, but yuh wouldn't have tuh do any of that if yuh would have just turned and looked at Owen this morning. Ah stared at him. Ah tried tuh give yuh a sign ... tuh just see his reaction when Ah stood tuh speak."

Loretha shifted and placed her left hand on the dashboard, quieted her tone, and placed her eyes back on the road. "Yuh know John, yuh are cold, cowardly, unfeeling, and more worried about keeping yuh position at the church than keeping yuh family together. The only reason yuh want them home is because yuh worried about what the church will do. Ah won't be a part of that. What 'Lizabeth needs now is love. Not love for yuh benefit, but yuh unconditional love for her and the baby. Yuh threw her out, now yuh want tuh pull her back only because it suits yuh needs." Loretha's left hand remained on the dashboard, and this time she smiled when she spoke. "Ah know yuh sorry about the emancipation, but Ah thank the good Lord for it. Ah'm just happy she was smart enough tuh realize what was best for her and her son."

John pressed the brakes, slowing the car before pulling off on the shoulder of the road and shifting his eyes to Loretha. Loretha was quiet. She had just struck another nerve, and John's actions were unpredictable. She shifted her weight, held her pocketbook to her chest with her left hand, tightened the collar of her coat with her right, and kept her eyes focused on the road. She could feel John's eyes penetrating the left side of her face as she heard the grunts of anger he made. Suddenly, he was quiet and moments passed. He calmed down before speaking.

"Loretha, yuh putting a strain on our marriage. Don't yuh realize that?"

"The only strain is yuh attitude." Loretha turned to look at him and spoke quietly. "Ah love yuh for better or worse. Now, Ah'm experiencing the worse, but Ah'll continue tuh love yuh even if Ah think yuh not doin' the right thing. There is only one thing that will strain this marriage. So please don't try tuh come between me, 'Lizabeth and the baby. Ah know how much yuh hurt, how much yuh been shamed, but when yuh start tuh be true tuh the teachings of our Lord, yuh'll live with a lighter heart." She reached and took hold of John's right hand, which was now resting on the back of the seat. "Don't yuh think Ah'm hurtin', too? But now that this has happened, Ah can't change it, so Ah'm gonna accept it for the part that's good."

Reverend Turner pulled his hand away, shifted the car in gear, and continued to drive. He didn't come back at her, matching opinions or fighting with words. Loretha began to believe she reached him, not about everything, but on some level. She wasn't angry, but she was disappointed and annoyed. She allowed her head to rest on the back of the seat and was relaxed by the rhythm of the car.

"Ah promised yuh Ah won't come between you and 'Lizabeth, but what about me and Sarah? Yuh conspired against me. Yuh knew she was going tuh live with Mrs. Collins, why didn't yuh tell me?"

A little weariness weighed Loretha's words. Now, she wondered on what level had she reached him, if at all. "Sarah has been through more than you. Everyday she has had tuh face the kids at school. Ah know that's why she always finds an excuse not tuh visit 'Lizabeth. She's a chile and she's handling it. Ah understand how she feels, too … and Ah didn't tell yuh because …" Loretha took a deep breath, "because, Ah'm tired of the fighting … and there's nothing we can do about 'Lizabeth's decision. Remember, she's an emancipated minor. Please, let's just get along. We need tuh use our energy tuh keep this family together. If the church finds fault in yuh, then yuh need tuh do what yuh know is right."

Loretha didn't have any more words for Reverend Turner. She had to channel her anger into the energy she needed to be productive. When they finally arrived home, she changed from her church clothes, called Sarah into the bedroom, and asked how she was feeling. She didn't wait to hear her response. She could see she was feeling just fine.

"Ah need yuh help before dinner. 'Lizabeth and the baby won't be coming home. Ah need yuh tuh help me take the crib tuh Mrs. Collins' house." Before Sarah could question, Loretha said, "Yes, she gonna live with Mrs. Collins. Ah'll explain later."

Loretha noticed Sarah wasn't overtly sad, but she didn't press her. She just continued to move the crib. They loaded it into the trunk, and

Loretha drove off by the time daylight slipped away. As soon as the crib was placed on Mrs. Collins' front porch, she drove Sarah back to the house and instructed her to pack up Elizabeth's clothing and other belongings. Sarah knew this was a trying period for her mother, so she worked quietly, without questions. When she finished with the packing, Loretha helped her load everything in the car.

"Sarah, Ah want yuh tuh warm up the dinner. If Ah'm not back by dinner time y'all go on and eat without me." Loretha spoke in a hurried voice before turning the car around and heading back to Mrs. Collins' house.

———⚏———

Mrs. Collins stood at the front door and watched Loretha get out of the car, pick up a section of the crib, and walk toward the door.

"Chile, what's the mattah wit' yuh?"

"It's John. John is wrong with me. Ah love him so much, but for the first time, Ah'm seeing a whole new side of him. Yuh heard him in church. He lied. He hurts me and angers me at the same time. Ah didn't know that was possible. Ah thought Ah was married to a man of God, a man blessed with integrity."

"C'mon now. Yuh need tuh sit for a while and relax. Ah have some coffee ready. Yuh need tuh calm down."

"Okay, just let me put the crib and 'Lizabeth's things in the room, and then Ah'll try tuh relax. Ah can set up her room tomorrow."

"Okay, Ah'll be fixin' the coffee."

With the same level of displaced anger, Loretha hauled each section of the crib into the house and positioned it against the wall in the right front bedroom on the side of the house near the kitchen. She made several trips to the car. When she finished, she went into the kitchen, sat for a few moments and took several deep breaths.

"Yuh-know … Ah didn't think John could ever make me feel this way. He told the church what he thought they needed tuh hear. Then, he tried tuh get 'Lizabeth tuh come back home. When she refused, he thought he could badger me. Ah really stood up tuh him … and that's why Ah'm so angry … but Ah won't give him the satisfaction of seeing me this way."

"C'mon now, drink yuh coffee. Do the Reb know 'Liz'beth is comin' here?"

"Oh yeah!" Loretha smiled and nodded. She held up her coffee cup and placed her elbow on the table. "He was really upset. He's not upset because she's coming here, but because she's not coming home. He thought, if she had nowhere else tuh go, she would have tuh come home. Now he doesn't know what tuh tell the church, because he has no control over what she does." She stared into her coffee cup, took a sip, and looked at Mrs. Collins. "Yuh-know … she would've come home, but she saw right through him. As a matter of fact, she gave him a hard time. Ah was kinda proud of her. She told him she didn't think it would be best for her or the baby. And yuh-know, she's right." Loretha took a deep breath, and another sip of coffee. She placed the cup on the saucer and reached to hold Mrs. Collins' hand. "Ah should be happy Ah raised such a strong, sensitive chile. On the way home, Ah had tuh tell John off again. Ah don't think Ah'll have any more problems with him."

"Ah see yuh beginnin' tuh feel better." Mrs. Collins gently squeezed Loretha's hand. "Keep talkin' 'bout it. It seems tuh he'p."

Loretha laughed. "Ah do feel better. Yuh must've thought Ah was crazy, just dropping the crib off in yuh front yard and not sayin' anything tuh yuh."

"Yeah, Ah was wonderin' what was happenin'. Thank God yuh came back."

"'Lizabeth said the doctor was letting her out of the hospital on Tuesday or Wednesday … if all goes well."

"Tuesday or Wednesday, yuh say? Dat be real good. We gone have the car by den, and we'll jest go pick 'em up and bring 'em here."

"That's great. Ah do feel better. Ah'll just finish my coffee and get on home."

"Yeah, drink up and git."

"Oh! Now yuh putting me out."

"Yeah, git. Go take care of yuh family," Mrs. Collins ordered, then she broke out with a pleasant smile.

"Ah'm gonna go home now and try tuh spend some good time with John."

"It's good yuh feelin' better. Yuh-know, yuh got tuh keep a man happy. The Reb may be wrong, but lak yuh said, he's hurtin', too. Now, go make him feel better," Mrs. Collins ordered. "And don't make no mo' babies."

"Oh, go 'way from here," Loretha said, she laughed aloud. It made her feel good to hear herself laugh again.

Loretha knew she was in the middle between John and Elizabeth, and she knew John believed Elizabeth had come between them. John and Elizabeth were her family, and now there was Little Johnny. And poor Sarah just seemed to be out there scratching for whatever affection and attention she could get.

—⁓—

Loretha knew Mrs. Collins was right. She believed it was time to show Reverend Turner how much she loved him and offer him some support. She spent the evening catering to him and returning to her affectionate self. She was comfortable that Elizabeth was going to be okay.

"John, please don't worry. Don't try so hard tuh make things work out yuh way. Let it be. Yuh made yuh decisions, and yuh must stick by what yuh think is right. Ah'm happy things will be all right with Elizabeth. Ah know things will be all right with the church, too. Ah love you and Sarah. Now, Ah'm gonna let go and let God. Can Ah give yuh a hug? Ah love yuh so much."

"Ah love yuh, too, Loretha. Ah really needed tuh hear yuh say those words. Ah've been so deep in despair, Ah couldn't see the blessings. Yuh right, Elizabeth is all right. Ah guess Ah deserved the way she treated me tuhday. Ah won't ask, push, or criticize yuh. We've been through a lot, so let's just try tuh get back tuh being a family."

Reverend Turner removed himself from his chair and approached Loretha just as she stood. They hugged and held each other. Their differences had not been reconciled, but were put aside because they loved each other.

Sarah entered the room, and Loretha called to her. They each held out an arm, and the three were in a supportive embrace.

"Mama, can yuh tell me what's going on?"

Loretha wanted Reverend Turner to explain the details about Elizabeth to Sarah. Reverend Turner and Loretha sat on the sofa and Sarah sat on the hassock. She would explain the details that John wasn't familiar with.

"Well Sarah, 'Lizabeth has made the decision tuh live with Mrs. Collins. Yuh know Ah said 'Lizabeth couldn't come home. Well … Ah was wrong, and Ah shouldn't have said those things tuh her. Ah was so upset … Ah wasn't able tuh think straight. Ah asked her tuh come home, but she believes it's best if she goes tuh Mrs. Collins. Ah'm not going tuh try tuh stop her."

"Daddy, Ah want her tuh come home with the baby," Sarah lied, saying what she thought they expected her to say.

"Maybe, one day, she will come home. She feels she needs a change, but she'll be just down Rehoboth Road. Yuh can see her and the baby whenever you want," Reverend Turner continued.

Sarah loved Elizabeth, but it was okay she wasn't coming home. Now she could have the best of both worlds. Her parents had shown her they still loved each other. Their feuding had caused her more concern than Elizabeth's dilemma. They all spoke freely about the changes in their lives. A calming solace came over them. Each had their own agenda, but as long as it didn't interfere with the family's unity, for the moment, it seemed acceptable.

Loretha returned to her bedroom. She and John enjoyed each other's company for the first time in over a week. They understood there would be no agreement over Elizabeth, but the craziness was put aside.

⚬⚬⚬

The next morning was chilly, and Loretha had planned her day with a purpose. She decided to walk to Mrs. Collins' house, taking the shortcut through the woods. With each step, she looked along the sides of the path and wondered which area was the place where Elizabeth was raped. It was quiet and peaceful, except for the crunch of the fallen leaves from the oak; maple and other trees that slept during the winter. Various varieties of pine and cedar trees were forever faithful, holding their greenery until the sleeping beauties awakened. The slight blustering winter breeze caused all the trees to gently sway.

Loretha could see Mrs. Collins' house in the distance, and warm tears began to roll down her cheeks. An overwhelming feeling swelled from deep inside where she had pushed her emotions, where she had set them aside because she needed to be strong to keep her family together. The solace of the woods caused her subconscious to release her inhibitions, allowing her to openly sob. Her pace slowed as if her tears robbed her of her energy. She sat on a fallen oak, the diameter of it caused her to believe it must have been more than two hundred years old.

Yuh must've held a lot of secrets befor' you laid down here to return to dust, Loretha thought "Thanks for being here for me," she said while patting the log.

Loretha cried and used her apron to capture her tears and empty the heaviness that pressured her heart. Everything was working out, now she needed to cry; to let all she was holding in pour out so as not to stifle the energy she'd need to continue her work.

By the time she reached the clearing, her eyes were red and her face puffy. She felt better, lighter, like weights had been removed from her shoulders. She could take deep breaths and not have her wind cut off by the fear of not knowing what would happen to her family. Her emotions swelled again, and she returned to the woods, seeking the comfort of the old log. She knew God was watching over her, giving her the strength to be strong, guiding her to do the right thing.

It had only been a few days, and she had gone from a time of extreme fear of the unknown during that Tuesday morning drive to the hospital; to the shock and dismay of her daughter's dilemma; to seeing her family falling apart; to deceptive behaviors; to acceptable solution. She had a grandson who was born without fanfare, but nonetheless, his arrival was a blessed event. She had Mrs. Collins. She never realized how much she loved her. Loretha cried out, "Oh Lord! Thank yuh, Lord. Yuh been so good tuh us."

Mrs. Collins was waiting for Loretha. When she finally reached her house, Loretha tried to hide her feelings, but her emotions were still surfacing.

"MaDear, the Lord has many blessings waiting for yuh."

"What yuh talkin' bout, honey?"

"Ah think Ah would've had a nervous breakdown if it weren't for yuh." Loretha began to cry again.

"Honey, don't cry. Ah know yuh been through a lot. Yuh whole family been through a lot. Ah'm here fer yuh. Ah don't think the Lawd would be takin' me from yuh now. Last year Ah prayed He'd take me. Ah was so lonely, and Ah had no purpose. Now it done all come tuhgether fer me. Ah kinda understand. Now we's got things tuh do. So don't yuh be cryin' no mo'."

"Oh … it feels so good tuh cry. Ah don't think Ah'm crying because Ah'm sad. Ah think Ah'm cryin' because Ah know everything is gonna be all right. Ah'm cryin' because Ah have yuh. Ah'm so happy tuh have yuh."

Mrs. Collins stood over Loretha. "Well … yes, lil' lady, yuh sure got me … yuh got me fer keeps. Now, if'n it makes yuh feel good tuh cry, then, yuh jest keep on cryin'. Yuh can jest cry all day whilst we work. That's if'n cryin' don't steal yuh energy."

When Loretha and Mrs. Collins' eyes met, they broke out in laughter. Loretha stood, put her arms around Mrs. Collins and held her.

"C'mon, honey, we's got work tuh do."

"Ah'm gonna get started, but remember, yuh said Ah could cry when Ah wanted to."

"Yep, as long as yuh keep workin'."

Loretha wiped her face on her apron, looked at Mrs. Collins, and began to laugh-cry all over again. "Okay, Okay, let's get tuh working."

They both decided to work in the bedroom while they waited for the mechanic to bring the car. Then, they would be off to town, to the bank, and then finish the shopping.

"MaDear, Ah was pleasant tuh John last night," Loretha bashfully announced with a shy smile on her face. "He's a different person today. Now, Ah still don't think he's changed as far as 'Lizabeth is concerned, but he's trying tuh put forth a good image."

"See, Ah tol' yuh tuh be nice tuh him and give 'em some lovin'. As long as he's willin' tuh let yuh have yuh way, chile … jest count yuh blessin's. God's been lookin' over us. Jest look at what he's he'ped us tuh do. Yes, honey, God is mighty good."

"Yes, MaDear. Praise the Lord."

CHAPTER 11

It was Thursday before Elizabeth and Little Johnny were discharged from the hospital. Loretha and Mrs. Collins arrived in Mrs. Collins' large shiny black automobile, which provided style and a small amount of fanfare for Johnny's homecoming.

Johnny was dressed in his new clothes and wrapped in a warm blanket. Mrs. Collins held him in her arms while Loretha drove the car.

Elizabeth sat in the rear, resting her head on the back seat. She thought about her life as it had been and the reality of her new life. She had turned to the extreme right on the crossroads of her life. All of her dreams were just memories. New dreams had already replaced the old ones, but that didn't stop her from wondering what would have been her fate on any of the other roads. To her left, she thought of her death. Straight ahead would have been her old life. At her right, on her new road, memories of her dreams and wishes for her future were still with her, but she knew she was living her new reality, and she was afraid.

When Elizabeth walked into her new bedroom, her fears faded. It looked almost like her old room, with her curtains, throw rugs and bedspread. The furniture was arranged in a similar position, and Johnny's crib was the new addition.

Johnny was placed in his crib and slept most of the afternoon. When he woke he was changed, fed, played with, held and caressed until he slipped back to sleep.

Elizabeth stood in the door with her arm around her mother when she first saw Sarah walking down the road. She didn't know her mother had ordered Sarah to make an attitude adjustment and take the school bus to Mrs. Collins'. It wasn't necessary. When Elizabeth called to her, Sarah quickened her pace. They greeted each other with hugs. For a moment it seemed that nothing had changed, until Sarah broke away and hurried to the bedroom to see Johnny.

"Oh! He got so big. He's beautiful. Ah haven't seen him since the day he was born. He's grown so much! Ah want tuh wake him up. Can Ah wake him up?"

"Well, yuh can try, but Ah don't think yuh can," Elizabeth said. "When he sleeps, he really sleeps. He only wakes up when he's hungry, and he just finished his bottle."

"Can Ah hold him?" Sarah asked.

"Okay, sit on the bed. Ah'll hand him tuh yuh."

As the late evening approached, Loretha and Sarah had taken Mrs. Collins' car and left for home. Elizabeth was exhausted. Johnny woke up on schedule every four hours, and Elizabeth quickly learned about the nighttime feedings. Her mother had advised her to try to sleep whenever the baby slept. She was happy to be out of the hospital, but wanted to be home. She wanted her old life, her school, her friends, and most of all, her father.

It would have been much easier if the memories of her old life could have been erased. But Johnny was hers. God gave him to her, and that was wonderful, but she still wondered why He selected this time in her life, the circumstances of his conception, and the turbulent outcome. Her mother had explained "free will," but the Lord was all-powerful and could make anything possible. She lay in her bed and allowed her mind to drift back to the carefree times. "Oh Lord!" Elizabeth cried softly. "Johnny's here now …" She drifted off to sleep while still in prayer. It was as if God had soothed her crowded conscience.

Christmas and New Years came and went. Loretha, Sarah, and MaDear tried to make the holidays nice for Elizabeth, but it was during this time that she learned the two sides of being a mother. There was the side that came with the bonding of her baby. She felt the kind of love she never knew possible. It was then that she understood how it was possible for her mother to risk all and stand by her. She loved Johnny, and now that he was here, she couldn't imagine how it felt without him. Even that love didn't dissolved the pain she suffered, but it made her stronger. It made her want to live. She'd hold him, feel the warmth of his tiny body and, during those moments, nothing else mattered.

Then, there was the other side of being a mother. The demands of an infant were trying. Overwhelmed with so much to learn and do, Elizabeth believed her life was no longer hers, and she had little time for herself. Her mother and MaDear were a big help, teaching her the things she needed to know, but she didn't want to be a burden.

Elizabeth thanked God Johnny was a good baby. For the first month, he slept most of the time. She had learned his schedule and arranged her schedule around him. MaDear was there for those times when he just wanted to cry, and Elizabeth didn't know what to do to comfort him. Elizabeth wished he were older. He was no fun as a needy infant. She wanted him to be a little boy. When she was alone, she thought of the years to come; when he would be more independent and could walk and talk and tell her when something was bothering him; when he could tell her what he liked and didn't like.

Along with these thoughts came the feelings of guilt. She thought she was the only mother to feel this way, and was ashamed of her selfish thoughts. Depression soon set in. She'd cry for no reason. It had nothing to do with her experiences. No matter what she was doing, she would just start to cry.

Loretha and MaDear noticed the onset of her depression, and decided it was time to talk to her. MaDear understood it was her mother's place to intervene.

It was a mild day around the end of January. Elizabeth welcomed the chance to be alone with her mother. She wasn't thinking she needed help with the baby. She wanted time away from him. She rested her head on the back of the car seat and turned to look out of the passenger side window.

"Honey. Yuh seem so depressed lately."

"Oh, it's nothing, Mama." She turned toward her mother.

"No. Ah'm gonna tell yuh what's wrong. Ah've felt that way, too. Yuh have a depression that many mothers have after they have a baby. Ah could ask yuh what's wrong and wait for yuh tuh feel it's all right tuh tell me ... but Ah know yuh won't. Now there are all kinds of depression, but Ah'm gonna tell yuh about the depression Ah had after you were born ... and most of the time it's the depression yuh feel after yuh have a baby. Now, it don't happen tuh all mothers, but it's common."

"Mama, Ah'm not depressed. Ah think Ah'm just real tired." Elizabeth turned to pull the sun visor down and returned her attention back to her mother. Occasionally she would look down at her fingers, but only for a moment.

"Yeah, well being depressed comes with being real tired. Yuh feel uncomfortable about being a mother. Yuh may even want yuh ol' life back, but Ah don't think it's all about that. Ah've watched yuh with Johnny. Yuh a fine, natural mother ... but yuh just overwhelmed. Taking care of a little baby is hard. It's even harder when yuh didn't expect tuh be a mother at such a young age." Loretha put her right signal on and pulled the car off the road near an old, closed down gas station. "Ah need tuh see yuh face when Ah talk, and Ah can't do that and drive."

"Ah'm listening, Mama." She pulled her legs up on the seat and sat facing her mother.

"Honey, babies need a lot of attention. Yuh devote yuh life tuh them, and yuh know yuh love 'em more than anything, but it drains yuh 'til yuh intuh a period of depression. Ah wanted yuh tuh hurry up and grow up." Loretha ran her fingers through Elizabeth's hair, and then down the side of her face. "Ah wanted time for myself. Then Ah felt guilty for feeling that way, especially when yuh were so little and helpless. Ah felt trapped … so all Ah could do was cry. Ah cried when Ah had tuh care for yuh in the middle of the night. Ah was so tired. Ah'd stagger tuh yuh crib tuh get yuh. There were those times when yuh just started crying, and Ah didn't know what tuh do. Ah felt inadequate, and there were times … Ah wished Ah didn't have a baby."

Tears began to crawl down Elizabeth's face, and she wiped them away with her hands. Loretha reached in her pocketbook, handed her a handkerchief and beckoned her to move closer to her.

"'Lizabeth, Johnny won't always be a helpless demanding baby. Ah know yuh want him tuh hurry and be a little boy, like Ah wanted yuh tuh hurry and be a little girl." Loretha rubbed Elizabeth's arm as she spoke, and Elizabeth continued to wipe away the tears. "Honey, Ah cried just like yuh crying. Then, Ah'd cry for feeling guilty, and that made me cry even more. It seemed no matter what Ah felt, or how hard Ah tried tuh make things better, it only made me cry more. Ah'd pick yuh up, hold yuh and Ah knew how much Ah loved yuh. So … what yuh feel is natural. It doesn't matter how many people are around yuh, yuh still feel alone."

Elizabeth sat up and turned to face her mother. "Mama, how'd yuh know Ah was feeling that way? Ah really love Johnny, and Ah'm happy tuh have him, but it's so hard, so confining … and so much work."

"Ah'm yuh Mama, and Ah just know." She threw her arm around her and kissed her on the cheek. "Now c'mon 'Lizabeth. It's a beautiful winter day. Let's get out of the car. The sun ain't as bright as it is in the summer, but it's still kinda nice. The air is clean and crisp. C'mon, take a deep breath." There was an old bench next to the building and Loretha had a blanket in the trunk of the car. "C'mon, we can sit over here,"

Elizabeth lifted her kerchief over her head, tied it under her chin, buttoned her coat and pulled on her gloves.

"Chile! Ah know yuh ain't cold on a day like this." She spread the blanket over the bench, and she and Elizabeth sat. "At least yuh behind will be warm." She laughed and hugged Elizabeth.

Elizabeth relaxed in her mother's arms, placing her head against her shoulder. "Mama, Ah never go anywhere. Ah don't have any friends, and Ah can't go tuh school. Is it so terrible tuh want a life again?" She wanted to glance up at her mother when she spoke, but she enjoyed her comfort more.

"Listen honey, it would be a good idea if yuh tried tuh rebuild yuh life. Ah know yuh can't go back tuh school. But there is a correspondence course that the state gives. Yuh can get yuh education, but it won't do much for yuh social life. The people at Concord are always asking about yuh, but Ah don't think yuh should worship there. Ah'd leave, except for yuh father. Yuh have a lot of friends at Bethlehem Baptist. Some of yuh teachers are members there, and when yuh didn't come home after Johnny was born, some of the member from Concord moved over tuh Bethlehem." Loretha removed her hand from Elizabeth's shoulder when she sat up and turned to face her.

"Mama, if they loved me so much, how come no one ever came tuh visit me? Ah've been at MaDear's for a month, and all those loving people never visited me … not even Mrs. Thea … not even Daddy."

"Sweetheart, some people are afraid of pain. When they think someone is hurting or sad and they don't know how tuh help, they tend tuh just stay away. Ah know real friends should stick together no matter what … but the way things should be and the way they really are is something different." Loretha took her hands. "Ah'll go with yuh tuh Bethlehem a couple of times, then Ah'll drive yuh tuh service and come back and pick yuh up until yuh learn how tuh drive. Yuh'll be happy there. Yuh can worship in peace, reacquaint with old friends, and yuh can have Johnny christened."

"Okay, Mama, maybe yuh right. Besides, Ah have nothing tuh be ashamed of. Ah want Johnny tuh be christened, but no one has asked tuh be his godparents."

"Well, when yuh start going tuh church again, yuh'll find someone. It's okay tuh ask someone, and if they love yuh and Johnny, they'll consider it an honor." Loretha put her arm around her again.

Elizabeth was quiet for a few moments. It was comforting to feel her mother rubbing her arm and holding her a little tighter. A slight wind blew, and the forest of tall Georgia pines swayed as if dancing in rhythm. "Mama, Ah wanna go back tuh church, but Ah wanna go tuh my church." Elizabeth sat up and looked at her mother waiting to see her reaction.

Loretha sat forward. "Elizabeth! Why would yuh want tuh go tuh Concord and have tuh face Reverend Oliver after what he's done tuh yuh?" She turned to see Elizabeth's eyes, hoping the true answer would be there.

"Ah want him tuh see what he did tuh me, and Ah want him tuh see what Ah have that he can't have." Elizabeth's eyes had focused inward, in her mind. She didn't blink because she had a vision of what her return to Concord would be like. "Ah been seeing that man all this time ... all these months ... Ah'm not gonna run away now." Her tone was defiant and definite. She turned and faced her mother. "Mama ... Ah ain't running. Maybe Ah can make him feel like runnin'. And Daddy ... Mama, Ah think Daddy expects me to run away and hide, then he can say Ah was lying 'bout Reverend Oliver. That will make him feel he was right about me. But on the other hand, if Ah come tuh church, it'll make him look good, but at the same time put some questions in his mind." Elizabeth had that "eyes focused inward" appearance again. Suddenly, she blinked, "Mama, yuh could be a big help if yuh would tell Daddy Ah'm coming tuh church and ask him tuh keep an eye on Reverend Oliver's actions. Ya-know, if he acts a little nervous with me around, 'cause Ah'm gonna lay my eyes on him like stone."

"All right, 'Lizabeth. If yuh want tuh come tuh Concord," Loretha shook her head in despair, "yuh know yuh father is gonna show off. He'll love tuh see you at church. It'll make him look good. Ah didn't want yuh tuh know, but the deacons really gave him a hard time about yuh. He's had tuh answer tuh them, and he's still answerin' tuh them.

Yuh know, yuh were right that day at the hospital. That's why he wanted yuh home. Maybe things would have gotten better between you and him, but who's tuh know? Ah just want yuh tuh know Ah'll support whatever decision yuh make, even if yuh change yuh mind later and decide to change churches." Loretha was as honest as she could be, and it was what Elizabeth needed.

"Okay, Mama, for now it's Concord." Elizabeth kissed her mother on the cheek.

"'Lizabeth, Ah just want yuh tuh feel better. Let's not talk about the church anymore. Now that Ah have yuh out, why don't Ah give yuh your first driving lesson. That should make yuh feel better. Just think, once yuh learn tuh drive, yuh can go anywhere yuh want. Honey, driving means freedom."

Loretha removed the blanket from the bench and returned it to the trunk of the car. "Ah'll drive the car back tuh Rehoboth Road, then we'll switch seats. Ah need tuh see how much yuh know."

Loretha kept Elizabeth on the back country roads. The new experience of handling a car quickly pushed her troubles to the back of her mind.

—⧟—

Johnny's first outing came on a cool, brisk Sunday morning in early February. Anxiety was etched into Elizabeth's face and pronounced in her slowed movement. Mrs. Collins pranced around getting ready. This was Johnny's "coming out" day, and she was eager to show him off.

Elizabeth was a wash of emotions. She wanted to hide in the serenity of her new life. She felt secure at home, and no matter how many times her mother told her of the love and acceptance she would find at church, she had her doubts. She knew she couldn't hide forever. She would have to face people sooner or later.

By the time Loretha and Sarah arrived, Elizabeth had managed to get dressed. She was beautiful, but she didn't feel beautiful. She knew what she had to do was not just for herself; it was for her mother and Johnny. MaDear and Loretha fussed over Johnny, dressing him in his sweater-set and blanket. MaDear surprised Loretha and Elizabeth with a beautiful baby bunting she had crocheted.

Over the weeks, Elizabeth had many driving lessons, and Loretha insisted she drive to church. "Listen, honey, yuh going tuh do just fine. Ah'll leave John's car here and pick it up when we return. If yuh have trouble parking, Ah'll park the car for yuh. Ah promise yuh'll have a wonderful day. Ah told everyone yuh were bringing the baby tuh church, so don't be surprised when yuh surrounded. They're all so happy things are working out for yuh, and they're dying tuh see the baby."

"And Daddy?"

"Honey, yuh'll see a difference in him. Ah can't tell yuh if he's sincere. Yuh have tuh judge that for yuhself, but he'll show the church that he's proud of his new grandson. Don't be surprised if he ask yuh tuh stand before the church with Johnny. He needs tuh prove his sincerity and show how much he's accepted Johnny. Ah'm telling yuh this because Ah want yuh tuh be prepared."

"Ah understand, Mama."

Elizabeth pulled the car up to the side of the walk leading to the front entrance of the church. Kids were running all over the dusty, dirt-packed parking lot, and some of their parents were standing around waiting for the start of the morning service.

Elizabeth got out of the car and assisted MaDear. Loretha handed the baby to MaDear, slid over to the driver's seat and pulled away. Everyone ran to Elizabeth and said all the nice things they were supposed to say, but Johnny was the center of their attention.

"Oh, Ah cain't let y'all see the baby out here in this chilly air," Mrs. Collins said. "He ain't use tuh havin' cold air on his lil' face. Now, jest lemme git inside, and Ah'll show yuh mah pretty Johnny-boy." Mrs. Collins walked up the steps to the church and down the aisle of the sanctuary to the second pew and took her regular seat. Elizabeth and Sarah sat in their regular seats, and Loretha soon joined them. Mrs. Collins handed Johnny over the seat to Loretha, and she placed him on her lap before going about removing his bunting. Johnny was asleep and didn't stir for an instant. By the time Loretha dressed him down, a small crowd of children and adults were surrounding them.

Mrs. Harris, Deacon Harris' wife, reached for Loretha to let her hold Johnny. Without hesitation, he was handed forth. Mrs. Dotson waited in turn to hold him while the others circled to just see him, tickle him, and coo at him.

Elizabeth glanced around at all the people and acknowledged their warm greetings.

"So, this is our miracle child. He's a beautiful baby," Mrs. Harris said. "Yuh have what the good Lord chose not tuh bless me with. Cherish him."

"Ah will, Mrs. Harris," Elizabeth responded.

"Chile, how yuh doin'? Yuh had a rough time, but see how God's blessed yuh. Yuh as pretty as yuh always were," Mrs. Harris said while she handed the baby back to her.

There were only a few more minutes before the service was to begin. More and more people wanted to touch or hold Johnny and wish them well. They didn't seem to be just curiosity seekers. They all knew what had happened and were genuinely happy to see Elizabeth again.

Elizabeth sat, holding Johnny. The smile on her face expressed the gratefulness she felt.

Loretha and MaDear sat with their heads held high. There was no mistaking their pride. Sarah tried to appear excited, but jealousy held her back.

Mrs. Phillips', Thea's mother, was holding Malcolm while Thea was preparing to start the service. As soon as the people began to take their seats, Mrs. Phillips walked over to Elizabeth and handed Malcolm to Loretha to hold, then stretching out her arms, she said, "May Ah hold yuh baby? Ah've been waiting tuh see him."

There was no place for Mrs. Phillips to sit, so Sarah gave up her seat and took Mrs. Phillips seat on the front pew of the next aisle.

Reverend Oliver sat to the right of the pastor's chair in the pulpit. When Reverend Turner entered wearing his fine robe, he gave Elizabeth a warm smile, which she returned, then shifted his eyes between Loretha and Mrs. Phillips and the two babies. The music began to play, and the Senior Choir began their march. Reverend Turner took his seat in the large chair in the center of the pulpit and sang along with the choir. Elizabeth knew he wasn't sure which baby was Johnny or Malcolm.

Earlier, Reverend Oliver had been shifting his eyes between both babies. Elizabeth smiled because his sons were side by side again, like they were in the hospital's nursery.

When the music ended, Reverend Turner stepped up to the podium. "Let us pray." He raised his hands, signaling the congregation to rise.

After opening the service, Reverend Turner did exactly what Loretha said he would do.

"Ah would like the church tuh welcome my daughter back," he said. The amens echoed from the congregation. "Elizabeth, would yuh hold my new grandson up?" Elizabeth was handed Johnny. Reverend Turner smiled and was a little surprised to see it was the baby Mrs. Phillips was holding. A slight rumble of laughter came from the people. Reverend Turner gave out a slight chuckle, then held up his arm and brought his open hand down slowly to calm the congregation.

"Church … it gives me the greatest pleasure tuh introduce yuh tuh John Robert Turner … my grandchild. Would yuh all join me in a prayer tuh thank our Lord for such a wonderful gift?" The congregation bowed their heads.

"Dearest Lord, we come before you again tuh offer our thanks for the many blessings you've bestowed upon us. This chile … this chile is a most precious gift. Help this chile tuh learn yuh ways … and bless our dear 'Lizabeth. She was given the task of bringing forth this chile under the most difficult of circumstances. Yuh loved her and gave her the strength tuh give life tuh this chile. Thank yuh Lord for bringing 'Lizabeth back tuh us. We love her so …"

Elizabeth believed in prayer, but she wanted her father to stop. *He doesn't love Johnny. He doesn't love me. He only loves his position in the church. If he could erase me from being, he would have. Having us here just strengthens his position with the church. He's so happy we're here, but he never visited us. Stop praying, Daddy. Stop! Stop!*

"…These and all other blessing we ask in Jesus' name. Amen."

"Amen," the congregation sang out.

Elizabeth was happy it was over. She had to stand before the congregation and pretend to be content. He used her to reinforce his hypocrisy. She was happy to take her seat and let the service continue.

After the service, the excitement over Johnny was as great as before. This time Thea was there. She held Johnny and cuddled him. Reverend Oliver joined the crowd, and, to the surprise of Loretha, Mrs. Collins, and Elizabeth, he asked to hold Johnny. Thea handed Johnny to Reverend Oliver, then they continued to make over him as if he were their own.

Reverend Oliver cradled him in his arms, and tickled him under his tiny chin. It was the first time he'd held this son. More than a month had passed, and he felt safe. Elizabeth hid her feelings. This wasn't the time to speak out, it wouldn't change anything, but she didn't want him to hold her baby. She reached for him and gave the excuse that she had to go. Reverend Oliver gently handed the baby over.

"Honey, Ah'll get the car. Sarah, do yuh want tuh go with me?"

"No, Mama. Ah'll wait 'til yuh come back tuh get Daddy."

Loretha pulled the car up to the walk and slid over to the passenger seat. Mrs. Collins got in the back seat, and Elizabeth handed Johnny to her, then she got into the driver's seat. Sarah stood on the steps and watched Elizabeth drive away. She made a right turn from the church driveway and drove down Rehoboth Road, at what seemed to Sarah, as a steady pace.

—m—

Elizabeth squeezed the steering wheel so tight it frightened Loretha. "Mama, Ah shoulda listened tuh yuh. Ah shoulda never gone back tuh Concord."

"Relax, honey, Ah didn't teach yuh tuh hold the wheel like that. Yuh could run off the road when yuh come up on that curve. Just relax. Forget the church and get us tuh MaDear's safe, and then we'll talk." Loretha was holding to the dashboard and the seat. Stress lines creased her forehead, and a quick glance at MaDear in the back seat confirmed that Elizabeth was frightening her, too. "Slow now, the curve is coming up. Take it slow and stay on yuh side of the road." She kept an eye on Elizabeth and held her breath. "Okay now, stay loose with the wheel. Yuh doin' much better. Don't think of anything but the road." Loretha exhaled and sat back on the seat. She removed her hand from the dashboard and placed her right arm over the seat.

Elizabeth arrived at Mrs. Collins' home and turned off the ignition. "Chile! Yuh lak tuh scared me tuh death. Whut wuz dat about?" She handed Johnny to Elizabeth while Loretha helped her out of the car.

"Ah just can't go tuh Concord anymore."

MaDear had one leg out of the car, and she stopped and looked up at Elizabeth. "Sha, chile, Ah coulda tol' yuh dat."

Elizabeth carried Johnny into the house. "Mama, yuh can go back tuh the church. Yuh told me so. Reverend Oliver showed no sign of bein' guilty. We can talk about it later. Ah'm tuh tired tuh go intuh it now."

"Okay, baby, Ah'll see yuh later." She kissed Johnny on the fore-head and pressed her cheek against Elizabeth's cheek. "See yuh later, MaDear," she called out as she hurried from the house. She could barely hear MaDear saying, "So long" as she was leaving the front porch.

"MaDear, Ah'm gonna feed and change Johnny, and then take a little nap. Okay?"

"Yes, honey, Ah think Ah need a little nap, tuh."

Elizabeth put Johnny down. Her body told her she was tired, and her bed was inviting. She tried to relax, but her mind raced to seek out the day's activities. Elizabeth and Mrs. Collins had arrived at the same conclusion about Reverend Oliver and Reverend Turner, agreeing they couldn't continue to worship with ministers who were unclean in thought and deeds, each in their own manner, but unholy to the same degree.

The people were excited to see her and the baby. She wanted her baby christened, but she knew she would have to move to another church. Her mother had suggested Bethlehem Baptist Church on the Southern end of Rehoboth. She would ask her mother to drive her to service there. Elizabeth lay in her bed and allowed her thoughts to speak to her until sleep took over.

Ah'm not sorry Ah went to Concord. If Ah didn't go, Ah would have never known, and Ah would have always wondered if Ah did the right thing. Maybe Deacon and Mrs. Harris would like tuh be Johnny's godpar-ents. Mrs. Dotson and Mrs. Harris showed interest in Johnny. Mrs. Dotson has a house full of little ones, but Deacon and Mrs. Harris are alone. Johnny can be baptized at Bethlehem.

CHAPTER 12

Over the next six years, Elizabeth's accomplishments were many: she was a perfect mother, had learned to drive, was teaching Sunday school at the Bethlehem Baptist Church, scored a perfect grade on her high school diploma correspondence course, and landed a job as a cafeteria worker at the Booker T. Washington school. She was no longer dependent on her father or the state for support. She had friends from church and work, most of them married with children.

There were no men in Elizabeth's life, in spite of the many who expressed an interest. She had resigned herself to raising Johnny alone, not having fully recovered from her earlier experience, or having any faith in men.

When Johnny asked about his father, Elizabeth, Loretha, and MaDear told the same story, "he had gone away." This explanation was disheartening to Johnny. His thoughts were of a person who had physically left town, and that was what the women wanted him to believe. As he grew older and asked more questions, more answers were given, but even then, he would only be told what he needed to know to satisfy his curiosity. The women believed the faithful, benevolent, and amiable Reverend Oliver had indeed vanished; only Owen was left, a sinner of the worst kind.

Reverend John Turner remained absent from Elizabeth's life, but Loretha and MaDear were still her major supporters. Sarah was in her second year at college and estranged from her sister. She was living the dream her father had once held for Elizabeth.

Over the years, Reverend Oliver secretly tried to satisfy his conscience with anonymous mailings of a fifty-dollar bill wrapped in a single white sheet of paper, the first of every month. He began doing this the month after Johnny's birth. This was definitely a hardship for him, but not nearly enough as the suffering he had caused Elizabeth. He was sorry, and thought the money could give him some peace. Elizabeth knew why the money came and who the benefactor was. It angered her to no end, but she kept her head level and decided her contempt for Reverend Oliver would not be allowed to deprive Johnny of the money.

Every penny was put in the bank in her name for Johnny's use when he came of age. She had the opportunity to return the money. She saw Owen every day at school. He would escort His third grade class to the cafeteria and glance at her, but Elizabeth had the willpower to see him as transparent while she continued to heal. Her only concern was that he would be Johnny's teacher at some time or another. There was only one other third grade teacher in the school. When the time came, Elizabeth would be sure to request her. She knew this would mean Johnny and Malcolm would be in the same class. The school would never allow Reverend Oliver to be his son's teacher. When she thought about it, there would probably be many classrooms that Malcolm and Johnny would share.

When the state stopped paying Mrs. Collins for Elizabeth's living expenses, Mrs. Collins refused to take money from Elizabeth, but she did allow her to purchase the groceries, and she registered the car in Elizabeth's name. She often spoke of how the emptiness in her heart left by the loss of her own family had been filled by Johnny and Elizabeth. She'd lived her four score and some years. Her health was better than it had been in years, and she attributed this to her new purpose. She thanked the Lord for his many blessings.

Johnny had grown from that tiny, helpless infant to a loving little boy. He was as mischievous and energetic as any male child, but he was also a lonely child. Elizabeth was happy he would start the first grade in August. She would sit in the window and watch him amusing himself with his few toys, spending hours in some imaginary place. She would read to him every evening, and watched the story themes become the settings of his games. Bright and eager to learn, he was hungry for knowledge. By the time Johnny was five years old, he had learned to read simple stories, could write his name and all the letters of the alphabet, and was a little whiz with numbers. Elizabeth used her time teaching him and fostering his joy of learning. She knew that education was his only avenue to escape the poverty the Negro man had to endure in the Deep South.

Johnny was as excited and frightened as most children on their first day at school. Some of the other children cried, believing their parent would never return, but Johnny knew he would be attending classes in the same building where his mother worked. Elizabeth knew he was happy she was nearby, but she also knew the day would come when he would move more toward independence. She wasn't looking forward to that. For a brief moment, her mind slipped back to the days of his infancy, when she didn't want an infant, but a little boy. Now he was a little boy and she wanted to keep him that way forever, even though she knew one day she would have to let him go.

Elizabeth saw Johnny during lunch and at recess. It was no surprise Malcolm was in his class, and Elizabeth knew this would be a common arrangement. It was Elizabeth's responsibility to serve Reverend Oliver's students during lunch, and Reverend Oliver had to perform his share of lunchroom duty. Over the years, their eyes met several times. Elizabeth didn't feel any pain or shame. She hated him, and whenever she was in his presence, she only spoke to him when it was job related, and then her tone was sharp and strictly business.

Other than Elizabeth, there were two more reasons for Reverend Oliver to be in the cafeteria. He would spend as much time as he could at Johnny and Malcolm's lunch table. Then he would make his rounds throughout the cafeteria, but always ending up back at the boys' table, and it wasn't for Malcolm's sake. He could see Malcolm anytime he wanted, but Elizabeth had sheltered Johnny from him, even leaving Concord Baptist Church to avoid him. The cafeteria and playground were the only areas in Johnny's world where he had the higher rank; not higher than a parent, but higher than a cafeteria worker. Elizabeth could have attempted to stop his contact with Johnny, but she would have had to give an acceptable reason.

Reverend Oliver had to be careful not to give Johnny more attention than he gave Malcolm, so he attended to all the children, but when it came to Johnny, he got that special something; that extra long hug, that eye to eye contact, and the warm smile that communicated that he was special to him.

———◦∞◦———

When Johnny was seven years old, he began to ask more questions about his father. Elizabeth realized it was time to tell him what he needed to know, and she hoped all the questions he would have in his lifetime would be answered. He was told he was the result of a rape, and she didn't know who his father was. It was a shock that packed a painful blow. He only knew the word "rape" was a bad word for a bad thing having to do with a man hurting a woman. He had no visual image of rape, but he summarized he was the result of something bad.

The news dropped him to his knees, reduced him to silence. The pain of knowing he existed as a result of violence, rather than love, hurt him to his heart. Elizabeth held him as tight as she could without squeezing him. She tried to console him, knowing he had to be able to protect himself against words that hurt.

"Mama, do yuh mean that Ah'm not suppose tuh be here?" Johnny cried.

Elizabeth tried to absorb his pain. She continued to hold him, and asked God to put the words in her mouth that would soothe his pain.

"Honey, all that matters is that Ah love yuh," Elizabeth whispered softly. She kissed the side of his face near his ear. "Ah can't imagine what my life would be like without yuh."

Johnny's sobbing made her heart ache. He stopped asking why. He just cried.

MaDear reached over and coaxed Elizabeth to let her hold and speak to Johnny.

"Johnny-Boy," she called to get his attention. "Johnny-Boy, do yuh believe in God?"

Johnny looked up at her with wide, swollen, saddened eyes. He nodded his head and lowered it to rest on her chest.

"Well, den if yuh be believin' in God, yuh believe he be all powerful. Yuh believe he knows what gone happin' 'fore he do anythin', am Ah right?" She waited to feel Johnny's head moving up and down, and didn't expect to hear him say anything. "Well, Johnny-Boy, if yuh be believin' all dat, den yuh gotta be believin' the Lord don't make no mistakes. Do yuh believe the Lord don't make no mistakes, Johnny-Boy?" She pulled Johnny back so she could see in his eyes.

"Yes, ma'am." He sat up and wiped the tears rolling down his cheeks, then cuddled back in MaDear's lap and snuggled his head against her large, spongy bosom.

MaDear looked over at Elizabeth and smiled back in acknowledgment of her gentle, thank you, smile.

"So, Johnny-Boy, if the Lord don't make no mistakes, den yuh is here fer a purpose. We know what one purpose is, but Ah been thinkin' it be more dan dat. Yuh bring us love. Johnny-Boy … yuh done brought us so much love … yuh added years tuh mah life. Yuh is a gift from God."

Elizabeth rubbed Johnny's back. "Honey, it doesn't matter how yuh came tuh be. Yuh here, and Ah thank God every day and all day long for giving yuh tuh us. There's only one reason we told yuh, and that's because most people 'round here remember when yuh where born. We didn't want yuh tuh hear about it from someone else. Ah love yuh too much tuh see yuh hurt."

"Yes-sir-r-e-e, Johnny-Boy! God's got mighty strong plans fer yuh. Yuh gone make a difference in people's lives. Yuh already done made a difference in mine." MaDear hugged him and rocked him in her bosom until he forgot how bad he was feeling.

Elizabeth turned her back and wiped the tears from her eyes.

When Johnny was in the third grade, he made a special request to ride the school bus instead of traveling to school with Elizabeth. It was just another step toward independence, and Elizabeth had a hard time letting go. On the second day, during the ride home, Malcolm and Johnny got into a fight. The bus driver had to pull the bus off the road. He grabbed Malcolm, pulling him off Johnny. The bus was rocking from the jumping and excitement of the other children.

"Whatcha grabbin' me for? He started it," Malcolm screamed at the driver.

The driver was holding Malcolm by the back of his shirt and gave him a punishing jerk for his rudeness. "Who yuh think yuh talkin' tuh, Mr. Oliver? Don't yuh be gittin' smart mouth wit' me. Ah don't care who yuh daddy be. Yuh don't be jumpin' on no one on mah bus. Ah heard what yuh said tuh Johnny about a toilet … Ah'd a punched yuh in the face, too."

Johnny sat back on the seat and watched Malcolm being humiliated while all the children on the bus laughed. For the remainder of that school year, Johnny was assigned a seat behind the driver, and Malcolm had to sit in the front seat across from him.

Elizabeth believed it was Malcolm's fault, and the irony that Reverend Oliver's child would be the one to bring up the conditions of Johnny's birth gnawed at her. The next morning, Elizabeth arrived at school earlier than usual and waited outside Reverend Oliver's classroom.

"Hello, Miss Turner," Reverend Oliver said as he approached her.

"Ah'd like to speak with you before yuh class begins. I think it would be in yuh best interest if we walk tuh some place where we can have some privacy." Elizabeth was angry and ready for Reverend Oliver.

"Come in the classroom and close the door. Ah don't expect the children for another twenty minutes. We won't seem suspicious if we sit across from each other at my desk. Ah know why yuh here, and Ah'm sorry."

"Do yuh! Then why did it happen? Yuh know … Ah would call yuh a son-of a-bitch, but yuh mother can't be blamed for yuh disgusting behavior. You hurt me and my family, now yuh son is tryin' to hurt our son. Yes 'our son,' and yuh better put a stop tuh it. Yuh-know … my father silenced me when Ah was a child, but Ah'm not a child any more, and yuh can take that any way yuh want. Ah just want yuh tuh keep Malcolm away from Johnny unless they can be friends. The only reason Ah allow yuh tuh give Johnny attention is not because yuh his father, but because it makes him happy."

"I understand, Elizabeth, and Ah'll talk tuh Malcolm."

"Oh … and Owen," Elizabeth said as she stood to leave his classroom. "Stop milling around me, and keep yuh eyes off me. Ah see yuh taunting me, and Ah want it tuh stop. If yuh don't stop it, Ah will."

Reverend Oliver removed his handkerchief from his back pocket and wiped it across his forehead, then blotted it over his lips. "Ah … Ah … had no idea Ah was doing that. Ah'll pay particular attention that it won't happen again."

"Thank yuh," Elizabeth nodded, turned, and left the classroom.

—m—

Thea didn't know Malcolm the way Reverend Oliver and Elizabeth did. She saw him as her obedient son, always polite and tactful. They saw him in his school environment, on the school grounds, playing with the other children. He was a confident, take-charge child, with many followers. He had been that way since the end of the first grade.

If he didn't get his way, he would cast the unfortunate child out of the play circle, leaving them to wander around the playground, wanting to be let back in. That decision was Malcolm's alone.

Most of the children wanted to belong to Malcolm's circle, but there were a few who were emotionally stronger and saw Malcolm's behavior as unfair. These children had different interests and wanted to keep their distance. Not because they feared him, but they were smarter and more mature. Johnny was one of them. There were no leaders in his circle of friends. They were just friends.

Of the two groups, Malcolm's was perceived as the "in" group. Johnny and his friends were "the outsiders," the smart kids, the ones who were different. So when the boys fought on the bus, Elizabeth knew it was Malcolm's fault. Reverend Oliver loved both boys and saw Malcolm's behavior as an example of his more dominant personality, and not as a flaw in his character.

—ɯ—

Elizabeth believed Johnny needed to be strong. The cruelties he would suffer as a child were nothing like the cruelties he would suffer as an adult. Other than her conversation with Reverend Oliver, she let the incident pass and offered Johnny comfort for his dilemma and strategies for avoiding another incident of physical contact.

During those first eight years at school, Johnny and Malcolm had several verbal and emotional conflicts. Malcolm knew Johnny wasn't afraid to physically defend himself, so he never pushed him to that limit. Johnny liked Reverend Oliver, and Malcolm believed he had no rights to him. For Johnny, it was not a question of rights, he just liked him, and enjoyed being in his company. He was the man he needed in his life. He could tell him anything, and was never ridiculed or reprimanded, just directed, redirected, and loved.

Malcolm would see them sitting together in the playground. He felt like an outsider when the conversation ceased as soon as he came into hearing range. There were times when Johnny would ride his bike over to Reverend Oliver's house and make himself at home. Thea questioned the relationship, but dismissed it as a young boy needing a father image. Johnny planned his visits when he knew Malcolm wouldn't be home. This was possible on any week day afternoon when Malcolm would be down the road visiting friends. Johnny would wait out of sight and watch for Malcolm to leave, visit with Reverend Oliver, and always depart before Malcolm returned home.

Johnny believed as long as he was welcomed and his mother or MaDear didn't object, there was nothing wrong with being friends with Reverend Oliver. Elizabeth didn't object. She knew Johnny loved and admired him. When MaDear frowned on their relationship, Elizabeth remarked, "What harm could it do tuh allow him a little piece of his birthright?"

That first fight on the bus was just the beginning. They had no real knowledge of the motives for their entanglements, only their misunderstood feelings of their own identity, their possession, and rights to territory. Neither could boast about winning, because the battles were fought on different grounds.

Johnny could make Malcolm feel insignificant and incompetent in the classroom. He always won the favor of his teachers. Malcolm's only battle ground was the playground. He said things that hurt and dug deep. It was no secret Johnny didn't have a father. Most of the children didn't care. Some of them didn't have fathers either. Some of them had a different father than their siblings, but none of them were born in the girl's bathroom in high school.

In spite of Reverend Oliver's scolding and punishments, Malcolm continued calling Johnny a bastard, saying, "Yuh don't have a father. Yuh a bigger bastard than most, 'cause yuh were born in the toilet."

Elizabeth was furious with Reverend Oliver, but never acted on her threat. Through it all, Johnny seemed to grow stronger.

These were the painful words Elizabeth tried to prepare Johnny for. Johnny had fought Malcolm because of these words, but now his refusal to fight and the confident way he could flick off his aggression was frustrating to Malcolm. The other children weren't sophisticated enough to understand what Johnny was doing. All they saw was Johnny receiving a verbal blow and not retaliating, but Johnny always won. The more Malcolm tried to humiliate Johnny, the more he was humiliated. Johnny and his friends understood. If Malcolm could incite Johnny into physical violence, maybe he would win the fight, but Johnny would win the battle.

Johnny seemed to be able to skim away at Malcolm's self-confidence until it left him feeling inadequate, a feeling he didn't like, a feeling he only felt after an attack on Johnny. It was as though Johnny had some magical powers that controlled him, and by the end of their eighth grade, Malcolm tried to distance himself from Johnny.

Johnny appeared to come away from every skirmish untouched, but he internalized the anger of Malcolm's attacks. He knew he had won, but his anger dug a groove in his soul. Talking about his feelings, or even physically acting out, would have been an antiseptic, an antibiotic to aid toward healing. But Johnny never spoke about it, or complained. Those early school years were just the proving ground for what would come later in life.

Time continued to pass, with one conflict after another. Johnny and Malcolm's had reached the end of the eighth grade and were preparing for graduation. Johnny was the honor student his mother prayed he would be, while Malcolm grades were just passing.

There were some differences in size between the two boys. Both were handsome in their own unique ways. Although Elizabeth thought Johnny would have her father's dark complexion, as he grew older, his complexion grew lighter and closer to Reverend Oliver's. By the end of the eighth grade, Johnny was taller than Malcolm by an inch. It was apparent he would be a large man, but at that time, he was just a tall, thin, lanky, clumsy adolescent. People would comment that he could be a great basketball player, but Johnny had no aptitude for sports. His gift was his intelligence, and he had been named the valedictorian at his grammar school graduation.

Malcolm had a slightly darker complexion, a handsome brown that complimented his muscular build. Reverend Oliver and Thea were lighter and had searched their family's lineage for relatives that he resembled. Owen realized that, of the two boys, Johnny's physical attributes resembled him more than Malcolm's, and those people who knew the truth also witnessed this fact.

The personality differences between the boys could be attributed to the differences of environment and rearing, rather than inheritance. Having a man around was a major factor in Malcolm's dominant personality. And being in the presence of women during his formative years seemed to make Johnny a more caring and studious individual.

CHAPTER 13

MaDear was aging, and accepted it gracefully as the normal process of life: her walk was slow, her steps deliberate, but her memory was sharp. Elizabeth worried about leaving her every morning, and called her twice a day. Loretha visited her daily for lunch, and sometimes stayed until Johnny's arrival from school. MaDear loved television, and most of the time she would sit in her chair and watch her favorite programs.

"Boy? … Boy? … Is dat yuh?" MaDear called out every day just as Johnny entered the house. She used to call him Johnny-Boy, but the "Johnny" seemed just too much of a mouthful for her to roll off her lips.

"Ma'am," Johnny answered.

"Did yuh have a nice day?"

"Yes, ma'am. Can Ah get anything for yuh?"

"Boy! If'n Ah wanted somethin', Ah would've got it by now. Ah can still do. Ah is ol', but Ah can still do. Ah wish yuh mama would stop worryin' 'bout me. Ah guess yuh think Ah'm gonna die soon."

"MaDear, please don't talk like that again."

"C'mere, Boy. Sit right down here by me and let me tell yuh somethin'."

Johnny sat on the floor next to MaDear and rested his head against her leg. It was a common ritual, and he did as he was told because it pleased MaDear. He'd look up at her, and she'd rub her soft hands over his hair and down the side of his face.

"Ah know Ah's ol'," she'd say. "Ah's ol'er dan anyone in mah family, and Ah done out lived all dem. Boy, Ah was born in July 25th 1872, and dis here be May of 1963. Ah know the Lawd gone call me soon. He's been good tuh me. Now … Ah ain't rushin' him … yuh know whut Ah mean, but Ah is ready when he calls, and Ah ain't 'fraid. Ah don't want yuh tuh be 'fraid either."

"MaDear, Ah know yuh not afraid. Ah'm not afraid for yuh. Ah'm afraid for me. Please, MaDear, can we just change the subject? May Ah get up now?" Johnny waited to see her smile and nod. He kissed her on the forehead and left the room. It seemed, lately, she had the same conversation every day. It was as though she had forgotten they had spoke about it the day before, or maybe she thought she needed to prepare him for what was to come.

Johnny went into the kitchen and got a snack before taking his books to the corner desk in the sitting room to complete his homework. He didn't want to hear about MaDear dying, but if he allowed her to lead the conversation, he knew that was what she would do.

"MaDear, are yuh coming tuh my graduation on Saturday?" He listened for her response while he opened his notebook and reached for his textbook.

"Chile, Ah wouldn't miss dat fer nothin'. Ah might not be here when yuh have yuh next grad'jation."

"MaDear, there yuh go again. Please stop talking like that. Ah know the Lord is gonna call yuh one day. He's gonna call me, too." He began writing in his notebook while he spoke.

"No, chile, no time soon. Yuh is young and healthy."

"So, yuh is old and healthy," Johnny said, rocking his head, mocking her, but not being disrespectful. "How come yuh never talk like that when Gram'ma or Mama are around?" He stopped writing and turned toward MaDear.

"Ah don't know. Ah jest worry 'bout yuh bein' sad." She knew he was looking at her, but she continued to look at the television.

"Well yuh making me sad now when yuh start talking like that," Johnny said. Then he changed the subject. "MaDear, yuh-know Reverend King is planning a march on Washington for August 28th. Ah would sure like tuh go. Reverend Lipton said he received a letter from the Baptist Ministers Alliance. He read it in church. He said the Southern Christian Leadership Conference would contact the ministers with more information as the details of the march are completed. Reverend Lipton said the church would probably plan a bus trip for the march. Do yuh think Mama will let me go?" He put his pen down and went back to sit on the floor next to MaDear.

"Ah don't know, chile. Maybe she be plannin' tuh go, too. It be somethin' tuh think 'bout."

"Yeah, Ah been just standing by watching as other people fight for freedom and Ah'm the one ... well, not just me ... but people my age will have the most tuh gain. Yuh saw what they did to those people in Birmingham last Thursday. MaDear, they were spraying them people with high pressured fire hoses and putting the dogs on them. They even did this tuh the women ... and the little children." Johnny removed himself from the floor, placed his hands on his hips and began pacing between MaDear's chair and the television and shaking his head in disbelief. "Ah been watching it on television, and Ah been reading about it in the papers, but what Ah've been seeing on television is nothing like what Ah read in the papers. White folks sure know how tuh twist the truth. MaDear, why do they hate black people so much?" He stopped in front of her chair and turned his attention toward her because she was the elder, and wise enough to have the answers to most of his questions.

"Well, honey, dey jest cain't turn loose the old ways. We ... being dey slaves ... way back ... and all dat." She eased herself out of her chair and pointed at the television. Johnny hurriedly switched it off. "Dey believe we is 'pose tuh still be dey slaves. Yuh-know ... Ah was born jest nine years after the Civil War ended ... dat be when slavery ended, and dat makes me ninety-one years old. Ah ain't know nothin' 'bout slavery. Ah mean Ah ain't lived in it." She pulled the kitchen chair out and sat in it. "Boy, would yuh put a fire under dat kettle. Ah be liking some coffee."

"Yes, ma'am." Johnny set up everything she needed for her coffee and set in the chair across the table from her. "Tell me more, MaDear."

"Oh, where was Ah? Oh yeah! Well, when Ah be growin' up, Ah ain't see no difference 'tween them folks that use tuh be slaves and a so-call free man. Yuh-know ... when Ah say 'free man' ... Ah mean our people. Dem white folks was still hangin' and beatin' our men and rapin' our women. Dey say the rapin', beatin' and lynchin' got worse after slavery." MaDear's voice had captured Johnny. He was now kneeling in the chair with his elbows on the table, his hands supporting his chin, and he was laying on every word MaDear spoke.

"Boy ... if yuh keep crawlin' on dat table, yuh gone be in mah lap." The vibrations of her laughter pulled her body into motion.

"C'mon, MaDear, keep tellin' me."

"All right, all right. Well ... some folks say some colored folk be livin' better cause dey still live in the old Massa's house or on dey farms, cause dey lived in the old ways. The massas didn't be callin' dem 'slaves' cause dat be 'gainst the law. Dey called dem 'darkies' or 'Niggres' or 'gal' or 'boy' or 'pick-a-ninny' or 'sunshine.' Dey called 'em anythin' but 'Negroes.' Ah think dey hate us 'cause dey cain't control us. Boy, Ah want yuh tuh know somethin' dat be real import'nt." MaDear leaned over and Johnny crawled closer to her. She whispered softly as though she was hiding something. "All white folk ain't bad. Dey don't all hate us. But the good ones are 'fraid tuh act good, specially when other white folk be 'round."

The kettle whistled and Johnny jumped. He was completely caught up in what MaDear was saying. He shimmied backward off the table and hurried to the stove to prepare her coffee. "Ah know that, MaDear. Just like Ah don't hate all white folks." He poured hot water over the instant coffee in MaDear's cup. "Ah'll get the milk for yuh."

"Gemme dat can milk, Boy." She stirred a teaspoon of sugar in her cup. Johnny placed the canned milk on the table. "Thank yuh, Boy."

Johnny went back to his seat and placed his elbows back on the table. "Well, Ah hope Mama wants tuh go on that march. ... Even if she can't go, Ah hope she'll let me go. Yuh-know ... if they have that march ... Ah know Reverend Oliver will go. Ah'd like tuh go with him, but Ah don't want tuh be around Malcolm."

MaDear was set back when Johnny mentioned Reverend Oliver's name. "Well, Boy, yuh be needin' tuh talk tuh yuh mama. Yuh be gittin' mighty close tuh Reverend Oliver. Yuh be talkin' 'bout him all the time."

"Yes, ma'am. May Ah be excused? Ah have tuh get back tuh my schoolwork."

MaDear nodded and lifted her hand to shoo him away. "Go on, Boy." She tilted her head downward and shook it slightly. Her lips turned downward in a frown, and she watched Johnny walk toward his homework. She took a deep breath, then a sip of her coffee.

—✺—

Johnny had trouble concentrating on his homework assignment. The more he thought about the march, the more he felt he had to be there. The idea of going on the march never entered his head until his conversation with MaDear. Even then, he wasn't seriously thinking about going, he was just trying to change the subject to keep MaDear from talking about dying. Now the march was all he could think about.

It would be another hour before Elizabeth was due from work. Johnny had to push thoughts of the march aside so he could complete his homework, but once he closed his books, he was free to allow his mind to wander. He thought about calling his grandmother, but was afraid Reverend Turner would answer the telephone. He thought about calling Reverend Oliver, but he didn't want to risk speaking with Malcolm. He decided he would just have to wait for his mother. Johnny surprised himself. He never acted impulsively before. He thought about his friend, Drew. Tapping his pencil on his teeth, he was trying to decide if he should call Drew or wait until after he spoke to his mother.

It wasn't long before Elizabeth arrived home. When Johnny saw the car coming down the driveway, he ran out to meet her. Just as she stepped out of the car, he started, "Mama! Remember Reverend Lipton announced the church would sponsor a bus trip if Reverend King had the march on Washington?" Johnny was beside himself with excitement.

"Johnny, this is Thursday, yuh knew about the possible trip since Sunday. Why the sudden urgency?" Elizabeth dropped the keys in her purse and reached for her bags.

"Ah don't know, Mama. Oh, hello! Ah got the bags, Mama. How was yuh day?" Johnny gave her a peck on the cheek, then he started all over again about the trip to Washington. He grabbed up the bags in both arms and pushed the car door shut with his backside.

Elizabeth began walking toward the house with Johnny walking at her side. "Johnny, let me get in the house and catch my breath, then yuh can tell me about this trip."

"Okay, Mama." Johnny hurried ahead of his mother, holding the door for her and following her into the house. He took the bags into the kitchen and set them on the table near where MaDear had been sitting. She had finished her coffee and returned to her chair in the sitting room. Johnny began putting the groeceries away and watched as his mother walked into the sitting room.

"Hi, MaDear, Ah'm home," Elizabeth spoke softly. She walked over to her chair and gave her a kiss on the cheek.

"Hi, baby," MaDear said. "Ah thought that boy was gone have a breakdown or somethin' thinkin' 'bout goin' on dat march. It come on him lak a fallin' rock."

"Ah know, we're gonna talk about it as soon as he's finished in the kitchen. Reverend Lipton was talkin' 'bout it in church last Sunday."

Johnny walked into the sitting room and sat on the couch and turned to face his mother. "Is now a good time, Mama?"

"Yes, honey, now's a good time." Elizabeth turned to face Johnny. "Honey, if there is a bus trip, it would have tuh be at least three days long, and it could cost as much as fifty dollars a person each way. That would mean at least a hundred dollars for you and me, and that doesn't cover food or spendin' money. And, Johnny, it could even cost more." Elizabeth shifted her eyes from Johnny to MaDear and back to Johnny.

"Ah know, Mama. Ah figured it out. Ah'll get a job as soon as school lets out. Mr. Jenkins is always looking for kids tuh help in the fields. Ah'll save every penny Ah make. Last summer Ah made near three hundred dollars. If Ah work hard, Ah can do as well as Ah did last summer and have enough for you and me?"

"Johnny, yuh thirteen years old, and yuh never really asked for anything. We'll work together, but yuh got tuh work hard and do without a lot of things."

Johnny wrapped his arms around his mother. He knew he could save the money by working for Mr. Jenkins, and he could go around and ask everyone he knew if they needed him for odd jobs.

Elizabeth stood looking at him, she could almost see the wheels of his mind working. She knew, without a doubt, he would raise the money.

Johnny left the sitting room and went into the kitchen. "Mama, would yuh like me to warm up that pot of beef stew for dinner?"

"Yes, Johnny, and would yuh heat up the oven to warm up those biscuits, too?"

Johnny had the stew pot in his hand. "Sure, Mama," he called out.

———〰———

"Yuh-know, MaDear, Ah was thinkin' about the march on Washington too, but Ah'm glad Johnny brought it up. Ah'll let it be his responsibility tuh get us there if there is a bus trip. It'll give him somethin' tuh look forward tuh and make it that much more important tuh him. Reverend Lipton said he'd be gettin' more information about it in the next few weeks. Ah'll just let Johnny start preparin' for it."

"Ah guess we be hearin' 'bout dis-here trip the whole summer, but it gone be good fer him. He needs tuh be thinkin' bout dat Civil Rights

Movement. Dat Martin Luther King is gone change the way colored folks be treated. Dat's gone make a better world fer the boy. He needs tuh be involved. Dat's a smart boy yuh got, baby."

"Yeah, MaDear." Elizabeth smiled and placed both hands against her chest. "Remember when you and Mama told me he was gonna be somethin' special?" Elizabeth didn't wait for a response. "Ah'm seeing the beginnings. He is somethin' special. If he continues this way, he'll really be somethin' special tuh our people and this community one day."

"Listen, honey, Ah jest want yuh tuh know dat Johnny been talkin' kinda fondly 'bout Reverend Oliver here lately. Ah reckon he be seein' him a lot at school," MaDear whispered.

"Ah know. That's been goin' on for years. Sometimes when Ah see 'em at school, Ah smile. Johnny's mine and he can't have him. Ah been watching them. Ah don't have no hate left, and Ah'm not worried. If Johnny is happy, then no harm can be done." Elizabeth got real close to MaDear and whispered in her ear, "Reverend Oliver can never tell him he's his father." Both women smiled at each other and agreed to watch the situation closely and just let it be.

❧

Saturday came quickly, and it was almost time for the Booker T. Washington Elementary School graduation. The sixty graduates, their parents, siblings, and other relatives and friends were excited about the big day. The children were dressed in black pants or skirts and white shirts or blouses. The boys wore black ties and the girls had black ribbons tied in a neat bow to complete their outfits.

Both eighth grade teachers sat on the stage along with Dr. Lacy, the Campus Principal; Mr. Daniels, the Assistant Campus Principal; Reverend Turner, Reverend Lipton, and Denise Shore, the high school valedictorian. The elementary school choir sat in the neat rows of seats to the left of the stage, and the graduates sat on the front center rows of chairs.

Loretha, Sarah, Elizabeth, MaDear, and Deacon and Mrs. Harris, Johnny's godparents, sat behind the graduates in the seats closest to the aisle. Pictures had to be taken, and it was important to be in a good location when Johnny made his speech.

Denise gave her speech first, then introduced Johnny as the elementary school valedictorian. He was nervous, but his friends cheered him on with encouragement. Reverend Turner stood when Johnny walked on stage, then everyone stood. Johnny looked at his grandfather, who was approaching to offer his congratulation. Johnny was taken back by his sudden affection and signs of admiration. He didn't know if he should smile and be accepting or stand stiff and cold. He shook his hand and allowed a coy smile to cover the seriousness of his feelings.

Johnny had prepared his speech very carefully. It was appropriately called "Getting Ready." He wanted to speak about the future, about the movement, and being ready when the time came. Elizabeth had some apprehension, but she also had confidence in his ability.

Johnny greeted the adults on the stage, the guests, and his fellow graduates, then he began.

"We have all been following the Civil Rights Movement. And … we all know of the Reverend Martin Luther King Jr. Some of us know of the many others who are the point men of the movement." He had placed the notes containing his speech on the podium, and looked up at the guests as he spoke. "We know of Mrs. Rosa Parks, she had the courage tuh stay steadfast on a bus and not give up her seat tuh a white man."

"That's right, son, tell 'em 'bout it," some man called out from the audience.

Johnny looked in the man's direction. "We've witnessed the 'movement,' and maybe some of yuh have helped the cause in one way or another. We can march, we can sit-in, we can go tuh jail, we can be

beaten, we can pray, but most of all we need tuh be 'getting ready.'"
Johnny paused and ran his hand over his head.

"Tell 'em young man, tell the young people what they need tuh
do." A lady stood and waved her hand.

"Amen," someone else yelled.

Johnny turned and looked at Reverend Oliver, and he smiled. "Yes,
fellow class mates, If we do nothing else, we owe it tuh ourselves and
tuh those who are on the front lines tuh be ready when equality comes.
That's what the movement is all about, *equality*."

Teachers and guests began to stand and shout out, "Tell 'em whut
they need tuh do."

"Amen, son."

Johnny had to lean into the microphone and speak louder to be
heard over the excited audience. "Things aren't so equal now … not
equal at all. Our people have always had tuh work harder … tuh
produce more with less … and endure the cruelty of degradation."

"We got us a young Reverend Martin Luther King right hear from
Rehoboth!" a man yelled out from the back of the audience.

Johnny smiled.

Someone else called out "Sho' nough."

"One day our time will come," Johnny continued to speak into the
microphone, "and we need tuh be ready. It would really be a shame if
they struggled so hard, and we weren't ready. Ah can see myself being
anything Ah want tuh be, being the best that Ah can be and nobody
can stop me, but me."

"Yes you can, Mr. Turner," a tall dark stranger spoke from the side.

He was different and caught Johnny's attention. Johnny smiled at
him and turned to face the entire audience before continuing. "We all
owe it tuh ourselves and tuh our families, tuh be ready, tuh be
prepared. When Ah saw the brutality our people were forced tuh
endure over in Birmingham, Ah thought tuh myself … they're doing
that for me. They were suffering like that for you and me. Some of
them were children just like us, and they were on the front line."

The audience was still charged, but Johnny wanted to finish. He raised his hands and brought them down slowly, the way Reverend Lipton did when he wanted to quiet the church, and the people took their seats. He smiled. "We are the next generation. We just can't let sufferin' like that go on in vain. Tuh all the students here at the Booker T. Washington School, Ah like tuh say, Our Lord blessed each one of us with a special talent. Identify yuh talent and polish it … study hard … we got tuh be ready when it's our turn tuh make a better America for our people. Thank you."

The audience stood and applauded as Johnny took his bows. He said what he thought all young people should be thinking, and was surprised that not only his classmates, but everyone at the graduation, was applauding him with such vigor. He took another bow before walking from the stage and returning to his place with his classmates.

Loretha and Elizabeth hugged MaDear; they hugged Sarah, they hugged Deacon and Mrs. Harris, then each other. They were so proud.

"Mama, Johnny said he was gonna get us tuh that march on Washington. Ah know he will. Ah'm so proud of him," Elizabeth announced.

"Mah boy is really somthin'," MaDear said in a just audible tone, with her eyes closed and shaking her head. "Oh he's special. He's so special. Thank yuh Lawd. Thank yuh Lawd."

"Ah told yuh he was special and would make yuh proud of him … and yuh ain't seen nothin' yet," Loretha said.

Across the aisle, Reverend Oliver and Thea were applauding Johnny.

Dr. Lacy thought back to the day Johnny was born, and remembered the horror of that time. He wore a smile of adulation. Then he leaned over and whispered to Mr. Daniels, "God bought that young man intuh this world on the lowest rung of the ladder. He had nowhere else tuh go but up, and there are a lot of rungs tuh go before he reaches the top, but oh what a man he will be."

Mr. Daniels smiled. "Ah believe you're right about that."

The ceremony was over and all the children hurried to be with their families, including Johnny. Mr. Baker wanted to congratulate Johnny and a special feeling came over him when Johnny hugged the beautiful woman he had seen in the cafeteria a week earlier while Mr. Lacy was taking him on a tour of the campus. Nathaniel Baker was the newly hired high school math teacher from Gainesville, Georgia. Reverend Oliver introduced him to Deacon Wren and his wife, who lived in Rehoboth. They had renovated their house after their children left home and had a small apartment to rent.

Mr. Baker stood back, waiting for the photos to be taken and for Johnny to receive his congratulations from his family. He wanted to meet Johnny, shake his hand, and tell him he was looking forward to having him in his freshman math class. Elizabeth's beautiful smile caught his eyes, and he prayed there was no man in her life. He stood waiting for the right moment; now it wasn't for Johnny, but for her. Sarah saw him first.

"'Lizabeth, Ah think yuh have an admirer." She used her eyes to draw Elizabeth's attention to Nathaniel Baker. "Now that's what Ah call a man. Look at that beautiful chiseled face and how he fills out that suit. Big sis, Ah think yuh have a suitor. Just look at him.'"

"Stop it, Sarah," Elizabeth smiled. "Ah don't have time tuh be courtin'."

"Honey, yuh missing out on life," Sarah said.

Johnny was still busy receiving his accolades when Mr. Baker walked directly to Elizabeth.

"Ah was waiting tuh congratulate young Mr. Turner when yuh caught my eye. Yuh must be his mother," Mr. Baker said.

Elizabeth smiled and nodded her head. "Yes, Ah'm Elizabeth Turner. It's a pleasure meeting yuh."

"It's more my pleasure," Mr. Baker said. "I remember seeing yuh last week during my campus tour with Mr. Lacy. Ah'll be teaching math at the high school."

"Then, Ah guess Ah'll be seeing a lot of yuh as soon as school begins."

"Ah hope so."

Sarah was standing close behind Elizabeth with both hands on her shoulder like she was going to push her into his arms.

"And may Ah ask who you are?" Mr. Baker said, nodding at Sarah.

"Oh. Um. Ah'm Sarah Turner, Johnny's aunt."

"Nice meeting yuh, Miss Turner."

"Well hello, young man," MaDear said. "Mah name is Anna May Collins. Yuh say yuh a teacher at dis here school?"

"Yes ma'am …" He had been captured by MaDear.

While MaDear had his attention, Sarah pulled at Elizabeth until they had turned away from him.

"'Lizabeth did you hear that voice … and that smile. C'mon girl, live."

"Please, Sarah," Elizabeth said. She turned from Sarah and called Johnny away from her mother and Mr. and Mrs. Harris, giving them a "thank you" smile.

"This is Mr. Baker, he wants to meet yuh." Elizabeth and Johnny waited until Mr. Baker finished talking to MaDear. It was a little funny. MaDear really had a hold on him.

"Yes, ma'am. Yes … yes. Ah know Ah'll be seeing a lot of you. Now if there is anything Ah can do for you, just let me know. As soon as Ah get my telephone Ah'll get my number tuh yuh. May Ah excuse myself?

Ah was waiting tuh congratulate young Mr. Turner. It was nice meeting yuh, Mrs. Collins."

MaDear smiled and glanced at Elizabeth with knowing eyes as Elizabeth introduced Johnny to Mr. Baker.

Mr. Baker extended his hand, and Johnny took hold. "Young Master Turner with the wisdom tuh see the future. Ah'm Nathaniel Baker." He turned loose of Johnny's hand.

Johnny smiled and nodded his head. "Ah haven't seen yuh around here before."

"Oh, Ah'm sorry. Ah'll be teaching math in the high school beginning next semester." Mr. Baker glanced at Elizabeth and back at Johnny. "Ah hope my outburst didn't throw off yuh speech. Yuh were so inspiring. Ah'm looking forward tuh having yuh in my class."

Johnny finally spoke with Drew. Together they planned the trip. During the next few weeks it became a reality. Johnny and Drew had paid more than half the money as their down payment. Johnny also paid Elizabeth's down payment, and knew he would have the expenses for both of them paid by the due date. Loretha wanted to take the trip too, but with Johnny and Elizabeth going, she knew it was more important to stay back and watch over MaDear.

Drew had been Johnny's friend since second grade, but most of the time they only got to see each other at school. They lived on opposite sides of Bibb county, a long-distance telephone call away. Sometimes Johnny would take the school bus to Drew's house. Elizabeth would pick him up after work or, sometimes, he would sleep over and take the school bus back to school the next morning.

In 1963, the first Sunday in June, Elizabeth, Johnny and MaDear returned home from services at the Bethlehem Baptist Church. Johnny was so excited, he could hardly sit still in the car.

"Mama! Mr. Baker joined our church. Ah thought he was gonna join Concord. Yuh-know he lives in that apartment at Deacon Wren's house."

"Ah know, Johnny. Ah'm happy he chose Bethlehem over Concord, too."

"Ah like him, Mama. Maybe he's gonna go on the march."

"Ah'm sho' he will," MaDear said. She slowly turned her head and looked at Elizabeth, smiling.

Elizabeth turned onto MaDear's bumpy private road. The car bounced when it rode over a large oak tree root. All of their heads wobbled, and they laughed. It wasn't about the tree root. They all knew he would be going on the march.

"Mama, can Ah ride my bike over tuh Deacon Wren's and visit Mr. Baker?"

"Only if yuh call him first. Ah'll have yuh gram'ma get his telephone number from Deacon Wren."

"Thanks, Mama."

Elizabeth thought about Sarah. This was the kind of things sisters would call each other and talk about. But Sarah and Elizabeth didn't have that kind of relationship. When Sarah came home she'd ask for an update, but she'd never take the time to call or write. When Elizabeth called her, Sarah always seemed to rush through their conversation, never seeming excited for her or laughing and giggling over the silly things. So when Elizabeth found out Mr. Baker would be riding with them to D.C., she didn't have her sister to share this tender moment with.

On August 28, 1963, Loretha and MaDear watched the television all day. There were hundreds of thousands of people in Washington, but for some reason they had hoped they would see Johnny, Elizabeth, and Drew on television, knowing that was almost impossible. Mr. Baker was Reverend Lipton's assistant, and it was his responsibility to provide information to all the passengers: check suitcases, coolers, assign motel rooms, and keep track of everyone, making sure they arrived home safely.

Reverend Lipton, a small man in his early fifties, had a charming smile and eyes that could put a person at ease. His wife died of cancer when his two daughters were young, and he was left to raise them to adulthood alone. His grandfather was the founder of the Bethlehem Baptist Church, donating five acres of roadside land, and the black community known as "Victory" came together to built the structure.

Victory was approximately seven miles west of the community of Rehoboth. Like the Concord Baptist Church, the Bethlehem Baptist Church was the cornerstone of that community. Reverend Lipton was the first of his family to receive the calling to preach the gospel, and when a minister was needed for the church, more than twenty years earlier, he was voted in by the members. Most of the deacons and trustees were in their twilight years, and it wasn't long before Nathaniel Baker became Reverend Lipton's right hand man.

It had been three months since Mr. Baker met Elizabeth. She told him she didn't take company, but agreed to accept his friendship.

"Then we'll just have to be friends until yuh ready," was Mr. Baker's response.

He sat beside her all the way to Washington D.C., and would keep the same seat during the return trip. They talked and laughed until sleep came over her. His heart raced as he watched her resting her head on the back of the seat. He turned to keep her in his sight. Elizabeth squirmed and shifted. The headrest on the seat was designed for a taller person, and caused her to bend her neck in an uncomfortable position. She squirmed and shifted her body again and found comfort when she placed her head against Nathaniel's chest. His arm was on the armrest, but suddenly it was under her, supporting and cushioning her back from the armrest.

Nathaniel held his head up with the side of his face against the back of the seat. He took deep breaths and exhaled slowly so as not to disturb her. This was a period of time he wanted to hold onto forever. *Oh, Lord, keep this woman for me. Ah'll wait for her forever. Ah love her so much, and Ah really believe she loves me.*

After an hour or so, Nathaniel fell asleep. He realized several hours had passed when the bus stopped in upstate South Carolina so the relief driver could take over and they were on their way again. Elizabeth stirred, and Nathaniel prayed she wouldn't wake up. He knew it would be a long time before he would have her that close to him again.

Hours later, the bus reached its final destination at the Lincoln Memorial. Nathaniel had to attend to the duties assigned to him, and leaving Elizabeth was very hard to do.

—⧓—

Reverend Turner, Sarah, Malcolm, Thea, and Reverend Oliver had taken the bus from Concord Baptist Church, but Loretha and MaDear weren't looking for them. They hadn't worked so hard to get there, so it didn't seem to mean as much to them.

The bus trips from Bethlehem and Concord Churches were truly independent of each other, even though their destinations were the same. The buses were scheduled to stop at a designated spot in Alexandria, Virginia. All those who wanted to march into Washington with Reverend King could got off there. Others could use the time to check into the motel, and then take the bus to the Lincoln Memorial.

Elizabeth decided to stay with the bus, and prayed this would allow her to get a good, up close spot. She looked at the boys who were willing to go along with whatever decision she made. Drew's brown skin and dimpled face were a contrast to Johnny's very serious look. She observed the two boys with the same dreams and aspirations, who expressed their excitement in two entirely different ways. Tall, skinny, lanky Johnny and short, round, pudgy Drew were as different in appearance as two boys could be, but they both believed in the promise of change and a better life for their generation. Elizabeth prayed it would be so.

Johnny and Drew were moved by the thought of seeing Reverend King. When the bus arrived in Washington, they fought to be as close to the podium as possible. It took hours to get there, so instead of resting or eating, they stepped lightly through the thick crowds until they could see the faces of all the people setting up the equipment on the stage. Elizabeth had a small metal cooler stored with food and drinks for the day, and Johnny and Drew took turns carrying it. When they found a good spot, they knew they had to remain steadfast to keep it.

It was hot, and Elizabeth thought she was going to faint. Even if she wanted to leave to find shelter from the heat, there was no way she could get through the thick crowd. The boys were drenched with perspiration, but they didn't seem uncomfortable. They were standing in a good spot, midway between the man-made lake and the steps of the Lincoln Memorial. Elizabeth looked back at the shade trees surrounding the lake and decided to endure the heat for the opportunity to see and hear Reverend King in person.

"Boys, do yuh have clean handkerchiefs?"

Both boys nodded, and then looked at each other wondering why she asked about their handkerchiefs.

"It's so hot out here. Ah'm afraid we all might have a heat stroke. Take yuh handkerchiefs and soak 'em in the ice water from the cooler. Then tie them around yuh necks. Yuh can even take some of that cold water and wet yuh hair. That should keep yuh cool."

The boys did as they were told, and Elizabeth could see the relief on their faces. She used her wet handkerchief to pat her face and neck.

"Here, Mama, put some water on yuh head. It really feels good."

"Oh no, Johnny! Yuh want my hair tuh kink up? Ah wish Ah could … Ah tell yuh what … pour a little on the back of my blouse. That should cool me off." Elizabeth was so hot she didn't care what the other people thought, but when she looked around, other people were doing the same thing. When the cold water hit her back, she made a soft startled sound and arched her spine backward. "Aaahhh! That feels really good," she cooed.

———✳———

Johnny had lived his short life in a segregated society and was amazed at the composition of people. The enormous gathering of people looked like black pepper with sprinkles of salt. "MaDear was right. All white people don't hate blacks," he mumbled.

"What did yuh say, Johnny?" Elizabeth asked.

"Mama, look at all the white people. MaDear told me all white people ain't bad."

"Yuh right, honey, but never let yuh guard down."

The roar from the assembly of the chattering people made it difficult to hear. The multitude was thick. The excitement of a promise of change, of freedom from oppression, of equality, glittered in everyone's eyes. The power. Everyone could feel the power. The power supported by the masses. The speeches from the movement's leaders and the songs of the entertainers set the stage for the man of the time, "The Reverend Martin Luther King Jr."

Suddenly, it was quiet enough to hear a still breeze. Elizabeth looked at Johnny, who appeared mesmerized by this man and the words he spoke. Words that challenged the nation's conscience. Enchanted by the soothing, rhythmic sounds of the eloquent words, words spoken so beautifully, Johnny was able to capture the concept of his themes. He could visualize Lincoln signing the Emancipation Proclamation and the Negro slaves rejoicing at the thought of freedom.

Ah never thought of it that way … The Emancipation Proclamation was a promissory note. A check. A bad check. For one hundred years, it has been a "bad check."

"Yes!" Johnny responded, while the people roared. *He's demanding that the nation honor its check.*

"Yes!" he yelled out again.

Ah like those words, cash the check and give us the "riches of freedom and the security of justice." They can cash the check and change the laws, but they can't change the way white people think. That was what they did with the Emancipation Proclamation. But he said the "security of justice." The "security of justice" will ensure the "riches of freedom."

"Now is the time!" Johnny heard ringing between the roars of the crowd. "Now is the time to make real the promise of democracy," Reverend King said.

Now is the time tuh cash that check. Johnny listened and looked around at the waves of people. His people, black and white. If they were there, they were his people. *MaDear said all white people ain't bad.*

Johnny was roused by the repetitive phases highlighting his message. "Now is the time … ," "We can never be satisfied … ," "I have a dream … ," "With this faith … ," "Let freedom ring …" and finally "Free at last." Johnny absorbed the words. He absorbed the message. He wanted more. He wanted to hear it again, and again.

Suddenly, the enthusiasm of the populace broke through the quiet with the cheers and cries for the possibility of a promise, for the realization of a dream. Johnny was too overwhelmed to speak. He couldn't yell or cheer. He could only stand there, hanging on the poetic words of a man that gave him a promise of a vision for his success in life. He wanted more, to hear more. Johnny didn't want the moment to end.

There were more songs and words of inspiration. When it was over, Johnny, Drew and Elizabeth were shuffled along by the crowd to the waiting buses. Johnny and Drew shared a room at the motel. Elizabeth roomed with one of the ladies from the church.

They were tired and hungry. The small restaurant attached to the motel filled with people waiting for service. Elizabeth and the boys ordered take out meals and ate in the quiet of the boys' room. They watched the news coverage of the day's events on the small black and white pay TV, which swallowed up a dime every half an hour. Someone knocked on the door, and Elizabeth hurried to answer it.

"Hello, Elizabeth. Ah hope Ah'm not intruding, but all my duties are complete, and Ah was hoping Ah could spend a little quiet time with yuh this evening."

Elizabeth looked back at the boys, eased the door closed, and stood in front of it. "Ah can't do that."

"Oh, Elizabeth, it's a beautiful night. Please just come out and sit on the bench with me. Just friends. Please, just for a little while."

"Mr. Baker, it's late, and we've both had a long day. Yuh should be gettin' some rest. We'll be sittin' together all the way home."

"I'll let yuh out of it this time, but yuh have to promise me one thing."

"What is it?" Elizabeth whispered softly. She blushed and allowed Mr. Baker to take her right hand.

"Do you think you could call me Nathaniel? If you can't, Ah'm gonna have my last name changed tuh Nathaniel."

Elizabeth laughed. "Okay, Nathaniel. Ah kinda like callin' yuh Nathaniel. Ah'll call yuh Nathaniel when we're together. Is that okay? Ah'll see yuh in the mornin'."

"It's a start. Ah'll see yuh in my dream tuhnight."

Elizabeth blushed and smiled, then backed into the motel room door.

———— ∽ ————

The bus was scheduled to leave at 6:00 A.M. the next morning. People began boarding by 5:15. They were exhausted, which was evident by their sluggish movements and the weariness in their faces, but there was a glow in their eyes. Nathaniel Baker assisted people, placing their coolers and bags in the luggage bays under the bus. He carried a clipboard and checked off their names as they boarded, reminding them to let him know if they got off the bus for any reason. Reverend King's inspiration surrounded the passengers, and for most, this would be their only active participation in the Civil Rights Movement. Some felt guilty that so many had suffered for the cause while they stood back and followed the events on the newsreels and in newspapers.

Although the movement was nonviolent, the responses from the white resisters were to the contrary. Some blacks vowed they would become more active in the movement, while others dug deep in their pockets to fulfill their obligations, and still others spoke about what they were going to do, only to procrastinate and do nothing.

CHAPTER 14

Fall, October 17, 1963, MaDear slipped away to be with her Lord. Elizabeth missed her in the kitchen fussing and fixing breakfast. She missed the aroma of coffee seeping into her room, the smell of bacon and ham, the clanking of pots and pans. She missed the love of MaDear.

Elizabeth walked from her room into the kitchen; next she walked across the sitting area to MaDear's room. She called her name, tapped on her door before opening it. She noticed MaDear was still asleep, but a different kind of sleep. She looked so peaceful, a smile gracing her face. A smile that said, "So long, see you later, I'm going home now." Elizabeth knew her time had come. She walked back into the kitchen and called her mother. Just then, Johnny staggered into the kitchen.

The Almighty was ready for MaDear. She went home in the still of the early morning. Johnny remembered MaDear preparing him, telling him, warning him that her time was near. She was his MaDear. The warmest person he knew. He thought his heart was breaking. His crying continued for hours, and seemed to paralyze him with a stiffness that frightened his mother. Elizabeth called the doctor, and he was given a sedative that allowed sleep to shroud his sorrow. As the days passed, sleep made MaDear's passing bearable.

The only Negro funeral parlor was near Macon. It was hard for most of MaDear's friends to travel that far. The funeral was three days after her passing, and the wake that night. Loretha had explained to the funeral director the detail of MaDear's final wishes. She wanted her funeral in the old way. Loretha instructed him not to erase her "going home smile." MaDear's body would lay in her bronze casket in her living room. Elizabeth agreed, wanting to be near MaDear as long as she could before her remains went into the cold, damp earth. It would be placed against the back wall between Elizabeth and Johnny's bedroom.

The living room furniture was moved to the shed, and some of the smaller pieces were placed in the sitting room to make room for the wake and to receive MaDear's friends after the funeral. Forty wooden chairs were set up in four rows, with an aisle down the middle, and an additional ten chairs were set up in the kitchen and in the sitting room.

It was difficult for Johnny to see MaDear lying still in the casket. But if she had to leave him, it was okay for her body to spend its last days above the earth, in her home, near him. He was quiet during the wake. People couldn't help noticing how difficult MaDear's death was on him. Loretha sat in the front row of the first aisle and held him tightly with her arm around him most of the time. His eyes were swollen, his heart hurt, and his chest was heavy.

Mr. Baker sat directly behind Johnny in the second row with other church members and friends from work. Elizabeth, Sarah, and Reverend Turner sat next to Loretha. Malcolm and Thea were at the wake and sat in the third row in the second aisle, but without Reverend Oliver. Reverend Lipton said a few words about Mrs. Collins and led her friends in prayer. Nathaniel Baker led a few members of the choir in singing two songs: "In My Home Over There" and "I'll Fly Away."

Reverend Turner turned toward Thea and Malcolm, his eyes remaining on them for several seconds. He wasn't paying attention to the words of the song, but he could hear the melody. He searched his pocket for his handkerchief and covered his mouth about the same time Mr. Baker and the other choir members were on the second stanza of the first song. Reverend Turner stood and walked to the doorway of the living room that led to the kitchen. Tears were traveling down his face while his eyes searched every face in the room. He wiped his tears, smiled at Loretha and his daughters, and walked over to MaDear. He leaned over and kissed her on the forehead and whispered, "Thank you for being here for 'Lizabeth and Johnny."

Mr. Baker and the choir were just finishing up the first song when John walked past Loretha, wiping away his tears, and not looking at any of them. He hurriedly retreated to the sitting room, knelt at Mrs. Collins' chair and wiped away more tears. He held his hand up, covering the bridge of his nose with his thumb and forefinger.

Dear Lord,

Where is Owen? Are yuh telling me he is the one? Are yuh showing me, Lord? Ah'm the coward. Lord, give me the strength. Show me the truth.

"John," he heard Loretha calling.

Help me Lord. Ah ask in Jesus name. Amen.

He opened his eyes, and Loretha was standing in the doorway of the sitting room.

"Ah'm all right, Loretha. Mr. Baker's singing moved me." He walked closer to her at the same time she was walking toward him. The tears began to fill his eyes again. They embraced.

"The Lord showed me the love Mrs. Collins gave my family. Yuh have no idea the revelation that came tuh me from Mrs. Collins' passing. She was there when Ah wasn't, and Ah never thanked her. Now she's gone. It's too late, Loretha. Ah kissed her and thanked her for caring for my family," he sobbed. After a few moments, he released his hold on Loretha and sat on the wooden folding chair. Mr. Baker and the choir were just finishing up the second song. "Ah think we should return to the living room." He wiped his face again, and they walked back together.

Reverend Lipton was reminding the mourners of the arrangement for the procession. The benediction was said, and the wake was over. The mourners milled about for another fifteen minutes or so before the house was quiet and left to Elizabeth and Johnny.

Johnny went to his room to be alone. He laid in his bed, staring up at the ceiling. Suddenly, he witnessed images merging into a billowy haze that seemed to filter a bright blue-white light. He felt a floating sensation that lifted his body, spirit, and emotions. MaDear came to him. She said the words she had spoken almost daily about her time coming near. She told Johnny to be good, think good thoughts and do good deeds all of his life. She promised she would be with him again for all of eternity, and there would be no more good-byes.

She said, "Take care of yuh mama, Boy. Take good care of yuh mama." Her image and voice faded into the blue-white light, and she was gone. Johnny opened his eyes and searched the room. It seemed only moments had passed, but it had been several hours. "Was Ah dreaming? Maybe … but MaDear would find a way tuh talk tuh me one more time," he whispered. He went to the living room to see her again.

"MaDear. Yuh tried tuh prepare me, but Ah didn't wanna hear nothing about yuh dying or going home. Ah didn't know Ah could hurt so much. But yuh know … MaDear … Ah don't think anything yuh had tuh say could have prepared me for this. Ah remember yuh telling me that yuh weren't afraid, but yuh were afraid for me. Well … Ah'm all right now. Ah'm sorry Ah made yuh worry about me. Ah couldn't help myself. Ah had tuh cry, tuh get it all out. Then, the medicine made me sleep. Ah almost slept through yuh wake. But Ah'm gonna be okay. Don't worry about me no more. Ah'm gonna try tuh make yuh proud of me … and as soon as yuh get settled in up there, look down on me. Talk tuh me when yuh can …"

The following morning, Elizabeth walked around the chairs near the window to Johnny's bedroom. She wasn't startled when she didn't find him there. She knew he was in the house and would never leave without first telling her. She walked toward the kitchen and let her eyes quickly sweep the living room as she passed through. She could see MaDear lying in peace, but still no Johnny. Concern filled her thoughts, and an edge was attacking her emotions.

"Johnny!" she called out. She was afraid, but didn't want to over react. She waited a few moments for Johnny to respond, but when she didn't hear anything, she called his name again. This time louder, and she recognized the sound of fear in her voice. Suddenly, she located him on the floor between the wooden folding chairs.

"Oh my Lord! My baby," she cried out. She ran to him, got down on her knees and touched him gently on the shoulder. "Johnny? Johnny, honey! What's the matter, baby? Wake up, Johnny!"

"Oh!" Johnny said, waking up startled. "Oh, Mama! Oh!" he said after taking a deep breath. "Ah was talking tuh MaDear, and Ah must have fallen tuh sleep. Ah'm sorry if Ah upset yuh, seeing me on the floor like that."

"Are yuh okay, Johnny?" Elizabeth could feel her heart pounding while she gasped for a few deep breaths of air.

"Ah'm okay."

"Ah was getting a little panicked when Ah couldn't find yuh, but Ah'm okay now." Elizabeth cupped Johnny's face in her two hands and kissed him on the forehead. Then she pulled back and took a good look at him.

"What happened, Johnny?"

"Ah don't know, Mama. Ah was in my bed, and MaDear came tuh me. She reminded me that she didn't want me tuh hurt or be afraid. Yuh-know, Mama, Ah don't know if yuh knew this or not, but MaDear use tuh talk about dying almost every day. She knew her time was near, and she didn't want me tuh hurt. Ah wouldn't listen tuh her. Ah didn't want tuh talk about her death. Ah kept asking her not tuh talk about dying. She said she needed tuh prepare me." Johnny raised his arms and hugged his mother around her neck. Elizabeth kissed him on his forehead and helped him off the floor.

"So how did yuh get in the living room?"

"Ah woke up and wanted tuh be near her one last time. Last night was the only time Ah had tuh be alone with her. So Ah walked in, kissed her, and then sat on the floor. Ah was talking tuh her. Ah guess Ah just talked and talked until Ah fell asleep. She must have wanted me there.

Ah don't know why, but Ah can live with her death now. Mama … do yuh remember when Ah was little and would fall and skin my knee or elbow? And MaDear would say, 'C'mere Johnny-Boy, let me kiss yuh boo-boo and make yuh hurt go away?' Mama … last night … while Ah was sleeping … Ah think MaDear kissed my heart, and made my pain go away. Ah'm okay now. Ah'm really okay. Ah still love her and Ah miss her, but Ah don't hurt anymore. Ah'm sorry yuh had tuh worry about me and take care of everything for MaDear alone."

"Oh, honey, Ah'm so happy yuh feeling better." Elizabeth wrapped her arms around Johnny and kissed him again. "Oh, Gram'ma was a big help. Ah was a mess, too. Ah couldn't do anything. Ah couldn't even think straight. Gram'ma, Sarah, Reverend Lipton and Mr. Baker did most everything."

"Mr. Baker?" Johnny said. "Ah like him."

"Yes, Johnny. He's a good, trusted friend." She smiled and stole a fraction of a moment. "Ah kinda like him, tuh."

Elizabeth watched Johnny walk back toward his room and called to remind him that he had to be dressed and ready for the funeral by 9:00 A.M. She sat at the kitchen table and covered her eyes with both hands, trying to hold back the tears. Everything she did and didn't do reminded her how much she loved and missed MaDear. Then she thought about Johnny again.

He's better. It's like MaDear rocked him tuh sleep. She rocked him tuh sleep just like she did when he was a crying baby. She kissed him, took away his pain and when he woke, he was content. He has bright eyes again.

She wished MaDear could rock her to sleep, kiss her heart and make her pain go away. But if there was only one person to be soothed, she was happy it was Johnny. When she couldn't hold on any more, she removed herself from the kitchen table and went into the privacy of her bedroom and cried.

At 8:00 A.M. sharp, the long black limousine rolled down Collins Road. Soon after, old Bob, Mr. Ghee's sway belly mule, was driven to the house pulling the flatbed hay wagon. MaDear wanted her funeral to be in the old way—no cars in her procession. Most of the cars were left up at the church, others were packed full for the shuttle ride to her home. Several trips were made, until all who wanted to walk in the procession were present.

The house filled with friends. Everyone wore black or navy blue. The women openly carried handkerchiefs that were a bright contrast to their dark cloth gloves. Elizabeth glanced around the living room and was pleased that so many of MaDear's friends had decided to walk in the procession.

Reverend Lipton handed out papers with the lyrics to the songs. They were all specially selected by Elizabeth and Loretha because they were MaDear's favorite: "Precious Lord," "Rock of Ages," "In the Garden," "He Leadeth Me," "When the Morning Comes," and others. These were old country songs, and most of MaDear's friends knew them well.

The hay wagon was draped with black fabric. Johnny watched as MaDear's casket was loaded onto it. Flowers were neatly arranged around the casket.

Johnny, Elizabeth, Sarah, and Loretha were the closest to family MaDear had, so they would be first in the procession. Young men from Concord and Bethlehem Baptist Churches were the pallbearers. MaDear's home church was Concord, but Reverend Lipton presided over the service. Reverend Turner assisted with the service, and the choir from both churches sang a medley of her favorite hymns under the direction of Thea Oliver.

Reverend Lipton, Reverend Turner, and Reverend Oliver walked in front of the wagon, leading the march. They sang the songs the way they were written, in the old way, the way MaDear sang them when she was a child. The mourners followed their lead.

The procession reached the end of Collins Road, turned left onto Rehoboth Road and walked the freshly paved road to the church.

Johnny sang loud and strong and held his head high. As they passed the church cemetery, he could see the newly dug grave. Pain swelled and pounded in his chest. He felt weak. Loretha held him tight. He stopped singing and took several deep breaths to regain his strength.

The mourners sang until they marched into the church. Reverend Turner gave up his seat in the pulpit to Reverend Lipton. He and Reverend Oliver sat in the remaining two chairs. Reverend Turner gazed at Reverend Oliver longer than normal. The service began with opening prayers, scripture readings, and songs from the choir.

Elizabeth noticed Nathaniel sitting in the choir stand behind the pulpit. He gave her a sympathetic nod as she approached the pulpit. She was on the program to speak, and had selected Bible verses that had a special meaning to MaDear. Her voice was soft and soothing, and her soulful spirit brought tears to those in the congregation.

"Dear relatives and friends, we are all here tuh rejoice in the 'Home Goin' service for Mrs. Anna May Collins. We called her 'MaDear.' MaDear always reminded me, saying, 'Liz'beth, the Lawd has made a special time for everything.'" She spoke slowly, and her voice quivered as she wiped away the tears.

The congregation shouted, "Amen," "Praise the Lord," and "Thank you Jesus."

"Ah'd like tuh read tuh yuh from Ecclesiastes 3; verses 1 through 8." Elizabeth paused for another moment and allowed her eyes to sweep the congregation before she continued.

"Tuh everything there is a season and a time tuh every purpose under the heaven:

A time tuh give birth, and a time tuh die." Elizabeth's voice still quivered. She paused to push her sorrow to a place deep inside and wiped tears from the corners of her eyes.

"A time tuh plant, and a time tuh pluck up that which is planted.
A time tuh kill, and a time tuh heal;
A time tuh tear down, and a time tuh build up;
A time tuh weep, and a time tuh laugh;

A time tuh mourn." She paused, knowing she could not continue to speak and control her sorrow at the same time. She took several deep breaths and waited until the quivering in her lips subsided.

"… and a time tuh dance;
A time tuh cast away stones, and a time tuh gather stones;
A time tuh embrace, and a time tuh refrain from embracing." She paused, allowing her eyes to sweep the mourners. She spoke the next four verses from memory, her voice cracking from sorrow as she gazed off to a distant corner of the church.

"A time tuh get, and a time tuh lose;
A time tuh keep … and a time tuh cast away;
A time tuh rend, and a time tuh sew;
A time tuh keep silent, and a time tuh speak." A moment later she bowed her head and blotted her tears before they dropped and soaked the pages of her Bible. She continued to read.

"A time tuh love, and a time tuh hate;
A time of war, and a time of peace."

She looked up at the congregation. "… Ah would like tuh add that it's now a time tuh say so-long tuh MaDear. We loved her, but Our Lord loves her more."

The eulogy was delivered. All of which was a tribute to the fine lady, the kind lady, and one who set the example for tolerance, generosity, benevolence, and compassion. Reverend Lipton reminded the mourners, "Mrs. Anna May Collins has earned her place with the Lord. She has gone home. Ah know she's happy."

Loretha sat with her arm around Johnny. He appeared as though he was trying to hold back his consuming emotions, trying to be a man. Reverend Lipton's words seemed to remind him of how much he was going to miss MaDear.

Reverend Oliver looked at Johnny. The pain in Johnny's eyes caused him to brush his handkerchief over his face, pushing back the pain and sorrow he felt for his son. He wanted to go to him and hold him the way Loretha was holding him.

Loretha handed Johnny her handkerchief and rubbed his shoulder and arm. MaDear was his "Mother-Dear," and now she was gone. Loretha knew he would heal and go on.

Reverend Lipton called for the final viewing, and the funeral director opened the casket. Johnny turned and held tight to his mother and refused to experience another viewing. He had said his goodbye the night before. It was hard for him to walk past the cemetery and see the hole in the ground where she would be placed, and now he had to sit in the front pew and see her lifeless body again. Tears flooded his eyes, and soon his body began to shake. He kept his crying as quiet as he could.

The ushers started at the back of the church, directing people to take advantage of the final viewing. Soon Johnny felt a hand on his shoulder, and he realized Mr. Baker had come down from the choir stand and was asking permission to remove him from the church.

"Mama, may Ah leave with Mr. Baker? Ah said my goodbye tuh MaDear last night. Ah can't do this again," Johnny whispered.

Elizabeth looked up at Mr. Baker, nodded gently, and released her hold on Johnny. Reverend Oliver's eyes locked onto Johnny and Nathaniel Baker as they left the church. It was easy to see he wanted to be the one to comfort Johnny. He sat forward in his chair and held tight to the armrest. Reverend Turner kept a watchful eye on him and pushed his head back on the visiting pastor's chair, closing his eyes. He used his handkerchief to wipe his face and reach for the glass of water on the pedestal between the chairs.

Thea played "Abide With Me," and the mourners sang softly as they strolled past the open casket. Elizabeth and Loretha quietly wept.

The casket was closed.

The three ministers stepped from the pulpit and walked into the center aisle. The casket was wheeled behind them as they approached the door. Elizabeth, Sarah and Loretha followed the casket from the church. Johnny left Mr. Baker's side and joined his mother as soon as she left the church.

"Thank you," Elizabeth mouthed to Mr. Baker, and, in spite of her sorrow, she managed to give him a tiny smile.

Mr. Baker smiled, gave her a gentleman's nod, and watched her walk behind MaDear's casket. He stood at the church's step while others moved forward to the cemetery, then followed them.

The service continued at the cemetery, next to the graves of MaDear's husband and daughter.

At the end of the service, Johnny took a handful of dirt and placed it on the casket. Elizabeth moved to hold him, and Loretha held her back.

"Honey, he's got tuh say his goodbyes. Leave him be for a moment."

Johnny moved his hand, spreading the dirt over the casket. "Ah'm sorry, MaDear. Ah tried to be strong. Ah tried, but Ah'm gonna miss yuh. How can Ah live without yuh?" he cried. He hugged the casket, laying his face against its cold surface. The casket swayed on the canvas straps holding it above the hollowed-out grave. Nathaniel Baker pulled him back. Johnny clung to him, sobbing. He supported Johnny's weight as he led him away from the cemetery.

Reverend Oliver appeared to be visibly shaken at seeing Johnny clinging to Mr. Baker. The sides of his jaws moved to the grinding of his teeth, and his anger traveled down his arms to his hands. He had to slip his hands in his pants pockets to hide his balled-up fists. He missed Johnny, his visits at his home, and at school. Nathaniel Baker had taken his place, and all he received was just a greeting.

Sarah and Elizabeth held each other's hand, and tears flooded their eyes as they left the cemetery. Nathaniel and Johnny followed, and Loretha and Reverend Turner were behind them.

Many people had left their cars at the church, and they were filled for the ride back to MaDear's home.

As soon as the last of MaDear's friends left the house, Loretha decided to leave with Reverend Turner. Elizabeth promised to drive Sarah home. They hadn't seen each other since Johnny's graduation, and had a lot to catch up on. Elizabeth and Sarah were sitting on the sofa in the sitting room when Johnny came in. The ladies looked up, and Mr. Baker was standing in the entrance holding his hat. He nodded his greeting.

"Hello, Nathaniel. Ah don't know if yuh remember my sister, Miss Sarah Turner? She was at Johnny's graduation."

Nathaniel smiled. "Ah'm not sure, but it's a pleasure meeting yuh now." Nat turned his attention to Elizabeth. "Would it be all right if Johnny took a ride with me tuh Macon? Ah have tuh make a quick run on church business."

"Sure, Nathaniel." Elizabeth watched the two men she loved leave the room. There was a gleam in her eye that Sarah didn't let escape her, and she smiled.

"How come Ah didn't see you when we went on the March?" Elizabeth said.

"Oh, Mama didn't tell yuh the bus picked me up in Atlanta? Wasn't no need tuh come down here tuh ride back through Atlanta. Enough about me, what's goin' on with you and that Mr. Baker?"

"We're friends. We sat tuhgether on the bus tuh D.C. Ah know he really likes me, and Ah like him, too. He joined Bethlehem and joined the choir. Last Sunday we sang a duet—an arrangement of 'Peace, Be Still.' The choir came in on the chorus. It was beautiful. That man has a voice yuh could die for. We're both on the Missionary Board, and he was voted as the church's treasurer. Ah guess because of his math background. Reverend Lipson said he didn't know how he managed without him."

"Elizabeth, Ah know Ah've never been there for yuh. Ah can't tell yuh tuh date him, but it sounds like Mr. Baker loves you. Ah date all the time, and Ah've never found anyone Ah wanted to spend my life with, and yuh Mr. Right is right here."

"Ah could spend my life with him, but Ah'm not ready. We're friends, and Ah hope he remains my friend until Johnny is ready tuh leave for college."

"Leave for college? Big sis, yuh expect that man tuh wait for yuh for four years?"

"If he doesn't, Ah'll understand. It's better than being hurt."

"Who am Ah tuh talk. Ah've been running away from yuh since Ah was thirteen, and Ah'm still running. Ah couldn't wait until it was time tuh leave for college, Ah love yuh more than life, but the guilt pushed me away."

"Sarah, Ah'm not tryin' tuh be mean, but when Johnny was a baby, yuh use tuh come tuh see him. Yuh use tuh visit him until he was about three years old, then yuh stopped. Until this day, Ah don't remember yuh spending more than two or three minutes with him, but yuh come tuh all his events. What's the matter, Sarah, are yuh afraid of him, too?"

Sarah held her head down. It was impossible to face Elizabeth and be honest. "Ah don't hate Johnny, and Ah know our family's dilemma was not his fault, but when Ah see him, Ah don't know what tuh say tuh him. Mama use tuh make me visit y'all. Ah did, and Ah pretended tuh be happy about it. That person that raped yuh, raped all of us. Ah think Ah could kill him if it would bring back our old life. Ah love Johnny, but it's the pain. Ah'm hiding from the pain. Ah was young, and Daddy was hurting. Mama was hurting, too, but she had you, MaDear, and Johnny. Daddy had no one. Yuh-know, 'Lizabeth, it's what happened here. Ah associate this place with pain. Ah love Johnny. He's a wonderful young man, but Ah never allowed myself the time tuh get tuh know him. Ah only come home when Ah have tuh; when Mama or Daddy call me."

"That's so sad, Sarah," Elizabeth said. They hugged each other for the first time in more years than either of them could remember, and for longer than the normal duration of a hug.

CHAPTER 15

It was the end of Johnny's first year in high school. The way he saw it, it was the most trying year he had experienced in all of his fourteen years. He cried almost every night for MaDear. He believed the pain of losing her was almost more than he could bear. A month after MaDear's death, his mother's car refused to go another mile, and it wasn't worth the cost of repairs—another part of MaDear had slipped away. Elizabeth bought a brand new 1964 Chevy II fully loaded for $3,265.00, putting $1500.00 down and financing the remaining $1,765.00.

Johnny had a week before he was due to start his summer job. He always seemed lost without a grueling daily schedule. He had a few friends, but they lived in the communities that surrounded Rehoboth. Most of the boys in Rehoboth were Malcolm's friends. It was late May, and already too hot to ride his bike long distances during the heat of the day. Reading a good book while sprawled across his bed, with the window fan cooling the hot air, was a more acceptable option.

Elizabeth called Johnny into the kitchen. There was an issue she wanted to speak with him about. She sat at the table with statements from the bank, one for her and two for Johnny. She also had a letter from the county that she wasn't quite ready to share with him. She placed both elbows on the table and buried her fingers in her hair. A pile of paper rested on the table between her arms. Her head was bowed, and she looked like she was crying.

"Mama!" Johnny sounded worried seeing his mother like that.

Elizabeth raised her head slowly, frightening him more. "Oh, Johnny, Ah'm okay. Ah dozed a minute. Come here and sit." She patted the table. "Ah want tuh go over a few things with yuh."

"Yuh sure yuh okay?" He walked toward her slowly.

"C'mon, Johnny, Ah'm tired." She brushed her hair back and sat up a little taller. She began talking before he sat in his seat. "Ah never told yuh something, but now Ah believe yuh're man enough tuh know. It has tuh do with a lot of money yuh have."

Johnny slid into his seat. "Ah have a lot of money?"

"Oh that got yuh moving, didn't it? Well ... MaDear left yuh $10,956.46. She left that money for yuh in a trust fund. Do yuh know what that means?"

"No." He shook his head.

"Okay, that means yuh can't spend it 'til yuh eighteen, and with interest it'll be more by then. Now yuh also have $11,136.00 in the same bank. Ah been saving this for yuh. Every month a fifty-dollar bill comes wrapped in white paper, and the postmark is from Macon. Ah believe it's from the man who's yuh father. Ah'd say yuh a rich man."

"Who's the fifty-dollar bill from?" Johnny placed his hand on Elizabeth's hand to get her attention and stop her from talking.

"All Ah know is that it comes from Macon. There is no return address, and it's never signed. Ah just take it that it's meant for you, so Ah been savin' it. It started comin' a month after yuh were born and has come every month since then. Ah put it in the bank under my name, but it's yuh money. That money includes the interest it's earned over the years. Ah been savin' it for yuh education." Elizabeth knew he would need tuh be comforted. She let her depression force her words, but she withheld words about whom she believed his father to be. She pulled her chair close to his, put her arm around him, rubbed his face and kissed his forehead.

"So my father is alive, and he's out there watching me. He knows me, but Ah don't know him." Johnny was quiet.

"Johnny, please don't get sour on me. Yuh my little man. Ah pray every day yuh father will show himself. He cares or he wouldn't send the money. Ah need my little man tuh stay strong. Ah didn't tell yuh this tuh cause yuh pain. Ah thought yuh were old enough tuh know." Elizabeth kissed him on the cheek. "Now look at me. Okay. Yuh my man."

"Yes, Mama. Ah'm okay." He jumped from his chair and started hopping and skipping around the kitchen table. "Ah'm a rich man." He slipped back into his chair, a huge smile on his face. He started jotting down the figures and adding them up. "Mama! Ah have *twenty-two thousand, ninety-two dollars and forty-six cents* and it's growing. Thank yuh Mama for saving that money for me." He stood, went behind her chair and wrapped his arms loosely around her neck.

Elizabeth laid her head on his arm, and he leaned over and kissed her face.

"Mama, did yuh need me for anything else?" He stood, turned to face her and held her hand.

"No, Johnny, except that Ah would like tuh hold yuh forever."

"C'mon, Mama, remember, Ah'm yuh little man. Ah'm a little tuh big for that." He laughed.

"No. Yuh can go on, Johnny."

Elizabeth stood, followed him to the back door, and watched him take off through the path in the woods. She had watched him ride down that path many times. He rode fast and a little reckless. She only worried that he would fall from his bike and injure himself. She prayed to the Lord to keep him safe.

Johnny was out of the woods in less than ten minutes. Loretha was hanging out the wash in the back yard. She had her back to the path. Suddenly, twigs were cracking, and old leaves that carpeted the forest floor from winters past made a crunching sound under the bike's tires.

"Hi Gram'ma," Johnny called out as he coasted by, waving one hand high and smiling and singing out, "Ah'm a rich man, Gram'ma. Ah got love. Ah got love."

"Johnny stop! Where yuh going?" Loretha dropped the wet sheet back into the basket, removed the clothespin from between her teeth, and hurried after him.

Johnny circled his bike around and lowered it to the ground. He dropped his head and waited for his grandmother. "Sorry, Gram'ma. Ah guess yuh thought Ah was crazy coming out of the woods like that."

"Come up here on the back porch and sit with me." She turned and walked toward the screened in porch. The door screeched from the rusty spring when she opened it.

Johnny was right behind her. "Is Grandfather here?" He looked around, expecting to be greeted by his cold, unwanting eyes.

"It don't matter if he is. C'mon now, sit right here and talk tuh me. Do yuh want some lemonade? Let me get yuh some lemonade."

"No! No! Gram'ma. Ah'm okay." He grabbed her by the arm when she stood.

"Now, what this yellin', 'Ah'm rich, and Ah got love?'" Her brow picked up lines Johnny never noticed before.

"Mama was tellin' me 'bout the money Ah had. She told me 'bout the money she was savin' for me and 'bout how it came every month. She said she thought it was from my father." He rubbed his knees and turned away from his grandmother. He took a deep breath, threw his head back and stared up at the porch rafter beams. "Ah just figured he must love me, and y'all loved me, and when Ah added up that money and MaDear's money, Ah said Ah was rich."

"Johnny, look at me." Loretha waited until his eyes met with hers. "Did it make yuh feel sad that he was around and he never came tuh yuh?" She searched his eyes for the truth. He tried to turn away. "No, Johnny, look at me when yuh answer."

Johnny took a deep breath and kept his eyes on his grandmother. He fought back his emotions, believing making her sad wouldn't change anything. He took another deep breath. "No, Gram'ma. Ah'm rich with love." He held his teeth tight and his deep breaths kept his lips from quivering. He threw his arms around her. "Ah love yuh Gram'ma. Ah'll take that lemonade now." He laughed out loud, more out of relief than happiness.

Loretha hurried into the house and returned with a tall glass of lemonade. Johnny drank it down quickly, and told his grandmother he was going to Reverend Oliver's house.

"Ah hope Malcolm isn't there." He shrugged his left shoulder up to meet his head and smirked his face. "Anyway, Ah gotta go. Thanks, Gram'ma." He picked up his bike and rode away yelling, "Ah got love!"

"He's in yuh hands, Lord. He's Yuh special child." She pulled up her apron and wiped her tears. "Damn that Oliver."

———〰———

Johnny rode his bike to his waiting place near Reverend Oliver's house. He didn't see any sign of Malcolm, but Reverend Oliver was leaving his house and walking toward his car. Johnny mounted his bike and pounced down on the peddle, but the bike spun out, kicking up road dust and gravel from the back wheel. He tried it again, taking it easy on the peddle, just as Reverend Oliver closed the car door, and he had traction. He called out his name and road his bike as fast as he could. He managed to meet up with Reverend Oliver just as he was leaving his driveway.

"Johnny, it's a surprise seeing yuh here. Whatcha doing up this way before noon." He was so happy to see him all of his pearly whites were gleaming.

"Ah was hoping Ah could see yuh. Ah kinda miss yuh. Ah was waiting down there hoping tuh see yuh." Johnny turned and pointed down the road.

"Yuh hide out and wait tuh see me?" He raised his head to see better, but when his eyes met with his innocent face and the sun, he pulled down the brim of his fedora, and it blocked his view.

"Yes, sir!" Johnny said, bending over to see him.

"Hey, would yuh like tuh ride tuh Macon with me? Ah have a few things tuh pick up. Yuh can leave yuh bike here and call yuh mother for permission." He smiled up at him, and this time he let the sun shine in his face. "Don't worry, Malcolm's not home, and even if he was, he knows better than tuh bother yuh."

———m———

Elizabeth hurried to the sitting room to answer the phone. She smiled when she heard Johnny's voice and eased into MaDear's chair.

"Mama, can Ah go with Reverend Oliver tuh Macon? He has some errand tuh run, and said Ah could go with him."

Elizabeth's heart banged against her chest wall, and all her energy was sucked out of her.

"Mama! Did yuh hear me?" She heard Johnny say. "Ya, yes Johnny, go on, have a nice time."

"Thanks, Mama. Yuh have a nice day, tuh."

Elizabeth hung up the telephone and remained in MaDear's chair for a long while. She could feel MaDear's eyes watching her, and got up and turned the chair around. "Ah know, Ah remember yuh telling me about Johnny getting close tuh Reverend Oliver. He ain't got nobody else, MaDear." She rested her head and closed her eyes.

"'Lizabeth! Wake up 'Lizabeth," Loretha called and tapped her gently on the shoulder.

"Oh, hi, Mama." She stretched and yawned. "What time is it? Ah must've fell asleep. Did Johnny come back yet?"

"Where did Johnny go? The last time Ah saw him he came off of the path yelling 'bout being rich and about being loved." Loretha walked in the kitchen and took a seat at the table, and Elizabeth followed her. "We talked a while, and he told me about the monthly money. He didn't seem sad. Seem happy about being loved. He had some lemonade, and he rode off."

"Yes, Mama, Ah told him about the bank accounts. That's why this table is in such a mess." She started picking up papers and stacking them. "Johnny took a ride with Reverend Oliver. He called for permission, and Ah said it was okay."

Loretha stood, staring at her. She brushed back the hair that was tickling the side of her face. "Yuh said it was okay?" She turned away before Elizabeth could answer.

"Mama, he's so lonely. He has no one else. Besides, you should see how much time he spends with him at school. Mama, please." Loretha turned around, and Elizabeth placed her hand over her mother's. "Ah was happy tuh have Johnny away for a while. Ah need tuh talk tuh yuh about something real important."

Elizabeth picked through the papers on the table until she found the one from the county. "Mama, Ah have a letter here from the county officials telling me Ah have tuh move from MaDear's house and land." Her brown skin picked up a reddish tint and tears seemed to come from nowhere to run down her face. "As much as MaDear loved, protected, and tried tuh prepare us for her death, none of us knew she needed tuh make a will. Mama, the house and land is now the property of the state because we're not her real kin, and she has no real kin that they could find. MaDear changed the bank account and made Johnny the benefactor. There was $10,956.46 in the account in a trust fund for him, but we have tuh find somewhere else tuh live." She lifted her apron and wiped her face, but the tears continued to flow. Loretha had moved to be closer to her and was reading the letter from over her shoulder. "The letter said if we moved within thirty days, we wouldn't have to pay the back rent tuh the month after MaDear's death."

Loretha removed the letter from her hands and stood staring at it. "When did you get this letter?"

"Yesterday. Ah had tuh sign for it. As soon as Ah read it, Ah went tuh the county land office. Ah spoke tuh one of their officers. He was smiling and chewin' tobacco the whole time he was talkin' tuh me. Ah ask him if Ah could buy the land and house? And all he said was, 'Ain't fer sale, little lady.' He laughed and spit in a bucket near his desk. Mama, they stole MaDear's land. Ah don't know how tuh tell Johnny. He's lost so much in just one year."

Elizabeth stood and her mother wrapped her arms around her. They each needed the shoulder of the other to cry on. The shoulder tops of their dresses were wet from tears. "No matter how bad things seem tuh be, there is always someone who is worse off."

Elizabeth pulled back using the back of her hands to wipe her eyes. "Mama, what did yuh say?"

"Yuh heard me right. Now let's get down tuh business. Sit down." Loretha was ready to move on. She put on a fresh pot of coffee and sat at the table. "Are yuh ready tuh move on with yuh life?" Elizabeth nodded. "Okay we need a plan. 'Lizabeth, yuh know Mr. and Mrs. James? They have that cute little house across from Concord. They have eight acres and the house is nice and clean. Well, they want $15,000.00 for the house and land." Loretha got up and got the cups and saucers for the coffee.

"Mama, we can't afford that. Ah bought the car, and Ah only have $6,500.00 left." She went to the refrigerator for the milk and placed the bottle on the table.

Loretha picked up the pot and poured coffee in each cup. "Honey, yuh could probably get them tuh come down on the price a couple of thousand, and use some of Johnny's money tuh make up the difference." She turned to place the pot back on the stove.

"Mama, Ah can't touch Johnny's money." She stood, holding the milk bottle, almost frozen with disbelief. "The reason why that money is there has caused me more pain than yuh could ever imagine. Ah'd rather live in 'the bottoms' than use that money."

Loretha placed both hands on the back of the chair. "No, honey. The reason why that money is there has caused yuh more joy than yuh could ever have imagined. Yuh got Johnny. What caused Johnny tuh be, and how he entered this world, was the painful part, the money didn't come from that." Loretha moved closer to Elizabeth and placed her hands on her hips. Her head rocked on her neck like it was made of rubber. "Now yuh listen tuh me, yuh don't really know what living down there is like. People don't live down there, they just survive … and yuh don't have those kind of survival skills. 'Lizabeth … Ah can't believe yuh'd take Johnny tuh live down there, tuh the slum, the ghetto, and pay that high rent for a shack, rats, garbage, and dirt roads."

Elizabeth put the milk away and sat at her place at the table. "Mama! Look at Johnny. He's fourteen years old and smart. In four years, he'll be off tuh college. He's gonna need that money for school. Ah'm not worried about 'the bottoms' getting him. Yuh told me he's gonna be somebody someday. All that money, he's gonna need it tuh give him a boost. Ah know Ah can find a house tuh rent. Something Ah can afford … somewhere … and especially down there, if Ah have tuh."

Loretha was hurt and disappointed. She didn't want Elizabeth and Johnny way over on the other side of town, in the pit of hell, living in a three room, unpainted shack. Where the dirt roads were so narrow cars couldn't drive through. Where rents were high, the strong victimized the weak, where hope and aspirations didn't exist.

She knew Elizabeth would never come back home. Except for the public celebrations of Johnny's achievements when Reverend Turner gloated, there was no change in their relationship.

Elizabeth was afraid she had hurt her mother's feelings; that she had been disrespectful and unthankful for her help. "Mama, Ah'm sorry. Let's enjoy our coffee. Ah have some cake that we can have. As soon as Johnny comes in we'll have to tell him, and we'll take it from there."

Johnny and Reverend Oliver were on their way to Macon. The car windows were rolled all the way down, and Reverend Oliver was driving close to 55 miles per hour. Johnny sat quietly, not the talkative young man he knew. "What the matter, Johnny?"

"Ah'm a rich man. Ah got love." Tears were running down his face.

Reverend Oliver glanced over at him. It was a hot day, and he wasn't sure if it was sweat or tears on Johnny's face. It was so noisy in the car with the window's down he wasn't sure he heard him, but he was sure there was something wrong. He saw a clearing in a closed up store parking lot. He slowed down and pulled in, parking the car under the shade of a large oak tree. He got out of the car and hurried around to Johnny's side. "Come, Johnny, get out and come around back where it's cooler." He took his handkerchief and wiped the perspiration from the back of his neck. "Now, what did you say?"

Johnny dug one hand in his pocket, walked to the back of the car and rested his backside against it. "Ah'm a rich man. Ah got love."

Reverend Oliver checked out Johnny's eyes and handed him his handkerchief from the breast pocket of his suit jacket. "Johnny, what does that mean?"

"There's a man, Ah think he's my father." Johnny began to cry. There was no mistaking his attempts at trying to hold back his sobs, but tears poured from his eyes. "This man has made me rich. He sent my mother money every month—a fifty-dollar bill." He held the hand-kerchief over his eyes and a high-pitched moan escaped his body. It sounded like it was coming from the back of his throat.

Reverend Oliver reached to hold and comfort him.

"No! Ah'm a man." He wiped his face. "Ah'm okay."

"Can yuh continue?"

"Mama said Ah'm a man now, so she told me Ah had over $11,100.00. She saved every fifty-dollar bill. Now Ah know there's a man out there who knows me, and he is probably watching me. Ah hope he loves me. Ah don't know him. So Ah'm, Ah'm … rich … and Ah'm la … la … loved." He burst into sobs and turned to Reverend Oliver, leaning on his chest. Reverend Oliver held his arms up, he lowered them, and raised them and finally he wrapped them around Johnny, who was wailing, trembling, and making sobbing sounds.

Reverend Oliver strained so hard to hold back tears, blood vessels broke in his eyes and tears still escaped. Johnny could feel Reverend Oliver's heartbeat increase. Suddenly, Johnny lifted his head. Reverend Oliver quickly wiped his face.

"Why … is yuh … heart beating … so fast?" He huffed and sucked in air as he spoke.

"Cause listening tuh yuh is breaking my heart. Man, Ah'm happy tuh be here for yuh. Are yuh all right now?" He took off his suit jacket and folded it over his arm. "Johnny, anytime yuh need someone tuh talk tuh, please come tuh me. Man, Ah'm gonna always be here for yuh."

"Ah love yuh, Reverend Oliver. Ah'll try."

They walked back to the car doors. Reverend Oliver laid his suit jacked on the back seat. Johnny smiled at him when he got behind the wheel. He drove away from the shade of the large oak tree, and they continued to Macon.

—◯◯◯—

Johnny returned home around 4:00 P.M. Loretha had gone home and prepared her dinner and returned to Elizabeth's with plates for her and Johnny. Elizabeth knew Johnny left home after pretending all was well, but she knew he was just trying to keep her from worrying about him. As much as she hated to admit it, she hoped his day with Reverend Oliver helped cheer him up. She and Loretha agreed to let him have his dinner before they explained about having to move. They had debated over when was the best time to tell him, wait a few days or tell him on that day. Loretha argued that they didn't want to lose the opportunity to make an offer on Mr. and Mrs. James' home, even though the house has been on the market for some time. It could be their misfortune to loose out. Elizabeth argued Johnny had had enough for one day. Loretha argued it was better to give the bad news to him all at once than to drag it out. They agreed to give him the bad news and have a solution ready.

As soon as dinner was over and the table was cleared, Elizabeth explained the delimma surrounding the house and land.

Johnny's eyes welled up. "No, Mama, Gram'ma. It's okay. Ah'll be all right. Just give me a minute tuh get myself together." After a few deep breathes he was ready. "Okay shoot. Ah'm ready. Just tell me the plan. Ah can't take the worry." He sat up in his chair with his palms down on the table.

Elizabeth and Loretha sat at the table with him.

"Johnny, Mama wants us to buy that house across from Concord, but Ah don't know if Ah can get a mortgage," Elizabeth said. "They want $15,000.00 for the house and Ah only have $6,500.00. Ah don't like not having any money saved, and Ah don't want to put more than $3,500.00 down on the house."

"Mama, why can't we take the money yuh saved and buy MaDear's house?"

"Ah already asked that question. The land people said the house and land would be tied up for years in some kind of legal mumbo-jumbo."

"Okay, Mama, then buy the house down the road. Ah lost MaDear, Ah don't want tuh move away from Gram'ma. Mama, use some of my money for a bigger down payment. Ah'll still have enough for college and Ah can work, too."

Elizabeth looked at Loretha and Johnny. "No, Johnny, Ah will not use yuh money."

"Please, please, Mama! Ah don't mean tuh be disrespectful, but yuh said it was my money." He put his praying hands up against his face. "Please, Mama! It's the only house in Rehoboth. Ah don't want tuh leave Rehoboth. Please try tuh buy the house."

"'Lizabeth, let's go see the house. That's not too much tuh ask. Just see it and then sleep on it, and, honey, while yuh sleepin', dream of Johnny."

Elizabeth had seen the house almost every day of her life; it had indoor plumbing and central heat. "Yuh both right. Ah'll try tuh buy the house, but Ah still won't use Johnny's money. Ah'll use every penny Ah have first."

Johnny and Loretha hugged each other, and then they hugged Elizabeth.

"Wait … wait … wait a minute! Suppose the house is already sold, or, Ah can't get a mortgage?" Elizabeth said.

"Elizabeth, when the Lord closes one door, he always opens another. Ah believe this door is still open, but Ah don't know how long He plans on keeping it open." The ladies removed their aprons and hurried to the large mirror in MaDear's old room to brush their hair. "Well, it's still early. Let's go visit Mr. and Mrs. James. Ah know they're anxious tuh sell. They want tuh go tuh California tuh be near their daughter and gran' kids. Ah suppose we should call first." Loretha knew her daughter, and she was anxious for her tuh make a commitment before she changed her mind. She decided tuh call Mr. and Mrs. James.

Within minutes, Johnny, Elizabeth and Loretha arrived at the white shingled, wood framed house. Mr. and Mrs. James were waiting for them at the front door. Elizabeth noticed many impressive qualities about the house, most of all its charming atmosphere and impeccable cleanliness. It was the right size for her and Johnny; was close to her mother, and it was what Johnny wanted.

Mr. and Mrs. James agreed to sell the house and land for $13,000.00 and, if Elizabeth couldn't get a bank loan, they would hold the mortgage for her. Elizabeth agreed to put $3,000.00 down on the deal.

"See 'Lizabeth, Ah always told yuh, when God closes one door, He always opens another," Loretha said.

"Mama, Thank yuh for being my mother."

The bank approved the loan because they believed Elizabeth was more than qualified; the purchase of the car gave her a credit record, she held two accounts in her name; her personal account, and Johnny's account under her name of more than $11,000.00, which never had a withdrawal in fourteen years. Finally, the land and house had been appraised well above the asking price.

Having to move from MaDear's home was painfully difficult. They took everything that wasn't part of the structure of the house or belonging to the land. All of MaDear's furniture and precious things became the property of Elizabeth and Johnny. MaDear had three bedrooms of furniture, and the new house only had two bedrooms. Elizabeth couldn't bear to part with MaDear's bedroom furniture except for her mattress. So, she donated her own bedroom furniture to the church. Everything else fit nicely in their new home. MaDear's memories were everywhere.

Johnny and Elizabeth were strong, but not strong enough to move furniture from MaDear's house to the newly purchased house. During Sunday service, after the announcements, Reverend Lipton asked the church for volunteers, strong men and someone with a pickup truck. Nathaniel Baker was first to volunteer, and he volunteered his friend Steven Gregory, who owned a pickup truck.

"Next Saturday is the only time Ah can do it. Ah'd like to start early in the mornin'," Mr. Gregory said.

"That's great," Elizabeth yelled out from the choir stand. "Thank yuh, Mr. Baker and Mr. Gregory."

Mr. and Mrs. James moved from the house a week before Elizabeth was scheduled to move in. There were minor repairs that were required in the bathroom: a leaky drip in the bathtub, running water in the toilet, grouting and new linoleum on the floor. Johnny told Mr. Baker what needed to be done and took the liberty of asking him to meet him at the house when he knew his mother was there cleaning and preparing for the move. Nathaniel showed up with all the equipment and supplies necessary to do the work. Elizabeth stood back with her arms crossed.

"Johnny Turner! How did Mr. Baker know we needed help?"

"'Nathaniel' tuh yuh, remember? Johnny told me, and Ah said Ah'd be here. Ah'm gonna always be here for yuh. Remember Ah'm yuh friend, and that's what friends are for."

Elizabeth smiled. "You're a piece of work, but Ah'm happy tuh have yuh as my friend."

"Yuh tell me if there's anything else Ah can do for yuh." He smiled and winked. "Ah mean around here. Yuh know what Ah mean."

"Ah sure do," Elizabeth laughed while she spoke.

CHAPTER 16

Johnny and Malcolm were no longer boys, but young adults. It was the summer of their sixteenth year. School was out and Johnny already had his summer work schedule prepared. Working during the summer was as natural for Johnny as it was unnatural for Malcolm. Except for Malcolm's daily chores, he was as free as a breeze to do whatever he wanted. Reverend Oliver knew work would be good for him. It would make him a better man and develop his sense of responsibility. But Thea had watched her father work himself into an early grave. She would tell Owen, "Let the boy enjoy himself now. When he starts working, he'll be working for the rest of his life."

To a minor degree, Reverend Oliver agreed with Thea, but he knew it wasn't good for a teenager to have idle time. He believed that idle hands and minds could lead to mischief.

Malcolm began his day sleeping late, getting his chores out of the way, and then hanging with the boys. The lake was one of his favorite places, or hanging at a friend's home listening and dancing to Rock-N-Roll music. There were plenty of young girls that enjoyed the company of Malcolm and his friends.

Malcolm had mixed feelings about Johnny; indescribable and powerful feelings. He hated him because he liked and admired him. Emotionally immature, he dealt with his feelings the only way he knew how—he detached them and attacked Johnny.

Malcolm was accustomed to having things his way. He boasted about getting the best of Johnny, but his personal reality was that Johnny had beaten him in every battle. He had believed for years that his father enjoyed Johnny's company more than his. Most of the time he left Johnny alone because he couldn't predict the outcome, and he didn't want to risk being humiliated in front of his friends.

One June evening, just about dusk, Malcolm and his friends were coming from the lake, riding in one of the older boy's convertible. There were three boys, and each was in the company of a girl. Johnny was on the same dirt road, riding his bike home after a twelve-hour day, working in the cotton fields. It had been a hot day, and a fast moving summer shower had cleared the way for a more pleasant evening. The rain quieted the dusty road, but gave way to little muddy puddles and pools.

One of Malcolm's friends was the first to notice Johnny riding his bike. Malcolm was sitting in the front passenger seat next to the driver's girlfriend. Just as the car approached Johnny, Malcolm reached across the girl and jerked the steering wheel to the right, trying to splash muddy water on Johnny. But he hit the large puddle and forced Johnny off the road and into a ditch.

"Hey, man! Are yuh crazy? Whatcha do that for?" the driver yelled at Malcolm. He held tight to the wheel and gave it a hard jerk back to the left.

All the other passengers screamed at Malcolm. His girlfriend called him a "dumb, stupid, fool." They all turned back and saw a mud soiled Johnny pulling himself up and out of the ditch, just as the car was pulled to a halt. The driver breathed a sigh of relief that Johnny didn't appear injured. Malcolm wanted this little prank to be a joke, intended to make Johnny look stupid, but it had backfired.

Johnny was angry. The front wheel of his bike was bent so badly, he couldn't ride it. When he realized Malcolm was responsible, he yelled out, "Yuh gonna pay tuh have my bike fixed." He pulled up his shirt and wiped the muddy water from his face before picking up the bike and walking down the road, carrying it braced against his shoulder.

The driver of the car was angry, he ordered Malcolm out of his car right there on the muddy road. Malcolm was so humiliated, he was happy to get out. The driver backed up to where Johnny was standing and offered him a ride.

Malcolm's now ex-girlfriend tossed Johnny a towel to absorb some of the mud that had soaked into his clothing. Johnny nodded a "thank you" accompanied by a tiny smile, at the same time he raised his hand to catch the towel. He wiped his arms and hands and the remaining splatters of mud from the side of his face. While he was cleaning himself, the driver jumped from the car, opened the trunk and placed his broken bike in before Johnny could refuse his offer. Johnny took the towel and wiped his shirt. Before he got in the car, he wrapped the towel around his pants so he wouldn't get mud on the seat. No one looked back as they rode away, leaving Malcolm to walk the more than five miles.

Malcolm stood on the dirt road and watched his friends favor Johnny. He rested both arms across the top of his head, turned around and placed his hands on his knees. He turned around again and watched the car pull away. None of his friends looked back at him. He was so humiliated. When the car was out of sight, he squatted down and placed his elbows on his knees and covered his face with his hands. He remained in that position until his legs began to cramp. He stood to walk and limped with his first steps. The sun added an additional insult when it slapped his face and assaulted his vision as it made its way to its Western sunset. He hurried along, seeking the path where the trees shaded the road.

Johnny asked to be taken to Malcolm's house. Anger didn't allow him to say another word, and humiliation prevented anyone else from speaking. They didn't know what to say to let him know that they weren't like Malcolm, so they said nothing and hoped he understood.

As soon as the car arrived at Reverend Oliver's, Johnny got out and got his bike. He thanked Malcolm's friends. The only thing any of them could say was, "Yuh welcome," before they drove off. Embarrassment for Malcolm's stupidity continued to play on their emotions. He braced his broken bike against the front wall of the Oliver's home and gave a hard knock on the door. Reverend Oliver answered and was surprised to see a muddy Johnny standing before him with piercing eyes and tight lips.

In spite of how Johnny felt, he remained respectful when he spoke. He explained what happened and demanded Malcolm pay to have his bike repaired. He took a few deep breaths to calm himself, he continued explaining in a more polite, respectful and humble tone, he told Reverend Oliver that until his bike was fixed, he would have to walk eleven miles a day to work and back.

"Where's Malcolm now?" Without hearing Malcolm's account, Reverend Oliver shared Johnny's anger and decided how the situation should be rectified. He placed his hands on his hips and looked down the road.

"He's walking." Johnny looked up at Reverend Oliver. "Ah guess he's walking home. His friends put him out of the car. He's at least five miles away, over on River Road."

Reverend Oliver was visibly disappointed in Malcolm's behavior. He took Johnny's bike and walked hurriedly to the shed. Johnny followed and watched as he placed his bike against the wall and reached for and gave Malcolm's bike to him.

"Thank yuh! Ah'll bring it back as soon as my bike is fixed."

"No. This is now yuh bike. If Malcolm wants a bike, he can fix yuh bike and use it." Anger continued to plague Reverend Oliver. Johnny noticed how rigid his body movements were and how sharp his tone was when he referred to Malcolm.

"Oh no, sir! Ah can't do that, Reverend Oliver. Ah just want my bike fixed. Ah don't want tuh take Malcolm's bike. It's just that Ah need a way tuh get tuh work."

"Listen, Johnny, what Malcolm did was stupid and dangerous. Ah'm thankful yuh weren't injured, but yuh bike will need a lot of work. Malcolm doesn't have a job, he doesn't know how tuh fix anything, and he doesn't have any money, at least not enough tuh fix yuh bike. But, Ah'll make yuh a promise. If Malcolm can get yuh bike fixed, yuh can give him back his bike. If not, this will be yuh bike tuh keep."

Reverend Oliver's anger seemed to move to the side of his mind. It was like there wasn't room to be angry with Malcolm and feel the love he had for Johnny. He looked at Johnny and just wanted to hold him. He loved Malcolm too, but Johnny possessed all the qualities he wanted in a son.

"Ah don't see you much any more. C'mon, Johnny, sit a minute." They sat on the bench outside of the shed. He knew this wasn't the time, but it was the only time he had to speak to him. He missed his son and hated seeing him hurting like that. He just wanted to grab him and hug him before Nathaniel Baker took him away.

"Yes, sir. Ah been working hard. Ah knew Malcolm didn't like me, so it was just easier tuh stay away." Johnny tilted his head and shrugged his shoulders.

"What about at school. We use tuh talk at school." He rested his arm on his knee.

"Malcolm didn't like that either. Now, Ah spend most of my time with Mr. Baker. He's kind like you, Mama likes him, and he doesn't have any kids that hate me. Thanks for helping me, Reverend Oliver. Yuh're still my friend. Ah have tuh go now."

"Well … Ah just wanted yuh tuh know Ah miss yuh." Reverend Oliver stood and offered his hand to Johnny. When Johnny accepted it, he pulled him into a manly hug.

"Ah miss yuh tuh. Thank yuh for helpin' me. Why don't yuh come tuh my house? We can sit on the porch and talk like we use tuh do." Johnny straddled the bike and slowly road off.

"Ah'll try, Johnny. See yuh," he called out. "Come tuh his house," he whispered to himself. He rubbed fingers over his eyes and shook his head.

Thea came to the door just as Johnny was riding away on Malcolm's bike. She asked a few questions. Reverend Oliver told her he would explain when they got inside the house.

Elizabeth was keeping dinner warm on the back of the stove. Johnny wasn't late, but she expected to see him at any moment. Reverend Oliver's house was just down Rehoboth Road. Johnny passed it every day, to and from work.

Johnny entered his home through the back door, which led into the kitchen.

"Hi, Mama!" he yelled. "Do Ah have time tuh shower and change before dinner?"

"Hey, baby! Go ahead, clean up."

He walked through the kitchen into a short hall that separated the bathroom from his bedroom. He knew his mother was in the living room and only heard him come in.

Johnny went to his room for a change of clothing before heading for the bathroom. He was tired and annoyed, but surrendered his anger to the soothing spray of the tranquil shower. He could feel his muscles relax as thoughts of Malcolm washed away as easily as the mud that was caking his body. He knew there would come a time when he would have to explain what happened to his mother, and that would be the more appropriate time to bring the issue up.

It was about eleven o'clock when Malcolm finally arrived home. When he entered the house, he was sweaty and really angry. But he wasn't as angry as Thea and Reverend Oliver. They approached him as though nothing had happened.

"Ah'm gonna give yuh a chance tuh talk tuh me," Reverend Oliver announced in the calmest voice he could utter. Thea stood beside him and sadly looked at Malcolm. Malcolm knew what he had done, but he didn't know how much they knew. He figured there was a slight possibility Johnny had not told his parents.

"Mom ... Dad ... Ah'm sorry Ah'm so late. We had some car trouble, and Ah had tuh walk the last five miles from the lake." He was smooth and calculating with his emotions and expressions.

Thea and Owen just stared at him. They were surprised at the talented way he gave his explanation and completely eluded telling a lie. In fact, they were shocked and at a loss for words. They glanced at each other, then back at Malcolm and took a step backward to allow him to pass.

Malcolm knew exactly what he had done. He was just trying to be cool so his parents wouldn't know anything was wrong. He was angrier with himself than with Johnny. He knew he was wrong, but he didn't expect his friends to throw him out of the car and let Johnny take his seat—humiliating him, once again.

Thea and Owen weren't finished with Malcolm, but they decided they'd let him settle in and have his dinner. Thea and Owen were sitting at the table staring at him when he sat down to eat.

"What! ... What!" Malcolm shrugged his shoulders and faced the palms of his hands up at them. "Why yuh staring at me?" His next memory was when he landed on the floor and was looking up at his father who had snatched the chair from under him. It was all Reverend Oliver could do to control himself and prevent Malcolm from receiving the back side of his hand across his face.

Thea leaped from her seat and gasped for a gulp of air at the same time she covered her mouth with both hands. She wasn't used to any form of violence, and was afraid for Malcolm and Owen. She knew Malcolm had it coming, but she was startled by the incident. Reverend Oliver knew he had her support when she came to his side and squeezed his arm. As soon as she held his arm, she felt his muscles relax, but he was still angry.

"Well, Malcolm," Reverend Oliver began in a calm voice. "Ah know something, and Ah know yuh know something. Ah have tuh give yuh a hand." Thea and Reverend Oliver clapped their hands and applauded Malcolm while he was picking himself up off the floor.

"Yuh really talented. He's a natural, isn't he, Thea?" He nodded his head, and a cynical smile appeared on his face.

Thea nodded her head. He gestured for Malcolm to return to his seat at the table and he and Thea sat down again. "Now, let me tell yuh what Ah know. Now yuh listen tuh me. When yuh were talking, we didn't interrupt yuh, *SO DO NOT INTERRUPT ME!*" Reverend Oliver's voice escalated from calmness to a loud roaring shout.

Malcolm gave his parents his undivided attention. He held his head low and only occasionally glanced at his father with a humble slight tilt of his lowered head.

Reverend Oliver pushed his chair away from the table and stood in one smooth movement. "Yeahhh … yuh had car trouble. And Yeahhh … yuh had tuh walk five miles. But yuh caused the car trouble. And Yeahhh … yuh could've killed Johnny Turner." He paced back and forth and around Malcolm, being purposefully intimidating and nodding his head to the beat of each word.

Thea had removed herself from her seat and stood propped against the refrigerator, her arms crossed and nodding her head in agreement with Owen.

"Yeahhh … now yuh have a damaged bike, and Johnny Turner has yuh new bike."

Malcolm's head jerked up in defiance at the news. He stared at his father.

Reverend Oliver knew he hit a nerve. "Don't yuh eye-ball me boy!"

Malcolm jerked his head down and rested his elbows on his knees. He knew when he was being chastised he was to only look at his father using his peripheral vision.

"Yeahhh … next time, yuh tell me the whole truth, and don't take me fo' no fool! Yeahhh, mister bad guy … yuh'll spend the next two weeks around this house, and Ah mean 'around this house with no company and no telephone calls! Just one more thing. If yuh break these rules, yuh'll spend the remainder of the summer in this house." Reverend Oliver was angry, but cool, and Thea continued to be supportive. "Malcolm Oliver, have Ah made myself clear?"

Malcolm gave an affirmative nod. He had not had his dinner, and now he had lost his appetite.

"Oh, there is just one more thing. Johnny Turner doesn't want yuh bike. He wants his own. Ah told him he would get his own bike back if yuh fixed his. So yuh got a chance, but Ah don't think yuh'll ever see that bike again." Reverend Oliver's cynical smile returned as he stared at Malcolm.

Malcolm was so angry he could feel his hot breath tickling the tiny hairs of his peach-fuzz mustache, but he was smart enough to remain humble. He asked to be excused from the table. Leaving his dinner, he went directly to his bedroom. He carefully closed the door, making sure it didn't slam. Then, in a rage, he punched his pillow, taking rapid and forceful swipes at the air and whispering curse words. He wanted to scream because of his own stupidity, his humiliation, his father's anger, loss of his bike and his belief that Johnny had some controlling force that made him want to hurt him.

After the first few days, being shut-up around the house for two weeks wasn't so bad. Malcolm didn't want anyone to see him, and he didn't know how he would ever face his friends again. Two weeks passed rather quickly. He repaired Johnny's bike, not to return it, but to prove his father wrong. He spent most of the time thinking about what he was going to do to Johnny. This had been going on for years, and each incident was more malicious than before. This time he'd planned to get him while they were alone—where he wouldn't risk embarrassment if he failed.

It was early July 1966. Malcolm had been off punishment for a week. He was free to rejoin his friends, but preferred to remain at home. Sometimes he would sit at the window and peek out, watching and waiting for Johnny to ride by on his bike. There were those days when he sat in the front yard, near the road, and without saying a word, he would fix his eyes on Johnny. Instead of just allowing his eyes to follow him as he rode pass, he'd turn his head slowly to keep Johnny fixed in his sight.

A little more than three weeks had passed since the ditch incident. Malcolm rode Johnny's bike to an ambush place. He waited in the thick, overgrown bushes for about thirty minutes. He planned to jump Johnny as he rode home, catching him off guard and beating him with his closed fist until he felt avenged. He used the fury of his ride to fuel his anger with hate-laced thoughts, but the wait in the bushes was cooling him off. He knew he needed to keep the fury, so he cursed Johnny aloud. "That son of a bitch! That bastard! I'm gonna kill him! Who the hell does he think he is?"

It wasn't long before Johnny's approach neared. Malcolm could hear the crunching gravel and saw road dust in the distance. He prepared himself and crouched back on his haunches. At the right moment, Malcolm leaped forward onto Johnny. They both landed on the dirt road, leaving Johnny surprised and dazed.

Malcolm jumped to his feet with the intention of inflicting more pain. He drew back and gave Johnny a strong swift kick to his right arm. Johnny screamed in pain. Malcolm drew back to give him another kick, but stopped. He knew his kick shouldn't have caused him that much pain. He just stood there looking at Johnny who was holding his arm, twisting and turning in pain and kicking up the dirt.

"Johnny, yuh hurt! Ah didn't mean tuh hurt yuh! Yuh gonna be all right … Johnny, yuh gonna be all right." He stepped back and placed his hands on the sides of his head.

"Ah think … Ah think my arm is broken … my arm is broken! Oh! My side hurts, too. Help me! Ah need help." Pain distorted his face and body—the kind of pain that took his breath away.

Malcolm looked at Johnny's arm. It was swelling rapidly between the elbow and the wrist. Johnny was screaming, and Malcolm didn't know what to do. "Ah'm sorry Johnny," Malcolm kept repeating.

"Malcolm … Ah need help! Please … go get help!"

"Ah will, Johnny, Ah will. Ah'm gonna get help! Ah'll be faster if Ah take the bike." Malcolm's feet kept slipping off the pedals, and he had trouble establishing his balance. "Ah'm gonna get help! Ah'm sorry, Johnny! Ah'm sorry!"

Johnny yelled out in pain, "Go, Malcolm. Ah know … yuh … didn't mean it. … Just get help!"

Johnny had never trusted him, but this time he didn't have a choice. He had stopped squirming and now laid there motionless, holding tightly to his right arm. Between each difficult breath, he cried silently in pain.

Malcolm rode like he was in a marathon. He had caused the incident, and now Johnny was at his mercy. Malcolm reached his house and told his parents that Johnny was hurt. The three rushed to the car and hurriedly headed back down River Road. Malcolm sat in the front seat so he could show his father where Johnny was.

"What happened tuh Johnny?" Reverend Oliver asked.

"It was my fault. Ah jumped out of the bushes and knocked him off my bike, then Ah kicked him. Ah didn't mean tuh hurt him. Ah just wanted tuh get even with him for taking my bike." He was covered with perspiration, crying, trembling, his eyes twitching and telegraphing his fear.

"Yuh did what?" Thea screamed. "Oh Dear Lord, hurry, Owen."

Fear clawed at Reverend Oliver's belly. His heart pounded rapidly. Malcolm had lacked the morals to see the error of his ways, now Johnny could be seriously injured. He'd seen it for some time, but figured Malcolm would grow up. But it seemed he didn't grow up before Johnny got hurt. He remembered Elizabeth's warning all those years ago, but that was just a memory. He wasn't worried about it now.

"Mom … Dad … Ah'm so sorry. Ah'm sorry it got tuh this. Please believe me. Ah didn't mean tuh hurt him," he cried and continued to tremble.

"Yes yuh did," Reverend Oliver yelled back. Fear was written on his face. He made a sharp right off Rehoboth Road onto River Road. Sounds of the pebbles and gravel pelting the undercarriage filled the car and felt like hail during the worst of storms. Thea yelled for him to watch the road when he was driving dangerously close to the right bank. Only then did he correct himself, but he continued to yell at Malcolm.

"Yuh meant tuh hurt him. Tell me … how did yuh surprise him? How did yuh knock him off his bike if yuh didn't mean tuh do it?" He turned to look at Malcolm again and glanced back at the road. "Yuh said yuh didn't mean tuh hurt him the night yuh ran him off the road." Reverend Oliver was driving so fast on the dirt road the car was skidding, forcing him to fantail and overcorrect to maintain control, and still he yelled at Malcolm, throwing question after question at him and not expecting an answer. He wanted Malcolm to speak so he could give him the back side of his hand.

"Ah believed yuh. Ah believed it was just a stupid prank that went wrong. Ah thought yuh had learned yuh lesson. But this time yuh were trying tuh get back at him." He was so angry spit spewed from his mouth when he spoke. "Yuh meant tuh hurt him by catching him off guard and beating him up. So don't sit there and tell me yuh didn't mean tuh hurt him!"

Malcolm accepted his verbal bashing. He wanted his father to stop the car, pull off his belt and beat him. He wanted whelps to form where the belt lashed his flesh. He wanted to feel physical pain to replace the emotional pain, so he would feel better. He'd really hurt Johnny. He never knew how bad he would feel because he had never caused a serious injury to anyone. His emotional pain was equal to Johnny's physical pain. He wanted his to be stronger and more intense than Johnny's pain.

"Owen, please, we can talk about this later. Right now let's just try to find Johnny," Thea pleaded. She knew Owen was right about Malcolm, but it was hard for her to hear that her son was a bully. She was sitting forward, leaning against the front seat, searching the road for Johnny.

It was about dusk when Malcolm yelled out, "There he is, Dad!"

"Stop, Owen!" Thea shouted.

The car skidded to a halt, crunching road dust and gravel. Thea was out of the car before Reverend Oliver or Malcolm.

Johnny was still lying on the side of the road. It had been about thirty minutes, and his arm was severely swollen. The right side of his face was also swollen from large deep abrasions. His complexion was pale, and his breathing shallow, which caused Thea more concern than his visible injuries.

"Owen, be careful how yuh pick him up." She turned to Johnny. "Where does it hurt, Johnny?"

"My arm and right here." Johnny used his left hand to point to his chest area.

"Owen, Malcolm, Ah need yuh shirts."

Thea had Owen hold one end of the shirt while she twisted them around into a make-sift rope. She slipped the ends under Johnny while he lay on the ground, tying one shirt to hold his upper arm against his upper side ribs. The other shirt was used to brace his elbow and forearm to his lower side ribs.

"Now Johnny Ah want yuh tuh take yuh left hand and hold yuh right wrist against yuh stomach—not tuh tight now. Ah know it hurts, but we're gonna get yuh some help." She turned to Owen. "Would yuh bring the car closer? Ah believe we can help him stand, and we can help him in the car."

Thea got into the back seat of the car, then Malcolm and Reverend Oliver helped Johnny position himself on the seat, placing his head in her lap. Malcolm rode up front with his father.

"What happened, Johnny?" Thea asked. She already knew, but wanted to hear it from Johnny. Not that it would make any difference, looking at Johnny's injuries. She hated to believe her son had been so cruel.

"Ah … fell off … the bike … and hurt … my side and arm," Johnny struggled to answer.

Thea looked up at Reverend Oliver, and Malcolm looked back at Johnny. Together, Thea and Reverend Oliver looked at Malcolm. "Johnny, we already know what happened, Malcolm told us," Thea said.

Reverend Oliver started the car, and they started back up River Road.

"What … did Malcolm … tell yuh?" Johnny struggled between breaths to speak. He needed to know before he could dispute them.

"Malcolm said that he jumped yuh from the bushes. And then he said he kicked yuh," Reverend Oliver answered. He looked back at Thea through the rearview mirror. He couldn't see Johnny because he was lying with his head in Thea's lap.

"But that's … not the way … it happened. Maybe … Malcolm wanted it … tuh happen that way … but it didn't … Ohhh," Johnny moaned in pain as the car went over a dip in the road. After a few moments he struggled to continue. "Ah … Ah saw Malcolm … in the bushes … Ah knew … he was … still mad at me. When … when Ah saw him … Ah thought … he was gonna … come after me. Ah got scared … and … the bike … it skidded. Ohhh!" he cried out again. "Ah … fell off … and the bike … flew up in the air … and … then … it came down … on top of me. Malcolm came … running toward me. He didn't kick me … ohhh … on purpose … he stumbled over … the wheel … of the bike."

Reverend Oliver and Thea knew Johnny was lying, and for some reason he was trying to protect Malcolm. It seemed important he have the story told his way. When they tried to challenge his story, he became upset, and would cry out in pain, just enough so they'd let him have it his way. Still, they believed Malcolm's version.

Thea and Reverend Oliver couldn't understand what Johnny was doing. But Malcolm knew. By the time they'd reached Elizabeth's house, Malcolm realized Johnny had won the final battle. It was time to just leave him alone.

—m—

"Yuh know the Missionary Society agreed to visit the sick and shut-in in groups of two. We've ordered a basket of fruit for each visit," Nathaniel said. "Can Ah count on yuh tuh be with me?"

Someone pounded at the door.

"Hold on, Nathaniel, someone's at the door," Elizabeth said. She placed the phone receiver on the table.

"Miss Elizabeth!" Malcolm yelled. "Johnny got hurt. Mama and Daddy are taking him tuh the hospital in Macon. They think he broke his arm! They need yuh now!"

Elizabeth could feel her heart in her throat. "Nat, Johnny got hurt. Ah have tuh go tuh Macon, tuh the hospital. Bye."

"Wait! Wait! Elizabeth," Nathaniel said. He hung up the phone and ran to his car.

Elizabeth ran for her pocketbook, then slammed the door behind her and ran to the car. She took Thea's place in the car. Thea got in the front seat with Malcolm and Reverend Oliver. Everyone listened carefully as Thea told Elizabeth Johnny's version of how he got hurt, and Johnny gave a confirming nod.

Nathaniel was at the hospital when Reverend Oliver and Elizabeth arrived. He ran to Elizabeth's side as Johnny was wheeled on a gurney into an examination room. Meanwhile, Elizabeth completed all the paper work: consent to treat, insurance, family history, allergies, childhood illness, and the likes.

Elizabeth called her mother and told her what Johnny said happened. She explained that Johnny was still in the treatment area, and she hadn't spoke with a doctor. "Mama, Mrs. Thea said he was complaining about pain in the right side of his chest and in his arm."

"We're on our way," Loretha said

"Mama, Ah can call yuh back as soon as the doctor comes out tuh talk tuh us."

"No! No! Yuh father is already in the car."

"Daddy? Okay, Mama." Elizabeth hung up the phone. She stood looking at it for almost a minute. *Ah never thought Daddy cared. Lord, yuh sure works in mysterious ways.*

An hour seemed like forever, but finally a doctor came to the waiting area. "Good evening. My name is Dr. Sutton. First, I'd like to ask who tied young Mr. Turner up like that?" His eyes scanned the waiting room. He slipped his fingers in his pockets, leaving his thumbs out.

Loretha and Reverend Turner arrived. "Mama, Daddy." Elizabeth called out. "Ah'm sorry tuh interrupt. These are Johnny's grandparents."

Dr. Sutton nodded his greeting and continued with what he was saying.

"Ah did," Thea responded. "Ah was afraid he had fractured ribs. Ah'd seen symptoms like his before with my brother. Ah hope Ah did right."

"Great thinking … Yuh may have saved his life. Ah'll explain in a minute. Your name is?"

"Thank yuh, Lord, thank yuh." Reverend Oliver jumped up from the chair and ran his fingers through his hair, placed one hand on his hip and paced in short track in the waiting room. Malcolm sat in the chair and cried with no one to comfort him.

"Oh thank yuh, Jesus!" Elizabeth called out. "Thank yuh, Lord."

Loretha and Reverend Turner sat in the chair and whispered their silent prayers.

"Thea Oliver." Thea's hands were shaking when Dr. Sutton handed her the two shirts.

"Okay, now, I'll be caring for your son. Who are the parents?"

Elizabeth raised her hand. She was sitting so close to Nathaniel, Dr. Sutton assumed he was Johnny's father. Elizabeth cut her eyes at

Reverend Oliver and he lowered his head, dug his hands in his pockets and turned away.

"Okay! We are very lucky. Johnny will fare very well, but he was in serious danger. The X-rays revealed he had a closed fracture to the radius bone in his right arm, as well as breaks to the third and fourth right ribs. There were no injuries to his head, except for the nasty abrasion to the right side of his face. He will be admitted and remain in the hospital for several days. Now here is where the danger was. Those dislocated ribs could have easily punctured and collapsed his lungs in two areas, and Johnny could have died before he reached the hospital." Dr. Sutton sat near Elizabeth and drew a rough sketch of a right arm and chest area, then placed slash marks where the fractures were. He handed the sketch to Nathaniel, who shared it with Elizabeth. She passed it on to her parents. Reverend Turner handed it to Thea, who shared it with Reverend Oliver and Malcolm.

Dr. Sutton continued, "I'd say the good Lord has plans for this young man. He will require emergency surgery to set those ribs, and we'll take care of his arm, too. There were no fractures to his facial bones, just deep abrasions. Those wounds were cleaned, but in time they should heal without scars."

While the doctor was explaining Johnny's condition, Nathaniel placed his arm around Elizabeth to give her the physical support she needed. She collapsed back against him, closed her eyes, and raised her head upward. "Lord, thank you for protecting and keeping Johnny safe. Oh … thank yuh, Lord." Tears seeped down her cheeks. Nathaniel handed her his handkerchief.

Loretha and Reverend Turner moved to seats closer to Elizabeth. Loretha reached over and hugged her and greeted Nat.

"Ah prayed all the way here for the boy," Reverend Turner said. "Ah know he's gonna be fine." He nodded at Reverend Oliver and Thea.

Reverend Oliver returned the greeting, then suddenly left the room in a hurry. Reverend Turner's eyes followed him more intently than anyone else's.

Elizabeth walked over to Thea and sat beside her. "Thank yuh for being there tuh help Johnny. Like the doctor said, he may have died if it wasn't for you." The two ladies stood and embraced before Elizabeth walked back to her seat and placed her head back against Nat's shoulder.

Reverend Oliver returned from the men's room. Reverend Turner checked his watched and realized he had been gone almost twenty minutes. Reverend Oliver's eyes were red like he had been crying.

Reverend Turner stood and walked toward Owen. "Are yuh all right? Yuh look like yuh been havin' a rough time over this."

"Yuh don't know, John. Ah'll be tellin' yuh about it. Excuse me for a minute." He walked over and shook Nathaniel's hand. "Thanks for coming, man."

"Anything for Johnny and Elizabeth," Nathaniel said.

Malcolm began to cry as if his conscience had split wide open. He looked at his parents, and then walked over to Elizabeth and Mr. Baker. "Miss Elizabeth, Johnny told yuh he fell off his bike and that's how he got hurt, but that's not true. Did Johnny ever tell yuh what happened about three weeks ago … yuh know … 'bout the bike?" Malcolm began to confess.

Elizabeth glanced at Malcolm, then at Thea and Reverend Oliver before returning her attention to Malcolm. "No, honey, he never said anything about a bike."

"Well, my father gave Johnny my bike because Ah caused him tuh ride his into a ditch and messed up his wheels. He needed his bike tuh get tuh work. My dad put me on punishment for two weeks, and Ah was really mad. So, when Ah got a chance, Ah went hunting for Johnny tuh beat him up." Malcolm was holding his head down because it was very difficult for him to make eye contact with Elizabeth and Mr. Baker. In between the crying, sniffing, and wiping the tears and nasal mucus, he managed to tell his story.

Reverend Turner and Loretha stood and walked closer to Elizabeth.

Elizabeth stared at Malcolm. What he was saying was more than she expected to hear. She shook her head in disbelief. She didn't give her attention to Reverend Oliver or Thea, not even a glance. She watched Malcolm as he continued to speak.

"It's all my fault. Ah wish saying Ah'm sorry could make everything all right. Ah don't know why Johnny said it was an accident." The intensity of Malcolm's emotional state slowed his speech pattern, making it difficult for him to continue to speak fluently. His mind swirled, and he blinked, fighting back the tears. He cried.

Thea went to comfort him, but Malcolm pulled away. He was taking responsibility. Reverend Oliver recognized this and gently pulled Thea back and held her in place with a comforting arm embracing her shoulder. "Honey, let him do this alone. It's good for him."

"Ah promise Ah won't ever do anything tuh hurt him again, and Ah won't let no one else hurt him either. Ah promise, Miss. Elizabeth." He wiped the tears that were dripping off his chin. "Johnny may never want tuh be my friend, but Ah will always be there if he needs me. Ah promise yuh, Miss Elizabeth ... as soon as Ah can see Johnny, Ah'll tell him."

Elizabeth glanced at Thea. Then she stared at Reverend Oliver, before cupping her hands around Malcolm's face. "Honey, Ah've known you and Johnny weren't getting along for a long time. Ah didn't know it had gotten tuh this point. Johnny never told me about the bike, and Ah didn't notice, but yuh a real man. Yuh told the truth even when yuh knew it would hurt. It takes a real man tuh be responsible for his action, and believe me, there are not a lot of real men out there." Elizabeth's eyes communicated to Thea, telling her it was time tuh comfort her son.

It was way past visiting hours by the time Johnny was settled in the four-bed hospital room, and only parents were allowed to stay. Elizabeth and Nathaniel stayed with him. The hospital staff continued to assume Nathaniel was Johnny's father, and he never informed them to the contrary.

"Mr. Jenkins." Johnny spoke out in a slow slur, still exhibiting the effects of the anesthesia. "Mama … Mr. Jenkins." A moment of sleep took over, but Elizabeth and Nathaniel waited for him to wake and continue speaking. When he did, he continued right where he left off. "Could yuh call Mr. Jenkins … and tell him what happened?" He was asleep again. Nathaniel patted Elizabeth's hand, and they sat forward to get the rest of the message. "The doctor said Ah won't … be able tuh work the … rest of the summer." And Johnny was asleep again.

Elizabeth assured Johnny she would call him, then she kissed his forehead and rubbed her hand along the side of his face, and watched as he fell asleep. Nathaniel stayed with Johnny while Elizabeth went to the waiting room. She told the Olivers Johnny was resting quietly, and she would be riding back with Mr. Baker.

"Yuh know, Johnny asked me tuh call Mr. Jenkins. The doctor told him he wouldn't be able tuh work for the rest of the summer. That's all he's worried about," Elizabeth said softly as though she were letting her thoughts speak aloud.

"Miss Elizabeth, maybe Mr. Jenkins would let me work for Johnny. Ah could save all the money for him," said Malcolm.

"It's so nice for yuh tuh offer, but that won't be necessary. Johnny needed a summer without work, but thank yuh for offering."

"Well, Ah don't see anything so great about Malcolm's attitude or his asking tuh work for Johnny," Reverend Oliver spoke out with a twinge of anger and disappointment in his voice. "We have tuh remember that he's the cause of all this. Maybe if he was working, he wouldn't have had the time tuh cause all these problems."

"Owen, please, not now," Thea said. She held her head down, knowing he was right.

"Why not now, Thea? Ah know what yuh thinkin', but there is never a good time." Reverend Oliver quickly and briefly glanced back at Malcolm. "Listen, son, yuh done some rotten things, but Ah'm proud that yuh owning up. Ah know yuh feel terrible, and that's good, too. If yuh didn't feel that way, Ah'd be afraid of yuh. Johnny is going tuh lose his summer pay. Yuh should work for him. He should be compensated. And Ah think yuh lucky Miss Elizabeth isn't pressing criminal charges against yuh for assault."

Elizabeth stared at the back of Reverend Oliver's head and shook her head at the audacity of his last statement.

"Miss Elizabeth, please let me do something tuh help Johnny. Ah know Ah can't take back what Ah did, but it would help me tuh feel better."

"Okay, Malcolm. If it's okay with yuh parents and Johnny, yuh do what yuh think yuh need tuh do, but Ah can't let yuh give Johnny all yuh pay. Yuh work and give him only half. Yuh got tuh get something."

Johnny was placed on the adult surgical unit in a four-bed hospital room. His bed was located near the window and across from him, in a front bed, was an elderly black man who had tubes entering his body and another that captured his urine in a bag that was attached under the bed to a frame. The other two beds were empty. Johnny had just dosed off into a peaceful evening nap.

Elizabeth and Loretha looked around. "My, my, things have changed around here," Loretha whispered.

"Yes, Mama, but take a closer look. They've done some renovations, but everything is still segregated. All the nurses and aides are black, and all the patients on this side of the hospital are black. The waiting rooms and patient rooms are nicer, but Ah'll bet this is the side of the hospital the white people use tuh have and that new wing they just built is exclusively white." Elizabeth crossed her arms and whispered her assumption.

After about thirty minutes, Johnny began to stir. Soon he was awake, but groggy. He looked around and squeezed a small smile for his mother and grandmother. The right side of his face, including his eye, was severely swollen. He could open his eye to just a slit. His right arm was in a cast, and his chest was heavily taped. He was receiving high doses of pain medication through an intravenous tube attached to his left arm.

Johnny's version of his accident had gotten around Rehoboth. Reverend Lipton visited the hospital the next evening. Elizabeth and Loretha were sitting by his bed when he walked in, and they immediately stood. He nodded his head. "Please, sit." He smiled at the ladies and used his gesturing left hand to tell them to sit. "How are y'all tuhday? Ah heard young Mr. Turner gave yuh quite a scare, but Ah know he'll be fine. Hey, partner. Ah hear yuh have trouble staying on yuh bike. How yuh feeling?" He walked around to the left side of the bed and held Johnny's hand.

"Sore all over," Johnny said, looking up at him. He gave him a tiny smile, but it quickly faded.

"Ah understand how yuh feel. It's been quite an ordeal. Johnny, yuh the first on my visitor's list, because yuh my special man." He placed the palm of his hand on Johnny's head, and Johnny glanced up at him. "Ladies, let's hold hands. Elizabeth, if yuh would place yuh hand over mine." They bowed their heads as the reverend prayed for Johnny's healing.

As soon as Reverend Lipton left, Nathaniel Baker walked in. "Hello, Mrs. Turner, and Miss Turner … and of course the man of the hour, young Mr. Turner."

Loretha and Elizabeth smiled and returned the greeting. Johnny's swollen face brightened up. "Hi, Mr. Baker. Ah guess you heard about my accident?"

"Okay. Ah forgive yuh for not remembering me being here with yuh until late last night," Mr. Baker said.

"You were here?"

"Ah was here. So Johnny … now how do yuh plan on spending the summer?" Mr. Baker asked.

"Ah don't know? Ah guess Ah'll have tuh learn how tuh fish."

"Hey, that's a great idea. Ah love tuh eat fish," Loretha said. A shadow cast across the foot of his bed, and Johnny turned toward the door.

"Hello, Reverend Oliver," Johnny said.

Elizabeth turned away and crossed her hands over her pocketbook.

"Ah see yuh have a room full." He walked over to Johnny and touched his left shoulder. "Yuh look a lot better today. Ah did a lot of praying for yuh last night and this morning. Ah'll see the good Lord is taking good care of yuh."

"Reverend Lipton was just here prayin' over me. Are yuh gonna pray over me now tuh?" Johnny asked, looking directly in Reverend Oliver's face.

"Would yuh like me tuh?" Reverend Oliver spoke softly, believing it was Johnny's decision.

"Can yuh come back later? Nathaniel just got here. Ah want tuh spend some time with him right now." Johnny tried to read Reverend Oliver's face. He didn't want to hurt his feelings.

Reverend Oliver had been leaning over speaking softly to Johnny, but not so softly the others couldn't hear their conversation. He stood smiling and tried to weigh his words so he wouldn't stutter. Sometimes he stuttered when he was unprepared for a situation or upset. "Okay, Johnny, Ah'll come back later." He tried, but his face couldn't hold a smile except for Johnny.

He bowed to Mrs. Turner, Elizabeth, and Mr. Baker prior to leaving the room, but before he reached the threshold of the doorway, he was blaming Mr. Baker for stealing his son from him. *Now that Malcolm has promised to try to be Johnny's friend, maybe Johnny will come back to me,* he thought

Moments after Reverend Oliver left, Loretha and Elizabeth left the room, leaving Johnny to have some private time with Nathaniel.

"Mama, may Ah ask yuh something?" Elizabeth kept walking as she spoke.

Loretha looked over at her. "Yes, honey, anything."

They had reached the visitor's lounge and sat at the table opposite each other.

"Mama, there's something different about Daddy. He seems tuh care about us. It wasn't just last night … he's been different since MaDear died. He still stands back and has that coldness about him, but he looks like he wants tuh be accepted." Elizabeth looked directly in her mother's eyes when she spoke.

Loretha took hold of Elizabeth's hand. "Honey, Ah seen a change in him, tuh … like last night. Ah would've waited for yuh tuh keep me informed, but yuh father was in the car before Ah hung up the phone. He may be searching for the truth."

"Well, that's easy. All he had tuh do was look in Owen's eye and ask that magic question." Elizabeth turned her mother's hand loose, sat back in her chair and crossed her arms. "Mama, Ah want tuh kiss him and hug him the way Ah did when Ah was a child. Ah miss him so much."

"Then do it," Loretha looked serious. She leaned forward and slapped her hands on the table.

"Mama! Ah'd die before Ah'd set myself up for that kind of rejection." She pushed herself up from the chair. "C'mon, let's go back tuh Johnny's room."

"Ah'm sorry, honey." She stood and hugged Elizabeth. "Ah shouldn't have said that."

———ww———

All the apologetic attitudes, words, and expressions didn't make Johnny feel restored. He believed Malcolm was sorry, but sorry was not an anesthetic for real, physical pain, and it was less effective on emotional scars. It was acceptable to say Johnny would be a more stable person if the years of emotional scarring could heal as clean and clear as the physical injuries. By the end of the summer, Malcolm mailed Johnny all the money he'd earned working for Mr. Jenkins, not half, as Elizabeth suggested. He never tried to bully or hurt him again.

Johnny, on the other hand, had suppressed all of Malcolm's cruel activities over the years, pushing them down in his psyche. In time, the most awful experiences were not easily recalled.

CHAPTER 17

During the spring of 1968, the young adults of the Booker T. Washington High School would march in the last commencement program as a segregated high school. Johnny was once again valedictorian and had accepted a full scholarship to a prestigious, all black male college in Atlanta, and for the first time in his life, he would be away from his mother.

Elizabeth knew she was going to miss him, but she also knew she'd survive. She loved him more than life itself, but now she could resume living her own life, which she believed had now come full circle. When Johnny left for school, she would be alone.

One evening, Elizabeth sat swinging herself on her front porch and thinking back to two years ago. *Nathaniel and Johnny were working so hard enlarging the porch so that it spanned the entire front of the house, extending the roof, and finally screening in the entire area. She smiled when she asked Nathaniel why he and Johnny were doing all that work? Johnny didn't answer, but Nathaniel said he hated bugs and didn't like getting bit by mosquitoes. She asked Nathaniel when all this sittin' on her porch was gonna happen, and he said when he started tuh court her. Johnny laughed so hard he stretched out on the grass. "It gonna happen, Mama. Ah don't know why yuh fightin' it so hard." She stared out into space and smiled to herself, remembering the time as if it were still in the moment.*

"Mama," Johnny called out. "Mama! Mama!" He was standing in the front entrance leading to the porch.

"Yes, Johnny!" Elizabeth turned startled. "Why yuh yellin' like that?"

"Mama," he laughed as he spoke. "Ah been standing next tuh yuh, callin' yuh, and it seems like yuh mind was somewhere else."

"Ah suppose so. Ah guess Ah was thinking back," she said while twisting the corner of her apron.

"Well, Mama, the way yuh were thinkin', Ah hope yuh were thinkin' 'bout Mr. Baker."

"Johnny! Yuh gittin' in my business?" Elizabeth looked up at him with a serious face.

"No, Mama. Ah'm gittin' in our business." He sat on the swing close to his mother with his arm around her shoulder and pushed the swing with his foot, hoping to sooth her mood with the swing's smooth gliding motion. "Mama, Ah'm not tryin' tuh be disrespectful. Yuh've devoted yuh whole life tuh me. It's yuh time now. Ah hope yuh been thinkin 'bout Mr. Baker. He's been waiting for yuh for four years. Mama, the man is yuh soul mate. Ah really believe his love for yuh is off the scale."

Elizabeth turned to Johnny. "Now, what's that supposed tuh mean?"

Johnny threw his head back and laughed. He used his other hand to comfort her by rubbing her arm. "Mama, that means his love for yuh just can't be weighed or measured. It's just tuh strong and tuh deep." Johnny gave the swing another strong push. "Besides, he's a really nice person, and everybody knows he's interested in yuh."

"Oh? ... Who's everybody? Everybody knows he's my friend." Elizabeth seemed annoyed.

"Mama, the man loves yuh, and yuh love him. It's more than friend-ship and yuh know that." Johnny planted his foot on the deck of the porch, stopping the swing. She turned her face away, and he took his hand and gently turned her face back toward his. "Ah've grown from a child tuh a man, and Ah've watched yuh show yuh love for him. Ah love him, too. Mama ... if you don't love the man, let him go. He's been waiting for yuh for four years. It's not fair tuh keep him hanging on if yuh plan on remaining alone for the rest of yuh life."

She stood from the swing and walked to the side of the porch and wrapped her arms around herself.

"Ma, please! Why don't yuh give the man a chance? Mama, Ah pray that one day Ah'll have as much mutual love in my life as you and Mr.

Baker have. It's time tuh stop thinkin' about livin' for me and live for yuhself."

Elizabeth continued to keep her back to Johnny. She took several deep breaths and all the time she continued to hug her self. Suddenly, she turned. Johnny was sitting on the swing, his feet planted firmly on the porch deck. He was leaning over with his head down. He rested his elbows on his legs and held one hand over the other. It was quiet, too quiet. Birds should have been singing, a breeze should have been blowing and cooling Elizabeth's face, dogs should have barked. The only thing Elizabeth heard was her heartbeat and Johnny's words, *"If you don't love the man, let him go."*

"Johnny!" She cried out, "Johnny!" He answered, "Ah'm right here, Mama!" He ran to her and wrapped her in his arms. "It's all right, Mama."

"Yuh right, Johnny, Ah've loved him for a long time. Ah pray Ah love him as much as he loves me. Ah think that's what Ah'm afraid of." She pulled up her apron and wiped her tears.

"Don't worry 'bout that. Ah know yuh love him. Now tell him." He held her gently by her forearms and looked in her eyes. "May Ah use yuh car? Ah'll see yuh later." Before Elizabeth could object, Johnny was through the screen door and out of sight.

"Johnny!" Elizabeth called out.

"Be right back, Mama." Johnny sped away, waving his arm out the window.

He thinks he's grown, but he ain't grown yet. Elizabeth walked back and sat on the swing. She rested her arm on the back of the seat, and positioned her head on her arm. She crossed her legs at her ankles and only the tip of one foot touched the deck of the porch to give the swing motion. All the things Johnny said about Nathaniel played in her mind, and it saddened her that he had been so good to her and she kept him at such a distance. She wondered if she had it to do over would it have been different between the two of them. She loved him so much and for so long.

Thirty minutes passed when Nathaniel's car pulled up in Elizabeth's driveway. "Is everything all right? Johnny said you needed me," Nathaniel called up to her from the driveway.

Elizabeth thought as she watched him standing there out of breath. *All Johnny had to say was that Ah needed him, and he came tuh me.* "He did? Well, Ah do need yuh, but … it's nothing so urgent." Elizabeth stood with both hands up at the side of the screen. "Would you join me tuhnight for dinner?"

Speechless, Nathaniel stood by the hood of his car. He held his head up. The wise old oak tree blocked his view of the sky. He dug his hands deep into his pockets and kicked at the dirt. "Yuh not playin' with me are yuh?"

"Why, Nat, Ah wouldn't do that. Now Ah'm gonna ask yuh again. Mr. Nathaniel Baker, would you do me the honor of having diner with me?"

"Miss Elizabeth Turner, Ah'd be honored."

When Elizabeth prepared dinner, she hadn't expected company. It was just supposed to be for her and Johnny. But she believed Nathaniel to be her friend, and as her friend, her dinner was just fine. Elizabeth had prepared fried pork chops, mashed potatoes, gravy and string beans, biscuits, chocolate layer cake and iced tea.

"Elizabeth, that was great. It reminded me of my mother's cooking." He drank the last sip of iced tea and set the glass on the table. "Thank yuh. Ah'll clear the table, and we can sit on yuh porch." She laughed.

"My porch?" Nathaniel said, wearing a puzzled expression.

"Don't yuh remember telling me yuh were fixing the porch for when yuh started courtin' me? That yuh hated getting bit by bugs, especially mosquitoes."

"Sure do. Am Ah courtin' yuh now?" He smiled and squinted his eyes.

"Yuh not courtin' anyone else, are yuh? If yuh not, then yuh can court me."

"'Lizabeth. Beth. Ah like that better. Can Ah call yuh Beth?"

Elizabeth threw her head back and laughed. "Yes, Nathaniel."

"Great. Well, Beth, now about this courtin' thing. The way Ah see it, Ah don't know about you, but Ah'd say Ah been courting yuh about three and a half years, give or take a week or two. Now don't get me wrong, Ah still want tuh go sit on my porch. May Ah escort my lady?" Nathaniel stood and held out his hand.

"Nathaniel, the dishes. Yuh don't want tuh court me?" She was beginning to feel weak. She placed one hand on the back of the chair and the other on the counter. *Maybe Ah was tuh forward,* she thought.

"Don't ruin the moment, Beth. The dishes can wait. Oh! Now where was Ah?" He held out his hand again and stood tall and cavalier, waiting for Elizabeth to put her hand on his. "Beth? ... The hand. Put yuh right hand on top of my hand." He did all he could do to keep from laughing. Elizabeth appeared absolutely lost, but she did what he asked. He swung her around and pulled her close to him. "Will yuh marry me, my Lady Beth?" He had to hold her tight. He felt her weight against him. Her eyes glassed over.

She wanted to speak, but the words lingered in the back of her throat, and tears trickled down her face.

"Okay, Lady Beth, let's walk slowly tuh my porch. There's a beautiful swing waiting for us."

The strength returned to Elizabeth's legs and she managed to walk from the kitchen through the living room and out to the swing on the front porch.

Nathaniel locked eyes with her. "Ah'm sorry if Ah may have upset yuh, but Ah've loved yuh since the very first time Ah saw yuh. Ah understood all the pain yuh carried, and why it was so important for yuh tuh wait, so Ah waited with yuh. If yuh won't have me as yuh husband, Ah'll still love yuh."

"Yes ... Yes ... Yuh the only man Ah ever loved. Thank yuh for lovin' me and waitin'."

Nathaniel cupped Elizabeth's face in his hand and kissed her on the lips. She kissed him back, and they were locked in an embrace of love and emotion. Their hearts beat with a separate rhythm that seemed scattered, but with a single breath, their hearts came into sync and beat as one. Time passed, and they held each other on the porch as if they were trying to make up for all the time they had missed. Nathaniel promised to take her to a jeweler in Macon the next day to pick out her rings.

Johnny returned about an hour later. He was smiling when he approached the front porch.

"Hey, Mr. Baker. How's everything? Oh Ma, thanks for the use of the car. Ah guess Ah'll see yuh later." He opened the door to enter the house.

"Johnny, wait. Nathaniel and Ah are engaged." She wrapped her arm around Nat's waist.

"Dag, man, yuh work fast!" Johnny held out his hand, and he and Nathaniel shook hands and embraced.

"It's that way when yuh have a head start," Nathaniel said.

"Ah'd say four years is a real head start." Johnny hugged his mother and gave Nathaniel a manly hug. "Ah can't wait tuh call yuh Dad." He smiled and entered the house.

———m———

Two weeks passed, and Nathaniel and Elizabeth were down by the lake, sitting in the front seat of his car and listened to Lyle Steven's "The Heart of Soul" on the radio. It was one of those hot muggy, nights in late May, and they were more comfortable and relaxed than on previous dates. They snuggled in each other's embrace. Their eyes were fixed on the moonbeams that danced on the shimmering water. They held each other, intending to wait until their wedding night.

"Oh, Ah can't do this any longer," Nathaniel blurted out. He threw his head back on the seat and his arm out the window.

"Do what?" Elizabeth teased.

"Ah want yuh *now!*" He lifted his head and rested it on hers.

"Ah do tuh, but ... ," Elizabeth whispered.

Nathaniel was quick to respond. "But, let's take a ride over tuh Macon and check intuh a motel. Ah promise Ah won't have yuh do anything yuh not ready tuh do. We can just relax, and if the feeling moves us, we'll be ready."

"Nat?" Elizabeth said, while her old shy feelings returned. "If the feeling moves us? ... The feeling is moving yuh right now." She was tempting him. She wanted him, her body was throbbing to be pleasured, but at the same time, she had the fear that young girls have from the thought of their first experience.

"It's not moving you?" A smile graced his face, and his eyes were glassy and sexual. "Do yuh know what yuh doing tuh me?" He leaned down and passionately kissed her. "Hello, my Lady Beth."

"Hello, my Master Nat," she teased.

"How'd yuh hand get inside my shirt?" He held his teeth together and sensually sucked in air while throwing his head back on the seat again, then blew it out.

"Wel l l l l!" Elizabeth teased, drawing out the word while rubbing his hairy chest.

"Okay, baby." He raised his head and removed his arm from around Elizabeth while he spoke. "It's time tuh go." He put the car in gear and backed away from the lake, shifted the gear to drive and waited for Elizabeth to stop him. Within the next few minutes he pulled the car to the side of the road and leaned over and gave her a long passionate kiss.

"No! ... No! ... We got tuh stop or ... or we won't get tuh Macon," Elizabeth said, managing to squeeze out words and hide her passion.

Nathaniel stopped and stared at her. He'd heard her say, "Get tuh Macon," and he knew she was ready to do some loving. There was a small, clean, nicely decorated, black-owned motel in Macon. Nathaniel drove, and the radio played love songs.

Elizabeth sat in the car and waited for Nathaniel to return from checking into the Emerald Inn. She noticed the row of one level, detached, room and bath bungalows, and she nervously watched through the car window and wondered what was taking Nathaniel so long, but it was only a few minutes. Nathanial returned. He had done a quick and thorough inspection of the room before escorting Elizabeth in from the car.

As soon as they reached the privacy of their room, their bodies took control. Their sensual indulgence removed Elizabeth's schoolgirl shyness. Nathaniel was warm, gentle, patient and smooth. His foreplay was like the prelude to a soulful musical composition, and when he entered her, he moved as though he were floating on the aura of the melody.

This was her first loving, and it was all she dreamed it would be. When their nakedness first met, warm gentle shivers vibrated from their inner most parts to the sensitivity of their warm moist skin. They enveloped each other; they loved each other. The kind of love they only dreamed of. The kind of dream reserved for soul mates.

Johnny was floating in serenity. For the first time he felt his life had balance, a calmness. All that was important to him was falling in place. For years Nathaniel had been there for them. Johnny was so happy for his mother. Having her married to Nathaniel before he left for school was a perfect arrangement. It was akin to having someone watch over your loved one while you're away. Someone you could count on, trust and feel comfortable with, akin to the way a mother feels about the security of her child.

Sarah was happy to return to Rehoboth for Elizabeth's wedding. She and Elizabeth spent little time together, but when they did they spoke of Nathaniel Baker. Elizabeth thought about their conversation when Johnny graduated from the eighth grade, and Sarah saying, *"Listen, big sis, please call me when yuh two are an item."*

Elizabeth wanted to call Sarah in the evening at home, but Sarah always insisted she call her at work. She was a 32- year-old, single black female, who worked hard and earned her position as a journalist with the Atlanta Sun, thanks to the help of the Affirmative Action Laws. Elizabeth didn't think it was proper for her to receive personal calls at work, but she called her anyway, and Sarah was delighted.

Elizabeth wondered if Sarah's insistence was her way to reinforce to her big sister her status at work—to hear her secretary announce, "The Atlanta Sun, Miss Sarah Turner's Office;" to remind her of her professional status. "Naw!" Elizabeth shook her head. *Sarah knows Ah don't care about that stuff.*

She sat back in her lounge chair, the one that was MaDear's favorite; she'd had a custom slipcover made for it. *Ah've only had one depressing time in my life. From May 14th, 1950 until December 14th, 1950. Two days after Johnny was born, when my life took on a new meaning. And around every curve, my Lord has made a way for me. Ah can even feel Daddy coming back. So Sarah, keep yuh Atlanta Sun. Ah have Johnny, and a man that loves me more than he loves himself.*

Elizabeth pulled her legs up in the chair, rested her head on the side and bask in the warmth of her euphoric emotions. She never called Sarah, but it wasn't long before the telephone rang and interrupted pleasant moments.

"Big Sis, Mama called me and gave me the good news. Weren't yuh gonna call me? Ah can't believe that man waited for yuh all those years."

"He said he loved me the first time he saw me. Ah didn't believe him at first, but he was always with me, especially when Ah needed him. Ah loved him so long, Ah think it was that day yuh pointed him out tuh me, but Ah had tuh keep my feet on the ground." Elizabeth crawled out of MaDear's chair and began pacing the floor. She twirled the cord around her finger, unwound it and re-twirled it several times.

"Do Ah get an invitation?"

"Ah mailed them out tuhday. Well yuh always so busy. Ah knew Mama would call yuh, and yuh'd call me when yuh had time tuh talk." Elizabeth listened for Sarah to say something, but the line was quiet for a while. She hoped Sarah was reflecting on her past behavior. It wasn't long before she heard her breathing hard. "Sarah? Sarah, Are yuh still there?" Elizabeth was still pacing and twirling the cord.

"Ah'm sorry, Elizabeth. Ah didn't mean tuh treat yuh like that."

"Ah love you, Sarah. One day when we're old and gray we'll talk about that. For now, it's the wedding and the graduation. The wedding is Saturday, May 17th, and Johnny graduates on May 25th. Nathaniel and Ah plan tuh take a couple of days for a very short honeymoon and be home by Tuesday evening tuh help Johnny prepare for graduation." Elizabeth had curled up in MaDear's chair again, but she was still playing with the telephone cord.

"'Lizabeth, Ah'm so happy for yuh. You have what Ah've always wanted, but never found. Ah'll be at the wedding and the graduation. If yuh need anything, just call me."

"Ah will, Sarah. Ah'll talk tuh yuh later." Elizabeth held the phone until she heard Sarah hang up, before placing her handset on the cradle.

───ｍ───

Elizabeth and Nathaniel decided on a small church wedding and a gathering of family and friends at Elizabeth's home after the service. Since Johnny was the only man in Elizabeth's life, it was appropriate for him to give her away. Nathaniel's oldest brother would be standing with him as his best man.

On that special day in May, there was a wedding. There was so much love in this union; it was the most beautiful wedding the Bethlehem Baptist Church had ever been a part of. Everyone knew it wasn't the fresh cut flowers decorating the church's pulpit, or the large white ribbons tied to the end of each pew. It wasn't the elegant, coordinated attire of the wedding party. The guests had yet to see them. It was the warmth of love that radiated throughout the church. Every pew was stuffed with guests squeezed shoulder to shoulder, but that had not dampened their spirits. They were smiling, and some were weeping, men and women alike.

The pianist was playing a medley of spiritual wedding songs when Reverend Turner escorted Loretha to seats in the left front pew where Sarah was sitting. Loretha held her lacy handkerchief, smiled and dabbed at the tears that continued to flood her eyes. Malcolm and Thea were behind Sarah and Loretha. Reverend Oliver stood at the end of the aisle. He smiled with teary eyes, waiting to see Johnny walking his mother down the aisle.

Nathaniel and his brother stood and stepped closer to the pulpit, looking toward the rear of the church. All eyes were on them, admiring their basic black suits, eggshell white shirts, and burgundy and beige, printed neckties. Johnny wore an identical outfit. Reverend Lipton stood and walked to the pulpit. The guests turned to see Lisa Murdock, the matron of honor, walk down the aisle. She was wearing a classy, burgundy, chiffon and lace cocktail length dress, and carrying a single white rose.

The pianist sounded the beginning chords of "The Wedding March." The guests stood in one unified movement, and Nathaniel's hands began to tremble. His brother gave him a comforting touch, but he couldn't see the tears streaming down his face. Nathaniel's mother reached across the front pew and beckoned him to take her lacy handkerchief. He did and began to wipe his tears. Johnny escorted Elizabeth down the aisle. Nathaniel was realizing his dream.

Johnny smiled at Reverend Oliver as he passed him. Loretha held her handkerchief to her face, and her eyes were fixed on the two of them. Reverend Turner's eyes were attracted to the way Reverend Oliver's eyes attended to Johnny. He'd seen him look at him like that before, several times over the years. He longed for Johnny.

Reverend Turner had been watching him every chance he got since MaDear died. He knew Owen lost Johnny shortly after Elizabeth met Mr. Baker. That's when he noticed Owen seemed to be stalking Johnny.

Reverend Turner turned as Johnny and Elizabeth passed. He offered a tiny smile when Elizabeth glanced in his direction.

Elizabeth was absolutely beautiful. She decided against wearing the pure white dress and veil sanctioned by Reverend Lipton, wearing instead an elegantly fitted, egg shell white, two piece suit with a matching pill box hat and carried a bouquet of four long stem roses, one for every year she knew Nathaniel.

Reverend Lipton watched Johnny escorting his mother and remembered Elizabeth coming to him when he was just an infant, crying and asking him to pray for her and her child. He remembered christening Johnny when he was a baby and baptizing him as a boy when he stood just above mother's waist. Now he was a man giving his mother away to another man that he loved, admired and trusted. Reverend Lipton felt the pulse of his heart beating. He knew the Lord was telling him that this union had His blessing. Nathaniel and Elizabeth were married.

CHAPTER 18

Johnny majored in Business Finance and Economics. His college days were an indisputable contrast from that of his high school years. He was respected for his maturity, intelligence, articulation, and his display of leadership qualities, mostly in social and academic activities. The tall, skinny, high school boy had filled out during his college years. By graduation, he was a confident, tall, handsome, well-developed young man.

Johnny had all the credentials that would land a white man a banking position during his final semester prior to graduation. But it took the Equal Employment Opportunities Commission (EEOC) to level the playing field. The Legend Bank of the Americas in Washington, D.C. hired him as a mid-level manager with a starting salary of $39,400.00, comparable to his white counterpart and an excellent salary for a black man in the early seventies. As soon as he was settled, he accepted an educational grant from the bank and registered at historically black college to study for his Master's degree. That was where he met Julia.

Julia ordered a cup of coffee and Johnny ordered a cup of herbal tea. The waitress jotted down the orders on her pads, but she neglected to note the table numbers. When she returned, she gave Johnny the coffee and Julia the tea. Johnny was reading the financial section of the newspaper, and Julia was going over a legal brief. They were sitting in separate booths and facing each other, but their view was partially obstructed by the back of the center seat. They reached for their cups at the same time and realized the error simultaneously.

"Excuse me, Miss," Johnny summoned the waitress. "I ordered herbal tea, not coffee." He eased the coffee cup closer to the edge of the table.

The waitress turned and walked back to Johnny. "I'm sorry, sir."

"I think you have my order," Julia said, glancing over the seat at Johnny.

Johnny turned and was greeted by Julia's warm smile. Instant attraction. The contents of the cups no longer mattered.

Johnny stood. "Hello, I'm John Turner." Knowing it to be etiquettely incorrect to offer his hand to a lady, he took a gentle bow.

Julia smiled, and without standing she offered her hand. "Hello, I'm Julia Batten." A sophisticated chuckle slightly parted her lips.

Johnny accepted her hand as if he were going to kiss it instead of the cordial shaking, all the time gazing at her. Julia allowed a tiny laugh to escape her lips, and they smiled at each other.

"I've finally met you," Johnny said, gazing down at her

"Met me? You've been waiting to meet me?"

"Yes," Johnny responded in a voice so charming he even surprised himself. "You're the woman I've been dreaming about. You're real. I'm so very happy to meet you, Miss Julia Batten. May I share your table?" He continued to smile and gaze at her. He held one hand behind his back, and his posture remained as if frozen in a slight bow.

"Are you an honorable man, Mr. Turner?" Her tone was serious, but her eyes told him she wanted him to share her booth.

"I assure you I'm an honorable man."

She waved the palm of her hand over the table and Johnny slipped into the booth.

"Thank you, Miss Batten."

The waitress was still standing there. "I'm so happy I've brought the two of you together." A wide grin spread her lips. "Now may I correct your orders? It's on me."

Johnny looked at Julia. "Do you still want coffee, because whatever you're having, I'll have the same?"

"Coffee," Julia said.

Johnny nodded, agreeing to have the same.

The waitress smiled and walked away without writing anything down.

"So … are you a student here?" Johnny asked. He couldn't take his eyes off her.

"Yes, I'm studying law, and you?" She adjusted the corners of her papers continuously until the edges were as even as her law books. "And you?"

"I'm a business finance graduate student." He knew she was nervous. He wanted to hold her hands, and rub them and kiss them and tell her she could trust him.

Julia and Johnny were involved in an amicable conversation when the waitress returned with two cups of coffee, placing them on the table. Johnny was overcome with Julia's intelligence and beauty. She looked like a model rather than a person studying law. Her long, silky black hair, with its gentle curl at the end, fell at her mid back. Her sandy colored complexion was smooth and highlighted by her rosy cheeks and dark eyes.

Telephone numbers were exchanged and a date was made for another time in the near future. Their coffee was cold and untouched, but Johnny left a five-dollar tip for the waitress.

Having Julia in his life didn't deter Johnny from his studies. He worked hard, and eighteen months later, he had earned his Masters, and mastered the operations of the banking and investment world to the point where his ideas were revolutionary and profitable. He learned early that when profit was involved, race took the second seat.

Advancement was easy, but watching his back was a skill that required continuous practice.

With the compounded interest, Johnny had nearly thirty thousand dollars waiting for him in the tiny bank back home. Some of it his inheritance from MaDear, the remainder, the result of an anonymous act of penance. He had more money than most black men of the day. The month he graduated from college was the last of the fifty-dollar bills. Johnny withdrew all the money and invested it in the Legend Bank Of the Americas, some in stable income accounts, some in bonds and a small portion in stocks. He watched the stock market, and when the time was right, he'd do what he thought was the right thing.

While Johnny was advancing in the banking world, Malcolm was finally finishing college as a business major. It had taken him five years, including the summer classes, and his grades were just passing enough to qualify him for his degree. Employment was another issue. Johnny was home for a few days, and Elizabeth and Nathaniel were telling him that Malcolm had been working as a custodian at the high school for that past six months. They were all sitting on the front porch relaxing and enjoying the fresh lemonade Elizabeth made.

"Ah know Thea must be disappointed," Elizabeth said.

Nathaniel knew Malcolm well. He had been a student in several of his required math classes. "Yuh-know, Beth." Nathaniel was the only person to call her Beth, and she loved it. The first time he called her Beth was the evening he asked her to marry him. "It's a wonder that boy finished college. Ah guess Ah have tuh give him that, but Ah would've never believed it possible. Ah guess when college is a free ride, yuh take yuh time graduating, but Ah don't know how he did it. He lacked initiative, consistency and drive." He took a sip of his lemonade and allowed his eyes to wander the screen of the porch, in the direction of Concord Baptist Church, before turning his eyes back on his glass.

"Hanging out and showing off were his main sports. Owen and Thea let him play most of his life. He's had no struggles in his life. Now, he's paying his dues. He's a man now. A man's got tuh pay his dues." *Dag! That's some good lemonade.* He turned the glass up and took the last few swallows.

"Let me fix some more." She reached for the pitcher and entered the house.

Nathaniel didn't know about Malcolm and Johnny, sameness. He only knew of their differences, but he believed if a black man made it, he should return to his roots and help another black man. He wanted to say this to Johnny, but he knew and believed Malcolm had dues to pay before opportunity could knock.

Johnny wasn't thinking about paying dues. He was quiet, but he was listening to everything his mother and Nathaniel were saying. He sipped his lemonade slowly and crossed his legs at his ankle. He was thinking about all the terrible things Malcolm had done to him. The painful experiences of yesteryears were clear and vivid. They were children then, and some lessons were difficult and dangerously learned. It had been over eight years since the bike incident, and during the last two years of high school, Malcolm had kept his peace and distance.

He knew he could and would help Malcolm. He knew of the expectations to help a brother of the soul, but it would not be for Malcolm, it would be for Reverend Oliver. When there were conflicts with Malcolm, Reverend Oliver was always fair. Until Nathaniel, he was the only man who seemed to genuinely care about him. When he was young, he believed Reverend Oliver's goodness came from being a man of God, but as he grew older, he knew there was something else, something special he couldn't put his finger on. Grandfather Turner was a man of God, yet he only felt the nothingness seeping from him.

Johnny knew people in the business world. He had contacts, and he knew he could get Malcolm a good paying, respectable job. It would be a challenge because Malcolm's college transcript was below the standards recruited by the industry, but there were favors that had been delivered, and now there were favors to be retrieved. He would make the necessary arrangements and call in one of those favors, but he needed to remain anonymous. He believed it would serve no purpose to let Malcolm know he had a hand in helping his career. Instead, he would make the necessary arrangements to allow Malcolm to believe he had done one thing right in his life.

"Nat, you're right, we all have to pay our dues. Malcolm is paying now, and he should. It'll help him be a better man. Then, when his debt is clear, good things will happen for him." Johnny stood and placed his hands on his hips. "I took a minute and visited Reverend Oliver yesterday." He looked down at his feet and raised his head again. "It was weird, man. Reverend Oliver was so happy to see me I thought he was going to cry. I don't know why he acted that way. I visit him every time I'm home."

"That is weird," Nathaniel said.

Elizabeth returned the porch. "Y'all stop talking about Malcolm," Elizabeth said. "Seems like everybody worries about Malcolm, and he always comes up smelling like a rose. Johnny, Ah want tuh hear about that new bank they're opening over in Atlanta."

Nathaniel and Johnny looked at each other and didn't try to correct her. Besides she was all ready off on a new subject, and they were finished with what they had to say about Reverend Oliver. Both men understood Elizabeth and knew correcting her wasn't worth the thousand questions she would ask.

"Oh yes, Mama, they offered that bank to me. I don't want it. It would mean leaving the central office." Johnny turned and bear hugged her from behind.

"Shoo, boy! Shoo!" She flung her dishtowel sideways at him. "Nat, do yuh hear this boy?"

"He could be the first black banker in Georgia, and he doesn't know if he wants it," Elizabeth spoke out in disbelief, pushing Johnny away from her.

"Mama!" Johnny placed his hands on her shoulders to hold her in place. "If I take the bank and it fails, my career is over. The bank only wants me so they can boast they have a black man heading a local branch. On the other hand, if I remain in the central office, I will be working with some of the most influential men in the industry. No matter how that little bank does, my career will continue to grow. There are other black men in the office that want that bank, let them have it."

Elizabeth listened to him. She heard every word he said, but it was the way he said it, the proper tone of his words. He was her Johnny, but he sounded different. His dialect had changed; his words were what she called proper; Northern proper, as proper as a real businessman. And she loved to hear him speak.

"Yeah, man." Nat nodded his head "Ah know what yuh mean. Follow yuh instincts, man, yuh won't go wrong. Oh we have some good news, too."

Johnny sat up straight, preparing to hear what had them so excited. Elizabeth sat on the arm of the chair, leaned over and hugged Nat as they smiled at each other.

"All right! Are you two going to leave me to form my own conclusions?"

"We're sorry, Johnny," Nat said. "We're having a new house built, and we have a surprise for you. C'mon take a ride with us. We want yuh tuh see where it will be built."

"We could walk there, but then we'd have tuh walk back. Ah don't like walkin' in the Georgia heat," Elizabeth said. "C'mon get in the car. It's on the other side of Mama's house."

Johnny's mouth fell open when they pulled up on the land on Rehoboth Road that bordered Collins Road. He got out of the car, and his eyes glassed over.

"Mama, how did you get this land?" He felt so weak he had to lean against Nat's car. "Have you and Nat walked to the house? There's hardly any road left." He tried to talk and his emotions burst to sobs. He placed both hands on the car and cried.

"Man, let it out. Ah know yuh have a lot of emotions tied up in this land." Nat reached for his handkerchief and handed it to Johnny.

"Man, God is good. Two weeks ago Ah was sittin' and thinkin' Ah'd like tuh buy some land. Ah was hoping tuh find land here in Rehoboth, and there it was, a land auction for MaDear's land scheduled for the next day. Yuh mother cried and Ah prayed, but we were going to that land auction. It was right here where we are standing, and we were the only black folk here. Between yuh mama and me, we had $12,231.52 to our name, but we weren't gonna let the white man get MaDear's land. The Lord bought rain that day, and only three white men showed up, including the auctioneer. They bid and we bid, and they bid and we bid again, and we kept bidding. We won the bid for 10.4 acres of land for $6,550.00."

Johnny wiped his face, wrapped his arms around Nat and hugged him. He was still crying when he hugged his mother. "Let me pay you for the land. I can afford it. You're going to need the money when you start building your house. I want to give you $10,000 for the land and pay for the land survey. You know I have the money."

"Yuh can pay us later, man. We got it for now."

"Well, Nat, we may need the money for the new house," Elizabeth said.

"Okay, Johnny, but only for what we paid and the land survey for the acre cut away for our home."

They shook on it.

"Now are yuh ready for that walk?" Nat said.

"It's been 25 years since we left that house." Elizabeth said "Ah think yuh guys need tuh come back tuh the house and put on some coveralls, long sleeve shirts, hats and high-top work boots. Johnny, Ah think yuh can fit in some of Nat things. No tellin' what might be lurkin' in them woods, not tuh mention the snakes. Nat, yuh need yuh machete to cut back the overgrowth, and don't forget to take along some work gloves."

The men returned to Collins Road, looking as if they were returning from the cotton fields. Elizabeth was right. The forest had recaptured the road leading to the house. Nat had to cut a path with his machete.

"Man, how do I thank you for getting this land?"

"Don't thank me, thank the Lord. Ah never read the real estate section of the newspaper before. The Lord gave me a reason at the right moment because he wanted me to see the auction notice. Yuh-know, them folks were s'pose to set a poster on the land to let the people in the area know about the land auctioned. Wasn't nothin' posted. Ah know them folks didn't want tuh live over here. They just wanted tuh buy the land and sell it tuh black folk tuh make a profit."

A fallen Georgia pine lay across the overgrown road. The men stepped over it. Johnny's right foot landed on a black snake, holding it to the baked hard ground, and it wiggled in place. Nat laughed and Johnny cringed.

"Man, Ah can kill it or yuh can step up on the log and let it go."

Johnny stepped on the log. Nat bent over laughing. "C'mon, man, Ah see the house."

Johnny jumped from the log. He and Nat hurried along. The house was standing tall and straight. Nat used the machete to cut away the wild shrubbery, small trees and crawling vines. Johnny pulled the debris away from the house, and they walked all the way around, checking the rock and cement foundation and finding some loose areas. The tin roof was completely covered with rust. Johnny pried open the door and searched for water leaks. There were several in each room. All the windows had been nailed shut, but none of the panes were broken. Johnny didn't check the plumbing. He knew it wouldn't work without electricity.

"Nat, I'm not prepared to renovate the house yet, but I need to do some repairs to prevent further damage. Could you find someone to open the road and cut back the forest from the house, then patch the foundation and roof? As soon as I get back to D.C., I'll send you a cashier's check and include an extra thousand to cover the repairs. If you need more, just call."

"Sure, Johnny. Now let's fight our way out of here."

Thea and Reverend Oliver were content, even proud of Malcolm. Six months after Johnny's conversation with Nat, he called in one of his favors. He believed Malcolm had learned some humility and had paid his dues, as Nat put it. Malcolm was given a position with Landers, Landers & Fine Brokerage firm, in Atlanta. He moved to Jonesboro, Georgia. During the following year he met and married Theresa Coleman, a charming and beautiful brown-skinned high school English teacher.

CHAPTER 19

Johnny had two specific reasons for visiting Rehoboth. He was finally financially secure whereas he could set in motion plans to have MaDear's home restored to its original charm, and he wanted to keep MaDear's name alive by building a medical facility to service the local communities in her honor.

—⁓—

It was September 6th, 1982, when Johnny began to acquire the land to build the Anna May Collins Clinic. Johnny was brilliant at grant writing, and he was connected to the right people who ensured his grant landed in the hands of the right people. It wasn't long before he received a substantial Federal Grant to build, staff and purchase supplies and equipment for the clinic and emergency trauma center. Because it was a Federal Project to benefit the people of Bibb County, the County agreed to sell the land to the Federal Government for one dollar per acre. Johnny managed to select a twenty-five acre parcel of land that happened to have $50,000.00 worth of prime Georgia pine on it. The sale of the timber would go into a fund to provide medical care for the indigent patients.

The groundbreaking ceremony was held on December 5, 1983, and the clinic was opened on October 4th, 1984. All of the County, State and Federal politicians were present for the unveiling. Johnny requested that Reverend Oliver be the officiating minister. It was really one of those days. The politicians used the events to campaign for themselves or for other party members due for re-election.

Reverend Turner was very upset that Johnny had Reverend Oliver on the program instead of himself. Elizabeth decided to volunteer to assist with signing people up for the health screening program scheduled for later in the morning rather than seeing Johnny buddying up with Reverend Oliver. Nathaniel helped blow up helium balloons for the children. Reverend Turner, Loretha, Thea and Malcolm and his wife sat in the audience and listened to all the speeches.

Nat had maintained Collins Road, having the driveway blacktopped from Rehoboth Road up to the circular driveway. Johnny had an appointment to meet with Mr. Robert Anderson of Southern Gold Builders in front of MaDear's Cottage.

"Mr. Anderson, I need to be clear with you before you take on this project." Johnny rubbed his forehead with his fingers and kicked up the dirt with his boots. "This house must stand. Tearing it down and rebuilding it is not an option. I want you to restore it to its original charm. You may stabilize the old timbers, but you cannot remove them." Johnny looked at the front door and pinched the corner of his eyes when he thought he saw MaDear standing in her doorway. He smiled and began cleaning his sunglasses. "If the timber is diseased, kill the disease. Don't remove the beadboard ceiling; if its warped, sand it even. You may replace the roof with asphalt, but then cover the asphalt with tin. You may replace the windows and doors and build new porches in the exact design as the old."

Mr. Anderson stood listening to Johnny. He pulled a section of creeping vine away from the house and stripped the leaves away until he was left with nature's rope. "Yuh grew up here, didn't yuh?"

"Yeah, man. A new house would remove the smells in the wood and walls holding my memories. Does that make sense to you?" Johnny turned his head to the side and squinted at him, holding his hand to shade his eyes against the sun.

"Yes, sir. My grandparents lost their place tuh taxes. We had three years of bad cotton, but the county didn't care. Add that tuh other bad years, and we lost our farm tuh taxes." Mr. Anderson gazed up at the sky. He pulled the visor of his cap to shade his eyes. "Man, we had two hundred acres, a farm house, a barn, yuh-know … we had a home, then we were homeless, living in an old trailer a mile deep in the woods."

Mr. Anderson bent over a picked up a hand full of stones and began throwing them into the woods and continued speaking. He threw a rock harder with each sentence he spoke, and his body turned as if he were swinging a golf club. "There were nine of us kids, my parents and grand-parents. The land was in our family since the 1700s. When the land went, it took my grandpa, too." A rock hit the roof of the old shed. "Ah was near manhood, and Ah swore Ah'd never farm. All the land was sold, but Ah got the acre the house was on. Nobody lived in it for twenty-two years. My sister's doll still laid on the upstairs bedroom floor. My grandpa died so the house could rot."

He threw his last rock, brushed his hands off on his pants and faced Johnny. "My grandma died a sad and lonely woman. Man, Ah cried like a baby when Ah got that house back. Ah restored it and Ah live in it tuhday with my family. So, man … Ah know where yuh heart is. Ah'll take care of yuh house."

Johnny stood back with his hands on his hips. He knew Mr. Anderson could have been lying to him, but what made him a good busi-nessman was his ability to read a person. The costs to rebuild or renovate were the same. Mr. Anderson knew he had the job. He didn't have to share that piece of his life with him.

"Thanks for sharing, man." He patted Mr. Anderson on the shoulder and they began walking toward the driveway. "I have other business today, but if you draw up your contract, I'll meet with you this evening. My father will be handling this project and responding to your payment scale. My mother knows what the house should look like, so you may consult with her for details." The men shook on the job.

Reverend Turner laid on his back on the gurney looking up at the gray ceiling and the large bright lights flash at repetitive intervals as the gurney was being raced down the corridor of the Anna May Collins Clinic. He was frightened. An oxygen mask covered his nose and mouth. His shirt had been ripped open, the buttons scattering across the floor while lead patches were applied to his chest. He gasped for air in spite of the pain and pressure on his chest that seemed to prevent his body from taking it in. Slowly, his eyes closed and all sounds and voices slipped into the abyss.

It was all so sudden. Reverend Turner and Loretha were returning from a church meeting late that Thursday evening, on October 17th, 1985. Loretha was walking ahead while John remained at the car to keep the headlights shining at the door to light her way. Suddenly, Loretha heard the blast of the horn. She ran back to the car and found him slumped over the steering wheel with his left arm under his body pressing on the horn.

"John! John!" she yelled, pushing him over onto the seat. He was awake. His eyes revealed his pain and fear. He was aware of what was happening. "Don't try tuh talk." She ran to the passenger side, opened the door and managed to pull him across the seat only a few inches. "Don't move John, just be still. Yuh gonna be all right." She ran back around the car, squeezed into the driver's seat, backed the car out and drove off to the clinic. She called Elizabeth as soon as John was placed on the gurney and wheeled into the treatment room.

—⟋m⟍—

Loretha, Elizabeth and Nathaniel waited for the doctor to explain John's condition. When a man wearing a white lab coat with a stethoscope folded in his side pocket entered the room, they all stood. "Mrs. Turner?" A medium height, young, very dark-skinned, black man called out to Loretha.

Elizabeth and Nathaniel kept Loretha between them, and they all stood. Fear had weakened her, etching its markings on her face and exhibiting its symptoms in her body tremors. Elizabeth and Nathaniel supported her with their arms around her waist.

"My name is Dr. Obey Amutu. Reverend Turner has suffered a massive heart attack, and his prognosis is guarded."

Elizabeth and Nathaniel sat Loretha back down. Nathaniel reached, and shook the doctor's hand.

"Mrs. Turner, I believe your husband has a good chance of getting over this. Of course, he will require a lot of care, but because of this clinic, we were able to provide an early intervention. He would not have had any chance if he had to go all the way to Macon for a first response treatment. He is in coma now, but the body heals while in coma."

He squatted down and took Loretha's hand in his and rubbed it. "Now, you do not worry. Recently, we were able to add a heliport to this facility. Your husband is being prepared to be airlifted to Atlanta University Hospital. They have the best Cardiac Intensive Care Unit in the region. You may ride in the helicopter with him." He turned to Elizabeth and Nathaniel. "I am afraid only Mrs. Turner can go along with him. Of course you may see him before he leaves."

Loretha wiped her eyes. "Elizabeth, call Sarah. Have her leave for the hospital right now. Ah need her tuh be with me." Elizabeth grabbed her mother and held her tight so she wouldn't have to see any more pain and fear in her face.

"All right, Mama. Nat and Ah will stop by yuh house and get yuh some clothing and personal things. We'll be driving up in the morning." She dug in her pocketbook for her small telephone book and wiped her eyes with the side of her hand even though she had a tissue in her pocket. *Sisters are supposed to know each other's number by heart. But Ah have tuh call her at work. It's still early.* She had the book in her hand. She looked at the clock. *8:57 A.M. She's at work.*

Dr. Amutu turned loose Loretha's hand, stood and addressed everyone. "I will return in a minute to tell you when it will be all right to see Reverend Turner." He bowed, backed out of the room, then turned to walk away.

Loretha rested her head against Elizabeth while Nat dug deep in his pocket for change. He placed a moderate amount of coins on the ledge below the pay phone, then he took Elizabeth's seat and held his arm around Loretha.

"Ah have tuh call her at work." Elizabeth dialed the number, dropped coins in the slot, spoke with Sarah's secretary and finally reached Sarah.

"Hi 'Lizabeth," her voice was cheerful.

"Sarah, Ah have bad news, and Ah want yuh tuh brace yuhself." Elizabeth deliberately forced Sarah to think the worst, believing when she gave her the news she could handle it.

"What is it? Is it Mama? Is it Daddy?" Sarah's voice was trembling.

"Sarah, Daddy had a heart attack, but he's still alive. The doctor said he has a good chance for recovery."

"Oh thank God." Sarah's crying suddenly changed to hysteria.

"Sarah. … Sarah!" Elizabeth called out, but all she could hear was Sarah's hysterical crying. She hung up the phone and called back to reach Sarah's secretary.

"Atlanta Sun, Miss Sarah Turner's Office."

"Yes," Elizabeth said. "Ah'm Miss Turner's sister. Ah just called her tuh tell her our father had a heart attack. Please go and see about her. She's in her office hysterical. Ah need tuh tell her that they are transferring our father tuh Atlanta University Cardiac Intensive Care Unit." Elizabeth turned and glanced over to her mother and Nat. She had the habit of twisting the cord as she spoke. She turned back and looked at the phone as if she were speaking to a person. "Our mother is being air-lifted along with him, and she wants Sarah tuh meet her there." Elizabeth pointed to the coins on the tray.

Nathaniel asked Loretha if she would be all right and she nodded, then he hurried off to find more change.

"Ah will stay on this line until yuh can get her tuh talk tuh me."

The operator cut in, "Please deposit fifty-cents for the next three minutes."

Elizabeth dropped two quarters into the slots.

"Hello? This is Miss Turner's secretary. Ah hung up the other line. She's calm enough tuh speak now. Ah'm going tuh transfer yuh."

"Thank you so much for yuh help," Elizabeth said, exhaling after she spoke.

"Yuh welcome."

"Hello, Elizabeth. Ah'm so sorry. My secretary said they're air-lifting Daddy and Mama here, tuh Atlanta?"

"Yes, and Mama needs yuh tuh meet her at the hospital. She is a nervous wreck, so yuh need tuh be strong for her. So you had yuh moment of hysteria, now tighten up and get over tuh the hospital. It will only take the helicopter about forty minutes tuh get there. They are getting' ready tuh leave here now. Nathaniel and Ah are drivin' up in the mornin'. We'll bring Mama some clothes and personal items." Elizabeth had placed one hand on the wall and stared at the telephone, blasting orders at Sarah like she was speaking to a child. Nat returned with the change just as the operator cut in again. Elizabeth dropped two more quarters in.

"Is Mama with you now?

"Yes, they haven't called her tuh leave yet. Hold on." She called her mother and Nat walked with her to the phone.

"Here she comes."

"Hello, Sarah." Loretha dabbed at the tears in her eyes. "Yuh'll be at the hospital when we get there, won't yuh? Ah'm scared, Sarah. He's so sick. Please be there. Ah need yuh. Ah don't want tuh be alone if something happens tuh him."

"Ah'm leaving my office as soon as Ah finish speaking with yuh. Ah'm gonna try tuh be there before yuh arrive, but if yuh get here before Ah do, don't yuh worry. Just know Ah'm on my way."

"Okay, Sarah. Please pray for yuh father."

"Ah will, Mama. Ah'll meet yuh at the hospital. Ah love yuh. See y'all soon."

Loretha handed the phone back to Elizabeth and dabbed at her eyes again. Nat helped her back to her seat.

Dr. Amutu returned to the waiting area. "We are ready."

"Sarah, they're ready tuh leave. We'll see yuh soon. Stay strong for Mama. Ah love yuh."

"Ah love yuh, tuh. See yuh soon."

Elizabeth hung up the telephone and hurried with Nathaniel and her mother to see her father. A weakening spell came over her and her mother when they saw him. He was in some kind of oxygen chamber. Elizabeth couldn't even kiss him, so she kissed the chamber. She hugged her mother and assured her that her father would be all right. Her mother was trembling again. The technicians wheeled the chamber out to the waiting helicopter.

"Mama, look at all the trouble and expense they are going through for him. If they thought he wasn't going to be all right, they wouldn't be doing all this. I'll notify the church, and we'll start a prayer chain. Mama, yuh always taught me, our Lord knows best."

"Time to go, Mrs. Turner," Dr. Amutu said. He escorted her by the arm and out to the heliport where a member of the flight crew took her by the arm.

It was extremely windy from the whirling blades. Loretha held one hand on her head and moved quickly in a bent over position. As soon as she was in the helicopter, the door was secured and the entrance ramp was pulled away. The helicopter wasted little time lifting off.

Elizabeth rested her head on Nathaniel's chest and her emotions broke loose. She sobbed; he held her tight, rubbing her back. He let her cry. She had fought her emotions all night for her mother's sake, taking charge, putting on a strong face, and she couldn't even kiss her father good-bye. She had waited 35 years to kiss him, and now a piece of plastic stood between them. It didn't matter that he was unconscious. She only wanted to feel his flesh on her lips one more time in this life.

Nat placed his chin on top of her head and rocked and soothed her. Tears ran down his face as he felt her pain, and he let them drop of his chin because he didn't want to turn her loose.

Sarah picked up her office phone and hit #9 for an outside line. She called her significant other, Stephen Parker, the owner of the New Age Magazine. She had never introduced him to her parents, but it was in her immediate plan to do so. Now she needed him. She needed his broad shoulders and strong personality to support her. He was her rock and had begged her to marry him, but marriage and loss of independence was something Sarah was afraid of. Now she needed him to be with her, to drive her to the hospital and be her rock where she could acquire strength to support her mother.

"I'll be in front of the building in fifteen minutes," Stephen said.

Sarah did a quick freshening of her makeup, hugged and thanked her secretary and asked her to notify her boss of the emergency, then hurried to the elevator corridor.

Stephen was where he said he would be. He was waiting to open the car door as Sarah approached it.

"Thank yuh, Stephen."

He could see she had been crying and was still upset, so he drove quickly, weaving in and out of traffic. He was strategic and missed most traffic lights. Finally, he pulled up in front of the hospital. "I'll let you out here and park the car. I'll meet you in the Cardiac ICU."

Sarah nodded and hurried from the car. When she got off the elevator, she rushed down the corridor to the nurses station and asked the nurse at the desk if Reverend John Turner arrived by a medical flight from the Anna May Collins Clinic. The nurse told her they were expecting him in any minute.

"Thank yuh." She exhaled, turned her back to the counter and ran her fingers through her curly hair. She looked at her watch and turned back to the nurse. "Would yuh call me when they arrive? Reverend John Turner is my father, and my mother is on that flight with him."

"Yes, ma'am.

"Thanks." She gently tapped the counter and returned to the elevator corridor to wait for Stephen. She propped herself against an adjacent wall and watched the indicator lights for elevators that were coming up and signaling that it was going to stop. After approximately ten minutes of waiting, Stephen stepped off the elevator.

He took Sarah's hand and began walking toward the nurses' station. "Have they arrived yet?"

"No the nurse said she would let me know when they came in."

"Well, let's stop by the desk again." He continued to hold her hand.

"Any news yet on Reverend John Turner's arrival? He was due into the Cardiac ICU via a helicopter lift from the Collins Clinic, south of Macon."

"Oh, yes, that flight arrived five minutes ago. We tried to find the lady who asked about it to tell her in was in but …"

"Please, just tell us where to go. My wife's parents were on that flight."

The nurse leaned over the counter and pointed to the double doors of the intensive care unit. "Go to Cardiac Intensive Care Unit."

Sarah and Stephen walked with a quickened pace through the doors of the Cardiac Intensive Care Unit and passed the first door to right. Loretha saw Sarah and called her.

"Mama!" Sarah cried, and embraced her, before they sat on the sofa.

Loretha looked up at Stephen. "Hello," she said and nodded.

Stephen smiled, and Sarah stood and grabbed his hand. "Mama, this is my dear friend Stephen Parker."

Stephen bowed and smiled gently. "It's nice meeting you, Mrs. Turner. Everyone just calls me Steve." Then he took a seat.

"Mama, Steve told the nurse he was my husband because only immediate family members are allowed in here.

Sarah held her mother's hand. "How is Daddy?"

"Honey, he's still in a coma, but the doctors are giving him hope. Yuh'll be able tuh see him as soon as they make him comfortable. Elizabeth and Nathaniel should arrive sometime before lunch tomorrow."

Elizabeth had called Johnny and told him of her father's illness. She told him she met Dr. Obey Amutu and praised him for his selection of a clinic director. Johnny was concerned for how his mother was handling her father's illness. She told him she was praying every chance she got and that his fate was in God's hands. Johnny asked to speak with Nat and Elizabeth handed him the phone.

"Hello, Johnny. Yeah, man, Dr. Obey Amutu had yuh grandfather flown to Atlanta. He said it had the best Cardiac Intensive Care Unit in the region." Nat stood tall and rubbed his hand across his hair. He looked for Elizabeth, but she had left the room.

"How were Mama and Gram'ma?"

"They were pretty broken up. Yuh mama had tuh be strong for yuh grandmother. They put yuh grandfather in this plastic oxygen chamber. Man, it looked like a plastic coffin." Nathaniel sat in his lounge chair and rested his head on the back as he spoke. "After the helicopter took off, your mama fell tuh pieces. She said he would die before she could kiss him and that she hadn't kissed him in thirty-five years. Man, Ah had my hands full. We're leaving for Atlanta early in the morning."

"Nat, I'll try to get a flight out tomorrow afternoon. I have one important appointment tomorrow morning, so I'm free to leave tomorrow afternoon. I don't have to be back in the office until Monday. I'll try to make a reservation tonight. Would you tell Mama I'll be there as soon as I can?"

"Sure, Johnny. See yuh soon." Nat hung up the telephone.

Nat dialed Reverend Oliver's number and told him Reverend Turner had been airlifted to Atlanta University's Cardiac Intensive Care Unit. He asked that the church pray for him and reminded him to have the church to hold back on sending flowers and cards until he was out of intensive care.

Nathaniel told Elizabeth Johnny would arrive at the hospital some-time Friday afternoon.

"Thank you for talking tuh him, Nat. Ah would've never asked him tuh come. Daddy never did anything for him."

"Johnny is not coming for your father. He's coming for you and yuh mother. He's gonna meet us in Atlanta at the hospital tomorrow after-noon."

———ɯ———

Nathaniel and Elizabeth arrived at the hospital before noon the next day. Sarah and Loretha were at Reverend Turner's bedside, and had been with him most of the night.

Stephen Parker left late the night before and promised to return around noon to take Sarah to get her car so she could go home to freshen up and change.

Sarah stepped out when Elizabeth arrived. Only two people were allowed at his bedside at a time.

"How's he doing, Mama?" Elizabeth asked. She leaned over and kissed him on the cheek, holding her kiss longer than a normal kiss. Then she kissed him again, a short kiss.

"He' about the same. 'Lizabeth, yuh really wanted tuh kiss him."

"Yes, ma'am. Ah been waiting a long time tuh do that." Elizabeth sat at his bedside and held his hand. "Ah called Johnny last night, and he'll be here this afternoon. Ah had Nat call Reverend Oliver. He told him to have the church pray for Daddy. He also told him tuh hold off sending flowers and cards until Daddy is out of IC …" Elizabeth stared at her father; past all the tubes and tuned out all sounds. She stood and leaned over him closer—so close she could smell the cool freshness of his oxygen.

"Mama, do yuh eyeballs move when yuh in a coma? Get the nurse. Mama, Ah think Daddy is out of the coma. His eyeballs are movin' under his eyelids."

Loretha hurried to the nurse's desk inside the unit.

The nurse looked at the EEG monitor. "It does appear he is out of his coma. Let me call the doctor, but according to the monitor, it's reading he's in 'stage three sleep.' That's the 'dream' stage. They call it 'REM' sleep for 'Rapid Eye Movement.'"

—⁓—

… And the Lord spoke to Reverend Turner.

John, you asked me to show you a sign. I have given you many signs. I have given you sight, yet you cannot see. I have given you emotions, but you fail to use them even when a warm heart has come to you. You have ears, yet you failed to hear the cries of the elder of your seed, the only one to pass your seed on to the generations to come. You are a weak and cowardly man, and you fail to see the error of your ways, but you have dedicated your life to me. All that you have seen and suspected, know it to be true. Leave out the doubt, remove the excuses and explanation and see all situations as they are presented to you. In your coming months, you will remember the past, and I will show you all that you have failed to see. You must take the first step to rectify the wrong you have done. The help you need has always been with you.

—⁓—

"The doctor is here," the nurse said. "Would you mind stepping out while he examines Reverend Turner?" The nurse was pulling at the curtain when they left.

Elizabeth and Loretha returned to the waiting room to meet up with Nathaniel and Sarah. Their faces were bright and they were chatty, but they didn't want to be too sure before they got the report from the doctor.

"What happened, Mama?" Sarah said. She was ready to assume the worst until she assessed their disposition.

"We think he's out of the coma, but we don't know. Even the nurse wasn't sure, so she called the doctor. We were asked tuh leave the area while they examined him. Now don't get excited. Let's wait 'til they tell us something," Loretha announced.

Stephen Parker walked into the waiting room, and Sarah ran to him. He stood, wondering what was happening and who Elizabeth and Nathaniel were.

He looked down at Sarah and spoke softly, "Is your father all right?"

"We think he's doing better. We're waiting tuh hear from the doctor." Sarah had her head resting on his chest and her arm around his waist. Then she realized he didn't know Elizabeth and Nathaniel. "Oh, Nathaniel and Elizabeth Baker, my sister and her husband, Ah'd like yuh tuh meet my dearest friend, Stephen Parker."

Stephen extended his hand to Nat. "Steve, man." They shook hands. "Yeah, Nat, man."

"Elizabeth, it's very nice meeting you."

"Is this the Turner family?" A middle aged, medium height woman entered the room. "I'm Dr. Baynard. Who ever noticed the REM was very perceptive. Reverend Turner is indeed out of his coma and on the way to recovery."

Loretha, Elizabeth, Nathaniel and Sarah dropped to their knees and immediately thanked the Lord, while Steven and Dr. Baynard stood with their heads bowed. A minute later they were standing again and kissing each other. The doctor cleared her throat to get their attention.

Johnny walked into the waiting room. Elizabeth hugged him and quickly told him her father was out of his coma.

A week later Reverend Turner was moved to a semi private room. Loretha spent most of the day at the hospital and her nights with Sarah. She got to know Stephen Parker very well and enjoyed his company. Sarah explained that they met at a literary conference, but she didn't tell her mother that she had him give up his large apartment for a small studio and move into her apartment with her. He basically moved out while

REHOBOTH ROAD

Loretha was staying with Sarah. She spent a month in Atlanta before Reverend Turner was discharged from the hospital. Sarah and Stephen drove them back to Rehoboth.

CHAPTER 20

By the summer of 1986, Johnny had advanced up the corporate ladder to second vice president and regional director for all the bank branches in the Caribbean and Central American region. He had a luxurious corner office on the 16th floor of the Legend Building, the main headquarters in Washington, D.C., and his salary was in the upper six figures. Along with his market investments, he was a millionaire several times over.

Julia had been with Johnny since their graduate days at Howard, but they were both busy making their way and developing their dreams. They always loved each other. It had been an on-again, off-again relationship, not really breaking up, just drifting apart, each sharing the many reasons. Now their careers were in place. They were prosperous, mature and settled. There were no obstacles or boundaries to keep them apart, yet they were incomplete.

Johnny loved Julia. He believed they were meant for each other. It was their shared interest, their compatible physical appearance, their mannerisms, their attributes and their particulars.

Julia was the product of her black father and her Cherokee Indian mother, both from the Rocky Mount area of North Carolina. Poor, hardworking folks who had suffered the same oppression as any other Southern minority. Julia was the first in her family to have the opportunity to attend college. Like Johnny, she took none of it for granted.

It was January 28, 1986, when an impulse to call Julia had overpowered Johnny. For days she had been in his thoughts. He wanted her: to hold, to keep and to love forever. It had been several months since they spent time together. He invited her to his apartment for dinner. She accepted, and he sent a car to pick her up. Thanksgiving and Christmas had come and gone, both spending the holidays with their families, now they needed each other.

Johnny knew the approximate time to expect the car. He waited anxiously in the lobby. The chill of the January wind bit through his sweater as he ran to open the limousine door before the driver.

"Julia," he said. Intense emotions flavored his voice, while his rapid heartbeat removed the chill from his body. He took her hand and assisted her from the car to the lobby.

"I missed you, Johnny," Julia said, her voice soft and sincere.

They held each other and kissed with a new passion. Before the evening ended, they had committed themselves to each other.

It was a Friday evening in May of 1986. Sarah arrived at her parents' home just in time for dinner after taking half a day off from work. Johnny had announced his engagement, and that was the beginning topic of conversation at the Turner's dinner table until it turned onto Sarah.

Loretha was blunt and confronted her. "Ah know you and that Mr. Parker are livin' together. Ah ain't no fool. Ah saw signs of a man livin' at yuh apartment when Ah was up there."

"Mama!" Sarah glanced at her father and shifted her eyes back at her mother. "Stephen has his own apartment. We spend a lot of time together, but he doesn't live with me."

"Then why don't yuh marry him. Stephen told me he's been tryin' tuh get yuh tuh marry him for years. Sarah, that man loves yuh more than yuh know. Don't take him for granted."

"Ah don't want tuh be married. Ah don't want tuh play the dutiful wife. Ah like being my own person. One day Ah'll settle down with Stephen, but right now, Ah like our arrangement."

Loretha grabbed Sarah's right hand and held it sandwiched between both of hers. "Yuh mean yuh scared." She gave Sarah a sarcastic smile.

Sarah held her head down and was momentarily quiet.

"Sarah, yuh 49 years old," her father said. "A woman needs a man tuh love her and add security and stability tuh her life."

"What!" Sarah jumped from her seat, placed her hands on her hips and paced back and forth on her side of the table, shaking her head. She looked at her mother and she was doing all she could do to keep from laughing. "Daddy!" She leaned over her place at the table. "Ah know yuh don't still believe that." She laughed and walked behind him, wrapping her arms around his neck and kissing him on the cheek.

"Ah love yuh, Daddy, but yuh a little behind in the times. Ah don't need a man for that. Tuhday's women can take care of themselves." She continued to hug his neck and placed her cheek against his. He reached up and rubbed her arm. "Ah need my man tuh love me and be my best friend. Ah don't have tuh marry Stephen for that. We already have that."

"Ah wanted grandchildren," Reverend Turner said.

"Daddy." Sarah wasn't laughing any more. She returned to her seat at the table. "Ah love yuh more than any man. Ah don't mean tuh be disrespectful, but yuh have a grandson. No matter what, yuh know he's yuh grandson!" She slapped her hand on the table.

"Sarah!" Loretha yelled out and partially stood, the chair making a noise as it scraped against the floor.

"Yuh haven't been there for him, so why should Ah believe yuh would've been there if Ah had children." Sarah continued, before covering her mouth.

"Sarah! How dare you?" Loretha watched John sink inward, trying to escape into himself. She turned toward Sarah and stood pointing her finger at her. "Johnny's yuh nephew, where have you been?" she yelled.

The veins in her neck protruded outward and her lips squeezed tight, holding in her anger.

Sarah turned and looked at her mother. The truth had snapped back at her. "Yes, Mama, where have Ah been? Sorry, Daddy. Sorry, Mama. Ah don't know what brought that on." She went to her father and wrapped her arms around his neck and kissed his cheek again.

He sat there, frozen, with glazed over eyes. He didn't move when Sarah kissed him. He didn't nod, or smile, or glance at her. He knew it was the time the Lord had told him about, and he was afraid.

Sarah was quiet. She folded her arms on the table and rested her head on them.

Loretha placed her elbows on her table and rubbed her eyes, then worked her hands around to the sides of her head and massaged her temples.

Reverend Turner closed his eyes and remembered the Lord pulling him out of his coma when his daughter kissed him. Remembering the Lords words. *You are a weak and cowardly man, and you fail to see the error of your ways, but you have dedicated your life to me. In your coming months, you will remember the past, and I will show you all that you have failed to see. You must take the first step to rectify the wrong you have done. The help you need has always been with you.*

"Daddy, do yuh know who raped 'Lizabeth?" Sarah blurted out. Quickly, she covered her mouth with her hand. "Ah'm sorry, Daddy." She ran to his side, but backed away before touching him.

"The help you need has always been with you," Reverend Turner whispered. Tears ran down his face. He sat with both hands together, up at his lips, as if he were praying. He closed his eyes and his lips moved.

Loretha stood and stared at Sarah. "How could yuh?" Anger creased her brow.

"Mama, the words came from my mouth, but it wasn't like Ah was saying them. It was like they were just pushed out of me."

Sarah backed against a wall and was still. She wanted to disappear. She knew she had woke a topic that had been sleeping for many years, but Reverend Turner's inner voice never left him alone. There was a long period of quiet, then Loretha eyed John, and they both faced Sarah.

Reverend Turner had been seeking an avenue to relieve himself of his obligations to Elizabeth, and he believed Sarah to be the messenger the Lord spoke about.

"Ah'm so sorry, Daddy." Sarah was still backed against the wall, and sorry for allowing her impulses to envelop her reasoning. She didn't know a higher power was at work.

"No, Sarah, Ah'm sorry." He turned toward her. "Ah've held the truth for more than twenty years. Suddenly, Ah realized the blessing of the relief yuh've innocently offered. In the beginning, Ah didn't believe Elizabeth, but Ah still could've protected her and Johnny. Ah was a coward and Ah never sought the truth. The Lord pulled me out of the coma to set things right. 'Lizbeth kissed me, and Ah was pulled from the coma and into a dream state. The Lord said the help Ah needed has always been with me. That's you, Loretha, and you, Sarah. Ah was suppose tuh die from my heart attack, but Ah was awaken by 'Lizbeth's kiss."

"John, yuh remember when 'Lizbeth kissed yuh?" Loretha ran to him, bent over and hugged him while he sat in his chair. Tears ran down her face. "John, look at me." She cupped her hands around his face. "How could you remember that?" She stood and wiped the tears from her face.

"The Lord showed me. He let me remember. She kissed me twice. One long kiss and one short kiss. Ah came out of the coma feeling her lips on my face. Ah could hear her voice, and that's when the Lord began tuh speak tuh me."

Sarah glanced at her mother. She kissed her father as he spoke and went to her mother and wrapped her arm around her waist. Loretha bowed and Sarah, watching her mother, bowed her head, too. They placed their hands on Reverend Turner's shoulder.

"Sarah, that's the way it happened. Ah was there when 'Lizbeth kissed him and she was the one to notice he was dreaming. Sarah maybe it was the Lord who just spoke through you? Oh! Praise be tuh God. Thank yuh, Lord." Loretha held her hands up and pulled Sarah's left hand up, too.

Sarah lifted up her right hand and held her head down. "Hallelujah! All Praises to yuh, Lord!" Sarah and Loretha wrapped their arms around Reverend Turner, their cheeks pressed against his. It was quiet for several minutes. Soon the women returned to their seats wiping tears from their eyes.

"Sarah, Ah've been so wrong about this whole thing for so many years. At first Ah believed Ah was doing the right thing, but what Ah was really doing was taking the easy way out. Ah've caused so much pain tuh this family. Ah've lost my only grandson. Ah've influenced yuh relationship with 'Lizabeth and robbed yuh of yuh right tuh yuh family unity. But worst of all … Ah allowed a man tuh go unpunished for a crime committed against my child and this family." He choked up. "Ah should have protected her. Lawd, help me. Ah can't do this any longer … 'Lizabeth told me. … She told me Reverend Oliver raped her."

Sarah froze and cast a paralyzing stare at her father. Time seemed to just stand still. She didn't see her mother race to her side. She only felt the weight of her arms surrounding her body. It was as though her mother had to hold her together, or she would have shattered into tiny pieces.

"Daddy! Reverend Oliver? Why?" Sarah whined and used the heel of her hands to clear the tears flooding her lower eyelids.

Reverend Turner evaded her question. He didn't know why it was Reverend Oliver, it just was. He felt offended. He had nothing to do with what Reverend Oliver did. His only crime was doing nothing about it. Sarah was about to step over the barriers of respect and remind him of how he'd failed to protect his family.

"Yuh mother and Mrs. Collins believed her … but Ah didn't. Now Ah know Ah didn't … because it was easier and less complicated for me. At least, Ah should've questioned Reverend Oliver … but Ah didn't. Your mother and Ah fought because she wanted tuh confront him … when Ah wouldn't."

"Daddy, how could yuh? Why didn't 'Lizabeth tell more people? Daddy, that was so unfair," Sarah shrieked as she pulled away from her mother and invaded her father's space. Her father's religious revelation didn't prevent her from feeling anger and disappointment. She used her palms to flick away more tears from her soggy cheeks. "All these years, Ah let my relationship with my sister and Johnny slip away! Ah feel like Ah've been violated! Daddy, we've all been violated! Daddy, we've been robbed. Yuh didn't protect us. Don't yuh know that? Daddy … how could yuh? How could yuh betray yuh own child?" She flopped in her chair and sobbed like her heart was breaking. Her mother rubbed her back and allowed her comforting hands to rub her to massage her neck, back and shoulders.

Reverend Turner turned away, looking humbly toward the floor. He accepted Sarah's verbal drubbing, believing he deserved it. It was a small price to pay to have the weights lifted from his heart and soul.

While Sarah sobbed, he lifted his head and glanced humbly at Loretha, allowing his eyes to find hers. It hurt him to watch Sarah cry and express so much pain.

Sarah was quieting down some, so he believed he should continue. "If Ah didn't support 'Lizabeth, what good would it have done for her tuh tell more people? None of the blame should ever have been placed on her. She was just a child … and then tuh have the baby in school …" He tried to explain, but Sarah was so emotional, it didn't matter what he said.

Loretha wanted to say something in John's defense, but she knew Sarah was right. She also knew John had carried this burden for half of his life, he was sorry, but he still wasn't doing anything about it. Whether he deserved it or not, she knew she had to keep a soothing hand on the situation.

"Sarah, Ah know it's hard for yuh tuh hear all this, but yuh have tuh stop now, yuh need time tuh absorb. Ah just want yuh tuh know this secret has gone on for so long, Elizabeth and Johnny may be hurt more than Reverend Oliver if the truth came out now. Elizabeth has never told Johnny or Nat."

Sarah's body was hot from pain and disappointment. Sarah continued to rest her head on her folded arms. Loretha fanned her and continued to rub her shoulders. "Cool down, baby. Rest now, and think things through, All they know is that 'Lizabeth was raped. So, now, yuh have tuh slow down and absorb. Sleep on it, and we'll talk about it tomorrow morning. Okay?"

Loretha looked over at Reverend Turner. "Is that all right with yuh? We'll talk about it tomorrow, okay? Ah don't know if we should do anything about Reverend Oliver after so many years, but yuh both can start tuh be real family tuh 'Lizabeth and Johnny."

Loretha's evening meal sat cold in the serving bowls. The dishes were still sparkling. Sarah retreated to her bedroom. John sat sunken in his chair. It was beyond quiet. It was serene. Loretha cleared the table, retreated to the den, slumped into her chair and let a tranquil smile grace her face.

On that same spring evening, Johnny and Julia arrived at MaDear's Cottage. It was near midnight. The lights were out at Elizabeth and Nathaniel's home, so they drove on, heading down the asphalt paved private road. It was the first time Julia visited Johnny's Georgia home. He had never described it to her. So she was surprised that with Johnny's wealth, he would have such a quaint little cottage, with its tiny little rooms. The entire cottage could fit in her Washington apartment and there would be plenty of room left over. But coming from meager beginnings herself, she knew that Johnny's cottage was more than its material value. Besides, despite its size, it was beautiful. Just like the dollhouse she had dreamed of having.

Johnny carried their bags into the living room and dropped them on the floor just as Julia stepped into his most cherished place. He took her on a tour. She was amazed at the beauty and condition of the furnishings. Johnny pointed out all the pieces he had reupholstered and refinished. He gave her an approximate age for each piece as she ran her hand over the fabric and wood grain in admiration. She questioned why the furniture wasn't covered and why there wasn't a speck of dust anywhere. The house was fresh: fresh-cut flowers in the vases, fresh candy in the candy dishes, fresh linen on the beds and in the bathroom. Not the stale odor of a house closed up waiting for life to return.

"Johnny, your home is beautiful." She ran her hands over the furniture; the unique carving on the upper back of the sofa, the fine brocade fabric covering the chairs, and the matching lampshades. She swung herself around toward Johnny and held her hands crossed at her chest. She was so excited. "I know these walls hold many stories. It's so clean. It's alive. Are you sure no one lives here?"

"No … No one lives here but me." He laughed at her excitement while he walked closer to her. "I have a lady come in three times a week to clean and do little things to keep it alive." He kissed her on her forehead. "How do you know that?"

"How do I know what?" She looked up at him.

He stood looking down at her. "How do you know about the stories the walls hold?"

She put her arms around his neck. "Because of the sparkle in your eyes. You love this house and all old houses have stories. One day will you tell me the stories?"

"What stories? This is just my little Georgia home." Johnny pulled her arms down, wrapped them around her waist and pulled her back close to him. He buried his face in the bend of her neck and kissed her, sending a tingling sensation over her body. She turned and kissed him gently. He took her hand and they walked out to the porch, arm in arm. Julia rested her head on his arm. He looked up at the clear sparkling sky. "Yeah, Julia, this house has many stories: it's my roots, my rock, my foundation. One day I'll tell you about MaDear's cottage."

Julia looked up at him. *MaDear's Cottage?* "Your home has a name?"

"Yeah, like Tara," he said with a chuckle. "Come, let's settle in, we're going to have a busy day tomorrow. I want to show you my little piece of earth. Wait until you see the garden and flower beds."

———— ⚬⚬⚬ ————

The call of the early morning whippoorwills, robins and jays chirped in harmony, providing a beautiful symphony to awake to. The scent of the fresh lilacs mingling with the wild country flowers; the smell of the morning dew; hot rolls, smoked ham, fresh fried apples and fresh coffee. Julia's senses were stimulated, and her twilight sleep took her back to her early days in Rocky Mount. "I'm coming, Mama," she called out. "Tell Bobby to put that wood in the stove, the fire is going down under that ham and them roll ain't gonna come out right."

Johnny sat up. He had to get out of bed because he started laughing so hard his body began to shake. He knew Gerta's cooking had taken Julia back home, to an earlier time in her life, in her dream. He backed up against the wall and watched the aroma of fried smoked ham mingle with that of sweet rolls and country fried apples make her smile. He smiled when he realized Julia was stirring to the beauty of the morning and Gerta's fresh breakfast.

Gerta, the housekeeper, had arrived early just to stir the morning. Johnny had called, asking her to work Saturday and Sunday, before and after church. It would be a surprise to Loretha, Elizabeth and Nat when they found out Johnny was home with his beautiful fiancée.

Johnny walked around to Julia's side of the bed and kissed her on the lips. "I have to go see my girl. Hurry, come out and meet Gerta."

"Who's Gerta?" Julia squinted up at Johnny, looked around the room, and back at him again before it came to her where she was. "Oh my God, Johnny. I thought I was a little girl back home. I was helping my mother with breakfast."

"I know." He laughed. "You were talking in your sleep. Who's Bobby? Seems like he wasn't putting the wood on the fire fast enough."

She slung a pillow at him. "Bobby's my brother."

"Well Gerta's my other girlfriend. She's the one responsible for keeping the warm feeling in MaDear's cottage." He pulled his arm in the remaining sleeve of his robe and struggled to keep his balance while he slid his feet into his slippers. "I'll be in the kitchen. C'mon, hurry now. I can't wait for Gerta to meet you." He disappeared through the half-opened door.

Julia wasn't far behind Johnny, but not before she did a quick brush of her silky hair. She hurried to the kitchen and stopped suddenly at the door. She had only heard about Gerta moments before, but she had likened her to be a short plump, dark-skinned, matronly lady, with a kind of "Aunt Lula Bell" look. But there was Gerta, holding Julia at the door with her appearance.

Gerta was a gracefully attractive, tall, sandy colored woman in her early forties, not the matronly type at all, but more like a young graceful schoolteacher. Julia walked over to greet her. At the same time she mentally blasted herself for forming the stereotype.

"Mrs. Gerta Mae Tyler, I would like you to meet my fiancée, Miss Julia Batten."

"Johnny, yuh out did yuhself this time. Hi, Julia. It's very nice tuh meet yuh," Gerta replied in her Southern articulate manner.

"It's nice meeting you, Miss Gerta."

"Miss Gerta?" She waved her hand. "Honey! Just call me Gerta, Ah ain't that old." She laughed and gave Julia a country hug. "Now come eat before this food gets cold."

"Gerta, just let me do a quick wash, and I'll be ready for breakfast," Julia said.

"And I have to call Mama and Nat and let them know I'm home," Johnny said as he hurried toward the telephone. "It's Saturday and they might get out early."

Julia brushed her teeth, washed her face and was back at the table before Johnny. "Gerta, let me help you with something."

"Oh no, honey, yuh man pays me well tuh do this. So yuh just relax and let me wait on yuh." She set a small polished silver tray on the table that held appropriate bowls and small containers for the proper dispensing of cream, sugar, sugar substitute, salt and pepper, ketchup, butter, strawberry preservers, and grape jam.

Julia smiled gracefully and was taking a few sips of her coffee when Johnny returned. "They want to come up here right now to meet you. I told them we'd come down to their house sometime before noon. I want to show you around here, and I want you to see Gerta's flowers."

"Gerta … Johnny told me you take care of his house. You do a wonderful job."

"Keeping this house is easy, no one lives here. Johnny hired me tuh give it that 'lived in look' when he's not home. This is the best job in the county. Ah got six kids at home. Ah just tell my husband Ah have tuh go tuh work, come over here and live in Johnny's house tuh get some peace, and he pays me a great salary." Gerta cracked the eggs and whipped them up in a moderate sized bowl and poured them in the cast iron frying pan. "Yuh-know, sometimes Ah come over here and cook dinner for my family so the food smells can get in the furnishings. When something needs fixing, Ah ask my husband tuh take care of it. Ah love tuh garden, so whenever Ah plant something at home, Ah just bring some over here and plant it around the house." She moved the eggs around the pan, cooking them gently until they were scrambled to a medium consistency. Gerta lifted the heavy pan from the heat and began removing the eggs and placing them in the center of the platter, in between the smoked ham and the home fries potatoes. "This here is such a good job, my husband takes full charge of the yard and helps me with the vegetable and flower gardens for nothing. There yuh go." She brushed her hands against her apron.

Gerta set a platter of ham, eggs and fried potatoes on the table. She returned to the stove and was back with a tray holding a bowl of fried apples, a smaller bowl of grits and a basket of hot rolls.

"Don't let her fool you, Julia. This lady earns her salary. It's really hard keeping a house alive."

Johnny blessed the food while Gerta stood with her head bowed.

Gerta fussed over them during breakfast, then cleaned the dishes when they had finished. Julia and Johnny dressed and took that long walk on the land. Johnny told her some of those stories from the walls. Then he spoke about MaDear, Loretha, Nat and his mother, and listened while Julia talked about her home and family. When they noticed the time creeping closer to noon, they returned to the cottage, got the car and drove to his parents.

Elizabeth and Nathaniel hurried from the house to greet them. Johnny made the introductions. Poor Julia was on her own, moving between the gentle hugs and kisses. Johnny knew how she felt. He had to endure the same greetings from her family. It was nice, but it made him feel somewhat awkward and uncomfortable.

The occupants of the Turner home were trying to restore balance to their lives. Breakfast was late. Reverend Turner and Sarah wandered into the dining room, not eager to resume their discussion about the family's skeleton, but knowing they had to finish what was started.

Elizabeth called earlier that Saturday morning. When Loretha heard her excited voice, she thought Sarah had been busy, very early. Her heart pounded. She felt tingling throughout her torso, fingertips and toes. She was angry and momentarily speechless. But before she could think of something to say to defuse what she thought she was going to hear, she heard Elizabeth telling her that Johnny and his fiancée were home, and she wanted them over for lunch and to meet her.

Loretha was deflated and elated at the same time. She accepted the invitation for John and Sarah, but explained that they were just about to have a late breakfast.

Loretha returned to her dining room table. Her mind skipped forward from Elizabeth's conversation. Now she was listening while Sarah explained that Johnny had a right to know who his father was.

She didn't tell them Johnny was home, but did interrupt Sarah when she said Johnny had a right to know.

"Who gave yuh the right tuh decide what Johnny's rights are? Yuh haven't spent a total of fifty hours with him in his entire life. Ah know yuh mean well, but Ah think it's 'Lizebeth's decision, not yours." Loretha's facial expression and stiff ominous posture gave Sarah a clear indication of how she felt about the subject.

Sarah sat quietly and listened while her mother spoke. She understood what she was saying, but disagreed with her. She looked at her silent and motionless father and reached over and touched his hand. "Daddy, don't yuh think it's time tuh say something tuh Reverend Oliver?" Reverend Turner remained motionless and Sarah lowered her head, slightly tilting it to make a visual empathic connection. All he thought about was that Sarah was his disciple to deliver his message, and he knew Loretha would have a part to play, too. He remembered the Lord saying, "The help you need has always been with you."

"Why! Why!" Sarah said. "Why didn't yuh ? Why won't yuh?"

"Daddy we could call Reverend Oliver over here. Three of us could confront him. We just can't let him get away with what he's done."

"Sarah, thirty-six years have passed," Loretha interrupted. "This is yuh father and 'Lizebeth's business. Yuh *HAVE* tuh stay out of it. If yuh want tuh do something, try tuh make up the time yuh lost with 'Lizebeth and Johnny. For now, Johnny and his fiancée are over at 'Lizebeth's. They came in last night. Sarah ... yuh have tuh promise me yuh won't bring this issue up while he's here. We were invited for lunch, so let's go over and try tuh have a nice day. John, will yuh be joining us?"

"Sure, Loretha, Ah have some quick errands tuh run. Ah'll meet yuh there." Sarah wasn't ready to tuck this information back into its hiding place. It wasn't settled, and she had lost a night's sleep questioning her father's decision. "Daddy, why can't yuh just let 'Lizebeth know yuh finally believe her? Please, Daddy!"

"Sarah, Ah don't want tuh go intuh this again. Not NOW! *To every thing there is a season and a time to every purpose under the heavens ... a time to keep silent and a time to speak. Ecclesiastes 3:7. He wiped* his hands and face with his napkin and removed himself from the table to put some distance between himself and her.

"Daddy!" Sarah called out, trying to get her father's attention again. Reverend Turner ignored her pleading. He walked out of the dining room and didn't turn back.

"Sarah! Please! Yuh father has said more tuh yuh than he's said since Johnny was born. Please, let it be. Ah'm sure he knows what needs tuh be done. He'll do it in time." Loretha was adamant. "Just leave it alone … Please! We're gonna go tuh 'Lizabeth's and Ah don't want tuh hear about this again today."

Sarah had just been "hushed," and she didn't like it. She was her own person and had not been "hushed" since she was a teenager. Deep-rooted parental respect forced her to be quiet. She jerked herself back in her chair, sucked her teeth and sulked like a child.

Loretha continued sipping her coffee and gave Sarah an occasional glance. She whispered softly, not meaning for anyone to hear her. "If, only if, and if 'ifs' came true, poor men would ride in limousines."

"What, Mama?"

"Oh nothing, just thinking out loud. Would yuh like some more coffee?"

"No thank yuh. Please excuse me," Sarah said. She was upset, but had remained at the table so her mother wouldn't see how deep her anger went. While her mother was talking to herself, she was thinking back over the years. She knew what she had to do, and how, and when she would do it. It wasn't because she was angry. It was because she thought she would be doing the right thing. She gave her mother a gentle smile and assured her they would have a nice day.

When Sarah and Loretha arrived, poor Julia had to go through the hugs and greetings all over again. Elizabeth had prepared a nice lunch and served it on her finest china. She wanted to create a positive first impression. Julia's parents had done the same when Johnny visited. Reverend Turner arrived a little later. He had never made amends with Elizabeth or Johnny, so Loretha and Sarah always stayed close to him whenever he was in an awkward situation. Johnny had asked Nat to make sure Reverend Turner was comfortable.

Johnny managed to steal Loretha away while everyone was entertaining Julia. He took her by the hand and led her toward the back door. Loretha pointed back toward Reverend Turner like she was leaving her child behind.

"He'll be all right, Gram'ma, and I'll only have you for a few minutes. He won't even miss you." He looked back at his mother and mouthed, "Take care of Julia." She gave him the OK sign.

"Gram'ma, I want you to sit for a moment. Now just be still while I pull up a chair."

"Johnny what is this all about?" She looked at the back door as if she expected to see Reverend Turner standing there.

"Don't worry, I got Nat taking care of him, only he doesn't know it." Johnny smiled. He sat on the edge of the chair. "Now I want you to just give me a minute of your time, and I don't want you to speak until I'm finished talking. Can I get that from you, Gram'ma?"

Loretha reached over and touched his face as she nodded. Johnny took her hand, kissing her palm before she held it against her lips.

"Gram'ma, I'm a rich man. I'm richest with the love of family. I'm rich because I had a person like MaDear in my life. I have you, Mama and Nat. I feel Aunt Sarah coming closer and Grandfather's presence. I've found the woman of my dreams. I'm rich because I'm from a little place called Rehoboth and all the money in the world couldn't make me happier." Loretha kept watching the door. "Gram'ma if Grandfather should come looking for you, it's all right. He can sit out here with us."

Johnny got down on his knees. "Gram'ma."

"What yuh doing, Johnny? Get up from there. Yuh gone get yuh pants all dirty."

"Now ... now, Gram'ma." Johnny held both her hands to keep her still. "I have two cashier's checks. One is for you for $9,999.00—the extra dollar is in the envelope. Mama and Nat will drive you to your bank. According to tax law, I can give you a tax-free gift of under $10,000.00 every year. So expect this every year. If you want a new house, I'll have one built for you. That is if Grandfather doesn't object. Anything you want, just ask. I have another envelope for the church. It's for $50,000.00, and the church is free to use it as they see fit. All I want from the church is a receipt for my taxes. I've also given Mama and Nat their gifts and an envelope for Bethlehem Baptist Church."

Loretha got on her knees with Johnny and she said a prayer of thanksgiving.

CHAPTER 21

A week later, Johnny and Julia decided on a small, quiet wedding. They had a few close friends as their witnesses, the church on a Saturday morning and a Baptist minister. There was no white dress, no tuxedo, no bridesmaids, no crying mamas and nervous papas, no red carpet runner, and no limousine—just their love and nuptials.

Julia and Johnny knew their families would be disappointed, but they had a better surprise for them. They decided that on their first anniversary, they would repeat their vows for their immediate families during a three days and two nights Caribbean cruise. They figured they had a year to plan, and that would only require setting the dates that were convenient for both families, booking the reservations and paying the bill. Their secretaries would make all the arrangements.

All of this excitement put a damper on Sarah's plan. She was happy about the marriage and the cruise. But she had a growing compulsion to make Reverend Oliver pay. She allowed several weeks to pass before her unrest became unsettling. The more she thought about it, the more impulsively she reacted. She called her parents several times, but was always given the same argument, "Leave it alone!"

She wondered why she was given this information if nothing was to be done with it. Loretha and John pleaded with her, but they knew she wouldn't rest until the matter had closure.

Sarah knew it was more Elizabeth's decision than her parents, but she didn't know how to talk to Elizabeth. She decided to speak with Johnny, believing he had a right to know the identity of his father. By the second week in July, she decided to call him at his office. For several days, she left messages with his secretary. When he finally returned her calls, arrangements were made for them to meet at a lounge at Dulles International Airport in Northern Virginia on the following Wednesday. She told Johnny she had something to tell him that was very important—too important to tell him over the phone. She lied, telling him she had to cover a story in D.C., so she could meet him at the airport before her 4:30 P.M. return flight.

The important information or Sarah's urgency didn't cause Johnny to feel any undue anxiety. His relationship with her was somewhat distant. When he was young, he wanted more of a loving relationship with her, but she had put up a thick invisible wall with a secret one-way opening where she could come through when she wanted to show warmth and affection. When Johnny tried to return his love, he could feel his emotions splatter against her sturdy wall. Now, when Sarah spoke with such urgency, Johnny made the appointment with a casual tone.

Each morning Johnny's secretary informed him of his daily schedule. He had forgotten about his two o'clock meeting with Sarah. He decided to have his driver take him to the airport so he wouldn't have to worry about parking. Sarah was waiting at the agreed-upon meeting place, a secluded corner table in a dimly lit area of the airport's bar and restaurant.

"Hello, Aunt Sarah." Johnny's approach was cold and distant. His only reason for attending the meeting was because she was family.

"Johnny, Ah'm so happy yuh could meet with me," Sarah whispered as she gave him a peck on the cheek.

"May I order a drink for you?" He sat facing her at a small square table in a far corner of the bar.

"Sure, Ah'll have a vodka sour."

"Uh, waiter," Johnny called out while motioning for him with the wave of his hand. "Give me a rum with cola and a vodka sour for the lady." As soon as the waiter walked away, Johnny turned and stared at Sarah, waiting for her to tell him why she dragged him all the way over to Dulles. "Okay, Aunt Sarah. You said you had something important to tell me. Well … I'm waiting."

"Yes, Johnny. It's really important, and Ah don't know how tuh start. Now, don't get all excited. Everyone is healthy and fine."

"Then, what is it?" He clinched his lips, crossed his arms and patted his foot on the floor loud enough for her to hear it.

Sarah sat facing the bar and could see the waiter returning to the table with their drinks. She looked at Johnny, before lifting her eyes in the direction of the waiter. She was telling Johnny she would begin when the waiter delivered their drinks and left their table. Johnny relaxed his posture.

The waiter placed the cocktail napkins and drinks on the table, then placed the bill face down near Johnny.

"Johnny … a few weeks ago … Ah found out who yuh real father is." Sarah began as soon as the waiter walked away. She didn't continue to speak, but looked at Johnny, waiting for his reaction.

Johnny was quiet and still. He wondered if Sarah was telling him this to help or hurt him. He sat, his eyes fixed on his drink and stirring it with the plastic cocktail straw. "Is that so?" he casually remarked.

"Johnny, don't yuh want tuh know who yuh father is?"

Johnny's anger was beginning to show even though he was flaking apart piece by piece. "Sarah, if you have something to tell me, then tell me. I'm not going to ask you to do what you came here to do. Please don't play games with me." Trying to appear aloof, he took a sip of his drink, not that he needed to drink, but he needed to do something to hide his building anxiety.

"Johnny, Ah'm not trying tuh play games with yuh. Ever since you were born, Ah was told yuh mother was raped. Hell, Johnny! Yuh knew that. Everyone knew that. But what Ah didn't know was, 'Lizabeth told Daddy who the person was that raped her, and Daddy didn't believe her. Only Mama and MaDear believed her, but Daddy wouldn't let Mama do anything either." Sarah stopped talking and reached for her drink. She began twirling her straw around the edge of her glass. Tears began tuh fill her eyes, and she let them roll down her face.

Johnny decided to lighten up and be more sympathetic. He'd heard her words, only words, she hadn't told him anything he didn't already know. He always felt very uncomfortable in the presence of teary-eyed women. He'd heard her say his mother knew who raped her, and that Gram'ma and MaDear also knew; these were words that had meaning.

Sarah caught the tears with her cocktail napkin and took a deep breath before she continued. She turned to Johnny and wondered why he was just sitting there staring at his drink and not screaming questions at her.

"Johnny, yuh mother always knew who raped her, but Daddy wouldn't let her say anything. The reason you and 'Lizabeth lived with MaDear was because Daddy threw her out of the house ... because he thought she had been wild and got pregnant. Daddy just couldn't believe Reverend Oliver raped her."

In an involuntary move, Johnny used his hands to push himself up from the table. His chair tilted back and crashed to the floor. He stood, holding on to the table and looking at Sarah. He wasn't angry with her. It was the shock of what he had just heard; it was how she said what she said. It jerked him to his feet and seemed to leave him hanging onto the table. Sarah didn't say, "Your father is ..." She slipped what she wanted him to hear in between the words of another sentence, catching him off guard.

"Reverend Oliver? Reverend Oliver raped my mother and is my father?" Johnny said in a tone loud enough to be heard and just short of shouting.

"Yes, Johnny. Ah didn't want tuh hurt yuh, but Ah couldn't rest without telling yuh. It's been a family secret for 36 years."

Johnny picked up his chair and sat down again, "Oh my God ... Reverend Oliver. Reverend Oliver is my father? Malcolm is my brother?" He gulped his drink down and raised his hand to order another. A clammy appearance came over him. He placed his hand over his face and rubbed his eyes. He stared as though in a daze at the empty dark corner of the room behind Sarah.

"Johnny … please, Ah didn't want tuh hurt yuh. Ah just thought yuh had a right tuh know. Back then, Daddy didn't believe 'Lizabeth and refused tuh question Reverend Oliver. Now, he believes her, but he still can't find a way tuh confront Reverend Oliver. 'Lizabeth never told you or Nat because of the years she was forced tuh keep her secret. She believed it wouldn't serve any purpose tuh have yuh relive the scandal she had tuh live through. Daddy loves you and 'Lizabeth so much, but he's so weak minded; too weak minded tuh do the right thing. Ah pleaded with him tuh confront Reverend Oliver. Ah even told him Ah would stand with him, but he just couldn't do it."

"Of all the people in the world, I would've never thought Reverend Oliver was my father and Malcolm my brother." He stood up again, walked around the table, fixed his eyes up toward the ceiling, then down at the table again, picked up his second drink, gulped it down and ordered another.

Johnny flipped his chair around. He swung his leg over the seat, sat and folded his arms across the back of the chair. "Damn! Damn!" he repeated, giving more emphasis to the word each time. "I never understood why Grandfather seemed to hate me. I always thought it was because Mama was raped, and he didn't know who it was. Now I understand." He sipped his drink and stared off in the distance. "It was never about me. It was about his cowardliness. Every time he looked at me, he saw the dark side of himself." He leaned over the back of the chair to get closer to Sarah. "You're telling me that Grandfather never questioned Reverend Oliver?"

Sarah twirled the straw around in her drink and held tightly to the security of her pocketbook. "Honey, that's the way Ah understood it. Ah believe it has been eating him from the inside out. He was never the same after you were born. Nothing was the same. Owen didn't just rape yuh mother—he raped our family. Daddy seemed tuh hurt so much when he was near yuh, it made me hurt, too. Ah'm so sorry for how

Ah've been. Ah was so young when all this happened. Ah didn't even know what the word 'rape' meant. All Ah knew was Daddy cried a lot, and Ah knew it was because of you and 'Lizabeth."

Sarah sat back and looked at her empty glass. Johnny raised his hand and snapped his fingers.

"Mama and MaDear stayed close tuh you and 'Lizabeth, but Daddy had no one but me. Ah just found out about this a few weeks ago. It was the weekend you and Julia came home, but Mama forbade me from saying anything then, even now. After all these years, Ah finally asked Daddy who yuh father was, and he told me. He knows me. He knew Ah wasn't gonna shove this kind of information back in the dark corner of our lives and do nothing. Ah know Daddy wanted me tuh tell yuh, why else did he tell me. Ah pray yuh can forgive me for a lifetime of my distance. Ah loved yuh the best way Ah knew how. Ah didn't want tuh see Daddy hurt, and Ah didn't want tuh hurt either."

Sarah had allowed the years to harden her, but her emotions struggled to surface and succeeded. She took a long sip of her drink and tried to blink back her tears.

Nothing else was said for some time. Johnny drank his third drink slowly and was up pacing, turning, and pacing some more, trying to absorb everything. Suddenly, he took his seat again.

"Johnny, there are a few things Ah feel yuh need tuh understand," Sarah said, breaking her brief silence. "There are people who will be hurt by this information. Innocent people. Nathaniel would be hurt and so would yuh mother. Nathaniel may feel he can't trust 'Lizabeth because she didn't tell him. Then, there is Thea. She is nothing but goodness, even though she's married tuh a rapist. Ah know you and Malcolm had yuh problems when yuh were young, but yuh can't blame him for his father's sin either." Sarah was talking to Johnny, but Johnny was again focusing in that dark corner behind Sarah. "Johnny! … Johnny!" Sarah whispered.

Johnny sat down in his chair again and continued to repeat himself. "Damn! Damn! Reverend Oliver is my father. Malcolm is my brother." After a brief pause, he stared across the table at Sarah. "Yes, Sarah! I heard you. I heard everything you said, and I'll handle this the best way I can."

"Johnny, can yuh promise me yuh'll be gentle with Daddy? He's suffered over this for so many years. Ah believe the stress over this caused his heart attack. He's a coward, but he can't help that." Sarah repeated herself because she wasn't sure Johnny heard or understood everything she said. "Johnny please understand, after all these years, he didn't have tuh tell me about this. But … Ah guess he did because he knew Ah'd do something about it … because he couldn't. Please, promise me yuh'll forgive him."

Johnny took thirty dollars from his wallet and placed it in the black folder containing the check. "Sarah, the only thing I will promise you is that I'll pray over this. I'll discuss it with Julia. I won't do anything right away. I need time to think and to sort things out." He leaned over and gave her a gentle kiss and walk away. Slowly, he turned and glanced back at her. "I'll call you as soon as I can. I will promise you that I'll call you before I do anything. I have to leave now."

Sarah had another hour before her return flight to Atlanta. Johnny didn't want to leave her sitting there, but he had to get away. He needed time to think. He loved Reverend Oliver. He felt like he had been stabbed in the chest. He was torn and confused, and his head was in a whirl from the three drinks. He called his chauffeur so the limousine would be waiting at the main entrance.

Sarah worried about Johnny. She rationalized that the truth had to come out, but the whole ordeal continued to plague her.

Johnny was pale and perspiring profusely when he arrived at the limousine.

"Mr. Turner, are you all right?" asked his chauffeur.

Johnny entered the limousine and stared at the front window. The chauffeur stood in the open rear door and repeated himself. Still Johnny didn't respond until the chauffeur put his hand on his shoulder.

"No! No! Oh yes, Stan! I'm okay. Just take me to my office."

"Yes, sir," the chauffeur replied before closing the door and taking his place in the driver's seat. He was still very concerned about Johnny's first response and periodically watched him in the rear view mirror.

Johnny used his handkerchief and wiped the sweat from his color-drained face. He loosened his tie, put his head back on the rear seat and closed his eyes. Stan continued to periodically glance at him as he pulled onto the I-495 Beltway. The air conditioner was blowing at maximum, but beads of perspiration continued seeping through Johnny's pores. He removed his tie and opened the top two buttons of his shirt. Suddenly, Johnny instructed Stan to pull the car over. He leaped from the car before it came to a complete stop, bent over and spilled the content of his stomach onto the grass.

Stan ran to him. "Sir, please let me take you to the hospital?"

Johnny shook his head "no" and gestured with his hand. Stan stood with him and handed him a clean handkerchief. When Johnny's stomach settled, he sat down in the rear seat, threw his head back and covered his face with the palms of his hands.

"Stan, I'm okay. It must have been something I ate. I feel better now, but we should stay here for a few minutes."

"Yes, sir, but would it be all right if I pulled the limo up a little?"

Johnny nodded. Stan closed the door, hurried to the driver's seat and pulled the car up about thirty feet.

"Would you like me to open your door again, sir?"

"No, I'm okay. Let's just sit here a little while longer," Johnny replied.

They sat on the side of the road for the next fifteen minutes. Johnny knew he didn't owe Stan an explanation, but he thought of him as a friend. "I need to learn to hold my liquor. I downed three mixed drinks in less than thirty minutes. I should've known better. I'm not really a drinking man, but in this business, sometimes you just can't refuse. I think I need to find a better way of doing business."

"I'd say so, sir."

"Stan … stop with the 'sir.' Just call me Mr. Turner. Hell, you can call me John if you want to." Johnny always had a problem with older black hired help referring to him as "sir." He believed he could have been Stan's chauffeur if he came along in a different time. The bank hired Thomas Stanley. With the exception of Gerta, Johnny always hired white domestics.

"Thank you, Mr. Turner. I'll reserve the 'John' for a later, more appropriate time, if that's okay with you?"

"Stan, I left my car at the bank, so I'll give you a call in the morning and let you know what time to pick me up."

"Yes, sir."

"Sir?"

"Sorry, sir. Uh … I mean … Uh … Mr. Turner." He flashed Johnny a smile from the rear view mirror.

Johnny smiled back and didn't say another word until he arrived home. His head was pounding and his stomach was churning. It took all of his energy to convince Stan that he could find his way to his apartment alone.

—m—

"Hello, Marian, I'm home. I think I may have some kind of virus, so I left work early," Johnny called out to his live-in housekeeper and cook.

"Good afternoon, Mr. Turner. Would you be needing anything?" Marian came running out of the kitchen, wiping her hands on her apron.

"Will Mrs. Turner be home on time?"

"She didn't call, sir."

"You may continue with what you were doing."

Johnny decided to rest. If he didn't feel better by the time Julia arrived, he knew he would have to call the doctor. He tried to relax to relieve the pounding in his head. He knew he was experiencing a severe anxiety attack. The more he tried to put Sarah's news aside, the more it plagued him, and the worse he felt. Julia was due home within the hour. Johnny was beginning to feel there had to be something more seriously wrong. He decided to call his doctor and was told to come to his office. He called down and had the doorman hail a taxi.

—m—

Johnny returned home an hour after Julia. The doctor had given him an injection to relax him and a prescription for a mild anti-anxiety drug. His blood pressure was within normal limits and, other than what the doctor called a panic attack, he was fine.

Julia greeted Johnny. She was concerned. Marian told her he came home early and didn't appear to feel well. Johnny was mellowed-out and Julia questioned if he had a business date and a few drinks. He didn't seem sick to her. In fact, she was all keyed up and wished she was as mellow as he was.

"Oh yeah, I had a few drinks. They went down smoothly, but didn't want to stay down. I got so sick I had to go to Dr. Ricky's office, but I'm okay now. He gave me a mild relaxant, and I'm feeling much better. My stomach is kind of tender, so I won't be having dinner. I'll sit with you while you eat. Maybe I'll have some tea."

Julia knew there was something else bothering Johnny. He was always so upbeat and talkative. She became more concerned with his health and began to inquire further, but before she could say another word, the telephone rang.

"Mr. Turner. Ms. Sarah Turner calling," Marian announced.

Before Johnny accepted the portable phone, he whispered to Julia, "Something did happen today, I'll tell you all about it as soon as I take this call."

"Hello, Aunt Sarah."

"Ah just wanted tuh call tuh make sure you're all right. Ah didn't mean tuh upset yuh. Are yuh all right?"

"Yes, Aunt Sarah. You did upset me, but I'm happy you told me. You were right. It was something I needed to know. I should've known it all my life. Mama and Gram'ma had reasons. I'll visit with them and get the whole story. I suppose they're going to be very angry with you, and I'll try to soothe that over too. But I still don't know how I'm going to handle this. I'll try to call you so you'll be prepared."

"Ah was just worried about yuh. Ah'm a big girl. Ah didn't mean tuh hurt anyone, but what's right is right. Mama and 'Lizabeth will probably be angry with me, that's why Ah decided not tuh call them this evening. Ah figured they'd call as soon as yuh did whatever it was yuh were going tuh do. Who knows, maybe they won't be angry, maybe they'll be relieved. Ah guess Ah'll have tuh wait and see. Ah just wanted tuh make sure yuh okay. Ah'll be talking tuh yuh."

"Okay, Aunt Sarah. Be talking to you soon. I hope you know how grateful I am for the information. Thanks again. Bye now."

He clicked the phone off, looked across the table at Julia and thought of how lucky he was to have her. He placed his hand on his hips and walked to the window. The view of the city was spectacular.

"Johnny, what is it?" Julia's bewildered voice broke through his silence.

"Earlier this afternoon, Sarah told me who raped my mother. Who my real father is. Who my brother is. That, Mama, Gram'ma, Grandpa, and even MaDear knew all these years. Sarah only found out that weekend when we were home."

"Johnny, why did she wait to tell you?" Julia could see her man was upset. She didn't know Nat wasn't his father, but that didn't matter. She went to him, and Johnny opened his arms to receive her.

"Well, there was our marriage, and she didn't want to put a damper on our happiness. She flew into Dulles, met with me and then took a return flight to Atlanta. She didn't want to tell me over the phone, and she wanted to tell me while we were alone. She even tried to make me believe she had business in Washington."

Johnny didn't mention who his father was, and Julia didn't ask. She believed it was Johnny's place to tell her. Besides, she didn't know anyone in his hometown except his family. She didn't know his mother was raped.

Together, they left the dining room table and headed toward their bedroom. Julia informed Marian that they wouldn't be needing her for the remainder of the evening and would take their own calls. They wanted to be alone.

Marian said, "Goodnight," and retreated to the domestic suite.

"Julia, let's get comfortable, I want to shower. Then, I'll tell you what happened and as much as I know about this whole thing."

They walked arm in arm into their bedroom suite, engaging in small, unrelated chitchat along the way. They both retreated to their own private bathrooms. While Johnny showered, he could hear the water running in Julia's bathtub. He stood under the shower and let the massaging water spray against the back of his head and neck.

Between the warm shower and the effects of the doctor's injection wearing off, Johnny's defenses were beginning to crumble. The shower water mixed with his tears. For years, he wished Reverend Oliver was his father. When he was a young boy, he couldn't understand why Malcolm hated him so much. He didn't have anything. Malcolm had all of Reverend Oliver, and now he finds out some of Reverend Oliver belonged to him. How was he supposed to hate the man he loved so much? Nonetheless, he hated that man who raped and violated his mother.

"Oh my Lord! Help me! Show me the way!" Johnny cried, but his words were quieted under the shower's sounds. He placed his hands against the shower wall and sobbed with bobbing head and jerking shoulder. His tears and the secretion from his nose and mouth were washed away by the spraying water, but not the pain and confusion he felt.

Johnny was surprised to see the sunlight peeping through the separation in the drawn drapes. It was morning. He felt like he had only blinked while he was still waiting to talk to Julia. He was still wearing his bathrobe and was lying on top of the bedcovers, but he felt refreshed, even when he remembered what had been so plaguing the night before. He checked the clock. It was only six-thirty. Their alarm clock usually buzzed at seven-thirty. He thought about waking Julia so they could have that talk, but she was sleeping so soundly. He laid there trying to get back to the business of sorting out the details he was working on while he was waiting for her the night before.

Johnny remembered feeling sick. He was confused and hurt. Now, he was angry. He knew he had to see his mother and grandmother before he did anything. He still loved Reverend Oliver, but had turned his hate at Malcolm. All those deep grooves that had been gouged in his soul so many years ago were surfacing. He knew it wasn't fair to Malcolm. Malcolm didn't rape his mother, and he didn't know he stole his share of his father. But he was the easiest target, easier than his grandfather or Reverend Oliver.

When Julia stirred and stretched, Johnny prayed she would wake up. Easing out of bed, he began to concentrate on going home. He needed to talk to his mother and grandmother. But for the time being, he needed to think straight, and that took a strong cup of coffee.

Marian smelled the coffee brewing and hurried to the kitchen.

"Oh, sir! You're up early. Here, I'll take care of that," she said, reaching for the coffee.

"No, Marian, I prefer to be alone with Mrs. Turner this morning. You're free until we leave the apartment."

"That will be just fine, Mr. Turner." Marian immediately stopped fiddling with the coffee tray and removed herself from the kitchen.

Julia wandered into the kitchen shortly after the alarm clock sounded. Johnny was on his second cup of coffee and was enjoying his toast covered with some of his grandmother's blackberry preserves.

"Good morning, honey," Johnny said while rising and greeting her with a kiss. "I'm so sorry I fell asleep last night. You should have awakened me."

"Oh I wouldn't do that. You were sleeping so peacefully. Where's Marian?"

"I asked her to leave us alone this morning. Would you like me to serve you your coffee?"

"Yes, I guess that would be a great idea. You've spoiled me, then you sent Marian away, so ... I guess you'll have to serve me." Julia laughed at the position she had taken.

"Honey, I have to go home. I need to go alone. I told you I met Sarah at Dulles. She told me Reverend Oliver was my father. That he raped my mother when she was fifteen years old." Johnny slowly repeated the stories MaDear and his family had told him. He shared all that he knew, including his birth in the girls' bathroom at the high school. He apologized. He realized he should have told her more about himself before they were married, and he prayed she would understand. There were things he intended to tell her, but either he forgot, or the opportunity never presented itself.

Julia gave his hand a squeeze, stood and walked behind his chair and put her arms around him. She kissed him on the sides of his face and the nape of his neck. "Johnny, what do you really want to do now?" she whispered in his ear.

"I need to go home. First, I need to go to MaDear's cottage so I can think. What I really want is for Reverend Oliver to openly admit that he is my father. That's what I want. I want to hear my grandfather tell my mother how sorry he was. Oh! ... I don't know. I want to be near MaDear and talk to Gram'ma and Mama." The remainder of the tears that were resting on the ledge of his lower eyelids spilled down his face.

"Julia ... I love Reverend Oliver. I use to pretend he was my father. I'd make up adventures with just us, then I'd realize he belonged to only Malcolm. That Malcolm! The one who tormented me all the way through school. He made my life hell. Now I hate Malcolm so much,

I don't seem to be able to control how much I hate him. I haven't thought about him in years."

"Johnny, you and Malcolm were just boys. Reverend Oliver, not Malcolm, raped your mother. Think about it. If you really hated Malcolm that much, why did you get that job for him?"

"Because I loved Reverend Oliver. It hurt me to know he was worried about Malcolm. Anyway, I knew it was the right thing to do. I had a good job and connections. It was my responsibility to help another brother … I didn't know he was really my brother." Johnny picked up his coffee cup and walked to the window. He turned. "Honey, I know I'm supposed to hate Reverend Oliver, but the rape was what resulted in my birth. My mother suffered. My whole family suffered … and I suffered too, even though it happened before my birth. Malcolm use to laugh and call me 'toilet trash.' He'd say I was born in the toilet bowl. All the kids would laugh at me. I was very young, and it hurt. I've never completely healed. I just tucked it away. I know I have to confront Reverend Oliver. He has to answer to the pain he caused my family."

"Johnny, please, there are things you have to do, but you must remember Malcolm had nothing to do with your mother being raped." She stood close to him and placed the palms of her hands on his chest and looked up at him, her eyes pleading while she spoke. "He didn't know. He may have been a rotten kid, but you both have put away that time in your lives. You have to place the blame where the blame belongs. Go home and gain your strength. Talk to your mother and grandmother." She didn't know Reverend Oliver, but she worried about Johnny's conflicting feelings about Malcolm.

"Honey, I know you're right." He kissed her lips and hugged her for understanding. "Don't worry, I won't do anything stupid."

"When are you leaving?" They held hands and walked back to the table. He waited on her as promised, preparing her coffee.

"I'll try to get a flight out this evening or tomorrow morning. I have some important meetings at work today, and there are a few loose ends I have to tie up. Then I'll be free until at least Tuesday, but I'll try to get back by Sunday evening or Monday morning."

"Johnny, don't worry. You're a good man. Everything you've ever touched turned to good. Everything will work out."

CHAPTER 22

As soon as Johnny's flight arrived in Atlanta, he called Sarah to let her know he was in Georgia. Next, he picked up his rental car. By two in the morning, he was pulling up in front of MaDear's Cottage. He would spend the night talking to MaDear; not that she would answer him or give him advice, but her spirit was always consoling and gave him clarity and strength. Maybe it was just the comfort of being home. MaDear had always cuddled and consoled him when he came home saddened with heavy burdens.

Johnny called Julia to let her know he had arrived, and assured her he would keep a level head. Julia was right. His mother was the one who had been violated. He would sleep until morning, then call his mother and grandmother and ask them to meet him at the cottage. He prayed they would come alone. He was happy to have the remainder of the night and the entire next day to relax and think of what options he would present for dealing with Reverend Oliver.

Feeling wired and unsettled, Johnny's world had been turned upside down. He was grateful the secrets had surfaced, but now he needed closure. He thought of openly exposing Reverend Oliver to the church, school, and community. And if the beast within Malcolm raised its ugly head, he would break him down and destroy him. He had ways and resources to do the unthinkable. But, he was Johnny and although he was hurting, he couldn't condone the worst of punishments for Reverend Oliver.

He threw himself down in the large easy chair, MaDear's favorite. He needed to think, to remind himself that he had vowed to follow his mother's wishes. He needed to remind himself that

Malcolm was not involved and to keep his promises to Julia. Johnny needed a revelation from MaDear.

—m—

Gerta was not surprised to see a car at the cottage that Friday morning. Johnny never let her know in advance when he was coming home. He was asleep when she arrived, but she believed he would want breakfast when he woke up. Gerta wanted to fix ham, sausages, grits, fried apples, salmon cakes, hot homemade biscuits and freshly squeezed orange juice.

"Welcome home. Why didn't yuh call and let me know yuh were coming home?" Gerta said, noticing a sleepy-eyed Johnny standing in the kitchen door.

"Gerta, you know I only call when it's something special."

"Did Miss Julia come with yuh?"

"No. I had some business in Atlanta and decided to visit Mama and Gram'ma while I was in the area. Julia has to be in court this morning, and is expected to work through the weekend."

"Ah miss her." She turned from the stove, holding an unopened package of bacon.

"Not as much as I do." He walked over and gave her a warm hug. "Forgive me. I'm still sleepy.

Gerta recognized the sincerity in his eyes just before she hugged him back.

"Now I'm not here for you to fuss over me. My mama taught me how to care for myself. In fact, you're excused from working this weekend. I'll keep the house."

"Okay, Johnny, but yuh know where yuh can find me if yuh need me."

"Yes, ma'am. Oh, I mean yes, Gerta. I have to remember to drop the ma'am." Johnny smiled, and for a brief moment Stan, his driver, popped into his head. "I'm happy you came when you did. I have to call Mama and let her know I'm home before she leaves for work.'

Gerta replaced the bacon and tinkered around the house for a few minutes before leaving.

Johnny slouched down in MaDear's chair and looked up at her picture. "You knew. One time I heard you telling Mama that I was getting kinda close to Reverend Oliver. Well … now I'm counting on you to give me strength." He removed the telephone from the end table, held it against his stomach and dialed his mother's number. While he waited for her to pick up, he pulled himself up to attention in the chair and held the phone in his hand. By the time she answered the phone, he was sitting forward with his elbows resting on his knees and holding the phone and receiver in his hand. "Hi, Mama."

"Johnny? Is everything all right? Yuh never call so early in the morning."

"Yeah Mama, everyone is just fine. I just wanted you to know I'm here at the cottage. I came in late last night." He waved the phone base as he spoke.

"Whatcha doing here on a Friday morning?"

"I had some business in Georgia, so I figured I'd spend the weekend at the cottage. Before you ask, no, Julia is not with me. She has a heavy court case and has to work all weekend. So this time you got me all to yourself." He stood and glanced up at MaDear's picture to gain strength, to be charming and himself, so as not to ruin her day.

"Mama, give me a call when you return from work. Okay?"

"Sure, baby. What yuh gonna do today?"

He looked up at MaDear. "First I'm gonna call Gram'ma and let her know I'm home. Then, I think I'm gonna go back to bed and catch up on some sleep. I only had four hours of sleep. Gerta likes to get an early start."

"Okay, baby. Ah tell yuh what, Ah'll come directly tuh the cottage. Nat has a meeting this afternoon."

"Okay. I'll see you later. I'm gonna call Gram'ma now," Johnny said in his usual tone of voice, and he hung up the phone. "Yes!" he yelled out and shot his arm up in the air while still holding the telephone. He wondered how he was going to get to talk to his mother without Nat.

Johnny dialed Loretha's number and stood waiting with his hands in his pocket. When John answered the telephone, Johnny responded with his usual proper, bland, expression. "Good morning, Grandfather, may I speak to Gram'ma?"

"One moment, Johnny," John replied in the same bland tone. What he wanted to say was, "Hi, Johnny! Good to hear from yuh." But he was still sleeping in that bed he had made in what seemed like a hundred years ago. He called Loretha.

Loretha came running to the telephone with a huge smile on her face. Johnny always had a way of making her smile. "Hi, baby. Whatcha doin' callin' so early? Is everyone all right? Didn't yuh go tuh work? Where are yuh?"

"Hi Gram'ma. Questions, questions, questions. You always have more questions than I can remember to answer. Well, let's see. Everyone's fine, and I'm at the cottage."

"Yuh home? Baby, when did yuh get home? Did Julia come with yuh? Whatcha doing home on a Friday? Did you call your mother?"

"Hold on! Hold it, Gram'ma! There you go again. Yes, I called Mama. Julia's not with me, but she's fine. I just wanted to let you know I was home before you had a chance to go out. Mama is coming here straight from work. Can you come over around that time or anytime this afternoon? I want to catch up on some sleep this morning. I got in late last night." Again, Johnny made a special effort toward keeping a chuckle in his voice. He needed to sound content. He didn't want Loretha to suspect something was wrong and worry until they had a chance to talk.

"Okay, baby, yuh get some rest. Ah'll see yuh this afternoon."

The remainder of the morning passed quickly. Johnny went back to sleep as he had planned.

Around one-thirty in the afternoon, the sun had passed over the cottage and was heading toward the western horizon. On its way, it found a slight opening between the closed blinds and drapes covering Johnny's bedroom window, casting a beam of light across the left side of his face. Johnny stirred, squinted and covered his face with his pillow. He laid there for a few moments. Looking at his watch, he saw it was an acceptable hour before sitting up and moving toward the edge of the bed. He stood, stretched and headed toward the shower.

While dressing, Johnny heard Loretha pull up in the driveway. She was a little earlier than he wanted, but since he didn't really give her a special time, he couldn't complain. Loretha, on the other hand, had a reason for being early. While Johnny slept, she contacted Sarah to find out if she mentioned anything to Johnny, and let her know she wasn't angry with her. Then she told her she would call her as soon as they decided what they were going to do.

Johnny waited on the front porch for Loretha. He opened his arms and gave her his usual greeting. Loretha put her arm around his waist and walked him toward the porch swing.

"Johnny, sit next tuh me," Loretha said while she patted a place on the swing beside her. "We have tuh talk."

While Johnny was taking his seat, his eyes locked with Loretha's. For a moment, they seemed to enter each other's soul. Loretha saw confusion, deception and betrayal, mixed with love and pain in his eyes. Johnny read explanation, concern, disquiet, and alarm, circled in a bubble of love and protection wedged in his grandmother's eyes. Quiet filled the afternoon air while tears locked in their souls. They began to speak at the same time.

"Why didn't you …" Johnny stammered.

"Johnny, yuh don't …" Loretha cried.

A few minutes passed before they could utter another word.

The swing swayed back and forth. Johnny closed his eyes and held his head low. Loretha held her head high and stared off in the distance. They didn't dare look at each other because they weren't ready to speak the words they were there to say.

"Johnny, Sarah told me she told yuh."

"What did Sarah say?" Johnny said in a weary tone while unintentionally trying to get his grandmother to be more explicit. He just needed more time to think. He hadn't planned to discuss the issue with her alone, or before he had an opportunity to speak with his mother. He believed his mother was the one who owed him an explanation, but Loretha was the great protector, the defender.

Loretha turned her head away, ignoring his arrogance, believing it was the least he was allowed to feel or express. Johnny held his head down. Suddenly, Loretha asked Johnny to hold his head up and look at her while she spoke. She needed to gauge his pain and weigh her words accordingly.

Johnny continued to hold his head down, staring at the uneven boards of the porch flooring. He pushed against the floor, giving momentum to the gliding swing. *The boards are warping. I have to make sure I have them repaired. Yeah, those boards are warping. My life feels warped. I'm gonna fix that, too.*

"That yuh father is Reverend Owen Oliver," Loretha replied.

Johnny looked up and faced his grandmother, but his mind was listening to his own thoughts, the warped floor. The warp he had just discovered in his life. He hadn't had time to speak with MaDear. To allow the cottage to soothe him, for the walls to embrace him and kiss away his pain the way MaDear used to do. Now Loretha was there questioning him, needing to know how much he knew so she could develop a protection plan.

"She told me that and more," Johnny said in a more solemn tone. He was mentally drained and too weak to offer a respectable resistance, so he decided to cooperate.

"Johnny, please! Look at me. Ah know yuh hurting."

"Gram'ma ... why?" Johnny spoke while holding back the sobs and tears in his swollen tear ducts. He sounded like that little boy she held when MaDear died.

"Why is Reverend Oliver yuh father ... or why didn't we tell yuh he was yuh father?" Loretha responded, still looking at Johnny and now using her legs to give the swing momentum. She knew which question he was asking, but his subtle arrogance caused her to respond out of character.

Johnny struggled to complete his sentence. He looked over at the old magnolia tree and down at the dying blooms lying on the ground. "Why didn't Mama tell me he's my father?"

"Because she loves yuh. Oh Johnny … it was because she was protecting yuh."

"From what Gram'ma?"

"From the pain. From the shame. Johnny! Reverend Oliver raped yuh mother! She didn't tell anyone except MaDear until after yuh were born."

Johnny stood and walked to the edge of the porch and looked up at his perfectly formed magnolia tree again. *Beautiful*, he thought. He was wearing his slacks and an athletic shirt. Beads of perspiration had popped out all over him. He wiped his brow with the back of his arm and his face with his hands. He turned to his grandmother. "Are you hot, Gram'ma?"

"No, Johnny." Loretha sat back on the swing and shook her head.

Johnny hurried into the house and returned with a bath towel draped around his neck.

"Gram'ma, I know about the rape. I know I was born in the girl's bathroom. I lived through that shame until nothing was left in the stories to hurt me. If I knew Reverend Oliver was my father, it would have been his shame not mine, but if I had to, I would've survived that, too. The only other thing I didn't know was that Grandfather didn't believe Mama, but I understand why, even though I know he was wrong, that was no reason not to love me. Help me Gram'ma. … Help me fill in the blanks. … Tell me what I need to know, and I'll make a promise to you and Mama."

"What promise, Johnny?"

"That I'll only do whatever you and Mama want me to do."

"Johnny, yuh already know most everything."

Johnny gave her a deep stare, not threatening, but pleading and begging. He took the corner of the towel and wiped the perspiration from his face.

"All right, Ah'll do the best Ah can. Well, when yuh were born …" Loretha began. She told Johnny how the family felt: that it was painful for all of them, because of the shame Elizabeth had gone through and the shame that hovered over the family; that she was a minister's daughter, raped at fifteen years old; wasn't married, and had a baby in the girl's bathroom at school. Loretha told him Elizabeth was the love of her father's life; that she too, almost didn't believe Elizabeth, but MaDear did, how Elizabeth was a perfect young lady; how they thought Reverend Oliver was a perfect young man; how Sarah was forced to cope without emotional support, and how his grandfather emotionally died that day.

The afternoon heat had reached triple digits. Johnny interrupted his grandmother, taking her by the hand and leading her into the living room where she would be more comfortable. She sat on the sofa, and he pulled up a kitchen chair and sat across from her. "Gram'ma, I'm sorry, please continue. The heat was getting to me. I need air conditioning."

"All right, Johnny." Loretha crossed her arms and smiled. "Ah was willing tuh stick by yuh mother, no matter what. Even when Ah didn't believe she was raped. That's the way mothers are, but John's heart was split wide open and he turned tuh stone. Most likely because it was easier tuh feel cold and numb, rather than the pain."

Johnny stood and paced the living room. He was hurting, but he was all cried out, and he didn't want his mother to see him with reddened eyes. Loretha was happy he wasn't sitting staring her in the face, laying on every word that passed her lips.

"Johnny, Ah don't know, and Ah believe Ah do know why yuh grandfather didn't ask Reverend Oliver about the rape; why he refused tuh let me ask him. It seemed it was easier tuh give up his daughter and her child than tuh question Reverend Oliver. And Ah blamed yuh grandfather and Ah hated him. Ah went against him, and then, Ah stayed with him. Ah still loved that tiny part that was left in him and then Ah began tuh live in two worlds … 'Lizabeth's and yours and Sarah's and John's."

Loretha sighed, took a deep breath and continued, "but ... that's what Ah felt, Ah don't know what John really felt. He seemed cold and empty. He was a different person than the one Ah knew, loved and married. Tuh him, 'Lizabeth was dead. He said she was dead. He said she didn't exist, that yuh birth never happened. He never talked about her ... or about you ... for years. But, in the past fifteen or twenty years, he's been slowly coming back. He's been sorry about his behavior, but not sorry enough tuh put aside his fears and confront Reverend Oliver. He loves you and 'Lizabeth. He didn't know how to crawl back and ask yuh tuh love him the way he loved you. He believes the Lord spoke tuh him when he had his heart attack and he was sent back to make his amends. That's why he told Sarah. Ah think, he believes he needs tuh be punished. He knew she would tell yuh and you would do something about it. It's the coward's way out, but John believes he has tuh have this matter settled before he meets the Lord again. He didn't say that, but Ah know. Fifty-two years of marriage, and you just know."

Johnny walked to the window and rubbed his day old whiskers that were irritating and itching his chin. "But, why didn't Mama tell me about Reverend Oliver?"

"Ah believe, first she was afraid of yuh grandfather. Later, when yuh were older, Ah believe she didn't want to reopen an old wound. Yuh have tuh understand how traumatic those times were for her."

Johnny sat in the chair again and continued to rub his chin. He was quiet for a while. Loretha had put her reasons in his head even though they were second hand and expressed her beliefs. But she did manage to quiet him, to settle him, to give him food for his thoughts. She was honest. She could have soft-touched his grandfather's attitudes, reasons and behavior, but she spoke from her heart and about what she believed.

"You're right. Did yuh ever tell Mama that Grandfather told Sarah?"

Loretha sat forward on the sofa. "No ... all this will be a complete surprise. Ah knew what Sarah would do. The first thing Ah should've done was tell yuh mama. Ah remember Ah didn't want tuh upset her that weekend. Yuh-know, it was the weekend you and Julia were here, and she was so happy. Then, maybe Ah couldn't bear tuh think about the pain it was gonna cause her. Ah just kept puttin' it off, but now yuh here."

Johnny moved to the sofa and sat next to Loretha, gently holding her hand. "Gram'ma … it's important that we have closure. We've all paid a high price for all the secrecy, but another day won't make a difference after all of these years."

"What yuh talkin' 'bout Johnny? What yuh meaning tuh do?"

Johnny sat quietly for a few moments. "Well," he said. "Let's not tell Mama … I mean … just for tonight."

"Why, Johnny?" Loretha was surprised at what she was hearing. Although she knew it was going to be a painful weekend, she wanted to get it over with.

"Wel l l … I'd like to have a pleasant evening with Mama. I don't want her to come here, straight from work and have all this shoved in her face. I want her to know that I know and have some time to sort things out before she and I talk."

Johnny moved from the sofa back to the chair. He sat on the very edge of the chair and rubbed under his chin with the back of his hand. "Gram'ma, I think Mama should be told that I know." He gave his grandmother a pleading stare. His eyes were glassy. "Maybe you could tell her. And maybe you could tell her how much I know. Maybe you could tell her late tonight, then we could talk about it tomorrow. Would you do that for me?" He felt like the coward, but he just couldn't do it. If he had to, he would just return to D.C. and let the matter sleep forever.

Loretha patted the sofa where she wanted Johnny to return. "Well, Johnny, Ah think yuh may be right. Ah'll call her later tonight and tell her. Ah think she may want tuh talk tuh Nat. Ah know it's gonna be mighty upsettin' tuh her."

Johnny and Loretha were still sitting in the living room when Elizabeth drove up. They could hear her car as she pulled up to park and returned to the front porch. They gave each other one last reminding glance, then moved toward the steps to greet Elizabeth.

Elizabeth closed the car door and strutted toward the house like she was marching in the Sunday school parade. "Johnny, yuh got tuh start calling ahead and letting us know when yuh coming home," she called out, her arms flailing to the beat of her words.

"I'll try, Mama, but sometimes I start thinking of you, and before I know it, I'm home. I can't help it." Johnny smiled. His arms held her ever so tender. "Oh, Mama, I love you so much."

"Not as much as Ah love you. Ah'm truly blessed."

It turned out to be a wonderful warm-hearted afternoon. Loretha and Elizabeth left in enough time to prepare their dinner. Johnny remained at MaDear's cottage until a little after 7:00. His exhaustion had taken a toll on him, and relaxing in the embrace of MaDear's chair quieted his spirit. He needed all the energy he could collect to join his mother and Nat for dinner.

Elizabeth was in the kitchen fussing with dinner while Johnny and Nat were playing the father and son role in the den, telling jokes and sharing an evening of laughter. Then a period of quiet blanketed them, and they threw their heads back on the lounge chairs and were still.

Nat was happier than he had ever been in his life. He looked over at Johnny, using his peripheral vision, and wished he were his natural son. He didn't have any children and thought of all the years he loved Elizabeth and Johnny. He closed his eyes, shook his head and thought of all the lost time that would never be found again.

Johnny was wondering how Loretha was going to tell his mother and how it would affect her. He could see his mother's tears when she tried to explain to Nat why she kept this secret from him. He wondered what was going to happen when they all met and was thinking that his grandfather should be present.

"No! No!" Johnny yelled out, breaking the silence in the room.

"Whatcha talkin' 'bout, Johnny?" Nat asked.

"Oh! Oh! I must've been dreaming." Johnny panted and threw himself forward in the chair.

"Damn!" Nat said. "That must have been a hell-of-a-dream. What shook yuh like that, man?"

"I don't know, but whatever I was dreaming, sure jerked me back to reality." He saw what he didn't want to see. It was his mother's tears. He had only seen his mother's tears when MaDear died. He never wanted to see her cry again.

"Hey, man, Ah'm here anytime yuh need tuh talk."

"Thanks, Nat. Man, I think I'm going to need you real soon." Johnny gave Nat a definite look, and Nat seemed puzzled. Nat reminded himself that Johnny would always know where he was. The men put their heads back on the chairs and continued in their private thoughts, Nat sensing something was going on, and Johnny thinking about his mother.

"Okay guys, dinner is on," Elizabeth's voice sang out.

Johnny and Nat ate like hungry bears. It didn't take long for them to finish their meals. They shared small talk for the remainder of the evening. It was around nine o'clock when Johnny left to go back to the cottage.

"Mama, what time is it?" Elizabeth watched moonbeams shine through the window and streak across the bedroom. Her heart jumped when Loretha told her Sarah and Johnny knew all the details of the family secret and her father finally admitting that he believed her.

"Honey, let's get there about 9:00 in the morning. Now don't be anxious. Yuh don't even have tuh tell Nat yet. Johnny just wants tuh know what yuh want him tuh do. He promised tuh do whatever we want and no more. So please don't worry. Ah'll see yuh tomorrow. Now, yuh take care."

"Now don't worry!" Elizabeth repeated her mother's words while fear and anxiety radiated outward from the crevices of her mind. She sat up in bed, and by the time Nat turned the light on, she was shaking and beads of perspiration were clinging to her body. Her face was fixed, pale, clammy and cold like stone. Her eyes, shifty and flooded with tears.

"Baby! What's the matter? Are yuh sick?" Nat moved closer. He wrapped his arms around her. "Please, honey, Ah can't help yuh if Ah don't know what's the matter."

Elizabeth was in a trance brought on by fear, and Nat was in fear brought on by her trance. He was beginning to panic, and all he could think about was Loretha. "Honey, yuh were talking tuh yuh mother before this happened. What did she say tuh yuh, Beth? Honey, Ah'm gonna call yuh mother." He dialed Loretha and told her what was happening. Loretha said she would be right over.

Nat took the blanket from the bed and pulled it around Elizabeth. Elizabeth's severe trembling was alarming, and Nat feared she would die in his arms. Then the whining came. It was a pleasure to hear her whining. It was something. It let him know she was still with him. He released the air trapped in his lungs, his chest concaved and he pulled her closer to him.

Elizabeth took a deep huff of air and a loud howling sob escaped; it sounded as though her soul was leaving her body. She vibrated, trembled and cried a drenching, soaking cry. Nat continued to ask her what was wrong.

Elizabeth shifted her body and continued to sob. She tried to speak. It seemed like all the fears she had experienced in her lifetime were bursting out of the hidden caverns of her mind and crowding into her consciousness. Now it was all there, all at once; all the bad, terrible, awful and unmentionable memories. All that was suppressed was there; unsorted, confusing and paralyzing her with fear.

Loretha was pounding on the side door. Nat moved cautiously toward the bedroom door. He watched Elizabeth and readied himself to run back to her, believing she would tumble over without his support. He ran through the dark house, bumping into furniture before managing to turn on the light. He yelled to Loretha that he was coming. When the door was opened, Loretha rushed to Elizabeth's side.

"Nat, may Ah have a few minutes alone with her?"

Nat nodded, backed out of the bedroom and closed the door behind him. He retreated to the den to wait and worry. Loretha put her arms around Elizabeth the same way Nat had done.

"Ah know yuh think the Lord has forsaken yuh again. Honey, hush. Shush, baby … shush now." Loretha spoke in a soft comforting voice while she rubbed her hands over Elizabeth's hair, down her cheeks, onto her shoulders, cuddling her and all the time whispering in her ear to be still and quiet. "Honey, his blessings come in many forms, from many directions, and from out of nowhere. Maybe that's why it's so frightenin'."

"Mama," Elizabeth whimpered.

"Yes, baby."

"When did Daddy start believing me? Why didn't he tell me? Why did he say anything tuh Sarah?" She cried between each question. "That was wrong, Mama! Why does he keep hurting me? Why now?"

Loretha wrapped her arms around Elizabeth and held her tight. She kissed her forehead. "Baby, yuh father didn't deliberately set out tuh hurt yuh. He was just tryin' tuh ease his own sufferin'. Sarah kept badgerin' him, telling him she knew there was a secret, and demanding tuh know what it was. He's such an emotionally weak man, and over the years he's grown weaker. It was a surprise tuh me when he told Sarah. But Ah believe he told her because he knew she would stir up the old issues, and they'd be resolved. Ah'm sure he knew it would hurt, but Ah believe he thought it would be the last of the pain for himself and everyone else. It's easy tuh say he should've come tuh yuh, but it wasn't easy for him. He suffered the errors of his ways for so many years. He didn't know what direction was right. He loves yuh and Johnny so much, but he doesn't have the courage tuh say so, and saying so just wasn't enough unless he fixed what was broken."

"Mama why didn't you tell me Sarah knew?" She pulled at her comforter with both hands and used it to dab at her tears.

"Honey, Ah should've. Ah guess Ah was just hoping Sarah wouldn't do anything … and after so many weeks … but now the more Ah think about it … Ah wonder if Ah wanted her tuh do something."

"But, yuh could have still told me. Mama … how long has this been going on?"

"Yuh father told Sarah the day the family met Julia. And yuh right, Ah should've told yuh. Ah guess Ah'm a coward, too. So many years have passed and everyone was doin' so good, Ah didn't want tuh relive that time. Ah really thought she was gonna leave it alone. But, knowing, Sarah, Ah don't know why Ah thought that way. Ah don't know, maybe subconsciously, Ah wanted a resolution, too. Ah just don't know why. But, it's time. Johnny knows now. Now it's time."

Loretha held her tighter and pushed her hair away from her face. "Honey, Ah believe Ah didn't tell yuh because Ah was afraid yuh would react this way. Ah didn't want tuh see yuh hurt like this. Ah think Ah just hoped Sarah would let it go." Loretha shook her head, made a single chuckle sound and looked off in the distance. "I don't know why Ah thought that?" She turned attention back to Elizabeth.

"Baby, Ah'll never know the pain and fear yuh experienced, and Ah don't know why the Lord chose you. Now it's time tuh remove all this pressure from yuh heart. Ah spoke with Johnny. He's a wonderful young man. He loves yuh more than any person in this world. He said he would never question why yuh didn't tell him. He knew yuh loved him, and if yuh had a reason, then that was reason enough for him. He just wants tuh know what yuh want him tuh do."

Elizabeth continued to hold tight to the comforter. "Nothin',
Mama! Ah don't want Johnny tuh do nothin'!"

Loretha gently swayed Elizabeth, soothing her with rhythmic
movement. "Honey, Ah think deep down inside, yuh want him tuh do
something. Yuh want all this tuh end. It's hung over yuh so long, yuh
believe it belongs there, but it doesn't. Yuh can't have all that fear paralyzing yuh like this again. Ah think yuh greatest fear is facing Johnny
and Nat."

"Mama, what about Nat?" A few more tears on the comforter
didn't matter, so she wiped her face again and snuggled close to her
mother and waited for answers.

Loretha pulled away and held Elizabeth by her shoulders. "Honey,
yuh had yuh reason for not telling him the truth, but yuh must understand, 'A lie begets a lie.' If it were me, Ah'd tell him, no matter how it
turns out tomorrow. He loves yuh and he'll understand. Tell him everything … everything from the very beginning. Ah know Nat. Ah know
he'll understand and stay by yuh side. Don't let this lie beget another
lie."

"Mama … how can Ah face him and tell him that?"

Loretha placed her forehead against Elizabeth's. "First … take time
and pray. Yuh asked God tuh give yuh strength before, and he was
always with yuh, even when yuh didn't believe he was. God loves yuh,
and he's right here with yuh now. Talk tuh him. Ask him tuh help yuh.
Ah'll stay with Nat until yuh call for him."

Elizabeth knew her mother was right. The Lord seemed to be whispering in her mother's ears. A quiet had come over Elizabeth. The
crying stopped. The shaking and the shivering subsided. Her mother
had given her something real to do and think about. It was like a tree
suffering the pain of being moved, having its roots transplanted in a
different field. The roots grabbed hold to the good earth and formed
the foundation. The bark of the trunk became thicker and the sprout
of each branch was a person to love. Each branch returned with more
branches, and all of this started from the pain of that transplanted tree.
It was the tree of love and happiness. Elizabeth walked over to the

window and let the moon shine on her face. She began to talk with God.

CHAPTER 23

Loretha left the bedroom and sat with Nat in the den. "She'll be all right. She needs tuh talk with God."

"Loretha, she was fine until she spoke with yuh. As soon as she hung up the phone, she seemed to freeze like she was in pain. What did yuh say tuh her?"

"Nat trust me. Ah can't tell yuh what we talked about. That's for her tuh do. It's not my place. But believe me, it's not pain she's experiencing, it's fear!"

—ᴍ—

More than an hour passed before Elizabeth entered the room. She was quiet. Her eyes were pink and her face swollen.

Nat responded with a jerk when she called his name. "Oh, baby, are yuh all right?" He sprang to his feet.

Elizabeth didn't speak, but nodded her head.

Loretha smiled and nodded her head. "Everything is gonna be all right. Call me in the mornin'."

"All right, Mama."

Nat and Elizabeth walked to their bedroom. He spread the blanket out on the bed and pulled it up around her shoulders. He looked directly in her eyes, rubbed his thumbs across her cheeks and asked her if she wanted to talk about whatever it was that upset her. She stood and rested her head against his chest, holding the comforter at her neck with one hand and the other around his neck. He wrapped both of his arms around her, quiet and waiting.

Elizabeth would have preferred to wait until morning, but during her talk with God, she'd promised to be hasty and ease Nat's anxieties the way God had soothed hers.

"Honey ... Ah'm so sorry. Ah'm so sorry ... Ah put yuh through so much worry. Ah've done something terrible ... and ... and Ah have tuh tell yuh about it. Ah should have told yuh when we were first married, but ... Ah didn't. Ah'm so sorry, but, Ah had my reasons ... but that's no excuse. If Ah could continue tuh keep this from yuh, Ah would. Ah have tuh be completely honest, if Ah wasn't afraid yuh'd hear it from someone else, Ah wouldn't be telling yuh this now."

"What is it, Beth? It can't be that bad. Ah don't think yuh've done a bad thing in yuh entire life."

"Nat, it's not what Ah did ... it's what Ah didn't do. It was wrong, but ... but my intentions were good." She used the section of comforter she was holding at her neck to wipe the tears from her eyes. "One time yuh asked me if Ah knew who Johnny's father was." She paused to hear what Nat had to say.

"Yes Ah did, but Ah hope that's not what upset yuh." He rubbed her back.

"Nat ... Ah lied." She paused to measure his reaction again, then hurried to say what she had to say before she lost her courage. "His father is Reverend Owen Oliver. He's the man who raped me ... and ... and, he told me that my father wouldn't believe what he did and he was right. The only reason Ah didn't tell yuh was because Ah didn't want yuh to have tuh look at him and think about the terrible thing he did tuh me."

Nat was speechless. He made a special attempt to control his breathing. He held her tightly, and leaned over and kissed her gently. He held her tight again and ran his finger down the back of her curly hair and rubbed her back. All this because he was speechless. Until he could talk to her calmly, he would keep her calm and quiet himself. It was important to let her know everything would be all right.

Elizabeth couldn't see the strained movement of his clinched jawbones flexing his anger. At that very moment, he could have killed

Reverend Oliver. When he was completely composed, he said, "Ah understand, baby … Ah understand. Ah love yuh so much."

But he didn't understand. He didn't understand how a man could cause so much pain and still be able to live with himself. He didn't understand how this man could remain in the community for so many years and face his victim and her family. He did understand why Elizabeth didn't tell him sooner. But nothing could ever make him stop loving her.

This one important detail was the only critical point Elizabeth had never told him. They had discussed the rape, pregnancy, emancipation and MaDear's relationship. He even knew about the mysterious, monthly fifty-dollar bills. He believed her when she said she didn't know who Johnny's father was, and so he believed it had all been settled.

"C'mon, Beth, let's get in the bed. Ah'm gonna hold you, and we can talk. Did Ah tell yuh how much Ah love yuh and nothing this side of heaven can change that. Ah only want tuh know one thing. Baby, did yuh ever tell Johnny?"

Elizabeth snuggled with her head on Nat's chest. "Oh no! No, Ah couldn't tell him. The only people that knew were Mama, MaDear, Daddy, myself and of course Reverend Oliver. Ah didn't tell Johnny because by the time he asked, everything had quieted down. In fact, it wasn't long before it was no longer considered gossip. If Ah told Johnny, it would've opened up that terrible time in my life. Maybe Ah was selfish, but Ah had Johnny, and he was pure love. When he became a man, it seemed selfish tuh tarnish Reverend Oliver's image, Johnny loves him as much as he loves you. Oh my Lord … Nat, how is Johnny taking all this? He must feel terrible."

"Baby, how did he seem this evening?" Nat said. "Did he seem sad?"

Elizabeth lifted her head and turned to face Nat. She placed her elbow just under his armpit and rested her head on the palm of her hand. "No, he just seemed like Johnny. But Ah suppose he did seem tuh be a little tired. He really wasn't as upbeat. There was a quietness tuh his smiles. It was like he was thinking real hard. Nat, Ah just thought he was tired. Yuh-know, he works so hard."

"Honey, Ah think Johnny is all right. It's gotta be a bad time for him, and that's why he's here. He had yuh mother tell yuh late in the evening. That's just like him. He didn't want tuh ruin yuh whole day. Yuh gonna see him tomorrow, and Ah'm sure he's all right. But, Baby … what happened? It's been a very long time. Why is all this coming out now?"

She rested her head back on Nat's chest. He wrapped his arm around her again. "Daddy. It was my daddy. It was Sarah. Mama said Daddy began tuh believe me some years ago. You don't really know my father. When it comes tuh controlling the church, he's a master, but when it comes tuh his family and his personal life, he's a coward."

Elizabeth was calm. Nat's positive and open attitude helped her to continue to be as complete as she could.

"Daddy told Sarah, when he should have come tuh me," Elizabeth continued. "But he just can't help it. Ah use tuh think less of him because of his weakness, but Ah don't anymore. He just can't help himself. Ah never stopped loving him, but Ah don't know if he loves me. Mama says he does, but he has never shown me any kind of affection since the day Johnny was born."

"Beth, did Ah say Ah only wanted tuh know one thing? Well Ah have one more question." Nat said in a calm, just above a whisper, voice. "Why do yuh think Reverend Oliver needs tuh be protected? Why did yuh have tuh suffer all this and he comes away untouched and still have Johnny's love and admiration?"

Elizabeth turned over, placing Nat's left arm into the crook of her neck. Nat adjusted his weight to his side and wrapped his right hand around her. "It just happened that way. When Daddy didn't believe me and forbid Mama from saying anything, Ah had nowhere tuh turn. Ah was young, and there was so much going on. Ah just wanted it tuh go away. Ah was so hurt by my father's behavior, Ah was emotionally drained. Daddy said Johnny and I couldn't come home and MaDear took us in. Ah even tried tuh end my life. Ah didn't know the law and when Ah did, Ah was too weak tuh relive my past. Ah just wanted tuh live, take care of Johnny and be left alone. Ah wasn't protecting Reverend Oliver, he was just lucky Ah didn't have the energy tuh fight. Ah left Concord and joined Bethlehem Baptist Church, but when Johnny took tuh him, Ah just let him be. MaDear warned me, but Johnny was happy. Ah couldn't give Johnny a reason tuh stay away from him, so Ah just let him be. Yuh-know, Nat, every time Ah had tuh tell my story, or even think about it, Ah had tuh relive it. It got tuh a point when Ah just couldn't do it anymore. Ah just took life the way it was and refused tuh relive the bad times any longer. That is, until tonight and, Ah suppose, tomorrow …"

Nat listened as long as Elizabeth spoke, but when her words trailed off, he just held her in his arms. He closed his eyes, placed the side of his face against her head and the sweet aroma of her hair filled his nostrils. He was filled with thoughts of how much he loved her. Then thoughts of Reverend Oliver invaded his consciousness. He thought of the muscle relaxant his doctor prescribed to treat his strained back muscle. He lifted Elizabeth from his arm and slid his body from under her.

"Nat? How come yuh not in bed?"

"Ah want yuh tuh get some rest. Ah'm Okay. Ah was just going tuh the bathroom. Ah'm gonna get me a pills, and Ah think it'll do yuh good to take one, too. It's just 5 milligrams, and it will help yuh sleep. This has been a terrible night for yuh."

"Ah do feel a little jumpy," Elizabeth said. "But Ah never took anything to make me sleep."

Nat came to her with a 5-milligram tablet and a half a cup of water. Elizabeth looked up at the guarded expression on his face when she took the pill.

Nat lay on his side and placed his arm around Elizabeth's waist. His pills remained in the medicine jar. He wasn't ready to have his sleep induced. Reverend Oliver was still in his thoughts, and he planned to rid himself of his plaguing presence as soon as he was sure Elizabeth was sound asleep.

Around 2:00 A.M., Nat got out of bed and tucked a pillow against Elizabeth's back, hoping it would substitute the support he gave her when she snuggled close to him. He grabbed up his clothing and shoes and quietly left the room. Once in the living room, he dressed, then threw himself back in his chair. He was tired, but not for sleep. He was heavy with the need for revenge. He and Reverend Oliver had been friends at work, but never formed a close relationship. He remembered asking him to his house on several occasions, but Reverend Oliver always found a reason to decline. Now, it was clear to him. Now he understood his closeness to Johnny. He remembered how Reverend Oliver never seemed to look at him face-to-face and eye-to-eye the way men often did.

Nat picked up the telephone and dialed Reverend Oliver's number. It didn't concern him that he might wake Thea, or if she answered the phone. If she did, he would just ask for Reverend Oliver. When the phone rang, he heard the groggy sound of a man's voice.

"Owen!" The whisper-yell harshness of Nat's voice sounded through the telephone.

"Yes, this is Reverend Oliver."

"This is Nathaniel Baker. Something came up this evening, and it involves you. Don't say anything, just listen! Meet me in front of yuh house in thirty minutes."

"Man, is this a life or death situation? It's after two in the morning."

"Ah'd say it was, just be there," Nat demanded before slamming the phone down and leaning back in his chair.

Nat's headlights flashed across Reverend Oliver's front porch when he turned into the half-circle driveway. He was five minutes early, but Owen Oliver was waiting for him. He pulled the car to the end of the driveway and waited for Reverend Oliver to walk toward him. By the time Reverend Oliver reached the car, Nat had lowered the window and unlocked the doors.

"Hello, Nathaniel. Why do yuh have me out here so early in the morning?"

"Get in the car, man. Let's take a ride. We need tuh talk." He didn't turn to look at Reverend Oliver or take his hands off the steering wheel. It angered him enough just seeing him through his peripheral vision.

"Why don't yuh just come in the house?" Reverend Oliver waved his hand toward his home.

"No, man," Nat said looking up at Reverend Oliver. "Just get in."

Reverend Oliver looked back at his house, wondering if Thea was standing in their bedroom window. "Okay, but it would be a lot easier if Ah knew what this was all about."

As soon as Reverend Oliver was seated and the door closed, Nat raised the windows, locked the doors, put the car in gear and drove off. It was a warm moonlit night, a beautiful night. Nat knew what he wanted to say, but he wasn't sure what he would do to him. He drove down Rehoboth Road for less than a mile before turning onto a private road leading to a fenced cow pasture.

Owen slapped his leg. "Okay, Nathaniel, when yuh going tuh tell me what this is all about?"

"Well, Owen. Ah heard some disturbing information this evening. Ah know yuh know about it." His tone was soft and bland.

He looked over at Nat. "Know what, man? What yuh talkin' 'bout?"

"Well it's about something that happened about thirty-six years ago. Something yuh did." Nat never took his eyes off the road. He didn't care what Owen's expressions were. Elizabeth said he hurt her and that was all he needed to know.

Reverend Oliver leaned his head back against the seat and took a few deep breaths. He looked out of the car window at the moonlit pasture, then turned to Nat again. "Something Ah did? What yuh talkin' 'bout, man?"

Nat was still quiet. His movements were slow. He reached for the door handle and got out of the car. He walked to the passenger side, opened the door and gestured for Reverend Oliver to get out.

"Ah was told yuh were Johnny's father and yuh were the one that raped Elizabeth." The tone of his voice was calm, but he knew Reverend Oliver understood what he was talking about.

Reverend Oliver held his hands out, palms up, as though he were offering himself to Nat. His lips moved, but there were no words. His arms and hands began to move in circular gestures, and he turned to look at Nat, just as Nat pulled his closed fist from behind his back and smashed him in his jaw, sending him to the dirt road.

Nat leaned over, grabbed the front of Reverend Oliver's shirt, pulled him off the ground with his right hand, reared back and punched the left side of his face again. He lifted him up again for another blow, but stopped and threw him back to the ground.

Reverend Oliver didn't say "stop" or throw up his hands in defense. He just turned his head like a broken dog and began to cry.

"God damn yuh, Owen! God damn yuh! Ah could kill yuh, but then Ah'd be like yuh."

"Man," Reverend Oliver said, "Yuh could never know how sorry Ah've been all these years."

"Shut up! Shut up! Ah should beat the living hell out of yuh, but yuh seems like that's what yuh want me tuh do. Ah'm not gonna give yuh what yuh want." Nat walked away from him, put his hands on his hips and looked up at the starry sky. He turned and looked at him again from a safer distance. Reverend Oliver was still on the ground, wailing.

"Ah know why yuh didn't turn yuhself in," Nat said. "Ah know yuh greatest fear, but how could yuh do what yuh did and stay around tuh torment Elizabeth with yuh presence all these years? Why didn't yuh just take yuh family and move on? Hell, man … this isn't even yuh hometown." Nat bent over. At the same time he grabbed Reverend Oliver up by front of his shirt and yelled in his face. "Why did yuh keep hurting her?" He threw him back on the ground and walked away.

"It was because of Johnny," Reverend Oliver said.

"Johnny?" Nat said, rushing back to Reverend Oliver. He leaned on the side of the car and yelled down at him, "Yuh didn't deserve Johnny. And yuh shoulda been gone before he was born. Ah tell yuh what Ah'm gonna do for yuh. Ah'm gonna give yuh another chance. Yuh better be gone in one week or yuh greatest fears will come true. Pack yuh shit, quit the school, quit the church and be gone from here. If Ah see yuh after next Saturday, yuh'll regret it."

"Nat, yuh want me tuh quit the school without giving notice. School starts next week. Ah'll loose my pension if Ah do that. Ah need at least two weeks."

"No shit! Man, Ah think yuh got a real problem," Nat said. He turned to walk around the car to the driver's seat, then he walked back to Reverend Oliver. He pointed his finger down at him. "If you tell anyone about this night, it won't matter if yuh leave town, yuh won't have a reason tuh continue to live."

He walked back to the car and drove away, spraying Reverend Oliver with dirt and gravel from the spinning wheels. He knew he could have easily taken his life. He thought of how easy it would have been to smash his head with a rock, or choke him, or run him over with the car. But he didn't. He had the presence of mind to get himself as far away from him as he could. He was sweating and breathing heavy. He yelled out a loud throaty scream—no words, only angry sounds. He screamed again and again until tears dropped from his chin and soaked his shirt. He cried for Elizabeth and Johnny. He cried for himself.

"Oh thank yuh, Lord. Thank yuh for stopping me and holdin' me back." He sobbed as he drove around the back roads until he was calm enough to go home.

When Nat finally reached his house, he turned his headlights off before turning into his driveway. When he entered the house, he checked in on Elizabeth before going to the bathroom to take his pills. It was almost 4:00 A.M., and he needed it. It was another hour before he fell asleep. He knew he didn't want Reverend Oliver to leave town. He wanted to expose him, to punish him, to disgrace him. His thoughts rambled through his head. When the morning came, the events of the last evening seemed like a bad dream.

—⟋⟋⟋—

Elizabeth informed Nat that she and her mother were going to see Johnny at 10:00 A.M. He asked if he was needed.

"No, honey, we're going tuh talk with Johnny. Mama said Johnny just wants tuh know what we should do about Reverend Oliver."

"Then yuh need me there because if it's left up tuh you and Mother, nothing will happen."

"Honey, Ah promise, something will happen."

Nat smiled a satisfied smile and looked away from Elizabeth. "Okay, yuh tell me what yuh decided tuh do when Ah see yuh later."

Loretha waved at Nat when she pulled into their driveway.

Johnny was on his second cup of coffee and was a little nervous, but he tried not to show it. When he heard the car coming up the road, he took his coffee, stood on the front porch, and casually leaned against the porch post.

Elizabeth had already climbed one mountain and believed the second would be easier, but that didn't stop the butterflies in her stomach. Johnny was waiting for them, he didn't appear upset or angry. In fact, he seemed pleased to see them. This eased some of Elizabeth's anxieties and made it easier for her to approach him. They greeted each other with hugs, went into the kitchen and sat around the table. Johnny began to engage in small talk because he didn't know where to start.

"Okay Johnny, now yuh know Reverend Oliver is yuh father, and Ah guess yuh wanna know why Ah didn't tell yuh." Elizabeth began with words that were reflective, but with an attitude that was humble.

Johnny got up and threw his arms around his mother's neck. "No, Ma. I think I know why you didn't. I don't want to talk about why. Whatever your reasons, it's good enough for me. Nothing can change the past. I was shocked and hurt, but I've given it a lot of thought. You know how I feel about Reverend Oliver. That's why I'm not questioning your reasons. I know what you did or didn't do was in my best interest. Now, I just want to know what you want me to do?"

Elizabeth watched Loretha who was sitting quietly, determined not to enter the conversation unless a question was directed at her. She turned toward Johnny. "Johnny … up 'til last night, Ah didn't want yuh tuh do anything, but now Ah'm not so sure. Yuh-know, Ah know how much yuh love him. In spite of everything that's happened, Ah've never tried tuh come between that love even though Ah despised him. Ah wanted to spit whenever Ah saw him. What he did tuh me was unthinkable, but Ah can't deny what he left behind. Nat knows and yuh know. Ah was only protecting y'all. Ah think it's time Reverend Oliver answered tuh someone. Ah don't know what yuh should do, but now Ah need something tuh be done. Ah want it over."

Johnny and Elizabeth looked at Loretha at the same time. "Gram'ma, what do you think?"

Loretha smiled. "Yuh need a voice of experience. Ah have an idea of what might be an acceptable solution." She stood and walked around the kitchen and talked all the while. "Now Ah would have Reverend Oliver bring Thea, Malcolm and his wife to my house and confess in front of Johnny, Elizabeth, John, Julia, Nat, Sarah and herself. He can say whatever else he wants tuh say, but he must say, 'Ah raped 'Lizabeth and Johnny is my son.'"

Elizabeth smiled. "Ah like it. What about yuh Johnny?

"I like it, too." Johnny said. "There's just one thing. I need to have this meeting take place this weekend. I know Julia isn't here, but I can't go home and have this hanging over me."

"Okay, Ah'll call Reverend Oliver as soon as Ah get home and tell him we'll expect him and his family tomorrow. It'll be up tuh him tuh make sure they all come. Ah'll call Sarah and tell her tuh be here. She got this ball rollin', so she better be here. Ah don't know how John will take this, but at this point, Ah don't care. So let's say 3 o'clock, tomorrow at my house."

There were no happy feelings about the plan. In fact, they were all very anxious. The thought of it finally being over was of some relief to Elizabeth. They all believed Thea, Malcolm and his wife had to be there to hear the truth about Reverend Oliver.

Loretha hurried home and went into her den. Reverend Turner was out on hospital rounds. She sat in her high back wing chair and rested her legs on her ottoman. She called Reverend Oliver's house and Thea answered the telephone. Loretha had to be her usual pleasant self and engage in small talk before asking to speak to Reverend Oliver.

Thea called Owen. She was concerned that the left side of his jaw was covered with a large, reddish-blue bruise and his left eye was bloodshot. Owen explained that he had slipped on the porch steps the night before and banged his face on the banister post. She handed him the telephone and told him she was getting an ice pack for his face. "Ah think yuh need tuh go to the medical clinic, looks like yuh jaw may be fractured," She said as she walked toward the kitchen. Loretha could hear almost everything Thea was saying to Reverend Oliver.

"Yes, Loretha. How are yuh today?" Reverend Oliver answered in his usual proper tone, even though his head felt like it was splitting in two.

"Reverend Oliver, something very important has come up. First, Ah want yuh tuh know that everyone is well. How is yuh family?"

"Everyone is fine, Loretha. What's going on?"

"Wellll, Ah think yuh should be sitting down, and Ah need tuh warn yuh, it's going tuh be shocking." She could hear the hush at the other end of the line, but she knew he was still there. She was thinking he knew what she was about to say.

"We know the truth about what yuh did tuh 'Lizabeth. We've always known." She could hear a gasping sound contrasting against the quiet. Reverend Oliver was too overwhelmed to respond.

In a demanding tone, she said, "Ah want yuh tuh make sure you, Thea, Malcolm and his wife are at my house, tomorrow at three o'clock."

"Loretha! ... Loretha!" Reverend Oliver tried to cut her off, but Loretha cut back in before he could get past her name.

Loretha removed her feet from the ottoman and sat forward in her chair. "Listen, Reverend Oliver! Yuh just listen tuh me! Ah've believed 'Lizabeth all this time, and yuh know Ah did. Since Johnny was born, Ah believed her. And Ah think John did too, but, he was too much of a coward tuh do what was right…"

Reverend Oliver cut her off again, "How do yuh know she was telling the truth?"

Loretha stood. "Owen, don't you know your choice of words are too wrong to say to a mother about her child? Too wrong to say to someone who had always known the truth? Now yuh just listen tuh me, Mr. Oliver. Yes, Mr. Oliver!" Loretha said, stripping him of his religious title."

"Loretha!" Reverend Oliver called out. "Loretha!"

"Ah'm not going tuh get intuh a debate with yuh. If y'all aren't at my house tomorrow, Ah'll publicly expose yuh. Yuh lucky Johnny loves yuh so much. Now, Ah'm gonna tell yuh what Ah expect yuh tuh say, and Ah'm not asking yuh tuh say it, Ah'm demanding yuh say it. It's yuh word against 'Lizabeth's, but would yuh be willin' tuh risk public exposure?"

"Ah'm not gonna let yuh threaten me!" Reverend Oliver whispered so Thea couldn't hear.

Loretha cut him off again. "*YUH WILL SAY THAT YUH RAPED 'LIZABETH AND YUH JOHNNY'S FATHER, AND YUH WILL SAY THIS IN FRONT OF YUH FAMILY AND MINE!!!* Then, Ah hope yuh begin tuh live the hell yuh put my family through and my family can begin tuh heal. Just be here with yuh family!" Before Reverend Oliver could say another word, Loretha slammed the phone down.

Loretha smiled a satisfied smile. *Oh! Thank yuh, Lord. Thank yuh for the satisfaction. Thank yuh for the courage. Thank yuh for the opportunity. Thank yuh for the wisdom. Thank yuh, thank yuh Lord.*

When Sarah heard her mother's voice, she knew it was about Reverend Oliver and was very happy to drop any plans she had for the weekend.

When Reverend Oliver hung up the telephone, he sat rubbing his hands over his face and eyes. The pain in his jaw was a throbbing reminder of the hell he would continue to experience. Moments later, he picked up the telephone again and held it while the dial tone hummed. Soon, the dial tone changed to a busy tone and Reverend Oliver placed the phone back on the receiver.

He threw his head back on his lounge chair and closed his eyes. He believed the Lord had already forgiven his sin in heaven, but on earth, his devil's work was bound to face these inevitable consequences. His most difficult penance would come from confessing to Thea. "Ah'll tell her tomorrow morning," he said to himself.

A few minutes passed, then he picked up the phone to call Malcolm. He wondered where Thea was with the ice bag. It was still early, and he hoped he would catch him at home. When Malcolm answered the phone, Reverend Oliver explained in his most urgent voice that he needed him and his wife to come home. Malcolm said he had plans for the weekend, and it was impossible for him to change them.

"Malcolm, yuh must be here no later than tomorrow noon. Ah don't want tuh hear what yuh weekend plans are. If Ah were dying, would yuh drop everything and come?"

"Yeah, Dad, but yuh not dying."

Reverend Oliver sat up quickly. His head felt like it was splitting open. He eased himself back against the chair. "How do yuh know that? Please, Ah'm begging yuh tuh be here." He hung up the telephone.

Thea entered the room carrying an ice pack and tried to comfort Reverend Oliver's physical pain, but he didn't want relief. It was his mask for his emotional pain. *My Lord, first Nathaniel, now Loretha.*

—⁓—

The next morning, Reverend Oliver watched Thea sleeping peacefully. He thanked the Lord for giving her to him. They had their disagreements like most married couples, but that was one of the things that made their life together interesting. She wanted more children, but no more came. Reverend Oliver wondered if she was paying for his transgression. He had two sons, but Thea always spoke about the daughter she never had. Now she hoped Malcolm would give her many grandchildren.

Sliding the covers away from his body, Reverend Oliver got out of bed and sat in Thea's bedside chair. He wanted to savor the remaining calm of the morning. He had been awake most of the night from his emotional and physical pain. By morning his face was so badly swollen and discolored, he looked like his pain should have been unbearable. But he had set his pain aside, accepting it as his punishment. He spent the night praying and thinking, but still, he lacked a solution. He prayed for Thea, but not for her to forgive, or to stand by him. He would take his punishment. The punishment was not the important issue, how was he going to tell Thea what plagued him. He prayed it wouldn't be unbearably painful for her.

Ah'm the one who did this terrible thing, and Ah've been paying ever since. Ah wished Ah'd paid up then, whatever the price. It would be over by now. A moment of passion has cost me a lifetime of agony. When he noticed Thea stirring, he felt his heart push up into his throat. He swallowed a big silent gulp of air. First, he knew she would be wondering why he was sitting in her chair watching her. He knew he could charm her into her first morning smile.

"Good morning, Owen." She smiled and took a tiny stretch. She glanced over toward the clock. "Six-thirty? Why yuh sitting in my chair watching me? Are you in pain? Do yuh need to go tuh the medical clinic? Yuh face looks terrible."

"Oh, Thea, Ah'm all right. My face seems worse than it is." He didn't want to cause her any undue anxiety because of his appearance. *Ah should wait. Give her time to wake up and have a tiny taste of the beautiful morning. Not now. It's too early. Ah'll wait 'til breakfast.* "Ah have something tuh tell yuh that happened a very long time ago."

He couldn't wait. He stole her beautiful morning. Now he gave little thought of how he was going to tell her. It was more important to just get it out. "Thea, what Ah'm trying tuh say is … in all these years, Ah prayed Ah would never have tuh tell you this, but …"

"Owen, what are yuh talking about so early in the morning? Yuh scaring me."

There was no time left to be silent. "Honey, Ah'm trying tuh tell you about something Ah did that was so terrible Ah never spoke about it tuh anyone. Ah don't know how all these years passed and this terrible thing was allowed tuh go unpunished."

Thea turned to the side to see Owen better, staring at him wondering what terrible thing could he have done. "Owen, please, yuh makin' me nervous. What are yuh tryin' tuh say? Please! … . Just say it!"

He continued to hold his head up high because of the pain in his face, but his eyes were on Thea. Tears ran down his face. "Ah'm trying, but Ah don't want tuh lose yuh."

"Lose me! What could possibly make yuh lose me? Please tell me!"

Reverend Oliver looked at Thea, then at the window where the bright new sun had removed the gloom of the night. He held his head high because the pain was unbearable when he lowered it. He let his thoughts say what he needed to say and what seemed like seconds to him, were minutes to Thea.

Thea, Ah'm the one who raped Elizabeth. Johnny is my son! That's what Ah should say. There's no way tuh make it sound good. That's how Ah have tuh say it at the Turner's.

"Owen ... what is wrong with yuh? Yuh still scarin' me."

"Thea, Ah'm the one who raped Elizabeth. Johnny is my son."

These words caught Thea's attention. She sat straight in the bed. She was speechless. She heaved and filled her lungs with air. She held her breath. She couldn't speak. She exhaled slowly with little quivers of air and looked at her husband with wide eyes and an open mouth. She closed her eyes, opened them again, and when she saw Owen again, she closed her eyes and kept them closed for several moments. She moved her lips, but no words came.

Reverend Oliver watched her suffer the agony of his words. He wanted to hold her, but when he touched her, she shook his hands off and continued to wave her arms like she was fighting away demons. He backed away, turned and faced the corner of the wall like a child being scolded. He lowered his head and allowed the pain in his face to smother his emotions. Tears rolled down his face for the pain he was causing his Thea.

"Owen!" Thea said, heaving her voice. "Owen! ... Leave me alone. Just go ... get out of the room."

Reverend Oliver stood staring at her. His lips moving without sound forming.

"Get out! Get out! ... I don't want to see you right now!"

He continued to stand there staring at her. He wasn't finished. He needed to tell her about the meeting.

"Leave me! Leave me, Owen! Get out!" She slammed her fists on the bed.

He stole one more peek at her and in that moment, he saw all the pain and agony one person could inflict on another. Thea wanted him to leave. She didn't want to hear, "I'm sorry," or "Please forgive me." She needed time to cry, time to say why, time to be angry and time to pray.

He stepped backward out of the room without taking his eyes off her.

If he'd remained for just one moment longer, she would have screamed a piercing scream. She didn't want him to walk backward. She didn't want to see his face. She wondered how he could bear to see her after what he had revealed.

Reverend Oliver knew it would get worse when he told her about the meeting.

He had to select the right words, be honest. He knew it was bad enough telling her what he had done. Now he had to tell her she would wear part of his shame.

CHAPTER 24

Loretha decided not to tell Reverend Turner until early that morning. Perhaps at breakfast or maybe just before leaving for church. She wasn't sure, but she knew she would tell him long before the scheduled meeting. She also knew he had lost most of his control over the family. This secret had weakened him—nearly killed him before reducing him to a fragment of a man. She wasn't the least bit intimidated by him. Those days had long passed.

It was already nine-thirty, and Sarah still had not arrived. Loretha knew she would be there as soon as she could, but that didn't stop her from searching up the road every time she got near the front poarch. Reverend Turner was already sitting at the table. It was just another Sunday to him.

"Thank yuh, Jesus," Loretha whispered when she heard Sarah's car turn into the driveway.

"Oh, Sarah is here?" Reverend Turner said. "That's good, it's been a while since she's been home. She's just in time for breakfast and morning service."

"Well, yuh just go on with yuh breakfast while Ah go out tuh meet her," Loretha ordered. John smiled and went about doing what he was told to do.

Loretha hurried out the front door and she turned to see if John had followed her. "Hi, baby, Ah was kinda gettin' worried," she said.

"Ah overslept and got a late start. Ah suppose Ah should've called, but Ah left so early," Sarah said, and without so much as a blink, she added, "So Mama, what's the plan?" She was like a little child, giggling for revenge.

She believed Reverend Oliver's crime impacted her outlook on life. He stole her ability to love, share, and be considerate. He stole her emotions and caused her to live within herself. He made her afraid to care, because caring could be painful, as painful as the pain her family felt over the years.

Johnny was the good that came out of all this ugliness. She had allowed the good to elude her. Johnny was as distant to her as a stranger in the street. She blamed this on Reverend Oliver, but the fault of this loss belonged to her. So now she was here at her parents' house to feel revenge, but she would soon learn that the only satisfaction of revenge would come through forgiveness.

Loretha and Sarah stood against Sarah's car while Loretha explained the details and informed her that her father didn't know about the plan. "Ah was waiting for yuh before Ah told him. Ah really wanted tuh tell him before church."

"Ah don't know, Mama. It might upset him so much, he may not be able tuh function in church. Church is over between 1:30 and 2:00. Ah think an hour is good timing, and Ah want tuh tell him."

Sarah and Loretha walked into the house like two schoolgirls. Sarah greeted her father with a kiss and a tender hug, then sat at her place at the table and hurriedly ate her breakfast.

Reverend Oliver knew he wouldn't be going to church that morning. It was just as well because he couldn't face the Turners, especially Loretha. He was also expecting Malcolm and his wife before noon, and all hell was going to break loose at his house before the three o'clock meeting.

He called Deacon Bains and told him he wouldn't be at church and was unable to reach Reverend Turner on the phone. Then, he went back to his bedroom and stood outside the door listening. He could hear Thea whimpering, and tears filled his eyes again. He tapped lightly on the door, only to hear Thea yelling at him to stay out. He knew there was no comfort he could offer her and, deep inside, he was happy to keep his distance, but at the same time he wanted to be near her. He didn't know how he was going to face her. He felt awkward and empty, believing he had to say something.

"Thea, Ah asked Deacon Bains tuh tell John we weren't coming tuh church. Thea, please let me come in. We need tuh talk. Ah know how yuh feel. Ah never wanted tuh hurt yuh. Please let me in."

Thea was quiet for a long time. "No yuh don't know how Ah feel!"

Reverend Oliver slid down to the floor, leaned against the door and cried. Thea had never heard him cry with so much emotion. His sobbing sounds jerked the strength back into her. She got out of bed and walked over and opened the door. An uneven heartbeat weakened her when she saw Reverend Oliver on the floor. She was still too hurt to say anything. She walked back to bed and laid her head on her tear-dripped pillow.

Reverend Oliver crawled into the room, then stood. He covered his eyes with his hands and continued to cry. Crying seemed to get Thea's attention, so he decided to just let his emotions take over until he could think of what his next move should be. Thea let him back in the room, but she had tears of her own and felt he deserved to cry. She turned her back to him, but couldn't block out his sounds.

"Thea, Ah'm so sorry," he cried. His face throbbed with pain and the jerking motion of his sobbing was becoming unbearable. He held his hand over his jaw and could feel the heat radiating from it. "All these years Ah wanted tuh tell yuh, but Ah didn't know how. Ah don't know what happened. What Ah did was so terrible. Ah…"

Thea cried a sobbing, jerking cry of her own. "Owen … please … just shut-up! Yuh'll … pay dearly for this. God will … tell me what tuh … do when the time is right."

Owen had stopped sobbing. His eyes were red and puffy. He wiped his face with his damp handkerchief. "Malcolm and Theresa are coming home today."

"What!" Thea sat up in the bed, turned toward Owen, and screamed, "Why today? Ah don't want them tuh see me like this. Why'd yuh tell me this when yuh knew they were coming home today?" She slammed her hand down on the bed and turn away from him again.

"Thea, there's more. Ah have tuh tell yuh more."

She quietly sobbed, her shoulders shaking and her breath quivering. "More! What else have Ah missed?" Her heart skipped again, stealing some of her breath as she wondered if Owen had raped anyone else, but she didn't turn toward him.

"Ah have to tell Malcolm and Theresa, and then ... we all have tuh be at the Turner's house by three o'clock."

"No! Why?" Thea yelled out. "Ah'm not going tuh the Turner's. Yuh did this terrible thing all by yuhself."

Owen stood and walked to the bed. Thea never turned around, so he began to speak. "Thea, please! Ah don't know how yuh will ever forgive me, but please be with me tuhday." He stood so close to her she could feel the heat from his body. "Thea, you are the most important person in my life. Ah did something awful. Ah've prayed for forgiveness. Ah'm not sure if it will count against me in the hereafter. How can our Father forgive me, when Ah can't forgive myself?" Ah would have taken this terrible thing tuh my grave, rather than hurt yuh."

Thea didn't exchange a word. She continued to keep her back toward him. She didn't know why, but probably thought if she didn't see him, nothing he'd said was true. There was still more she had to know.

"Loretha called me yesterday and gave me an ultimatum."

She turned toward Owen with a jerk "Ultimatum? Is that bruise on yuh face part of that ultimatum?"

Owen was much calmer now, but he was trying to calm Thea. He spoke softly, "No, Thea. This has nothing tuh do with it. Loretha only wanted tuh keep this between our two families, but she threatened tuh expose me publicly if Ah didn't do what she wanted me tuh do. Please, Thea. Ah need yuh tuh be with me. Whatever yuh want tuh do after tuhday, Ah'll understand. But Loretha wanted us, including Malcolm and Theresa, tuh come tuh her house at three o'clock. Ah have tuh say,

'Ah raped Elizabeth and Ah'm Johnny's father,' in front of her family. Then we can leave."

"Ah'll be there. But Ah'll be there for the Turner family. Ah want yuh tuh back away from me." She turned and allowed her eyes to trace the swirling pattern of the lace curtains. "Ah blamed John when 'Lizabeth left the church, but it was you. Ah don't know what Ah'm gonna do after Ah leave the Turners. Maybe Ah should leave yuh. Maybe Ah should go tuh Atlanta while Ah sort this thing out. Ah can't believe yuh did such a terrible thing. If Ah stand with yuh, it'll look like Ah condone what yuh did, or even forgive yuh when Ah don't. Oh, Ah don't know what tuh do."

Owen stopped crying and was resting his head on the back of the chair. His head was pounding and an unsteadiness had come over him. He felt dizzy and knew he needed to go to the medical clinic, but he didn't have time to think about himself. He wanted to tell Thea what Nat had done and said to him. He wanted to tell her he had to leave town by the end of the week. That he would leave the church. That they would need to sell the house, and if he couldn't think of a solution, he would lose his job and pension. But most of all, he couldn't bear to lose her.

The morning sun had risen. Malcolm and Theresa arrived early. Thea was out of bed, but the saddening gloom continued to lay over her like a veil, making her feel weak and without a purpose. Owen went to the front door to greet them.

"See, Dad, yuh not dying," Malcolm said. "But yuh look like yuh almost dead. What happened tuh yuh face?"

Owen placed his hand over his jaw. "It's nothing. Ah slipped on the porch. Good morning, Theresa. How are you this morning?

"How are yuh, Dad? Have yuh seen a doctor about yuh face," Theresa asked.

"No, honey, it's gonna be all right."

"Where's, Mama! Is she all right?"

"She's inside. She's fine," Reverend Oliver said. "Ah need tuh talk tuh yuh, Malcolm. Theresa can Ah steal yuh husband for a few moments?"

Just as Reverend Oliver was leading Malcolm off toward the den, Thea came out of the bathroom. She walked over and greeted Malcolm and Theresa. Thea was quiet, not her usual self, when she invited Theresa to join her in the kitchen.

—m—

"Dad, why yuh hurrying me off tuh the den like this?" Malcolm stood and waited for his father to enter before he sat in the high-back chair across from the sofa.

"Ah have something tuh tell yuh. It's something terrible, something Ah did just before yuh were born. This is hard for me and Ah'm not gonna waste words." Reverend Oliver slouched down on the sofa because the dizziness was coming over him again. "Ah already told yuh mother, now Ah have tuh tell yuh." He paused and took another deep breath, the kind you take when you need time to think before you exhale. "This afternoon Ah'll need you and Theresa tuh go tuh the Turner's house. Can Ah count on yuh?"

"Sure, Dad. But ..." Malcolm hung his mouth open. He had never seen his father act in such a vague manner before. He was clueless as to the cause.

"When Ah say what Ah have tuh say, yuh may not want tuh go. Can Ah still count on yuh?"

"Yeah, man ... what's going on?"

"Ah'm gonna tell yuh this terrible thing, straight and forward. Believe what Ah'm about tuh tell yuh, and believe that Ah'm so very sorry." Reverend Oliver stared at Malcolm, waiting for a reaction. A slight nod of Malcolm's head signaled him to begin.

"Back when Ah was a young man. Ah committed a crime that Ah've never paid for. Oh, Ah paid a little piece of myself every day since then, but Ah never answered tuh no one else. Malcolm ... Johnny is yuh half brother and the worst of it is, Ah'm the one who raped his mother."

Malcolm didn't speak. He closed his eyes and massaged his temples, then brought his fingers around and massaged his eyes. He stood and walked to the window. He rubbed his hand over his face again, then he walked back to his father and stood over him with his hands on his hips. "Damn you, Dad! You raped a child and tormented her with yuh presence all these years. Yuh stood in the church and preached the Gospel with a holier than thou attitude. Then you threw me intuh yuh cesspool of sin. It was easier for me tuh tell myself that Ah hated Johnny than tuh say Ah loved him. Ah thought Ah was gay. Yuh made me question my manhood. Yuh have no idea how yuh ruined my life. Today yuh hurt my mother. Ah'm sure yuh had her crying all morning. Yuh gonna embarrass me in front of my wife. If yuh weren't my father, Ah would hate yuh. Then yuh ask us tuh share the blame of yuh crime and Ah agreed because Ah never thought my father could do anything so awful."

"Malcolm, Ah'm so sorry. Ah've prayed for forgiveness every day of my life."

Malcolm returned to his chair. His jawbone twitched under his skin, and his eyes squinted. He tried to remain respectful, but his lips curled inward when he spoke, and his words were sharp. "Ah know yuh weren't gonna turn yuhself in 'cause yuh would of gone tuh jail, but why didn't yuh leave town?"

"She never told or if she did no one believed her," Owen whispered.

Malcolm slammed his hand down on the coffee table. The crystal candy dish and matching ashtray made a crashing sound, but didn't break. "Damn it, Dad! So that gave yuh a right tuh stay around tuh torment her? Yuh know, Dad, years ago when Ah hurt Johnny and confessed to Miss Elizabeth. She looked in my eyes, smiled and said, 'It takes a real man tuh be responsible for his actions, and believe me there are not a lot of real men out there.' Dad, she was talkin' about you."

Owen looked up at Malcolm and tears were running down both their faces. "Malcolm, Ah'm so sorry. Ah had no idea Ah hurt yuh like that. Ah hope yuh can forgive me. When a stone is thrown in a lake, the ripple effect is far reaching. Ah'm so sorry about yuh and Johnny. Ah hope Ah can help bring yuh together. Ah have tuh go tuh the Turners' this afternoon and confess tuh them. Ah need everyone tuh stand with me. Can Ah still count on yuh?"

"Yeah, Dad. Damn yuh! Ah'll tell Theresa, and we'll stand with yuh at the Turners. My God … what will Theresa think about yuh?" Malcolm stood and stared at Owen. "Is that how yuh got that nasty bruise on yuh face? Did someone beat yuh up? Did Johnny beat yuh up?"

"No! No! Malcolm, Ah fell and smashed my face on the rail post on the porch steps. Ah wish someone had beat me. Ah deserve to be beaten."

Malcolm had trouble believing what he heard. He turned away. "Ah need tuh go tuh Mama." He left the room and walked over to his mother with his arms opened wide.

Theresa's big brown eyes focused on the movement in the room.

"Are yuh okay, Mama? Daddy out did himself tuhday."

"Ah don't know, Malcolm. Ah just have tuh get through tuhday so Ah can think about tomorrow. He told yuh about the meeting and what he did?"

"Yes, Mama."

Theresa's eyes shifted between Malcolm and Thea. "Isn't anyone gonna tell me what's going on?"

"Ah'm so sorry, honey." Malcolm put his arm around her and walked her out near the front door. He whispered when he told her what was happening.

"That's so terrible! How could yuh father ever do something like that?"

"Yuh right. It is terrible. It's so terrible, we have tuh wait a few days just tuh talk about it. We need tuh use this time tuh just think. Ah believe that's how Mama is getting through this. So, Ah think it's a good idea if we do the same. But, yuh-know Theresa, yuh heard me talk about Johnny Turner, not Reverend John Turner, but his grandson. He's the one that helped me get my job. He doesn't know Ah know, but Ah have a friend in personnel who told me about the letter of recommendation from Johnny that's in my folder. Johnny is my brother. Ah wonder if he knew when he sent the letter? Ah wonder if he knew he was my brother then?"

"My Lord, Malcolm. Ah don't know what tuh make of yuh attitude. What yuh father did was terrible. It was terrible because it was rape. Yuh mother is so sad and hurt, and yuh father only appears tuh be somewhat withdrawn and remorseful. But you, yuh speakin' more of yuh new found brother than yuh father's crime. A crime that was compounded more because he is a man of the cloth and a school teacher." Tears formed in her eyes, and her chocolate complexion took on a reddish hue.

"Malcolm … stop thinking of yuhself. Think of the heartache and pain of this crime. Think of the suffering of this woman and her family. There's a lot more tuh all this than Ah'm being told, even more than yuh may know about. Maybe you're right, we need tuh just get through this day, and then take it one day at a time." Theresa wasn't open to hearing anymore. She walked back toward the kitchen, stopping in the doorway. Owen was sitting at the table, Thea sat quietly across from him. Theresa took a seat near Thea. Thea asked Owen to bless the food.

Reverend Oliver looked around at everyone. "Before we start, Ah just wanna thank this family for bearing with me on this day. It's been a painful morning, and the day is far from over. Ah'm not seeking an easy way out, but Ah think it would be easier for yuh all if we don't speak about this again tuhday except during our meeting with the Turners. Then if yuh want, Ah'll answer any questions yuh may have tuh the best of my ability. Ah know y'all think Ah'm out of line, and Ah'm thinking only of myself, so Ah don't have tuh face it, but Ah was the one who did this terrible thing. Ah don't want y'all tuh suffer anymore than yuh have tuh."

Everyone stared at him and held their mouths open like they had something more to say, but no one spoke.

"Ah would like tuh ask Malcolm tuh bless the food," Reverend Oliver said.

Malcolm said the blessing, and little else was said. Silence gripped the air. Reverend Oliver had committed the crime, but everyone acted like they were guilty.

The ride home from church in Sarah's car was the perfect place to tell Reverend Turner about the meeting. Reverend Turner sat in the passenger seat, while Loretha sat behind him in the back seat.

"Daddy, Reverend and Mrs. Oliver, Malcolm and Theresa, are coming tuh our house this afternoon, Johnny, Elizabeth and Nat are coming, too."

"What's the occasion, Sarah?"

"It's showdown time!" Sarah sang out like a child and blew her father a kiss. "Reverend Oliver is coming over tuh confess, then maybe this family can start tuh heal."

"Sarah! Who gave yuh the right?"

"You did, Daddy. And yuh know it's the right thing tuh do. That's why Reverend and Mrs. Oliver weren't in church today. That's why Johnny is home. Daddy, that's why Ah came home. Yuh'll see, everything is gonna be all right."

Reverend Turner began to shake his head and blow off his anger. "Loretha, did yuh know about this?"

Loretha moved to the center of the seat and sat forward. "Yes Ah did, John." She placed her hand on his shoulder. "Now Ah want you tuh calm down and remember yuh conversation with the Lord. Now yuh told me what the Lord said, and Sarah and Ah were just following yuh wishes. Didn't yuh say the Lord told yuh, 'Yuh must take the first step tuh rectify the wrong yuh have done. The help yuh need has always been with yuh.' Is that what yuh told us?"

John looked off in the distance while Loretha quoted the Lord's words. "Yes, Loretha. That's what the Lord said tuh me."

"Daddy," Sarah called softly. "Do yuh want us tuh call off the meeting?"

"No. Yuh doing what the Lord said tuh do."

Loretha patted John's shoulder. "We know yuh nervous. But They're suppose tuh be at our house by three o'clock. Yuh don't have tuh do anything but sit with the people who love yuh. We're getting older, and Ah'm not willing tuh take this tuh my grave. Ah believe that's why the Lord gave yuh a second chance. The Lord said yuh were a 'good servant.' We've worked out a solution that will finally hold Reverend Oliver accountable. We're gonna let his family punish him the way yuh punished 'Lizabeth and Johnny all these years. He's the guilty one. Ah believe the Lord will be happy with our plan."

Reverend Turner smiled sadly and didn't say another word. Sarah was excited. Ever since she found out the truth about Elizabeth, she had an overwhelming compulsion for revenge against Reverend Oliver. She believed she could never get back the years he stole from her and her family, and now he had to pay.

It wasn't long before Johnny, Elizabeth and Nat arrived at the Turner home. Loretha fluttered around nervously, and the thickness in the air was apparent. A few words were spoken, here and there—short quick conversations that were as superficial as discussing the air.

Sarah was the only one bustling about. She went around hugging and kissing everyone and was extremely talkative. It was as though she had been away for a long time and was finally home. Everyone else, including Nat, acted like they had large malignant lumps in their throats. The next thirty minutes seemed to pass as slowly as the previous 36 years.

"Ah wish this were tomorrow, or next week, or next year. Ah wish this was over and we were a family again and these uncomfortable feelings were something we could hardly remember." Loretha spoke what she felt, which seemed to represent the collected consciousness of everyone, except Sarah. Loretha seized their attention, and they nodded in agreement.

"Okay, everyone, here they come!" Sarah yelled out like a little kid waiting for a surprise party. The others tightened up.

Sarah hurried to the front door. The large bruise on Reverend Oliver's face startled her. She wanted to ask what happened, but she didn't. Without saying a word, she escorted the Olivers to the den.

Southern courtesies mandated that greetings be exchanged. Loretha pointed to the four dining room chairs lined up across the side wall, invited them to take a seat and offered them fresh lemonade.

"No thank yuh," Reverend Oliver said, speaking for all of them.

The Turners stared at the Olivers. His bruised face was of particular interest to everyone, but no one spoke of it. Nat's subtle satisfied smile and unblinking eyes made contact with Reverend Oliver's eyes. Reverend Oliver turned away, more from fear than from guilt.

Another minute passed before Loretha said, "Reverend Oliver, do yuh have somethin' tuh say tuh this family?"

Reverend Oliver knew he was only expected to say a few chosen words, but he wanted to say more, he also wanted to take his family and leave. Just saying those few words meant they would be out of the Turner's home in under a minute.

"My family is here because Ah asked them tuh stand by me, and Ah want tuh thank them."

Sarah allowed a tiny smile to part her lips.

Reverend Oliver scanned the room, paying particular attention to his family. Then, he directed his comments to Johnny. "Johnny, Ah'm yuh father. Thirty-six years ago, Ah did a terrible thing. Ah want everyone in this room tuh know that Ah'm the person who raped yuh mother." He paused again and looked around at all of the Turners. All but Johnny looked directly at him.

"Ah know Ah caused this family a lot of pain, especially you, Elizabeth." He looked directly at her, and for the first time in many years, she looked directly at him.

"Ah want tuh thank yuh for keeping this among us." Before the next word passed across his lips, tears filled his eyes and rolled down his cheeks. Sobs caused him tuh muffle and pause, before squeezing out more words. "Please ... forgive me ..." He sobbed. "... Ah'm ... so ... sorry ..." He sobbed again and sniffed.

"Come on, Dad. It's time tuh leave," Malcolm said.

Thea took a humble bow, stepped back and turned to leave the house. Malcolm was holding Reverend Oliver's arms and escorted him toward the front door with Thea and Theresa following close behind.

Johnny held his head down the whole time Reverend Oliver spoke, but Sarah stared at him with so much animosity she hardly blinked. Johnny was the only Turner that seemed to feel empathy for him.

Reverend Turner stood and stumbled over his words before calling Reverend Oliver's name. Reverend Oliver's family stopped and turned to look at Reverend Turner.

"Owen!" Reverend Turner yelled out again. Reverend Oliver stopped, but still didn't turn around, so Reverend Turner just spoke out, "Owen! Ah'm giving yuh two weeks tuh hand in yuh resignation at church and yuh not welcome in this house again!"

Reverend Oliver nodded his head. Like a crippled, broken man, he was led from the house, with Sarah gloating like a child as she escorted them to the door.

Reverend Turner walked over to Johnny who was sitting with his head bowed. "Johnny, may Ah have some private time with yuh? Will yuh come with me intuh the living room?"

Johnny didn't say a word. He stood and quietly walked from the room and waited for his grandfather to enter before he closed the door. He remained standing until he was invited to sit and waited to hear what his grandfather had to say. He had no emotion to show or give this man that spent his lifetime ignoring him, and living a lie whenever he needed to show him attention.

"Johnny, Ah'm seventy-two years old. Ah'm not long for this world." He watched Johnny sitting in the lounge chair, looking down toward the floor with his arms resting on his knees and his hands clasped. He had hoped Johnny would look at him, but he didn't, so he continued. "Can yuh ever find it in yuh heart tuh forgive me?"

Johnny looked up. Forgiving his grandfather was harder than forgiving Reverend Oliver. "In time, Grandfather. I can only say that I'll work at it for Mama and Gram'ma's sake. You hurt my mother so much. Reverend Oliver raped Mama once, but you raped her heart every day since I've been alive. Please don't tell me how much you were hurt. That was your choosing. My mother loves you so much; even now. I could see it every time she was near you. You knew the truth, and at some point she didn't care if you said anything to Reverend Oliver or not. She just wanted you to love her. I can only work at forgiving you. Before, I never thought about you. I didn't use up any of my energy. Hating you would drain me, and I don't want to hurt myself. I don't love you, I never have … you never let me love you, and so I probably never will. But, I'll try to like you. That much I'll promise … and that's because my mother loves you. What you've done to this family is far worse than what Reverend Oliver did. He raped my mother, you raped my family."

Reverend Turner wanted to plead, but he wasn't a pleading man, so he put his hand on Johnny's shoulder. "Ah understand."

Just as Johnny stood, Reverend Turner held his hand out and waited. Johnny looked at his hand, and then looked up at his grandfather and walked away. "Not yet, Grandfather."

Johnny returned to the den alone, and Reverend Turner remained in the living room.

Ah sho' did ... Ah raped my family ... Ah ... raped ... my family.
When Ah didn't believe, Ah should've loved my daughter enough tuh stand
by her even if Ah didn't have the nerve tuh confront Owen. Johnny is right.
Ah've caused a lifetime of misery.

"Oh Lord lead me. Guide me. Show me the way." Reverend Turner removed his handkerchief, opened it, palmed it and wiped the sweat and tears from his face. "Help me win Elizabeth and Johnny back. Help me tuh show Sarah it's all right tuh live and love. Ah know my days are numbered, but Lord, let me have a little time tuh make it up to them."

He wiped his face again and shoved his handkerchief in his back pocket. "Thank yuh, Lord for yuh direction. Ah will forever be yuh faithful servant. Please, Lord. Ah ask this of you in Jesus' name. Thank yuh, Lord. Amen."

—⟶⟵—

Elizabeth watched her father return to the room while Johnny and Nat stood back near the mantle. All she wanted was for her father to hold her in his arms the way he did when she was fifteen. Now she was fifty-one years old. It was easy for her to forgive, because she never stopped loving and longing for him. She had kissed him when he was sick, now he could kiss her.

"Oh, baby, Ah love yuh so much. Ah hope yuh can forgive me. Ah'm such a weak minded man—a coward. For years Ah wanted tuh try tuh set things right, but Ah had dug my ditch so deep, Ah couldn't get out by myself. Ah should've called Sarah then." His sudden revelation seeded his smile, and he looked at Elizabeth.

"Daddy!" Elizabeth cried. "Ah love yuh, Daddy."

Johnny watched the tears roll down his mother's face and wondered how many tears she shed when his grandfather threw her away. *If I were God, I'd measure his sin greater than Reverend Oliver's,* he thought.

Sarah propped herself against the wall next to Johnny. "Ah just wished Ah got tuh Daddy a long time ago. It's gonna be nice having a family that's not carrying around sacks of wet sand," she whispered.

Johnny turned, put his arms around Sarah, kissed her on the cheek and whispered in her ear, "Thank you for giving me answers to the questions I didn't know how to ask."

"Thank yuh, Johnny, Ah felt really bad about upsetting yuh the other day. Ah really felt Ah had little choice. Yuh don't know how much Ah wanted my family back."

Loretha stood back and watched everyone come together. She smiled and clasped her praying hands against her lips. "Thank yuh, Jesus," she whispered so softly that only Jesus could hear her.

Johnny put his arms around Loretha and told her how much he loved her. "Gram'ma, I know how much it means for you to have your family together, and I promise, Grandfather will know I have good feelings about him, but it will take time. I'll try to come home more often and spend some time with him. No! I promise I will. I'm sure things will work out between the two of us. I'll give it my best shot for you and Mama."

"Johnny, honey. Ah'll pray the good Lord gives him the time yuh need," Loretha said.

"It won't take long, Gram'ma. I promise." Johnny gave her a warm hug and a kiss on the forehead.

CHAPTER 25

Malcolm had to support his father's weight, assisting him from the car to his house. Reverend Oliver was so distraught, they were afraid to leave him alone. Earlier, Thea had secretly planned to get away from him, to leave with Malcolm and Theresa. She needed to get away to clear her head and think about her future. Owen seemed to need her more than she needed to get away, but she would leave him anyway, at least until she could think clearly. She watched him, weak and sheepish. His appearance only angered her more. She turned her attention away from him. He was draining her. Her mind was made up. She would go with Malcolm.

It was after four o'clock and Malcolm and Theresa were ready to leave. "Mom ... Dad. We need to have a little talk before we leave. Dad it's been a terrible day for all of us. But we need tuh know that yuh gonna be okay. Promise me yuh'll have a doctor look at yuh face. Yuh say it looks worse than it feels, but Ah know yuh lying."

"Ah will, Malcolm. Tomorrow," Reverend Oliver promised.

Thea turned to Reverend Oliver who appeared sorry and pitiful, slouched in the dining room chair. He held his head back to reduce the pain, and he had closed his eyes. He seemed to be trying to escape into himself. Thea was close enough to hold his hand, rub his back, put her arm around him and let him know everything would be all right, but she remained in her chair.

"Malcolm, we do have tuh clear the air so this family can go on, but not today," Thea said, first looking at Malcolm and then directing her comments toward Reverend Oliver. "Owen ... there is no doubt about how much Ah love yuh or Ah wouldn't be sitting here telling yuh this. Yuh really tested that love today. As much as Ah want tuh get away from yuh, love wants tuh hold me back, but Ah'm going tuh leave you. Ah need time tuh think."

Thea turned from Reverend Oliver and approached Malcolm again. "Ah want tuh thank you and Theresa for dropping everything and coming home. No man should ever ask his family tuh do what he had tuh do tuhday. Ah want tuh ask yuh both if Ah could stay with yuh for a few days? Ah love Owen, but Ah have tuh get away."

"Thea, are yuh leaving me?" Reverend Oliver cried out in a weak voice.

"Yes, Owen," Thea said. "Ah need tuh be away from yuh. Yuh'll be okay. Just think of it as a healing process. Ah don't know how much time Ah'll need. Ah don't know if I'll be back. Ah don't know anything right now. Ah'm confused. Ah have tuh get away so Ah can think clearly. Yuh-know, Owen. Ah keep thinkin' 'bout the time just before Malcolm was born. It was right after Elizabeth had Johnny. Ah remember yuh being so upset yuh went out back and chopped a mess of firewood. There were other clues, too. The nervous spell at the hospital. And all these years, the way yuh took tuh Johnny. Sometimes, Ah wondered if yuh loved Johnny more than Malcolm. Yes, Owen, Ah got a lot of thinkin' tuh do."

"Are yuh sure, Mom? Yuh know yuh always welcome," Theresa said. Malcolm nodded in agreement.

"Ah'll just be with yuh for about a week, then Ah'll go tuh my sister's. She's alone in that big old house. Ah can't say anything for now. Ah can't even think straight."

"Mom, we'd love tuh have yuh stay with us for as long as yuh want. Ah really understand how yuh feel," Theresa said before she gave her a genuine hug. It was all Thea needed to feel and believe she was welcome, still knowing she would be going to her sister's house.

"Okay. It's settled. Ah'm going tuh pack my bags. Ah'll be back as quickly as possible. Ah don't want tuh hold yuh up."

"May Ah come with yuh?" Theresa asked.

Thea nodded and smiled, and the two women walked from the room. Theresa was as foresighted as Thea. She knew Malcolm needed private time with his father.

Malcolm's car pulled from the driveway and headed down the road. The taillights were still visible in the distance when Reverend Oliver entered his empty house. He was terrified of losing Thea. Of all the things he'd lost that weekend, Thea was the most precious. He had Malcolm, but he couldn't connect with him the way he connected with Johnny. Johnny didn't even raise his head while Reverend Oliver spoke. He believed he had lost him too. His life, the way he knew it, was gone: his family, his work, his church, his home and friends were all gone. His head hurt and the side of his face was pounding.

"Oh Lord, Ah believed yuh forgave me," he cried out. Misery and dispossession plagued him. "Oh Lord! Lord please don't take my Thea from me. Ah'm sorry, Lord. Must Ah pay a lifetime for a few moments of weakness?" Tears flooded his eyes and emotions made his body jerk with the kind of inner pain he had never experienced.

He walked to his chair and lowered himself to the floor. His legs were weak. His neck ached, his back, shoulders and chest ached and dizziness continued to plague him. "Thea! Please, Lord, don't let Thea leave me. Thirty-seven years of marriage. Ah can't lose her now.

"Lord, Ah prayed tuh Yuh. Every day, Ah'd asked for Yuh forgiveness. Ah've tried tuh live in Yuh light. What happened Lord? Why now? Why do Ah have tuh lose everything? Ah believed Yuh had forgiven me." Reverend Oliver prayed and cried.

He never removed himself from the floor. He'd rise to his knees only to roll back to the hard carpeted floor. His eyes were red and the pain to his face had sharpened. When his tear ducts dried up, his emotional pain continued to manifest, tightening his chest muscles and causing him to experience involuntary muscle vibrations. The hardness of the floor awakened his senses. He pulled himself to the sofa. He laid there with his eyes closed. When his dried up tear ducts filled again, he cried some more.

Nothing could change the circumstances created in a lifetime. Only love could make it bearable. Johnny was happy for his mother, Nat, Sarah, and his grandparents. He was happy for himself, but he was still caught between two worlds. What Reverend Oliver did to his mother was wrong, but he was the result of this wrong. He loved Reverend Oliver and was allowed to love him for as long as he could remember.

The afternoon had moved into evening; it had been a very long and trying day. It was time to leave. Johnny, Elizabeth and Nat left together. Nat drove and Johnny sat up front with him. Elizabeth sat behind Nat. Johnny sat sideways in the seat.

"I need to talk to both of you." He brought his fingers down over his eyes and interlocked them in front of his lips. His eyes shifted between Nat and his mother. "There's still something I have to do. Mama, you know what I'm trying to say, it's about Reverend Oliver. Nat, I love you and respect your opinion, too."

"Johnny, we respect how yuh feel. Reverend Oliver is yuh father. Before Nat, he was the only man who gave yuh any attention. Ah could've stopped it, but Ah didn't. Ah allowed yuh tuh be close tuh him, so Ah can't come between yuh now. We've talked about it, and he ..." Elizabeth looked at Nat and took his hand. "Nat agrees with me. What he did tuh me ... and what he stood back and allowed tuh happen tuh me ... Ah will never forgive him. Honey, Ah don't hate him, but Ah don't care how badly he hurts, and Ah don't care what he's going through. But, if yuh want tuh be his friend, then we'll respect yuh decision. We only ask that yuh keep him separate and away from us."

Nat pulled the car up in the driveway and parked next to Johnny's rented car. They remained in their car for a few minutes while they finished their conversation.

"I understand," Johnny said. "What you ask is more than fair. I promise, I will never put him before you or Nat."

"Okay that's settled." Elizabeth gently squeezed Johnny's hand. "What time is yuh flight?"

Johnny got out of the car and opened the door for his mother. As soon as she was standing, Johnny pulled her into his arms. "I love you, Mama." He kissed her on the side of her face. Nat was standing to her side. "I love you too, man." He shook his hand and they pulled into a manly hug, Nat patting Johnny on the back several times.

"Man, when's yuh flight?" Nat asked.

"I had planned to leave early tomorrow morning, but I think I'm going to leave this evening. Our family needs a lot of healing." He hugged his mother again and kept his arm around her while he continued to speak. "I think I'll start with Sarah. I was thinking I'd ride back to Atlanta with her and get a hotel room. We could use the private time together. I can turn my car in at the rental branch in Macon. I'm booked on the eight A.M. flight out of Atlanta. Right now, I'm going to the cottage, I need to gather my things and try to get a little rest. I'll call Sarah from there."

"Johnny, don't yuh want tuh have dinner before yuh leave?" Elizabeth asked.

"Next time, Mama. I had Gerta prepare dinner for me. I knew I'd want to be alone this evening. I know you understand. Julia and I will be back in a couple of weeks."

"Well, let me get my hugs now. Ah probably won't see yuh before yuh leave." Elizabeth threw her arms around his neck. Then Johnny gave Nat one of those manly, one-arm hugs, and a handshake.

"See yuh man. Good luck," Nat said. Elizabeth blew him a kiss.

"Bye, Mama. Bye Nat."

Johnny got in his car, drove to the end of the driveway and stopped. He thought about visiting Reverend Oliver's, but was too drained to have his misery laid on him. He turned right and promised himseld to call him as soon as he arrived back in D.C.

The sun continued to shine behind the tops of the tall trees that canopied the forest behind MaDear's Cottage. Johnny stopped the car before he reached the circular driveway. He remembered seeing the sight many times when he was a boy and had taken it for granted. He got out and rested against the grill of the car. "The Lord's beauty will only last a few moments. One day I hope I can show this to my children. I'll tell them that it's the Lord's magic ski, and they should make a wish."

Johnny entered the cottage and called Sarah. She welcomed his company. Gerta left a plate for him on the stove and Johnny only nibbled at it. He spent the remaining hours of the evening in the quiet, serenity and contentment of MaDear's memories. A large picture of MaDear hung on the wall opposite her favorite chair. He had placed it there as soon as the cottage renovations were completed. He loved to sit in her chair and look at her picture. He believed he could feel her smiling at him, and her smiles were the rays of warmth he felt when he drifted off to sleep. The phone rang, pulling him away from his dream. It was Sarah. She was ready to leave.

Johnny arrived at his grandparents' home before nine o'clock. Loretha and Reverend Turner stood on the porch with their arms around each other.

Sarah threw her arms around her mother and kissed her on the cheek. "Bye, Mama, I'll be home again real soon." When she moved to hug her father, she stopped. Johnny and her father's eyes were locked on each other.

Johnny stepped on the porch as Reverend Turner moved closer to him. Reverend Turner threw his arms around him. Johnny allowed it to happen for himself, not just for his mother's or his grandmother's sake.

Reverend Turner whispered in Johnny's ear, "Ah always loved yuh."

Johnny whispered back, "Yes, sir." They pulled away from each other, and then Reverend Turner grabbed Johnny for another quick hug.

Loretha smiled. She didn't have to say anything to Johnny. He knew what her heart was saying.

"Bye, Grandma. I love you so much."

Sarah hugged her father, pulled the strap of her pocketbook on her shoulder and said, "Okay. Okay. There's plenty of time for that later. We got a long drive. Bye Mama, Daddy. Come on, Johnny."

"She's a little tenacious, Johnny, but you'll get used tuh her," Loretha said while laughing.

Johnny laughed. "Tell Mama I'll call her from the hotel."

Sarah and Johnny pulled out of the driveway in their two cars, tooting their horns as they drove away.

—⚬⚬⚬—

Reverend Oliver sat up on his sofa. *My Lord! Ah never confessed. Ah was a coward asking for forgiveness and Ah never forgave myself. Ah never asked anyone tuh pray for me. Ah saw fault in others, asked them tuh confess, prayed for them and they were healed. Loretha made me confess. Ah have tuh call Reverend Lipton now and confess my sin; Ah'll ask him tuh pray for me.*

It was late Sunday evening. Reverend Oliver prayed Reverend Lipton was home or not already turned in for the night. His phone rang four times. Reverend Oliver was ready to hang up his receiver when he heard Reverend Lipton's voice.

"Reverend Lipton, this is Reverend Oliver. Ah know it's late, but Ah have a serious problem."

"Do yuh want tuh talk about it tuhnight?" Reverend Lipton said. He was concerned and asked why he wanted to confide in him instead of Reverend Turner.

"Ah'll explain when Ah see yuh. Ah would come tuh yuh tuhnight, but Ah have a bit of a problem, and Ah need tuh go to the medical clinic."

"Are yuh alone? Where's yuh wife?" Reverend Lipton asked.

"Thea's went to Jonesboro earlier this evening with Malcolm."

"Owen, Ah think Ah should come over tuh see about yuh now. Ah don't like the way you sound."

"Ah don't want tuh put yuh out."

"Ah'll be there in a few minutes."

Reverend Oliver hung up the phone and laid his head against the back of the chair. The left side of his face throbbed with pain. When he held the palm of his hand against his face, he could feel the heat radiating from it. The swelling went from his chin to his eye. He staggered to the kitchen and removed a bag of mixed vegetables from the freezer, wrapped it in a dishtowel and held it against his face. He was walking down the hall toward his study when he heard a knock at his door. He looked through the glass on the side of the door and saw it was Reverend Lipton.

"Thank yuh for coming." They went into the study and sat across from each other in the twin wing highback chairs. He placed the icepack against his face.

"My God, Reverend Oliver, what happened tuh yuh face?"

"Strange enough, Ah fell last Friday night and slammed my face intuh the ball on the banister on the front porch. Ah didn't think tuh much of it, but this evening it seems to be pretty bad. Ah know, Ah'm gonna have tuh go tuh the clinic tuhnight and have it looked at. But Reverend Lipton, Ah need tuh tell you about something Ah did years ago that was so awful it changed the complexion of Rehoboth. Ah confessed earlier this afternoon, because Ah was threatened with exposure. Ah prayed for forgiveness. Ah never sought my own church because Ah didn't believe Ah deserved it. Then tuhnight the scripture came tuh me;

'If we confess our sin, he is faithful and just tuh forgive us our sin, and tuh cleanse us from all unrighteousness. 1 John 1:9 and confess yuh faults one tuh another, and pray one for another, that ye may be healed. The effectual fervent prayer of a righteous man availeth much. James 5:16

"Reverend Oliver, why didn't yuh confess tuh Reverend Turner?" Reverend Lipton asked.

"Because it's his family Ah transgressed against. Ah'm the person that raped Elizabeth, and Ah'm the father of her son."

"Oh my Lord!" He leaned over, placed his hands on his knees, closed his eyes, inhaled in a deep breath, then exhaled slowly. It was several moments before he could look at Owen. He continued to breathe deeply and turned his head slowly. "Please just give me a minute tuh absorb this. It hit me kinda hard." He took out his handkerchief and wiped his brow and the perspiration over his upper lip.

"Is that why Elizabeth joined Bethlehem? Have yuh confessed tuh the Turner family … and your family, too? Owen did you confess tuh them of your own free will?"

"Ah was forced tuh confess tuh my family and the Turners. Loretha threatened tuh expose me all over Rehoboth."

"Owen, why did yuh call me?"

"Ah spent years praying, asking the Lord tuh forgive me. Two people, my own son was one, asked me if Ah stayed in Rehoboth tuh torment Elizabeth. At first Ah stayed because Ah wanted tuh tell her how sorry Ah was. Ah was afraid tuh tell her father because Ah didn't want tuh go tuh jail. Then, when Johnny was born, Elizabeth told her father, and he didn't believe her." Owen pressed his fingers to the sides of his head. He dropped the ice pack and held his head against the back of the chair. Pain froze his face, and paralyzing his speech.

"Are you going tuh be all right?"

Owen slightly nodded his head and clenched his lips. The pain seemed to come in waves. He took a deep breath, and his face relaxed enough for him to speak. "Ah didn't want tuh leave Johnny. Ah prayed for guidance, and when the law didn't take me away, Ah thought the Lord forgave me." He could feel his heart racing. "Ah sent anonymous support checks to Elizabeth from Johnny's first month until he graduated from college. Suddenly, this evening, those scriptures came tuh me. Ah would stand on the steps of Concord and Bethleham and confess to the congregation. Ah want to be free of this sin, please pray for me."

"Do yuh think yuh can get down on yuh knees and let me pray for yuh?"

Reverend Oliver nodded his head. Reverend Lipton knelt on one knee, placed one arm around Reverend Oliver and opened his Bible. He began by having Reverend Oliver repeat several Bible verses related to the remission of sin before he began to pray. He could feel Owen's rapid heartbeat against his arm and felt the need to pray with him even more.

"Dear, Lord, Ah implore yuh tuh hear this man's prayer and heal him. Heal those he's hurt, may it be physical or emotional ..." He and Reverend Oliver prayed for fifteen minutes. Reverend Lipton was about to call the session to an end when Reverend Oliver fell to the floor.

Reverend Lipton quickly said, "We ask these blessing in yuh name, Lord. Amen." He felt for a pulse and hurried to call the Anna May Collins Clinic for an ambulance.

He returned to Reverend Oliver and placed his ice pack on his head. "Oh Lord, if it is yuh plan tuh take this man now, forgive him of his sins and accept him into the glory of heaven. Let those he has offended forgive him, and remember him for the good he has done. Ah ask this of You in Jesus' name. Amen."

Just then Reverend Oliver began to stir and opened his eyes.

"Don't move, Owen. Ah called for the ambulance. They should be here in a minute or two. Where can Ah find yuh son's phone number? Ah need tuh get in touch with yuh family."

"Malcolm lives in Jonesbo ..." Reverend Oliver fainted again.

The emergency medical technicians arrived and began examining Reverend Oliver. They removed him from the floor and placed him on the gurney. One of the technicians was taking his blood pressure while the other was checking his blood sugar level. "What happened tuh his face?" the technician asked Reverend Lipton.

"He told me he fell on the porch last Friday and hit his face on the banister,"

"Sugar's okay, how the pressure?" one technician said.

"Off the scale," the other said. "We're taking him over tuh Collins Clinic, stabilize him, and then he'll be transferred tuh Macon General. They'll take a good look at his jaw when he gets there. Can yuh get in touch with his family?"

"Ah'll try," Reverend Lipton said. He walked to the corner of the house to give the paramedic room to work. *Ah have tuh call Reverend Turner tuh get help reaching his family,* he thought.

ABOUT THE AUTHOR

Anita Ballard-Jones is a native of Brooklyn, New York. In her mid-twenties, she and her family relocated to Suffolk County, Long Island, New York. She earned an Associate Degree in Early Childhood Education at the State University of New York (SUNY) at Farmingdale, and continued her studies in Elementary and Special Education, earning a Bachelor's and Master's degree from The C.W. Post Campus of Long Island University, in Greenvale, New York. Anita is retired from New York State after working twelve years as a teacher and twenty-one years as a Treatment Team Leader with children and adults having various forms of Development Disabilities. She is married and has three adult children and five grandchildren who have been very supportive in her new endeavor as a writer. She believes her reader's feedback is important and welcomes their input. Her e-mail address is **aballardjo@aol.com**.

Excerpt from

RISE OF THE PHOENIX

BY

KENNETH WHETSTONE

Release Date: August 2006

PROLOGUE

The bitter cold of the seventeen degrees outside clutched T.J. Stonewall's body and followed him into the home of his good friend and former junior high school basketball coach, David Martin, who was now coaching the girls' basketball team at Stuyvesant High School. David was a fifty-two-year-old physical education teacher with thinning brown hair and a dark half dollar-sized birthmark on the left side of his neck. He grew up in the Howard Beach section of Queens before moving to his current apartment in Brooklyn Heights.

T.J. quickly shut the door and let the comforting warmth overtake him as he placed his backpack down and shed his hat and coat. The frost in the air was gone in seconds, but the numbness of his fingers and toes lingered as he followed David past the open kitchen area into the living room so that they could watch the NBA game together on television.

"It's cold outside," T.J. complained. "I hate the cold. I can't wait until summer."

"It was freezing in Jefferson's gym today, too," David said, sitting on the couch using the remote control to change the channel.

"Oh, that's right, you played Jeff today. What happened?" T.J.

wanted to know.

"Well, first of all, I sat my point guard the whole game because she told me that she couldn't come to practice yesterday because she had to do something for her mother, but I found out before the game that she lied so that she could go see the boys' team play."

T.J. frowned in disappointment. "I never could understand why girls always do that."

David shrugged. "Me either. Boys sure don't duck out of their practices to go see the girls. The worst part is that she didn't even apologize or try to make amends. She just sat on the end of the bench shivering."

"It was that cold in Jefferson's gym?"

"Well, the game was close for the first one and a half quarters because it was so cold no one could shoot or even catch the ball. At the end of the first quarter, the score was 7-4. The problem was that they warmed up a lot faster than we did. The score at halftime was 27-14. They ran away with it from there. We ended up losing by twenty-something—59-32 I think."

"Wow, I thought the game would be a lot closer than that."

"So did I, but like I said, it took us way too long to warm up. But I can tell you this. They're going to have a much tougher time with us if we meet them in the playoffs. They're not going to be able to empty their bench like they did today. I'll tell you this, too. If I had one superstar, we'd beat them for sure."

T.J. got up and walked to the kitchen. "Do you plan on coaching this summer?"

"Nah, I'm going on vacation to Bermuda for three weeks as soon as school is out," David was more than happy to say. "And since you keep telling me how nice Puerto Rico was when you went there for your honeymoon a few months ago, I'm going there for three weeks, too. I'm gonna hang out on the beach all summer and get a real good tan."

"Lucky you." He helped himself to a cup of water. "But you're not going to be here for the New Attitude League."

"Yeah, I know. That tournament has everybody on the New York City Girls Basketball website all fired up. It's all anyone is talking about these days, and it doesn't even start 'til May."

"Later for those people on that site," T.J. grumbled. "They should just take away the message board because the people that post there have made a mockery of it. All they do is have stupid arguments over who's the best team, who's the best player and why this person is ranked high and that one isn't. They're even ranking junior high and elementary school kids now. That's just ridiculous. I could see if they were a bunch of experts, sports writers, etcetera, but it's just a bunch of people who think they know a lot more than they actually do."

"That's for sure."

"Why do you even bother reading it, then?"

"It's funny." David laughed.

"I guess you're right about that." He chuckled. "When this tournament starts, it's really going to become a circus on that site."

"Not just there, but everywhere else, too. Do you see the publicity it's getting in the newspaper already, five months ahead of time?"

"Yeah, five months ahead of time and they already have all ten teams for this region."

"They do?" David asked, surprised. "At seven hundred dollars a team? How can that be?"

T.J. guzzled his water and leaned back against the sink. "People jumped on it right away. They couldn't pass up a chance on taking their whole team to New Orleans for four days for seven hundred bucks. That's a damn good deal for whoever wins."

"Are you entering your teams into it?"

"I wasn't going to because of the entry fee, especially since they're not even giving out any jerseys but insist that every team has *full* uniforms. But the girls in my program deserve to be involved. It doesn't even matter if we get to go to the National Tournament in New Orleans. I think just playing against the competition that's going to be in this tournament will be good for us."

"I don't know." David scratched his head. "I think the same three or four teams that are always coming up short to the Roadrunners will be fighting for second place just like in every other tournament."

"Really? But they have four teams from New Jersey in this region, too."

"Yeah, but the New York/New Jersey region ain't like the Connecticut/Massachusetts region. Like I said, the same three or four teams will be fighting for second place. To me, that's just a waste of seven hundred dollars. You're going to play those same teams in every other tournament. In fact, you can add a hundred bucks to that seven hundred and pay for the West Fourth Street league, the Slam Jam Showcase and the Highland Park tournament all together. It doesn't make sense to me to spend your whole budget for four or five tourna- ments when the same money can get you into seven or eight."T.J. placed his glass on the counter and rejoined his mentor on the couch, staring at him as he spoke. He knew that what David was saying had some truth to it, but he had already made the commitment and paid the entry fees for the junior and senior divisions. "The girls will get a kick out of it. I always shelter them from this type of thing so that they won't be surrounded by negative influences. This time, though, I think we'll just go in, compete hard, have some fun and get a few more looks by some of the local college recruiters in the process, since they're all going to flock there anyway." David threw up his hands. "Okay, but I'm telling you, this is the type of thing that can be just as bad for kids as it is good. Don't let the negative stuff suck you in."

2006 Publication Schedule

January

A Lover's Legacy
Veronica Parker
1-58571-167-5
$9.95

Love Lasts Forever
Dominiqua Douglas
1-58571-187-X
$9.95

Under the Cherry
Moon
Christal Jordan-Mims
1-58571-169-1
$12.95

February

Second Chances at Love
Cheris Hodges
1-58571-188-8
$9.95

Enchanted Desire
Wanda Y. Thomas
1-58571-176-4
$9.95

Caught Up
Deatri King Bey
1-58571-178-0
$12.95

March

I'm Gonna Make You
Love Me
Gwyneth Bolton
1-58571-181-0
$9.95

Through the Fire
Seressia Glass
1-58571-173-X
$9.95

Notes When Summer
Ends
Beverly Lauderdale
1-58571-180-2
$12.95

April

Sin and Surrender
J.M. Jeffries
1-58571-189-6
$9.95

Unearthing Passions
Elaine Sims
1-58571-184-5
$9.95

Between Tears
Pamela Ridley
1-58571-179-9
$12.95

May

Misty Blue
Dyanne Davis
1-58571-186-1
$9.95

Ironic
Pamela Leigh Starr
1-58571-168-3
$9.95

Cricket's Serenade
Carolita Blythe
1-58571-183-7
$12.95

June

Cupid
Barbara Keaton
1-58571-174-8
$9.95

Havana Sunrise
Kymberly Hunt
1-58571-182-9
$9.95

2006 Publication Schedule (continued)

July

Love Me Carefully
A.C. Arthur
1-58571-177-2
$9.95

No Ordinary Love
Angela Weaver
1-58571-198-5
$9.95

Rehoboth Road
Anita Ballard-Jones
1-58571-196-9
$12.95

August

Scent of Rain
Annetta P. Lee
158571-199-3
$9.95

Love in High Gear
Charlotte Roy
158571-185-3
$9.95

Rise of the Phoenix
Kenneth Whetstone
1-58571-197-7
$12.95

September

The Business of Love
Cheris Hodges
1-58571-193-4
$9.95

Rock Star
Rosyln Hardy Holcomb
1-58571-200-0
$9.95

A Dead Man Speaks
Lisa Jones Johnson
1-58571-203-5
$12.95

October

Rivers of the Soul-Part 1
Leslie Esdaile
1-58571-223-X
$9.95

A Dangerous Woman
J.M. Jeffries
1-58571-195-0
$9.95

Sinful Intentions
Crystal Rhodes
1-58571-201-9
$12.95

November

Only You
Crystal Hubbard
1-58571-208-6
$9.95

Ebony Eyes
Kei Swanson
1-58571-194-2
$9.95

Still Waters Run Deep –
  Part 2
Leslie Esdaile
1-58571-224-8
$9.95

December

Let's Get It On
Dyanne Davis
1-58571-210-8
$9.95

Nights Over Egypt
Barbara Keaton
1-58571-192-6
$9.95

A Pefect Place to Pray
I.L. Goodwin
1-58571-202-7
$12.95

Other Genesis Press, Inc. Titles

A Dangerous Deception	J.M. Jeffries	$8.95
A Dangerous Love	J.M. Jeffries	$8.95
A Dangerous Obsession	J.M. Jeffries	$8.95
A Drummer's Beat to Mend	Kei Swanson	$9.95
A Happy Life	Charlotte Harris	$9.95
A Heart's Awakening	Veronica Parker	$9.95
A Lark on the Wing	Phyliss Hamilton	$9.95
A Love of Her Own	Cheris F. Hodges	$9.95
A Love to Cherish	Beverly Clark	$8.95
A Risk of Rain	Dar Tomlinson	$8.95
A Twist of Fate	Beverly Clark	$8.95
A Will to Love	Angie Daniels	$9.95
Acquisitions	Kimberley White	$8.95
Across	Carol Payne	$12.95
After the Vows	Leslie Esdaile	$10.95
(Summer Anthology)	T.T. Henderson	
	Jacqueline Thomas	
Again My Love	Kayla Perrin	$10.95
Against the Wind	Gwynne Forster	$8.95
All I Ask	Barbara Keaton	$8.95
Ambrosia	T.T. Henderson	$8.95
An Unfinished Love Affair	Barbara Keaton	$8.95
And Then Came You	Dorothy Elizabeth Love	$8.95
Angel's Paradise	Janice Angelique	$9.95
At Last	Lisa G. Riley	$8.95
Best of Friends	Natalie Dunbar	$8.95
Beyond the Rapture	Beverly Clark	$9.95
Blaze	Barbara Keaton	$9.95
Blood Lust	J. M. Jeffries	$9.95
Bodyguard	Andrea Jackson	$9.95
Boss of Me	Diana Nyad	$8.95
Bound by Love	Beverly Clark	$8.95
Breeze	Robin Hampton Allen	$10.95

Other Genesis Press, Inc. Titles (continued)

Broken	Dar Tomlinson	$24.95
By Design	Barbara Keaton	$8.95
Cajun Heat	Charlene Berry	$8.95
Careless Whispers	Rochelle Alers	$8.95
Cats & Other Tales	Marilyn Wagner	$8.95
Caught in a Trap	Andre Michelle	$8.95
Caught Up In the Rapture	Lisa G. Riley	$9.95
Cautious Heart	Cheris F Hodges	$8.95
Chances	Pamela Leigh Starr	$8.95
Cherish the Flame	Beverly Clark	$8.95
Class Reunion	Irma Jenkins/John Brown	$12.95
Code Name: Diva	J.M. Jeffries	$9.95
Conquering Dr. Wexler's Heart	Kimberley White	$9.95
Crossing Paths, Tempting Memories	Dorothy Elizabeth Love	$9.95
Cypress Whisperings	Phyllis Hamilton	$8.95
Dark Embrace	Crystal Wilson Harris	$8.95
Dark Storm Rising	Chinelu Moore	$10.95
Daughter of the Wind	Joan Xian	$8.95
Deadly Sacrifice	Jack Kean	$22.95
Designer Passion	Dar Tomlinson	$8.95
Dreamtective	Liz Swados	$5.95
Ebony Butterfly II	Delilah Dawson	$14.95
Echoes of Yesterday	Beverly Clark	$9.95
Eden's Garden	Elizabeth Rose	$8.95
Everlastin' Love	Gay G. Gunn	$8.95
Everlasting Moments	Dorothy Elizabeth Love	$8.95
Everything and More	Sinclair Lebeau	$8.95
Everything but Love	Natalie Dunbar	$8.95
Eve's Prescription	Edwina Martin Arnold	$8.95
Falling	Natalie Dunbar	$9.95
Fate	Pamela Leigh Starr	$8.95
Finding Isabella	A.J. Garrotto	$8.95

Other Genesis Press, Inc. Titles (continued)

Forbidden Quest	Dar Tomlinson	$10.95
Forever Love	Wanda Thomas	$8.95
From the Ashes	Kathleen Suzanne	$8.95
	Jeanne Sumerix	
Gentle Yearning	Rochelle Alers	$10.95
Glory of Love	Sinclair LeBeau	$10.95
Go Gentle into that Good Night	Malcom Boyd	$12.95
Goldengroove	Mary Beth Craft	$16.95
Groove, Bang, and Jive	Steve Cannon	$8.99
Hand in Glove	Andrea Jackson	$9.95
Hard to Love	Kimberley White	$9.95
Hart & Soul	Angie Daniels	$8.95
Heartbeat	Stephanie Bedwell-Grime	$8.95
Hearts Remember	M. Loui Quezada	$8.95
Hidden Memories	Robin Allen	$10.95
Higher Ground	Leah Latimer	$19.95
Hitler, the War, and the Pope	Ronald Rychiak	$26.95
How to Write a Romance	Kathryn Falk	$18.95
I Married a Reclining Chair	Lisa M. Fuhs	$8.95
Indigo After Dark Vol. I	Nia Dixon/Angelique	$10.95
Indigo After Dark Vol. II	Dolores Bundy/Cole Riley	$10.95
Indigo After Dark Vol. III	Montana Blue/Coco Morena	$10.95
Indigo After Dark Vol. IV	Cassandra Colt/	$14.95
	Diana Richeaux	
Indigo After Dark Vol. V	Delilah Dawson	$14.95
Icie	Pamela Leigh Starr	$8.95
I'll Be Your Shelter	Giselle Carmichael	$8.95
I'll Paint a Sun	A.J. Garrotto	$9.95
Illusions	Pamela Leigh Starr	$8.95
Indiscretions	Donna Hill	$8.95
Intentional Mistakes	Michele Sudler	$9.95
Interlude	Donna Hill	$8.95
Intimate Intentions	Angie Daniels	$8.95

Other Genesis Press, Inc. Titles (continued)

Jolie's Surrender	Edwina Martin-Arnold	$8.95
Kiss or Keep	Debra Phillips	$8.95
Lace	Giselle Carmichael	$9.95
Last Train to Memphis	Elsa Cook	$12.95
Lasting Valor	Ken Olsen	$24.95
Let Us Prey	Hunter Lundy	$25.95
Life Is Never As It Seems	J.J. Michael	$12.95
Lighter Shade of Brown	Vicki Andrews	$8.95
Love Always	Mildred E. Riley	$10.95
Love Doesn't Come Easy	Charlyne Dickerson	$8.95
Love Unveiled	Gloria Greene	$10.95
Love's Deception	Charlene Berry	$10.95
Love's Destiny	M. Loui Quezada	$8.95
Mae's Promise	Melody Walcott	$8.95
Magnolia Sunset	Giselle Carmichael	$8.95
Matters of Life and Death	Lesego Malepe, Ph.D.	$15.95
Meant to Be	Jeanne Sumerix	$8.95
Midnight Clear	Leslie Esdaile	$10.95
(Anthology)	Gwynne Forster	
	Carmen Green	
	Monica Jackson	
Midnight Magic	Gwynne Forster	$8.95
Midnight Peril	Vicki Andrews	$10.95
Misconceptions	Pamela Leigh Starr	$9.95
Montgomery's Children	Richard Perry	$14.95
My Buffalo Soldier	Barbara B. K. Reeves	$8.95
Naked Soul	Gwynne Forster	$8.95
Next to Last Chance	Louisa Dixon	$24.95
No Apologies	Seressia Glass	$8.95
No Commitment Required	Seressia Glass	$8.95
No Regrets	Mildred E. Riley	$8.95
Nowhere to Run	Gay G. Gunn	$10.95
O Bed! O Breakfast!	Rob Kuehnle	$14.95

Other Genesis Press, Inc. Titles (continued)

Object of His Desire	A. C. Arthur	$8.95
Office Policy	A. C. Arthur	$9.95
Once in a Blue Moon	Dorianne Cole	$9.95
One Day at a Time	Bella McFarland	$8.95
Outside Chance	Louisa Dixon	$24.95
Passion	T.T. Henderson	$10.95
Passion's Blood	Cherif Fortin	$22.95
Passion's Journey	Wanda Thomas	$8.95
Past Promises	Jahmel West	$8.95
Path of Fire	T.T. Henderson	$8.95
Path of Thorns	Annetta P. Lee	$9.95
Peace Be Still	Colette Haywood	$12.95
Picture Perfect	Reon Carter	$8.95
Playing for Keeps	Stephanie Salinas	$8.95
Pride & Joi	Gay G. Gunn	$15.95
Pride & Joi	Gay G. Gunn	$8.95
Promises to Keep	Alicia Wiggins	$8.95
Quiet Storm	Donna Hill	$10.95
Reckless Surrender	Rochelle Alers	$6.95
Red Polka Dot in a World of Plaid	Varian Johnson	$12.95
Reluctant Captive	Joyce Jackson	$8.95
Rendezvous with Fate	Jeanne Sumerix	$8.95
Revelations	Cheris F. Hodges	$8.95
Rivers of the Soul	Leslie Esdaile	$8.95
Rocky Mountain Romance	Kathleen Suzanne	$8.95
Rooms of the Heart	Donna Hill	$8.95
Rough on Rats and Tough on Cats	Chris Parker	$12.95
Secret Library Vol. 1	Nina Sheridan	$18.95
Secret Library Vol. 2	Cassandra Colt	$8.95
Shades of Brown	Denise Becker	$8.95
Shades of Desire	Monica White	$8.95

Other Genesis Press, Inc. Titles (continued)

Shadows in the Moonlight	Jeanne Sumerix	$8.95
Sin	Crystal Rhodes	$8.95
So Amazing	Sinclair LeBeau	$8.95
Somebody's Someone	Sinclair LeBeau	$8.95
Someone to Love	Alicia Wiggins	$8.95
Song in the Park	Martin Brant	$15.95
Soul Eyes	Wayne L. Wilson	$12.95
Soul to Soul	Donna Hill	$8.95
Southern Comfort	J.M. Jeffries	$8.95
Still the Storm	Sharon Robinson	$8.95
Still Waters Run Deep	Leslie Esdaile	$8.95
Stories to Excite You	Anna Forrest/Divine	$14.95
Subtle Secrets	Wanda Y. Thomas	$8.95
Suddenly You	Crystal Hubbard	$9.95
Sweet Repercussions	Kimberley White	$9.95
Sweet Tomorrows	Kimberly White	$8.95
Taken by You	Dorothy Elizabeth Love	$9.95
Tattooed Tears	T. T. Henderson	$8.95
The Color Line	Lizzette Grayson Carter	$9.95
The Color of Trouble	Dyanne Davis	$8.95
The Disappearance of Allison Jones	Kayla Perrin	$5.95
The Honey Dipper's Legacy	Pannell-Allen	$14.95
The Joker's Love Tune	Sidney Rickman	$15.95
The Little Pretender	Barbara Cartland	$10.95
The Love We Had	Natalie Dunbar	$8.95
The Man Who Could Fly	Bob & Milana Beamon	$18.95
The Missing Link	Charlyne Dickerson	$8.95
The Price of Love	Sinclair LeBeau	$8.95
The Smoking Life	Ilene Barth	$29.95
The Words of the Pitcher	Kei Swanson	$8.95
Three Wishes	Seressia Glass	$8.95
Ties That Bind	Kathleen Suzanne	$8.95
Tiger Woods	Libby Hughes	$5.95

Other Genesis Press, Inc. Titles (continued)

Time is of the Essence	Angie Daniels	$9.95
Timeless Devotion	Bella McFarland	$9.95
Tomorrow's Promise	Leslie Esdaile	$8.95
Truly Inseparable	Wanda Y. Thomas	$8.95
Unbreak My Heart	Dar Tomlinson	$8.95
Uncommon Prayer	Kenneth Swanson	$9.95
Unconditional	A.C. Arthur	$9.95
Unconditional Love	Alicia Wiggins	$8.95
Until Death Do Us Part	Susan Paul	$8.95
Vows of Passion	Bella McFarland	$9.95
Wedding Gown	Dyanne Davis	$8.95
What's Under Benjamin's Bed	Sandra Schaffer	$8.95
When Dreams Float	Dorothy Elizabeth Love	$8.95
Whispers in the Night	Dorothy Elizabeth Love	$8.95
Whispers in the Sand	LaFlorya Gauthier	$10.95
Wild Ravens	Altonya Washington	$9.95
Yesterday Is Gone	Beverly Clark	$10.95
Yesterday's Dreams, Tomorrow's Promises	Reon Laudat	$8.95
Your Precious Love	Sinclair LeBeau	$8.95